Praise for *Proving*

"Blauner's characters are complex and ⬚⬚⬚⬚⬚⬚⬚⬚⬚⬚⬚⬚
plot. His gritty portrayal of urban cri⬚⬚⬚⬚⬚⬚⬚⬚⬚⬚⬚⬚
Price and Dennis Lehane."   —*The Washington Post*

"A great thriller . . . I just kept turning those pages."
                    —Nancy Pearl, *Morning Edition,* NPR

"Edgar-winner Blauner hasn't lost his touch, as this page-turner demonstrates. . . . Blauner has crafted two strong and complex leads in Natty and Lourdes and given readers an intricate plot that never feels forced."
                    —*Publishers Weekly* (starred review)

"The murder of a liberal lawyer in Brooklyn puts his Iraq War veteran son and two detectives on a collision course in this complex, character-rich tale. . . . A top-notch crime novel that avoids easy resolutions and is all the better for its unanswered questions."
                    —*Kirkus Reviews* (starred review)

"With *Proving Ground,* Peter Blauner continues to prove why he's one of the most consistently bracing and interesting voices in American crime literature. A beautifully written and relentlessly exciting thriller."
                    —Dennis Lehane

"Over the last twenty-five years, Peter Blauner has proven to be a master of the urban dark side, his crime novels suffused with a knowing compassion for the bottom dogs who live in the minotaur's maze that is New York City. *Proving Ground* is one of his finest efforts."   —Richard Price

"Peter Blauner's new novel, *Proving Ground,* is an old-school page-turner, as war-damaged army vet Nathaniel 'Natty Dread' Dresden and police detective Lourdes Robles close in on the killer of Natty's father . . . and, maybe, each other. Taut narration, spot-on dialogue, and sharply etched action sequences make this one a must-read. I couldn't put the sucker down."   —Stephen King

"A new Peter Blauner novel is cause for celebration, and *Proving Ground* justifies the wait. This is a thoughtful, nuanced novel of crime and war and the human heart. Blauner's authentic and powerful writing is worthy of comparison to Richard Price and Dennis Lehane, and his story is coiled with emotional impact. Not to be missed."

—Michael Koryta, *New York Times* bestselling author of *Rise the Dark*

"Peter Blauner's first book in ten years, *Proving Ground*, is a showstopper. A tour-de-force of smart, gutsy, relentlessly entertaining storytelling that counts as one of the finest novels I've read in the past five years. Blauner has a painter's eye for detail, a playwright's ear for dialogue, and a film director's kinetic narrative vision. All combine to create a turbocharged reading experience. *Proving Ground* is a masterpiece of contemporary fiction."

—Christopher Reich, *New York Times* bestselling author of *Rules of Deception* and *Numbered Account*

"*Proving Ground* is a startlingly powerful tale of lost lives and lost souls with a crackling crime drama at its core. No one understands the NYPD, the backroom politics of New York, nor the heart of the city like Blauner. No one."

—Reed Farrel Coleman, *New York Times* bestselling author of *Where It Hurts*

"Like Richard Price, he has a bone-deep feel for New York's neighborhoods, a talent for making his characters fully alive, and the gift of turning descriptions into moments of found poetry on nearly every page. He's pretty handy with plot, too. Blauner is a terrific novelist and *Proving Ground* is proof of it. Is it selfish to ask him to turn off the TV and write nothing but novels in future? We don't want to wait another ten years for a book as elegantly written and engrossing as this one." —*Reviewing the Evidence*

Additional Praise for Peter Blauner

"The best New York thriller of the moment is Peter Blauner's *Slipping into Darkness*, with a title referring to both moral quicksand and failing eyesight. And this moody, location-specific story wears its urban authority with ease . . . layered and involving . . . Each of its main characters is life-like, and each is sharply defined by a sense of New York."

—Janet Maslin, *The New York Times,*
on *Slipping into Darkness*

"This isn't escapist fiction—Blauner's world is frighteningly real—but sales-wise that should serve the book well in the long run."

—*Publishers Weekly* (starred review)
on *The Last Good Day*

"The best novel I've read in years. It has great characters, a great story, a great heart. If you want comparisons, I can't give you any. There aren't any. I think Peter Blauner is better than Grisham, better than Patricia Cornwell. I loved *The Intruder*! Loved, loved, loved it."

—James Patterson on *The Intruder*

"Dig it. *Casino Moon* is a terrific crime novel. This book has it all: milieu, a terrific plot, characters so rich they reach out and grab you. . . . Peter Blauner is a brilliant young writer. . . . Read this book—it'll hang you out to dry."   —James Ellroy on *Casino Moon*

"Because Blauner tells the truth, his book is unforgettable."

—Patricia Highsmith on *Slow Motion Riot*

ALSO BY PETER BLAUNER

Slipping into Darkness

The Last Good Day

Man of the Hour

The Intruder

Casino Moon

Slow Motion Riot

PROVING GROUND

PETER BLAUNER

MINOTAUR BOOKS

NEW YORK

This is a work of fiction. All of the characters, organizations, and events portrayed in this novel are either products of the author's imagination or are used fictitiously.

PROVING GROUND. Copyright © 2017 by Peter Blauner. All rights reserved. Printed in the United States of America. For information, address St. Martin's Press, 175 Fifth Avenue, New York, N.Y. 10010.

www.minotaurbooks.com

Designed by Omar Chapa

The Library of Congress has cataloged the hardcover edition as follows:

Names: Blauner, Peter, author.
Title: Proving ground / Peter Blauner.
Description: First edition. | New York : Minotaur Books, 2017. |
    Series: Lourdes Robles novels ; 1
Identifiers: LCCN 2017011878 | ISBN 9781250117441 (hardcover) |
    ISBN 9781250117472 (ebook)
Subjects: LCSH: Women detectives—New York (State)—New York—
    Fiction. | Murder—Investigation—Fiction. | BISAC: FICTION /
    Crime. | FICTION / Mystery & Detective / Police Procedural. |
    GSAFD: Mystery fiction.
Classification: LCC PS3552.L3936 P76 2017 | DDC 813/.54—dc23
LC record available at https://lccn.loc.gov/2017011878

ISBN 978-1-250-11746-5 (trade paperback)

Our books may be purchased in bulk for promotional, educational, or business use. Please contact your local bookseller or the Macmillan Corporate and Premium Sales Department at 1-800-221-7945, extension 5442, or by email at MacmillanSpecial Markets@macmillan.com.

First Minotaur Books Paperback Edition: March 2018

10 9 8 7 6 5 4 3 2 1

To Mac and Mose,
Theme and Substance

PROVING
GROUND

PROLOGUE

The trouble started with the mask.

Soon after the surge died down, the commanders, in their infinite wisdom, decided that the handful of ballsy Iraqis who'd agreed to risk their lives interpreting for American military forces would no longer be allowed to cover their faces.

Word got passed to Second Lieutenant Natty Dread, a.k.a. Nathaniel Dresden, while he was in Mortaritaville. He was involved in a house-to-house search for a high-value target known as Ahmar the Red Beard, who had a reputation for personally executing suspected collaborators.

"That's a *negative*," Captain Paultz, the main fobbit at the base, told Natty when he questioned the order. "We're a professional army and professionals don't conceal their identities. If your terp is that scared, tell him to seek other employment."

Which meant Natty, a butter bar intelligence officer attached to the First Brigade Combat Team of the Tenth Mountain Division, had the stone privilege of walking down a crater-pocked street and breaking the news directly to the terp known as "Borat," because his long face, droopy mustache, and occasionally unseemly enthusiasm reminded some American soldiers of the only foreigner they'd encountered before deploying overseas.

"Please, no, Natty Dread." Jittery brown eyes stared out from behind a Polartec ski mask, watching Iraqi police officers help themselves to freebies from a fruit stall across the street. "It's not safe here. People are not how they seem."

"It's the army, B. Love it or leave it."

Knowing damn well that Borat couldn't afford to leave it because he needed cash to repair a family home badly damaged by Coalition bombs early in the war. A tiny mudbrick house near Balad with rebar sticking out of the walls, which Natty visited three days after the unmasking order came down. Now a group of individuals who needed no permission to wear balaclavas had just broken into the house, dragged Borat out of bed, and beheaded him in front of his wife and four young children.

"This cannot stand," said Captain Paultz. "This man was an important asset. It's like one of our dogs getting killed."

Resisting the urge to assault a superior, Natty channeled his aggressions into putting together leads instead, digging up information that led to Special Ops picking up a bunch of low-level insurgents for questioning. One of whom, nicknamed Crazy Eddie, literally coughed up a tip after a long adventure in what was euphemistically called Waterworld. An enhanced interrogation that Natty, the son of a civil rights attorney, observed with increasing discomfort bordering on physical symptoms over several hours. He'd just started to lodge a protest when Eddie suddenly recalled that *pendejo* Ahmar was laying up with a relative's family near the old cigarette factory in Sadr City. He was posting jihad messages by day and banging a twelve-year-old niece by night with selectively edited passages from the Koran as justification.

Hyped on bottles of Ripped Fuel 5X, Natty's unit scaled the front wall just after twenty-two hundred hours the next night. The sapper set a donut-shaped charge on the steel front door, while Natty, hanging back by the concrete shitter in the yard, noticed that even with night-vision goggles turning everything aquatic-green, the villa they were about to break into vaguely resembled the brownstone where he was raised in Park Slope, Brooklyn.

The charge blew the door off its hinges and put white noise between his ears. He hoisted his M4 and joined his staff sergeant, J. R. Cuddy, and four other joes in the stack, breaching the entrance and entering the front hall. Army cowhide and rubber soles stomped past a fading Persian rug with two pairs of sparkling silver women's slippers, a pair of men's Adidas shower shoes, and child-sized soccer cleats. He stepped over them gingerly, knowing they could have been rigged with explosives, his gunsights finding a black plate with Arab calligraphy over the doorway.

"Enter here in peace and security."

He lowered his gun sights, his hearing fading back in, realizing his parents had the same plate over their entrance. Along with the mezuzah by the front door, the "No Blood for Oil" bumper sticker, and the Bob Marley posters in the living room.

One fire team went off to a room on the left that had a running fountain while Natty followed Cuddy to the right, finding himself in a small den where the air was heavy with lavender and flavored tobacco.

A man his father's age in a white Oxford shirt, dark pleated slacks, and a Stalinesque mustache was already facedown on the rug, hands laced behind his head. A stocky woman in a lumpy red pullover and a black headscarf was waving her arms and shrieking in Arabic.

"Fayn Ahmar," Natty yelled at her, trying to fill in for his dead translator with the pidgin Arabic he'd retained from his army language program.

"Fayn Ahmar?" The lady looked confused, shifting her glare from Natty to the beleaguered husband on the floor.

"Fuckin' listen to him." Cuddy tugged on one of his big mudflap ears to illustrate, while driving the heel of his boot into the prone man's back. *"Samee-ya.* Okay?"

"Ahmar," Natty rubbed his own chin. "Fuckface Red Beard. Where is he?"

"Bit Amal." The woman screamed, the smell of cumin on her breath. *"Da gozee! Da baiti . . . "*

She pointed at the man on the floor, at the soccer game on the television, the water pipe on the end table, at the family photos around the room. Then she began patting her chest frantically as if to say, "You see? You see? We're the same. Our hearts beat just like yours."

"Sir, whoever you're looking for is not here." The man facedown on the floor was speaking in lightly accented English, calm as Obi-Wan telling the stormtroopers *"These are not the droids you're looking for."*

"Ahmar." Cuddy kicked him in the ribs. "Don't fucking tell me you don't know."

The rest of the team was casing the room. Nothing in the closets. Bunch of books on the shelves but, suspiciously, no pictures of any of the local "Death to America" fire-breathers, which were as common here as photos of the Pope in Carroll Gardens. Anyone who didn't have one had to be hiding something.

Cuddy grabbed a gold trophy on a white pedestal off the mantelpiece and exchanged a knowing look with Natty. Fucking A. The last house where they found a high-value target had a solid-gold table with a personal thank-you from the local Al Qaeda chapter inscribed on the bottom.

"Da ibn! Da ibn!" the wife was shrieking again.

"Shut the fuck up already," Natty raised his carbine, trying to silence her and figure out what was going on.

He was aware of the differing rates of respiration in the vicinity. At least a half dozen people breathing hard in a limited space, like they were all recovering from a marathon. But someone was conspicuously panting more than the others. Natty looked around until his eyes found a door at the back of the room. A pair of shadows were visible in the gap at the bottom, indicating human presence. He nodded at Cuddy, making sure he'd seen as well. Two days before, a joe from another fire team searching for Ahmar got fried to a living crisp at a similar house in Ramadi.

The shadows under the door moved and footsteps pounded up an unseen staircase, then tramped across the ceiling.

The husband on the floor tried to lift his head. "Sir, this is a misunderstanding—"

Natty was fast through the door, Cuddy at his heels. A short hall led to a stairway with a lime-green carpet. A wall to the right was shiny with a fresh patch of plaster, probably covering a hiding place for a weapons cache. Shattered glass in a back door looked out on a rear yard, where another fire team was coming over a wall. Natty's heart pummeled at thrash-metal speed as he took the lead up the steps, forgetting for the moment that his job was supposed to be intel, Cuddy close behind, joes in the other room still shouting at the couple not to fucking move.

He crept three-quarters of the way up the stairs and then stopped, hearing frenzy on the second floor. Ali Baba up to no good, preparations for counterattack underway. Cuddy joined him on the step, listening and then detaching a stun grenade from his belt. He carefully extracted the pin and rolled the charge across the landing. The dimpled avocado shell made a muted treading sound on the rug before it stopped a yard short of a doorway: maybe a dud. But then the concussive force of the flash-bang turned Natty's eardrums inside out again, leaving just a high, mournful keen above a low hiss.

Cuddy's round face floated beside him, mouth opening and closing without aural effect. Natty rested his hand on the banister, noticing that it was still vibrating. Someone continuing to move above them. Jihadi Terminator shit. Normal people would have surrendered by now. He tried to say as much to Cuddy but couldn't hear his own voice. He looked back and saw the shadows moving within a scalene triangle of light coming through the door which was now half open on the landing.

His right shoulder tightened as he raised his carbine and set it to burst, ignoring the voice in the back of his head second-guessing. Shut up, old man. I'm here. You're not.

The door creaked, the shadow lengthening, the scalene turning into an isosceles and then a trapezoid. He pulled the trigger and let go a three-round burst just as Cuddy mouthed the words "Oh shit."

Natty shut his eyes, deliberately counting to five. The stillness of the house had the submissive character of city streets after a blizzard. He opened them again and saw an empty child-sized sneaker sideways on the landing. A Nike knock-off with gold Lakers trim. And velcro straps. Just for style, he tried to tell himself. Because the alternative explanation was that the little boy in the white soccer jersey, who'd just been blown out of his shoe, was not quite old enough to tie his own laces.

Natty knew before he turned that the parents would be at the bottom of the stairs, looking up at him. The mother was hollow-eyed. She'd just seen to the end of her days and knew nothing she cared about was standing between now and then. The father had gotten a life sentence as well. His face was like a study in time-lapse photography, thirty years passing in ten seconds. He opened his mouth to speak, but all Natty could hear was the keen rising into an unbearable shriek inside his own skull.

He looked down, trudged past them dutifully, and went out into the cold desert night.

1

A helicopter with a searchlight is hovering low over Prospect Park, its juddering hum reminding Lourdes of a man deciding how to respond to an insult.

As she approaches the Fifth Street entrance, she sees ambulance guys smoking cigarettes, in no big hurry to do anything. Yellow tape cordons off the bike lanes, a big crowd behind it already, bathed in flashes of blue, white, and red from the squad car lights. An exclusive nightspot for people you wouldn't want to party with: white-shirted supervisors, regular uniform cops, and detectives in off-the-rack suits.

On first glance, it looks like the unusual event they've shown up for is a vacant parking space in No-Park Slope. But then she sees the fleecy white and red clumps, which turn out to be feathers, trailing back toward the sidewalk. They lead past inside-out latex gloves, snipped rubber tubing, and a bent syringe to a body facedown near an elm tree, stuffing coming out through the ruptured stitching of a Canada Goose parka.

Lourdes flips tin at the cop standing guard and ducks under the tape, not liking the way her trousers crackle with the bend. A month without carbs and she still can't get under 165. But fuck it, she's bootylicious and proud. Always been a big girl, with lots of bounce to the ounce. All creamy café con leche abundance busting from a halter top when she was waitressing undercover at the Golden Lady Gentlemen's Lounge, substantial and serious when she's wearing her Lane Bryant business suit in the squadroom. Either way, whoever couldn't appreciate that rearview had no class and could just move it along, nothing to see here, fellas.

"Detective Robles, welcome back." Captain Bowman, the CO from her patrol days, is just inside the tape, shivering in the spring chill. "I'll cue the balloons."

She smiles and bunches her cheeks up like brioche tops. Three months back in the detective squad and still catching grief from the trolls downstairs. What else could she expect? Even before she got in trouble, she'd been dangerously low on allies at the seven-eight. Pretty much everyone she used to work with had been pissed about her getting to jump the line before she'd even completed her eighteen-month rotation in Narcotics.

But none of them happened to be getting highlights at the Sophisticated Lady Hair Salon on Flatbush Avenue when a five-time loser named Tyrell Humphries tried to hold the place up with a .22, which he dry-clicked twice upside Lourdes's head after she ID'd herself as a cop. Somehow even with a smock on, she'd managed to wrestle the gat away before shooting him in the ball sack. Which, in turn, led to her getting promoted at a special ceremony attended by the mayor and the PC.

Her photo appeared in the *Daily News*, effectively ending her career as an undercover. And leaving her unprotected six months later when her fuckwit partner, Erik Heinz, got caught on a cell-phone camera verbally abusing an Arab cab driver for cutting them off on Ocean Parkway, with Lourdes standing behind him, silent and embarrassed. The clip became an instant YouTube sensation, seventy-five thousand clicks in the first three hours, earning Heinz a new assignment moving Staten Island barricades and Lourdes six weeks in a VIPER room, watching security monitors in a housing project basement. When she got out, she was no longer known as the "Heroine of the Hair Salon," but as "that fat girl who got in trouble."

"What do we got, Captain?"

"Deep breath, LRo. Taxpayer down."

"White guy?"

"Amazing. You're getting called in six hours after your tour ends and you figure that out on your own. No wonder they let you hang on to that little gold shield."

Four detectives from her squad are already at the scene, joining a couple of medical-legal investigators from the ME's office in Tyvek suits and booties. Two CSU techs take photos and make notes. The ghouls are parking the morgue van over by the parks administration building. She notices that every time she catches someone's eye, it darts away.

"The 9-1-1 operator patched the call through a few minutes past eleven," Bowman says. "Residents across the street reported hearing shots."

Lourdes looks over at the limestones and brownstones on the other side of Prospect Park West, lined up like nineteenth-century novels you needed perfect ACT scores to read. Each worth four million *easy* these days—more, if you could get a dentist or a shrink paying office rent on the garden floor.

It must be twenty years since the last murder in the park that white people cared about. A drama teacher got shot for his mountain bike near Swan Lake, back when she was in fifth grade and Brooklyn was still fierce.

Nowadays, the whole damn park is an ad for healthy urban living. At least when the sun is up. Private foundations and citizen volunteers had poured dollars and hours into protecting the trees, saving the ducks, bringing in the Metropolitan Opera, and chasing junkies from the band shell. Any Saturday or Sunday, the six hundred acres are fields of well-tended flesh: world-class runners, Tour de France wannabes, Audubon Society bird freaks, Olympian volleyball players, and Ivy Leaguers dragging their $500 congas to the African drum circle in the grove.

At night, though, the ghosts still come out. The Picnic House gets shrouded in mist like a castle from some old Shakespeare play. Homeless people still hide out in encampments in the woods, where they can lie down quietly with their sorrows in the moonlight. The occasional wolf pack still roams over from Parkside Avenue or Empire Boulevard. Every few years, a ninja with a sword shows up in the Vale of Cashmere, a vengeful spirit from the eighties slashing at gay men in the bushes. And every season or two, a lonely life still ends dangling from a low branch on Suicide Hill.

"See all the fluff that came out of the coat?" Bowman points out the wisps blowing away. "Must have been a big gun."

"Or defects in the nylon." Lourdes aims her chin at a flagrant rip in the stitching. "Eyewits?"

"The good news is, we found some screwball with a sleeping bag and a view of the crime scene just on the other side of the wall."

"The bad news?"

"He's not talking." The captain jerks a thumb over his shoulder.

Detective Robert "Beautiful Bobby" Borrelli from her squad is a few yards away, gesturing haplessly at a man wearing a hat with furry ears and a plastic shower curtain over his shoulders.

"It's not clear he speaks English," the captain says. "Or any other earth language."

"Like that matters." Lourdes unbuttons her coat as she strolls over. "What up, B.B.?"

Beautiful Bobby, Romeo-eyed with a Guido Elvis pompadour and a small pink baby butt of a bald spot, shrugs at his subject.

"Mork from Ork here. Ten minutes, no ID, *no hablo*. He's either deaf and dumb or thinks we're from the intergalactic border patrol."

"I'll talk to her," the homeless man says matter of factly.

"See that, B.B.?" She throws her shoulders back. "It's all about the attitude."

"I know you." The homeless guy adjusts the shower curtain like an aristocrat's cape.

"You know *me*?"

She studies the homeless dude more closely. He has the face of an Aztec warrior debauched by years of hard city living: high, bruised cheekbones and slanting almond eyes with tiny globs of mascara sticking to the lashes.

"I met you in the park," he says, with a hint of a Mexican accent. "Long time ago."

"Yeah?" She wrinkles her nose, hoping this isn't someone she once dated.

"I was living down under the bridge, by the ravine." He doffs the furry ears in tribute. "You were in uniform but I knew you were an angel."

"Yeah, I get that a lot." She rolls her eyes at B.B., knowing she'll pay for this later at the squad.

"It was ten below zero in the park." Little yellow whales crinkle on the shower curtain cape. "You gave me a twenty-dollar bill and told me to get the fuck out."

"*De nada.*" Lourdes nods. "Was I nice about it?"

"Nice enough."

"Anyway, tonight . . ."

"Tonight I'm sleeping by the wall, when I hear these people talking."

The homeless man pops his eyes open, to recreate the moment. "Old white dude says, 'Hey, guys, what's doing?'"

"'Hey guys'? Like it's someone he knows?"

"Dunno." The homeless man shrugs. "Then I hear, 'Whoa, whoa, whoa,' and *bap bap bap*. I drop back down behind the wall and I hear this other dude go, 'Kizz, kizz.'"

"'Kizz, kizz'? You sure?"

"More likely, 'Keys, keys,'" a deep, tired voice says behind her. "Like the victim dropped his car keys and one of them was saying pick it up."

A tall, red-faced man with 1977 sideburns and bloodhound eyes has lumbered over in a black raincoat, uniformed cops getting out of his way like meerkats fleeing an elephant.

"Kevin Sullivan, Brooklyn South Homicide," he introduces himself in the diffident grumble of a country priest with a Marlboro habit.

So this is Him: the Last of the Mohicans. His reputation precedes him, but he's actually more imposing than Lourdes expected. Maybe six-five, six-six, two fifty—the kind of big that makes everyone else have to adjust their seats when he gets in a car. Said to be peaceful of disposition until provoked—then potentially terrifying. Up close, he looks to be in his early sixties but his ruddy complexion is still so pockmarked from adolescent acne that it appears small animals have been gnawing on his face. He smells of Old Spice and patchouli. His mop of black hair has no shading or nuance. More Grecian Formula Apache than Sitting Bull Natural.

"Yeah, that must have been what they were saying." The homeless guy nods. "When I looked over the wall, they were getting in a Benz and driving away."

"Mercedes-Benz?" Lourdes makes a note.

"Yeah, I'd say an old 450." The homeless man registers Lourdes's questioning look. "I used to be a mechanic out at one of those garages by Shea Stadium." He glances away wistfully. "Anyhow, I look out and see the white dude's crawling along the sidewalk going, 'Help me, help me.' But by the time I got to him, he was gone."

"Can you describe the guys who jacked the car?" Lourdes asks, a little self-conscious about keeping her voice steady with Sullivan clocking her.

"No. It was too far from the streetlight."

"Excuse me, *how many* shots did you say?" Sullivan looms over the homeless man, more solicitous than threatening.

"Three."

"Sure about that?" Sullivan gives Lourdes a sidelong glance.

"I've seen better days, but I can still count to three," the homeless man says, a brief history of shame passing across his face.

"All right." Sullivan nods at Borrelli. "You got this?"

"Oh yeah, we're BFFs now." Beautiful Bobby helps the homeless guy keep his cape on. "I'll get him a hot chocolate and take his statement."

Lourdes watches them trundle off, then looks back toward the body as the CSU techs slip paper bags over the dead man's hands. Sullivan drops into a surprisingly agile squat and starts to count the evidence placards.

"I see five shell casings; he says three shots." He sucks his lips. "You find that odd?"

"I wouldn't take his word for anything." She shrugs. "He's out of his fucking mind."

"Watch the language, please." He doesn't meet her eyes.

God, another one of those lace-curtain Irish hypocrites, who swears like Lil Wayne around other men but blushes every time a woman lets a four-letter word drop.

"Good you got him talking though." Sullivan bounces on his haunches.

"What we do."

"White man dead by the park, in an $800 coat, with a Benz driving away afterward." Sullivan stands, wipes his hands on his coat. "There's going to be a lot of eyes on this."

"You telling me to back off?"

"Just saying. You have options."

So he's heard about Erik Heinz.

"You want me off, do whatever you have to do," she says. "But I'm not going willingly."

He looks her up and down. Other girls may have wanted to be ballerinas or princesses, but Lourdes never thought about being anything other than a cop. Spent her nights watching *Kojak* reruns and reading

Dorothy Uhnak novels while Papi was starting his bid upstate and Mami was out getting high. And now that she's finally made it to a detective squad, she's not looking back. Other people got into the job for the benefits or because they couldn't think of anything else to do. But Lourdes always knew she had the calling. While other girls she grew up with at the projects were getting pregnant too young and soft-minded with reality shows and self-pity, she was sharpening up like a Westinghouse scholar. Getting all sagacious and streetwise about human behavior. Even Erik Heinz couldn't quite kill her feeling for the work. After eleven years on the job, the girl loves having her own desk and coffee mug with the NYPD emblem, loves the dark science forensics and data-bank searches, loves the interrogation head games, and yes, even sometimes loves working with men instead of women—appreciating the simplicity of dealing with a bunch of coarse, hairy-knuckled guys who don't talk shit all day about their weight and how no one really appreciates them.

"Hey, detectives." Bowman is waving them over, a tech from Crime Scene with him holding up a wallet. "Know who this is?"

The vic has been rolled. An older guy, maybe mid-sixties, with a halo of wizard-white hair spilling out around his head and a kind of exhausted middle-class nobility to his leonine features. He wears a scruffy beard and the slightly perplexed expression of a man interrupted while making his morning coffee.

"That's David Dresden." Sullivan goes still.

"The lawyer?" Lourdes asks.

"Try the lawyer every cop in the city hates," the captain says.

Big mouth on the evening news, press conferences on courthouse steps, always carrying on about police brutality and racial injustice. Lourdes heard him referred to as "the white Al Sharpton" and worse long before she even became a cop. Despised not only for keeping criminals out of prison but for causing epic traffic jams with his protest marches.

"Scumbag." The captain breathes out a cold vapor. "I don't want to say 'what goes around comes around,' but . . ."

"Then *don't*." Sullivan turns away, broad shoulders hunched.

"Wasn't he just in the news, defending some raghead who wanted to blow up a bridge?" the captain asks, not taking the hint.

"*Suing* the FBI." Sullivan looks back over his shoulder, setting his teeth. "For a client who claims he was tortured. Slight difference." He eyes Lourdes. "Sure you still want in?"

"I come a long way to get back to the dance, daddy." She sticks her chest out. "Don't send me home early."

"Suit yourself." Sullivan takes out his notepad and ambles back to the body. "Just don't count on meeting any princes at the ball."

2

An old man with long gray hair is in a corner of the cell. Sweat stains form a harrowed *Scream* face on the front of his t-shirt as he hunches over, talking to himself. At least he *appears* to be talking to himself. Except every once in a while, he tilts up his scabby chin, fixes on Natty, and announces, "Well, you done it now, son . . ."

Natty averts his eyes, the back of his buzz-cut head sore and cold from the cinder block wall as he tried to sleep sitting up on the bolted bench.

The ghouls and goblins of recrimination were at him until dawn, much louder than the perps in and out of the pens. The system is overloaded. Last night, Ecstasy-addled fans pouring out of a Skrillex concert ran straight into hordes of angry Yankees fans tumbling from the bars after a brutal loss to the Tigers, resulting in dozens of arrests for fighting and public indecency.

"The fuck are you looking at?" The man with the long gray hair is staring again, some old wet brain in the late stages of dementia. "You want something to cry about?"

Natty bangs the back of his head against the wall again. Stop tripping, yo. Come on, be a man. You're thirty-three years old. You can take care of yourself. Still in good health, physically, with a thick neck and oversized shoulders from weight-lifting and mixed martial arts. "The kind of muscles that make it look like you're about to attack someone when all you're doing is getting in the shower," his father once said. No one's going to hurt you in here, except yourself. And you're *definitely* not going to do that. It's just normal procedure that the court officers took the belt from your khakis and the laces from your Timberlands. Right?

"Long way down, son." The wet brain is laughing. "Enjoy the ride."

The air smells of two-day-old urine, Vanilla Mist air freshener, and man ass. An old Chinese dude sits on the steel toilet in the corner crying. A skinny black androgyne with braided hair and an "I Luv Haiti" t-shirt knotted above the navel leans against the bars, talking quietly to a young Pakistani-looking dude with a hennaed beard and a ponytail, who keeps drawing back and falsettoing, "Nigga say wha?"

Natty crunches his eyes, trying to shut out the noise. Most of his cell-mates are what his father would have called *the disenfranchised*. Subway slashers, pocketbook grabbers, credit card snatchers, nickel bag dealers, bus stop boxers, dis cons, DVs, DUIs, and ACDs, with the occasional Ecstasy seller and child abuser thrown in. Men born mostly without privilege, who have tried and failed to reach accommodation with friends, family, women, the powers-that-be, and their own defeated ex-pectations. Waiting to be shipped off to Rikers, the island of no hope, where they might wait years for their cases to be called while the rest of the world goes about its business and forgets them.

How you like me now, Dad? I'm finally one of your people.

He rubs his face in the crook of his elbow, right below the tattoo that says "Everywhere Is War." His little revenge joke on the old man. Who used to play that fucking Bob Marley song all the time in the old Peu-geot with the "Coexist" bumper sticker and the skunky back seats.

Natty reacted by listening to nothing but death metal and gangster rap for years afterward. Until he got in the army and wrote the hated reg-gae nickname Dad had given him on his helmet, making "Natty Dread" his nom de guerre. Then he had the lyrics from "War" inked permanently into his flesh. Because by then he had learned a truth not often spoken about in Park Slope: That war was a natural universal state. War between nations, war between religions, war between races, war between men and women, and, yes, war between fathers and sons. *Iyaman*, Bob Marley. Everywhere is war.

He stops knocking his head and wrinkles his nose, disgusted by the smell of his own BO. The clock on the wall says it's almost nine in the morning, but it could be hours before he sees a judge. His hands flex as he tries to get his circulation going. There are red rims on his wrists from handcuffs being on too tight and something is stuck in the webbing between the fingers of his right hand. A fragment of a tooth lodged in the knuckles, with dried blood around it. His tongue feels around inside his mouth and finds all his own teeth present and accounted for.

"Hey, what are you?"

A large black man stands over him, with the pot-roast arms of a bouncer who works at a nightclub where they even have to check the purses for weapons. He wears an untucked striped polo shirt that makes him look like a member of the Peanuts gang turned ill thug by life on the streets. You a bad man, Charlie Brown.

"I don't know," Natty keeps his head down. "What do you think I am?"

In the P.S. 51 schoolyard, he was never really anything. A shade or two darker than most white kids, but too pale to be considered black or brown. Just lost in the middle when they sang "The Rainbow Connection" at the year-end assembly. By the time he hit his teens, his features had settled and become more conventionally Caucasoid, with Dad's nose prevailing over Mom's mouth, but inside he still didn't quite ID as anything. Not really majority or minority. Not really Jewish or Christian. Not really cool or a nerd. Not really rich or poor. Right or left. Probably half the reason he joined the army was just so he could be *something*.

"No, I mean what are you here for?" Thug-life Charlie Brown asks. "You a domestic? Arson? Drugs? What'd you do?"

"Why's that anyone's business?"

"Okay, don't tell me." Charlie Brown puts his hands up. "All I know is those dudes over there saying they're gonna fuck you up, first chance they get."

He moves aside so Natty can see there are two men across the cell glaring. Both white and brawlic, wearing navy-blue t-shirts with FDNY emblems.

"So you must have done *something*." Charlie Brown peels off as the older of the two comes over.

A Brooklyn redwood in Levi's and work boots, with salt-and-pepper commas of hair and the confident stride of a battalion captain who believes that the free swinging of his dong could wake the whole neighborhood like the tolling of the Liberty Bell.

"Hey," the captain says.

"Hey."

"You know what you did, don't you?"

He looms over Natty as his buckethead friend joins them, the two of them starting to do that chicken-wing limber-up that men do when they circle each other before a bar fight, raising their elbows to shoulder level and bending them back.

"Depends." Natty turns and gives him side-eye. "What do *you* think I did?"

"I think you fucked yourself," the captain says.

"Yeah? How'd I do that?"

"You jumped one of our brothers."

"He need jumping?"

"He's in the ICU now."

"Because of what *I* did?"

Unlikely this is a coincidence, being placed in a holding cell with people he'd had a conflict with earlier. Protocol should have separated them. Maybe it's just the overcrowding tonight. Or maybe someone is fucking with him, playing fast-and-loose with the rules because they figured out just who his father was.

"Here's the thing." The captain lowers his voice. "Our crew, we're a family. We eat together, we sleep in the same room, we put our lives on the line for each other. You hurt one of us, you hurt all of us."

"I don't know what the fuck you're talking about." Natty shrugs.

But little pinpricks of concern are giving way to a massive bubble of panic forming. He has literally no memory of anything after ten o'clock last night.

"When we get out of this place"—the captain lays a heavy hand on Natty's shoulder—"there's going to be a conversation."

"Whatever." Natty brushes it off.

"Not 'whatever.' This is going to happen."

All the other men in the cell are staring. This is a test, a proving ground, to see what he'll do. Backing down or offering a feeble apology would be a fatal choice for someone about to go in the system. Even his father, champion of the oppressed and defender of the underdog, would admit, after a few scotches, that no one loves a pussy who can't stand up for himself.

"You're crowding me," Natty says.

He stands up to his full five foot ten inches. The captain is at least a head taller, but Natty holds the bigger man's gaze for a full ten count before he allows himself to blink.

"There are fifteen thousand people in our department," the captain says. "You'll be safer in Rikers than you will be out on the street."

"You know what?" Natty pulls up on his belt loops. "If what you say about me is true, I must have issues. And you're triggering them."

A buzzer sounds and a heavy door opens down the hall. A couple of court officers walk up to the cell, having probably seen enough on their CCTV monitors.

"All right," says one of them, a municipal Medici with a clipboard and a Staten Island accent. "Gentlemen, some of your attorneys are here to speak to you before your arraignments. I have Alvarez, Pablo; Carter, Marcus; Dresden, Nathaniel . . ."

"Peace." Natty nods at the firemen.

The door opens and he joins the line of defendants being led to a series of booths in the hall between the pens and the courtroom.

His father's best friend and law partner, Benjamin Grimaldi, a.k.a. Ben Grimm, a.k.a. Benny G., is at a small table in one of the cubicles, a steel mesh partition separating him from the client side and making only a few fleshy sections visible at a time.

"Goddamn, kid," he says in his Brooklyn grand opera baritone. "Didn't anybody tell you the war is over?"

Tears of relief pump up behind Natty's eyes. Hallefuckinglujah. The cavalry is here. If the mesh wasn't in the way, he'd throw his arms around Ben.

As usual, Ben is dressed with the kind of pimpish, bad-ass Jim Dandy flamboyance that can only be pulled off with a Marine Corp bearing, a heavyweight boxer's physique, and a head shaved clean and round as a cannonball. On a lesser man, a purple Hermès tie and matching pocket square might seem—well, a little swishy, even when worn with double-breasted Hugo Boss pinstripes. But on Ben, with his iron jaw and his deviated septum, they looked like the heraldry of a warrior-king.

By contrast, Natty's own father, David Dresden, was a bit of hippie shlub in his old corduroy jacket with the patched elbows and his gasoline-rainbow ties. A decent man. An admirable man. An *estimable* man even. He took on unpopular causes, challenged the authorities, got innocent men out of life sentences and at least one off Death Row, and argued successfully twice before the Supreme Court. While usually getting home in time to have dinner with his family. He took his only child to pediatrician appointments, helped him with his math homework, pitched in on art projects, and tried to teach his boy how to play the guitar.

But Ben was the man Natty truly wanted to be.

The first call you'd make when you were in trouble. Natty's earliest memories are of his own sticky-stubby fingers tracing the smooth dome of Ben's scalp, instead of getting caught in Dad's stringy locks. And with only daughters at home, Ben was always happy to take Natty camping in the Catskills, where he taught the boy how to split wood and build a fire.

While Dad was off at protest marches with Pete Seeger and Harry Belafonte, Ben, a former Golden Gloves fighter, taught Natty how to box. Enrolling him at Landau's gym, getting him his first pair of Everlast gloves, and signing him up for his first junior tournament when Natty was twelve. While Ben wrapped his hands in the locker-room, Dad showed up in his Grateful Dead *American Beauty* t-shirt and said, "You don't have to do this." Trying to give his son an easy out. Not realizing it was the worst possible advice to give a boy trying to psych himself up for his first physical combat experience.

So once Natty was between the ropes, facing a beast built like middle school Mike Tyson, it was Ben's voice that he listened for calling out "stick and move . . . keep your guard up . . . stay off the ropes . . . pick your spots." He waited until he saw the opening, landed a solid shot through the headgear, and dropped the larger boy to the canvas. Then beamed as Ben got in the ring to hold his bony trembling arm aloft.

While Dad talked about "the importance of the struggle," Ben was just about winning. His wall had framed headlines about the Mafia cases he won as a state prosecutor and the acquittals he'd collected later as a defense lawyer. He kept a pair of old brass knuckles in a desk drawer and sometimes sported a .38 caliber service revolver in an ankle holster, which his own father had worn as a New York City police officer. He had a collection of watches that included a gold Rolex Chronometer he'd been given by Tupac Shakur as a thank-you for representing him in a traffic dispute years before. After Natty made it through basic training at Fort Benning, it was Ben, who'd served in Vietnam, taking him out for a steak dinner at Peter Luger's to celebrate.

But thinking back now on how the constant comparisons must have weighed on Dad, Natty feels a sting and contraction in the middle of his chest, as if someone had stuck a syringe into his heart and slowly pulled back on the plunger.

"Thanks for coming, Ben."

"What am I gonna do? Rack up billable hours while my best friend's son is in the can?"

"What do you hear from the DA's office?" Natty sits down.

"I won't lie. It's serious. They're going for the top count."

"Assault one?" Natty shows his palms. "These look like deadly instruments?"

"We'll get you bailed out," Ben says.

"What's the max I could get?"

"Twenty-five. But it's not going to come to that."

"Oh my God." Natty shakes his head. "Ben, I fucked up."

"We're not going to argue that now. The fact is, there's a probationary firefighter in intensive care at Bellevue, with a severe concussion and a broken jaw. And he's got an uncle who died on 9/11."

"Jesus . . ."

"Hey." Ben puts his palm flat on the mesh. "We are going to fix this. Okay? You're not some jerk-off who's already on parole. You did two tours in Iraq. You've got a half dozen commendations, a law degree from Duke, and—what?—two years as a prosecutor with the state attorney in Orlando, Florida. And if that wasn't enough . . ." He raises his finger, pausing for dramatic effect as he rehearses his pitch for the judge. "You've just suffered a tragic loss in your own family."

"Do we really have to bring that up?"

"Why wouldn't we? Your father's dead less than a week."

Natty crosses his arms, starting to feel sick to his stomach, remembering how he handled himself at the funeral over the weekend, getting up in his army uniform to read Rudyard Kipling's "If—" at Riverside

Memorial Chapel. A not-so-subtle fuck-you to the overflow crowd of lefty lawyers, media geeks, Occupy Wall Street types, and common criminals trying to pass themselves off as "activists." The so-called progressives who always acted like they had more of a claim on Dad than he did.

"Nathaniel," his mother said afterward. *"I'm a let you be you."*

"All right, what can you tell me about last night?" Ben rolls his neck.

"Nothing."

"I don't need to go into a lot of detail at this point." Ben opens his legal pad. "Just enough to start the negotiation."

"I don't remember anything." Natty drops his voice. "I think I blacked out."

"Seriously?"

"There's nothing past a certain point."

"What's the last thing you got?"

"Arguing with my ex-girlfriend on the phone, and then stressing about money with Mom afterward." Natty shakes his head again, sick to his stomach from remembering. "So I was like, 'fuck this, I've gotta get out of here. I'm bugging.'"

"Where did you go?"

"A bar called Rescue One on Fifth Avenue."

"I know it. A retired firefighter owns it." Ben's tone of voice is not approving.

"I was just gonna have a couple and watch a few innings of the Mets in LA. But that's where my highlight reel ends."

Ben taps a silver Cross pen on the pad in a steady metronome rhythm. "So let me ask: has that ever happened to you before?"

Natty clasps his hands on top of the table, the right trying to take custody of the left, before he nods.

"When?"

"Just a few times. Mostly in Florida."

"Have you been treated for post-traumatic stress disorder?"

"We really have to go there?"

"Yeah, we really do." Ben tucks his chin down and looks up from the tops of his eyes. "It's not clear if this firefighter is even going to make a full recovery."

Natty takes a deep breath, as if preparing to go underwater for a while.

"I went to a few group sessions at the VA in Orlando. But I got sick of the long wait to get an individual appointment and didn't think it was helping anyway. So I stopped. And never applied for disability."

"Uh-huh. You want to tell me why you had to start going in the first place?"

Natty looks down, watching his own knees bang together. "I was starting to have some trouble at work, spacing out, fighting with my supervisor. And a couple of times on the highway I hit the brakes when I thought someone was tailgating me."

"Oh, boy." Ben stops taking notes. "Anything else?"

"In the parking lot of a Publix supermarket, when I was with my girlfriend and her daughter, I had to deck someone. But it was for good reason. He'd knocked the kid over with a shopping cart and wouldn't apologize."

An unwelcome flash puts him back in the sunshine. With Tanya screaming, her daughter, Ariel, cowering behind her tawny leg, as a dude in a Marlins jersey cups his bloody mouth and screams "lawsuit."

"Let's just cut to the chase," Ben says. "Were you arrested for any of these incidents?"

"The police took a report after one of the tailgating things. And they showed up after I punched the guy in the parking lot. I got a deferred adjudication because I agreed to counseling."

"So charges were dismissed?"

"I didn't lose my army benefits, but it was strongly suggested I take a leave of absence from my job." Natty sniffs, his tongue touching a sore spot where he'd been chewing the inside of his cheek. "Not giving you much to work with, am I?"

Ben spread-eagles his right hand up against the screen again. "Let me ask you something else, Natty. Do you trust me?"

"You know I do."

"Do you believe I have your best interests at heart?"

Natty puts his palm up against Ben's, the mesh in between. "I do."

"Then I need you to listen to me. The answer is drug court."

"Ben, I'm not an addict." Natty slides his hand down. "I went out to have a few drinks because I haven't been able to sleep since the funeral . . ."

"Don't get hung up on the technicalities." Ben barrels over the objection. "It's a diversionary program. Treatment is better for every-body than prison. The judge who handles it was in Vietnam around the same time as me. He's taken over other cases where the defendant was a vet. If the other side is willing to deal, I might be able to get you counseling for PTSD instead of jail time."

"What about keeping my law license? Who's going to hire me if that's on my record?"

"I am trying to save your neck, son," Ben says. "If convicted, you will lose not just your license, but all your military benefits. And you will de-stroy your mother. Who just lost a husband. You want her to have to drive six hours and get felt up by some inbred redneck prison guard every time she wants to see her kid?"

Natty shakes his head and picks at the dried blood on his knuckles.

"Then let's get to it." Ben stands up, does the pocket mambo to make sure he's got everything, and then grabs the pad. "Oh, and Natty? One other thing."

"What?"

"I'm aware you and your father had your differences. But you should know David was always very proud."

"If you say so." Natty looks over his shoulder again, to see the court officers escorting out the firefighters and the wet brain who'd been pes-tering him in the cell.

"Enough." Ben gets up. "I'm gonna talk to the judge. See you out there."

Natty nods and watches him go, tongue touching the inside of his cheek again and then pulling back, the sore spot still too tender to probe.

3

Just after eleven that morning, Lourdes and Sullivan sit in a 2014 Chevy Impala parked across from the Dresden address on President Street, waiting for mother and son to get back from court.

When Lourdes was growing up at the Walt Whitman Projects, a couple of miles away in Fort Greene, this was her storybook dreamtime neighborhood: the alternative reality where a slimmer Lourdes, with *blanquita* skin, would raise a family of her own in one of the neat little row houses with the cherry blossoms and oak trees in front and the clean-swept sidewalks where relaxed-looking white people stood around talking like they had all the time in the world, never taking their eyes off their kids as they skipped rope and rode scooters, never smacking anyone upside the head for using chalk on the pavement, and walking dogs that looked better groomed than the people. But she never got the *blanquita* complexion and, truth be told, never got much slimmer, and if she couldn't afford the hood then, she certainly can't live here now, but like a lot of things in her life she's learning to adjust and be all right with what has to be.

They've been sitting here, saying nothing, for more than an hour. She'd been warned about the Sully silences. B.B. tried to convince her that Sullivan really was half Indian and this was some Native American war trance he went into from time to time. Andy Chen from the seven-eight detective squad claimed they were acid flashbacks. But Captain Bowman just said when you got ready to retire, melancholy fell over you sometimes for no good reason.

A silver Jaguar pulls up with a bald man at the wheel.

"Benny G. in effect," Sullivan says.

"Dresden's law partner?" Lourdes twists the mirror to get a better view.

"Piece of work. I knew him back when he was a prosecutor with the Brooklyn DA's office."

"He was a prosecutor? So why's he giving us a hard time about turning over Dresden's case files?"

Sullivan sighs. "Check out the widow and the son."

A young buck gets out on the passenger side: jarhead haircut, a gauze bandage on his hand, and an undersized peacoat. He opens a back door and extends a hand to help an elegant middle-aged woman with a mane of streaked tresses and golden-brown skin get out. Classy. The young man allows her to take his arm as they walk gingerly to the curb and the Jag takes off. Like what they've just been through makes them afraid to let go of one another.

Sullivan is already out of the car, again surprising Lourdes with his quickness. "Ms. Dresden? Nathaniel?"

Lourdes trails, noticing Sullivan doesn't bother to show his tin. Just takes his authority for granted while she has to take out the billfold and fully display the shield every time she passes a barricade.

"It's Ms. Ali-Dresden," the widow corrects him crisply. "And *excuse me:* what can I do for you?"

A long-backed Park Slope lioness with vaguely Eurasian-looking features. She wears a tailored red coat, pleated slacks, and purplish lipstick. Holding up well into her late fifties and irritating Lourdes by keeping her waist wasp-thin. A faint spray of suburban girl freckles high up on her sculpted cheeks offsets her air of grande dame seriousness. But the implacable set of that black-coffee stare is a warning not to play. No artificial sweetener here. One of those self-contained women that Lourdes sometimes has a hard time connecting with. Not cold or stuck-up necessarily, just way back on the shelf.

"This is Detective Sullivan and I'm Detective Robles. We're working on your husband's case. We know you've been talking to Detectives Borrelli and Chen, but we wanted to share a little information and ask for some help. Can we come in?"

"It's all right, Mom." The son pats her shoulder. "You guys been waiting awhile?"

"Not that long," Sullivan says without conviction.

Alice Ali-Dresden pulls out her keys to open the garden-level gate. "Don't mind the mess," she says. "I've been distracted."

Lourdes trails in after her, clocking the ceramic Jewish mezuzah screwed to the wall and the Islamic plate over the door, as she lets Sullivan pass and the son locks the gate behind them. Usually, there are certain smells that go with a death in the family. Unattended baby diapers in the garbage, flowers going bad in the vases, Chinese takeout left too long in the refrigerator because no one feels like eating. But this is one of the most orderly homes Lourdes has ever seen in the wake of a murder. Not a cracker crumb or a stray piece of clothing on the red-and-gold Moroccan rug in the living room, a book or magazine out of place on the tree trunk coffee table or the umber-colored sofa with the Karma Living throw pillows. African-style tapestries hang straight on the walls, depicting women in farm settings and men in prison yards, as if they were gifts from parolees who'd taken up arts and crafts behind bars. There are no dishes on the floor or glasses sitting neglected on the bookshelves, which are packed with hardcovers that seem somehow to be arranged in both alphabetical and size order. Lourdes knows without investigating that there will be fresh potpourri in the bathroom, and that the organic and inorganic materials will be separated in the garbage.

"Have you lived here a long time?" Lourdes asks.

"We've been renting the bottom two floors for twenty-seven years." Alice hangs up her coat and rewraps the kinte cloth shawl around her shoulders, nothing coy or lilting in her voice. "We were not part of the Great Bourgeois Real Estate Boom."

In other words, they missed out on buying low and selling high. People in this neighborhood talk about houses like they're superhero origin myths. *Can you believe a piece-of-shit brownstone that they bought for seventy-five grand just sold for two million?*

Halfway doing detective work and halfway indulging real estate fantasy, Lourdes starts looking around more carefully, aware Alice is watching her being nosy, as she clocks the original tin ceiling, the restored crown molding, the nonfunctioning fireplace. There are pictures on the mantle above it, and it takes Lourdes a second to make out the nappy-headed, gap-toothed child holding the hand of a frizzy-haired white lady in a peasant blouse as Alice. The black guy with the big Afro and a Malcolm X stare beside them must be the father. Some kind of big-deal activist himself. *Figures.* Another mongrel child, like herself. Being a little white and a little black probably taught Alice to be wary around everybody. Lourdes knows how that goes, from having a *blanquito* Dominican father and a dusky PR mother. Don't ask nobody for nothing, not even a cup of sugar. Just make sure your own cupboard is stocked. No wonder Alice is so far back on the shelf.

"So what's up?" The widow settles onto the couch, pointedly not inviting the visitors to sit down. "Did you find my husband's car?"

"Not yet," Sullivan says. "We've had an alert out in all five boroughs that's expanded to other states, but no hits yet."

"Probably has a different color and a different VIN number by now," the son mumbles.

Lourdes sees Sullivan has turned and narrowed his eyes at almost the exact second she did.

"What makes you say that?" Lourdes asks.

"Natty was a prosecutor in Florida." Alice waves the back of her hand. "He knows how these things go."

"*You're* a prosecutor?" Lourdes cracks a half smile at Sullivan, trying to see if he's registered the irony.

"Don't get too excited." Natty keeps his back to them, pretending to be more interested in studying family photos on the walls. "I was mostly just doing low-level cases involving prescription drug abuse and Medicare fraud."

"Modest like his father," Alice says.

"Speaking of which, I'm surprised your husband drove a Mercedes," Sullivan says, changing the rhythm. "I would've figured him more of a secondhand Prius kind of guy."

"Nothing wrong with having nice things." Alice pulls a pillow onto her lap defensively. "David worked hard all his life and most of his clients couldn't afford to pay him a damn nickel. That so-called luxury car was one of David's only indulgences, and he bought it for a song off one of his clients who was doing life in Dannemora."

"So were you having financial troubles, ma'am?" Lourdes reaches into her coat pocket for her notebook.

"*No.*" Alice hugs the pillow tighter, as if daring them to take it. "I have been over this six times with the other detectives. We all know this was not some money issue or some goddamn phony random carjacking . . ."

"Really?" Lourdes stares at her. "Then what was it?"

"David goes out to move the car at eleven o'clock at night, to avoid getting a ticket the next day, and two people are waiting by the park? No witnesses who can identify the shooter? No cameras that show where the car went? No identification of where the gun came from? Come on now, officers. Who do you think you're fooling?"

"Okay, then what *do* you think is going on?" Lourdes asks, striving for patience.

"Tell me it's not obvious." Alice splays her fingers against the hollows of her throat. "David was suing the FBI for twelve million. He had just beaten the government in a motion to dismiss the hearing and was getting ready to expose their secrets in open court. He was assassinated, plain and simple."

"You really believe that?" Lourdes can't help herself. She's giving the widow that look of duck-lipped sarcasm that somehow never makes anyone else happy.

"Yes, I do." Alice raises her tapered chin. "Officer, I'm going to give you the benefit of the doubt and assume you don't know your history. But I'll bet your partner knows who my husband was and how most members of your department felt about him."

"I do, indeed." Sullivan has crossed the room to study a *Village Voice* front page in a frame above a papyrus plant. Lourdes can read the headline from five yards away: DAVID DRESDEN IS ONE OF THE MOST HATED LAWYERS IN AMERICA—AND ONE OF THE BEST.

"You wrote this article, ma'am?" Sullivan gives Alice a slanted seesaw of a smile.

"I don't suppose you were a subscriber."

"I remember reading it when it came out," Sullivan says. "I just didn't realize you were the author."

"It was from before we were married," she says, her face and voice softening—like most writers, in Lourdes's limited experience, charmed by easy flattery.

"I met my husband on assignment and we fell in love after the article was published, in the spring of '79," Alice says.

"I knew your husband a bit, back in the day." Sullivan points at the accompanying photo of Dresden. "We were involved in a couple of cases, from opposite sides. He was, shall we say, a memorable character."

Lourdes comes over to take a look: Dresden, young and whippet-thin in a denim workshirt, a full dark beard, a defiant big nose, and an explosive Jewfro, grinning and giving the middle finger to a fish-eye camera lens. The resemblance to the son is subtle but noticeable. More in the attitude of the features than the posture of the body.

"Meaning you didn't care for him," says Alice, retreating back in exacting vinegary mode. "As David used to say, 'Take a number and stand in line.' Cops despised him. That's why none of you should be investigating this case."

"*Mom . . .*" The son, who's been off in his own world, studying photos on the mantelpiece, exhales heavily and knuckles the underside of his chin.

"You know it's true, Natty." She wags a finger. "Your father sued the police department more than a dozen times. I told those other detectives who were here that an FBI supervisor named Paul Kirkpatrick personally threatened David in a phone call. I wouldn't be surprised if you were all in on it."

Sullivan puts his hands behind his back. They'd been warned the widow might go off on them. B.B. and Andy had already gotten an earful about this murder being payback for Dresden suing the federal government because his client, an allegedly innocent Arab mailman, had been grabbed off the streets by agents in Bay Ridge and transferred to an overseas Black Site for a year and a half of "enhanced interrogation."

"And this Agent Kirkpatrick explicitly threatened your husband?" Sullivan asks, his face creasing with the kindly forbearance of a country priest.

"You people already know this. He said David better watch himself." Alice slips off her espadrilles and tucks her bare feet under her knees. "So now's the part where you start telling the old brown lady she sounds paranoid and crazy."

"No, ma'am." Sullivan shakes his head.

"Well, *excuse me*, but it's not always paranoia," Alice goes on, ignoring the attempt at conciliation. "My parents were both activists when the government infiltrated our movement . . ."

"Alice, believe me, I know anything is possible." Sullivan puts a hand up, a new firmness in his voice finally stopping her. "I've worked in Internal Affairs. But it's important *you know* that nothing and no one is getting excluded. Including members of our own department. I guarantee you that we'll look into every angle."

Lourdes gives him the stink eye, trying to gauge if he's serious. Is he suggesting a cop could have been involved? Or just blowing smoke to mollify her?

"Well, all right then." Alice nods.

Lourdes does a double take. The craggy old white guy with the dyed hair is the one developing the rapport here?

"And a way you could help us with that?" Sullivan puts his hands together, as if trying to get her to join in common prayer. "We want to make sure we're aware of anyone who had a problem with your husband."

"Now we're talking," Alice says.

"And that's going to require looking more closely at your husband's finances and his office records."

"Why would you need to do that, detective?" The widow draws her shawl snug around her shoulders.

"It's just standard to look at the finances, ma'am," Sullivan says, working a little harder to maintain the courtly tone, like a polite bartender making sure he knows where the baseball bat is behind the counter. "And as far as the office records go, we need to see if there are any former clients who might have had a beef."

"That is simply not possible." Alice's elbows suddenly come up like horns as she seizes the back of her hair. "My husband's clients loved him. David got holiday cards from prison every year."

"I'll bet." Lourdes nods.

A lot of criminals had a corny sentimental streak. Whenever he was out of prison, her own father was always bringing her paperback mysteries and comic books he stole from the Port Authority newsstands.

"We just need to eliminate people from the pool of suspects," Sullivan says.

"Then you'll have to get a warrant or speak to Ben Grimaldi about that." Alice crosses her arms. "It's out of my hands."

So much for the little Kumbaya moment, Lourdes thinks. The old gentleman soft-shoe will only get you so far with your social justice warriors.

"Mom, come on." The son rests his fingers on the bridge of his nose. "You could give Ben a nudge."

"*Excuse me.* The last thing your father would have wanted was police officers seizing his files and using them against his clients."

"Then *I'll* talk to Ben." Natty sighs. "Okay?"

Lourdes has been checking him out on the sly the whole time they've been here. Observing his sullen air as he moves around the room awkwardly, not speaking but occasionally pausing in front of a picture on the wall and taking a deep breath like he's just off a respirator. If she didn't know he'd just put a fireman in the hospital, she might have thought he was cute. Andy Chen said it took three other guys to subdue him in the bar fight. But he doesn't look that hurt, except for the bandage on his hand and a couple of light facial scratches. Which, she has to admit, is sort of hot in a screwed-up way.

"Incidentally, were you here in the city when your father was killed, Natty?" she says, getting to the business at hand.

"*Why?*" He regards her with sleepy eyelids.

"I don't think I have anything in my notes about where you were when your father died." She riffles through pages. "Did the other detectives ask you?"

"Why would they?" Alice interrupts. "Natty lives in Florida. He came for the funeral."

Lourdes tries to exchange a look with Sullivan, but he's preoccupied checking more photos. Not quite in sync as partners yet.

"So you weren't here?" Lourdes turns back to Natty for confirmation.

He shakes his head, bandaged hand disappearing into a pocket, not offering a verbal response.

"It might be good to speak to you on your own," Lourdes says.

"*Excuse me.*" Alice sits up, the mama lion ready to show her claws. "Didn't you just hear him tell you that he wasn't even in town?"

"He still might have some helpful information," Lourdes says, noticing he hadn't said anything of the kind.

"Anyway, do we really need to do this now?" Alice sighs, shawl sliding off her shoulders.

"It's true, I had a long night." Natty puts his good hand to his mouth to stifle a yawn. "But I'm guessing you guys know all about that."

"Separate matter." Sullivan stands. "Nothing to do with us."

A lot of pain here, Lourdes thinks. Can't blame someone for lashing out after losing the man of the house. At least she can't.

"Maybe we can talk when you've had a chance to rest." She reaches for her wallet and gives Natty her card. "That's got the office and cell numbers. Call anytime, day or night. I'm always working."

"Thank you." Natty pockets the card with a cursory look. "I'm on notice."

"Good to meet you." Sullivan bows to the mother and offers his hand to the son. "If you could follow up with Mr. Grimaldi, it'd help."

"We'll see what we can do." Natty takes the bandaged mitt out of his pocket and holds it out reluctantly.

Sullivan gives the fingertips a gentle shake. "I should've said it before, but I'm sorry for your loss. Your father didn't have a lot of good things to say about cops, but I respected the way he did his job. I hope you can respect the way we have to do ours."

4

"*She's* got a mouth." Mom is turned around on the couch, watching the cops out the front window as Natty comes back in.

"Takes one to know one," he mumbles, thinking he kind of liked the chubby little detective's smile.

He casts a look around the living room, wondering how it must seem to the cops. Where other people had regular family photos and maybe one corny studio portrait, they've got headlines and protest posters. Instead of a baby-in-a-blanket shot, there's a black-and-white *Times* photo with Dad giving a speech at an anti-apartheid rally in Central Park while Mom, skinny and chic in Jordache jeans and a Che Guevara t-shirt, holds newborn Natty in her arms.

The smaller frames hold a few concessions to tradition and convention. Family vacation snaps from Yellowstone Park and Nicaragua. Visits with Dad's parents in Midwood, and the hippie homestead on the Lower East Side where Mom grew up. A fishing expedition, catching stripers and flounders with Dad and Ben off Sheepshead Bay. Fleeting moments of joy that now feel like fresh wounds. The St. Ann's high school graduation, Natty with skinny shoulders and heavy metal fan ringlets in his cap and gown, while his parents make stabs at middle-class respectability on either side of him, Dad in his customary corduroys and patches and Mom in a violet dress that showed a commitment to progressivism did not prevent her from trying to eclipse every other mother in attendance. Next to that, Natty enveloping both of them in a red-robed hug four years later up in Ithaca, a graduate of the Cornell class of '04. Then a more somber picture from the Duke Law School graduation eight years later, after the war, the three of them together, each slightly thicker but not quite touching.

But naturally, there's nothing from the in-between time, nothing commemorating Natty's acceptance into officer candidate school in '05, or the special training programs at Fort Huachuca and Fort Irwin after that. Or either of his two deployments in '07 and '08.

He remembers the long bus ride down from Ithaca, on Columbus Day weekend, sophomore year, 2001, when he decided he had to tell them in person that he'd just signed up for ROTC. The trees somehow turning redder and more fragile-looking as he got closer to the city, where the towers had come down a month before. The thought crossed his mind that sometimes things were at their most beautiful right before they started to decay.

And so it was with his family. The moment before he broke the news, he realized he'd never loved them more and that he would go ahead and break their hearts anyway.

"Are you fucking kidding me, Nathaniel?" Mom said. "You're going to join *the army*?"

"We were attacked . . ."

"So you're going to let yourself be used to wage a phony war to help Halliburton and the oil companies improve their bottom lines?" She'd held her head as if it was about to explode. "No, child. You're *not* going."

"I don't see how you can stop me. I'm eighteen."

"Oh my God. David, say something . . ."

Meanwhile, Dad, home from representing a couple of Yemeni cab drivers accused of plotting a follow-up attack in the Holland Tunnel, was standing there with his tie undone and his thousand-yard stare, which Natty attributed at the time to weed, waiting patiently to have the last word.

"Well, whatever you do over there, Natty," he said and sighed, "I'm sure I won't want to know about it."

Thinking back on it now, Natty can see the old man was probably more scared than stoned. Once Natty finally got to Bagram six years later, there was a care package from Dad waiting. With a bulletproof vest and a terse note about the administration's failures to provide proper body armor for soldiers. And both parents were probably even more scared when he came back in '08. Because he wasn't the same. The child who'd unabashedly held his mother's hand at "Take Back the Night" rallies and went to watch his father's opening arguments was gone. Someone harder, more remote, and more potentially incendiary had replaced him.

Natty started finding reasons to avoid spending time with them after he came back. Choosing a law school down south; taking a first job at the Florida prosecutors' office instead of using Dad's contacts at Legal Aid; leaving their phone and email messages unanswered for days, even weeks.

He flinches, knowing it must have seemed like he was being deliberately callous. Punishing them for some unknown sin. When the truth was that he was just hiding, from them and himself, and the questions that would eventually have to be answered.

Somehow Natty always assumed he'd clear the air with Dad first. Years in the future, maybe after a wife and grandchildren entered the picture, he imagined a quiet Sunday and a football game on in the living room, with a couple of empty beer bottles already in the recycle bin. At some point during the halftime roundup, Natty would just casually start to talk about what happened in the regular interrogation sessions, about how he never crossed the line and violated the Geneva Conventions *personally*, though he knew people who did. Never waterboarded anyone with his own hands, never delivered a face slap or employed a full choke hold. But let's say there were exceptional circumstances sometimes, when you might have left the room or turned away.

If Dad could accept all that, he might bring up a certain situation that developed in Sadr City. *I never told you about this?* And then maybe Dad would patiently probe, not pressing too hard, giving Natty just enough space to tell the story. Instead of harshly interjecting or judging the way Mom might, he would help Natty put it in perspective. He'd talk about the larger context of war the way he talked about the social context that caused his clients to take drugs, do robberies, and, yes, occasionally commit murders of their own. Not minimizing exactly, but mitigating, balancing, transforming the monster into a human being again. Because as things stood, the question of why Natty deserved to have anything good happen to him again was lurking behind every moment of his life.

But now Dad would never be able to give him a way out. And the great reconciliation that Natty always held out hope for would never take place. What was broken would stay broken. There would always be fissures inside him, ready to crack and bleed. No mea culpa or mature acknowledgement would smooth things over. *It is what it is.* All he could do was keep banging his head against cinder block walls, wishing he could take back three-quarters of the things he'd said and tell the old man that he knew he'd been well loved, if imperfectly understood.

"You all right?" His mother is beside him, her head about even with his shoulder.

"It's all good." He puts his arm around her. "What about you?"

"I didn't spend the night in a holding cell."

"Then it was probably worse for you, because you were up worrying. I went right to sleep."

He feels the fragility of her bones through her sweater. A reminder that sometimes the reason he keeps going is so she won't have to deal with the ugliness of finding her only child's body and planning the funeral.

"I still don't understand what happened last night," she says.

"Just a dumb bar fight." He starts to cover another yawn, the webbing between his fingers still smarting where the tooth went in. "I don't want to talk about it."

"*Dayum*, son." She shakes her head. "That's the best you got for me?"

His mother. Graduate of Barnard College, class of 1978. Freelance writer for the *Village Voice* and author of *Our Bodies, Our Rights*. Member of the St. Marks Poetry Collective, fluent in Lacan, Chomsky, and Simone de Beauvoir. Wife of David Dresden. You can have all the facts and still never get the full 360 on your own parents. Because you're always too attached to get all the way around them.

"*Is this your mother?*"

He remembers the security guard looking skeptical when he got separated from her at Macy's on Fulton Street, a little sorta white boy being brought over to the sorta colored lady.

"*Does he really belong to you?*"

Twenty-five years later, he still wonders the same thing.

"I'm sorry I put you through it," Natty says. "Ben and I are going to handle it. I'll do my little diversion program, show some remorse, and be out of the woods."

It's just now sinking in that he'd been so out-of-control last night that he almost killed a firefighter from a 9/11 family.

"I just don't know where this is all going." She touches his cheek tenderly and then pulls her hand back, as if afraid his face will detonate.

"Everything is *irie*, Mama." He forces a smile. "No worries."

"That's what you said about the army." She drapes her shawl on the back of a chair. "You want tea?"

"Yeah, sure. Why not."

He'd rather have a beer, but he needs to think about getting on the wagon, for his program. Nominally.

He follows her through the dining room and into the kitchen, which hasn't been painted since his first deployment. *Irie, Mama.* Every little thing's going to be all right. Something about being in the space makes him think of Bob Marley songs and Jamaican spices. Dad letting Natty have his first Red Stripe at fourteen when Mom wasn't home, Mom going hard with the chile powder and the brown sugar in her jerk chicken recipe, the *Natty Dread* tape blasting on the Sony boombox, the vague smell of ganja and cinnamon in the cabinets. "Lively Up Yourself." "No Woman, No Cry." "I Shot the Sheriff." "Them Belly Full (But We Hungry)."

He tries to remember the good times. When he didn't feel resentful or displaced by the "foster kids" who sometimes cycled through. Children of Dad's clients, who were either incapacitated by drugs or incarcerated. Psycho Shamal who held Natty's arm over an open flame on the stove when they were both six. James the Jealous stealing Natty's Walkman and Gameboy, and then denying his culpability even as he played with them openly. And of course, 250-pound La Quinta who was subject to violent "seizures," which somehow caused her to grab Natty's head and bang it on the counter when she got excited.

Thinking back, he can feel a degree of sympathy for those kids, knowing the kind of extravagantly fucked-up scenarios they must have been coming from, but how he wishes it could have been just the three of them more often. Then there'd be more he could hold onto.

He watches his mother pad across the checked linoleum floor in her bare feet and start to go into her whole tea ceremony, channeling the WASP side of her family by putting her own mother's battered old Connecticut copper kettle on the stove and scooping up the peppermint leaves into a strainer.

"Ben really thinks you can get this knocked down to misdemeanor assault?" She turns the heat on.

"Be easier if the victim agrees to it."

Assuming he wakes up from his coma. But she doesn't need to hear that.

"And what are the chances of keeping your law license?" she asks.

"Fair to middling. A misdemeanor doesn't lead to automatic disbarment. Felony assault could be a problem. Ben thinks my service could help."

"The war, which messed you up in the first place . . ."

"Mom . . ."

"*Right*, I'm not supposed to say that." She leans against the stove. "So what are you going to do in the meantime?"

"I don't know. I have to stay in New York while I'm out on bail."

"How you fixed for money?"

"I'll get by. I passed the bar here before I went to Florida. Maybe I can pick up some work . . ."

He hears his voice trail off under the sound of the burners, as he tries to calculate his finances again. His army separation pay is gone and his paltry savings from his prosecutor's job in Florida have been drained by some of his recent insanity. Which means he's still living in the shadow of his student loans with less than $1,000 in the bank, $9,000 in credit card debt, and a serious risk of losing all his benefits permanently.

"What about you?" he asks, shifting gears.

"What about me?"

"How you holding up?"

"Emotionally or financially?"

"Both."

"Emotionally . . ." She takes a deep breath. "I'm still in shock that someone went and killed my man."

Somehow it hurts all over again, hearing her say it this way. No one warned him that when something fundamental gets broken, every day feels like the first day.

"When I'm not numb, I'm trying to get numb," she says. "Paxil helps,

a little. Drinking, not so much. And meditation is useless. But I'm hanging on. Barely. For your sake as much as mine."

You and me, Mama. He can't let go now; it'll kill her. The tautness
of her posture reminds him of a concert violinist trying to carefully tune
a string without breaking it.

"What about financially?" he asks.

"Honey, I'm a fifty-nine-year-old freelancer who can't even get paid
anymore for the articles they *do* print," she says, putting twelve kinds of
pissed-offness into a two-letter word. "How's that for a business plan?"

"You have savings, though, don't you?"

He goes to stand behind her as the wings of her shoulder blades come
out and touch his ribs well below his pectorals.

"Didn't Dad leave you set up for a big payday with this mailman rendition case?" he asks.

"For real now?" She pushes away from him to attend to a flame lick-
ing the bottom of her kettle. "Your father was a great lawyer but a terrible
businessman. He got all these people out of prison and then let other
lawyers cash in on the civil suits."

"But I thought it was going to be different this time."

"So did he. But the government kept fighting him every step, hoping that he'd go away. Every week he was sending them Freedom of Information Act requests, and they were finding excuses to try to classify
the material and hide it under the National Security Act. And in the meantime we've been going broke."

Natty massages the groove left by a cuff on his right wrist. "So how
deep in the hole are you?"

"Right before David was killed, we found out the landlord wants to
sell this house and kick us out on the street. We were counting on that
case to bail us out. After the judge denied the government's motion to
dismiss and accepted the tort claim to let the suit go forward, I thought
we were safe."

"Jesus, Mom." He exhales. "I had no idea . . ."

"Well, if you'd bothered to call . . ." She stops herself. "Never mind.
Your father used to say, 'Let 'im be, Alice. He's got a lot he's dealing with
already.'"

He watches her shoulders shake and the faint white jet stream shooting out of her kettle. Nice work, Natty Dread. You made your mother cry.

"You know what's funny?" she says. "All this time, you were the one I was worried about."

"Mom . . ."

"You were living down in Florida. Never talking to us. Never answering messages. We've had no idea what was going on in your life. I said to your father, 'Our boy is back and God how I miss him.'"

"Mom, I'm trying to get it together . . ."

Though he couldn't claim practice made perfect. VA appointments, marathon drinking, sex binges, and mixed martial arts barely helped his insomnia, let alone dented this massive inability to feel *anything*, except sudden bouts of panic and depression. One thing he could say about Dad getting killed: it woke him up just enough so he could see how much wreckage was spread out around him.

"I know you're trying." Her chin dives toward her clavicle. "It's just kind of scary, where I'm standing right now."

"What are you going to do?"

"I don't know. I haven't even figured out how I'm going to pay for your father's funeral. I bought the damn coffin on an installment plan."

He watches her take her teapot and a highball glass down from the cupboard.

"I can help," he says. "I'll get another job and we'll find you another place."

"Excuse me, Natty, but you *need* to get a job. Eventually. Not just for me, but for you."

She takes the kettle off the stove, puts the strainer in the teapot, and uses an oven mitt to pour the scalding water.

"Have you talked to Ben about your money situation?" she says.

He lays his hand on the table as the knuckles start to pulse. "It's embarrassing enough that he had to go my bail."

A $5,000 cash bond down on $50,000 bail to get him released on recognizance. Natty almost couldn't answer when the clerk quietly asked, "You related to that other Dresden?"

"You know he's talking about taking over your father's mailman case," she says. "He could probably use someone in the second seat."

"Mom, I was a second-year prosecutor, handling penny-ante fraud cases in Florida. I've never even had to prepare for a trial."

"The law is the law." She puts the cup down in front of him. "You've always been savvy."

"It's major federal litigation." He flexes his good hand before he picks up the tea. "You know how hard it is to sue the FBI?"

"You want some other low-life lawyer to come along and steal it?" She gives him a withering look. "That's *your* father's name still on all the papers. He had the relationship with the clients."

"But I'm totally unqualified."

"You can't just have a conversation with Ben? Seriously?"

Her fine features have gone as slack as an unironed dress on a wire hanger. Your mother. Who just lost her husband. Who knelt down and pressed your clammy little hand to her warm soft mouth when the Macy's security guard asked if you were truly related. Who kicked the foster kids out of the house because you couldn't get along with them. Who burst into tears when she walked in on you and Ben writing a last will and testament naming your parents as beneficiaries after you signed up for the army. Who wrote you letters every other day even after you stopped answering from Iraq.

"I have to go in tomorrow to talk to him about my case anyway," he says. "I guess I could mention it."

"Well, all right then." She opens a cabinet under the sink and takes out a half-full bottle of Macallan 18 single malt.

"What the hell, Mom?"

"I'm having a drink. What you put me through, I deserve it."

"Macallan 18? That's like $200."

"Blame your father. He got me into it. I used to be a strict white wine and mint julep girl. A client gave him a bottle of the 25 after he won a case a few years ago and David fell in love with it. $800. Part of him getting expensive tastes late in life. He's been trying to earn enough to buy another one ever since. Excuse me—he *had* been trying." She uncorks the bottle with an insouciant pop. "Anyway, the 18 is not bad if you give it half a chance."

"And you're giving me a lousy cup of tea?"

"I'm drinking for both of us," she says. "Don't give me any lip."

As she pours herself two fingers neat, he watches her face get old and sad, then young and hopeful, and then old again. And he yearns for the days when things were just as they seemed. She clinks the edge of her glass against his cup in a wordless toast and drains it.

5

When the pop-up appears in the corner of her computer screen, listing the bosses checking her progress, Lourdes's heart chokes like it's swallowed a blood clot. Three names down from the top, at 10:58 this morning, Joseph H. Gunther himself, chief of detectives, looked at her files. The black letters in twelve-point type throb before her eyes. The chief is probably up on the fourteenth floor of 1 PP right now, reporting to the commissioner about her work.

Her chipped red nails tap the edge of the desk and her mouth shrinks to a small dry circle.

She starts fumbling through her top desk drawer for a lipstick. Since that first night by the park, this thing has been a beast sprouting fangs and talons. The first couple of news cycles, David Dresden's murder was all over the media, with screaming tabloid headlines, the mayor holding a press conference, and everyone running that same goddamn photo of Dresden next to the little Arab mailman on the courthouse steps with his white mane flying and his fist raised. It didn't help that an unnamed "high-ranking law enforcement official" fed the widow's paranoia by being quoted in the *Post* suggesting the attorney got exactly what he had coming for representing the worst of the worst.

In the smaller follow-up stories, the nature of the pressure shifted and became more acute. The *Times* ran a long feature about the ex-cons whose exoneration cases Dresden worked on pro bono while taking in their kids for months at a time. The accompanying photo showed him sitting on his stoop on President Street, with his arm around a smiling Alice and a sort of tired good humor in his eyes that Lourdes found herself responding to. And in becoming more human to her, he became more of a burden as well, haunting her off-duty hours and distracting her at family dinners when her mother and sister were crazy desperate for her attention.

"Got a minute?" Sullivan sticks his head out of the break room.

"Yeah, totally."

She checks her makeup in a pocket mirror, grabs her pad, and heads past the row of desks laid out shotgun-style, the moldy lockers with "BIOHAZARD" and "COP SHOT" stickers, the stacks of cardboard evidence boxes, and one emaciated junkie wearing a toga-like bedsheet and buckled loafers in the holding cell, where Al Capone supposedly cooled his heels.

"We are in a mist and cannot know ourselves." He lays baleful eyes on Lourdes. "O that this too too sullied flesh would melt."

Sullivan and Bobby are in front of the stove with Captain Terry McKenna, all three holding coffee mugs as a sooty breeze blows in the barred window, flapping "Never Forget" posters, announcements for the Emerald Society's Shamrock Run, and a flyer for Andy Chen's side business selling precinct baseball caps sewed by two Mexican women in the basement of his house in Bensonhurst.

"All right, the Comeback Kid is here," says Captain Mac, one of those waxy-looking white men whose face looks perpetually boyish and shiny, except for the hundred-year-old eyes and the faint tracery of broken capillaries in his nose. "Let's go. Where we at?"

There's something a little fussy and pedantic about him, Lourdes thinks; he kept her an hour after her shift ended last week, telling her about his vintage collection of Yankee clippers in bottles and explaining in minute detail how to get a mast through a narrow opening.

"Still no hit on any of the slugs recovered from Dresden's body," Lourdes says. "All three were hollow-point rounds from a .45 that deformed on impact. But no links to any other shootings in the system."

"What about the shells from the .357 and the .22 that were lying next to the vic?" the captain asks.

"They don't match the rounds in the body," Lourdes says. "And our witness said he only heard three shots."

"Somebody is trying to throw us off by leaving them at the scene," Sullivan says. "Pretty slick."

"No other witnesses from the recanvas of the park and the surrounding neighborhood," B.B. chimes in. "And nothing new from tracking the cell phones that made calls from the area around the time of the killing. We've either accounted for all the subscriber phones in the radius or they were using burner numbers that we're still trying to chase down."

"Wunderbar." The captain rubs his stomach. "Did I mention I'm seeing Chief Gunther later today?"

"Can't manufacture evidence for him if we don't have it." Lourdes forces a smile. "Unless you really want us to."

No one laughs and her tongue sticks to the roof of her drying mouth. Three months out of purgatory and she's still on tenterhooks. And acting like she's got nothing to be self-conscious about is only making her more self-conscious.

"Still nothing on where Dresden's Benz could be?" the captain asks as Andy Chen walks in.

"Traffic cams lost track once it left the BQE by McGuinness Boulevard," says Andy, squat with the face of a Yuan dynasty warrior and maybe the heaviest knockaround Brooklyn accent Lourdes has ever heard. "TARU's going block by block trying to pick it up again."

"You guys know you're killing me, right?" The captain puts his hands behind his back, white shirt coming untucked and loose like the flapping sail of a listing ship.

"The upshot is this does not appear to be a random street crime," says Sullivan, reestablishing a center of gravity in the room with the weight of his cadence. "Murder in a low-crime area. High-profile victim. Minimal witnesses. Deliberately misleading evidence. No one on the street talking about it."

"So who's fucking with us?" Lourdes says.

Sullivan's ruddy complexion turns a shade redder, contrasting with the total crow blackness of his hair. "I'd rather we saved that language for the street, but that is the question."

"And they call *me* Captain Obvious." McKenna's belly quivers, eliciting a rare smile from Sullivan. "How did the reinterview with the widow and the son go?"

"She's a pain in the ass and he's a little edgy," Lourdes says.

Immediately, she feels herself nailed with reproachful stares from every direction. Four men judging her hard.

"Well, come on," she says defensively. "She's going off on us about the FBI threatening her husband and the son just put a firefighter in the hospital. It ain't Disney World over there. Not that they don't have a right to be stressed."

"How's the probie doing in the ICU anyway?" Sullivan asks Andy, who caught the bar fight case when it came in.

"Stabilized but he'll be taking dinner through a straw for a while."

"You know how hard it is to break a jaw with your fist?" B.B. asks, massaging his own jaw.

"The DA's trying to get the fireman's family to accept a deal to put it through Veterans Court and knock it down to misdemeanor assault, but they're not happy," Andy explains.

"Misdemeanor?" Lourdes asks. "I thought he put that dude in a coma."

"The bartender says he saw the probie acting like a dick and throwing the first punch after Nathaniel bumped into him and spilled his drink, but who knows?" Andy shrugs. "The bar's video camera is fucked up so we're still talking to other witnesses."

"Why do we care, terms of the bigger case?" Beautiful Bobby adjusts his shirt cuffs, like he's getting ready for a *GQ* shoot. "The son was out of town when his father got shot, wasn't he?"

"His mother said he was." Sullivan holds up a finger. "But let's not take anything for granted. Natty's a prosecutor when his father was a famous criminal defense lawyer. I'm thinking there had to be some tension."

Lourdes notices how everyone stops talking and takes a beat to readjust. The captain is a captain, but Oz has spoken. Whatever it takes, she decides she's going to stick by Sullivan and try to pick up on whatever mojo he's got.

"Okay, check the son's story." The captain looks at Andy and B.B. "Can't hurt. And where are we on getting Dresden's old case files and following up with the clients?"

"Benny G.'s straight-arming us so far, claiming attorney-client privilege for all his law partner's records." B.B. smoothes his quiff. "So we're letting the DA's office run interference and draw up the subpoena. Knowing Ben Grimaldi, he's gonna fight it every step."

"We may have to get in on that." The heaviness goes from Sullivan's eyes to his jaw as he looks at Lourdes, indicating a certain depth of feeling about the prospect. "Eventually."

She stares back, thinking she'd meant to follow up when Sullivan mentioned knowing Dresden to the widow.

"Let's just keep plowing forward on all fronts," the captain says. "Anything else?"

"You want to tell him?" Sullivan elbows Bobby.

"Don't hold out on me, B.B.," Captain Mac says. "No one likes a prickteaser with a bald spot."

The men do a collective "Ho!" of appreciation at the diss.

"Well, you know how Dresden had at least two different cell phones with at least two different carriers?" B.B. blushes ever so slightly.

"Yeah?" Captain Mac coughs, still enjoying the joke.

Bobby grabs a sheath of printouts off the lunch table with its gray gummy vinyl top and passes out copies to the captain, Andy, and Lourdes.

"TARU's still checking calls from his Verizon account and his Sprint account," Bobby says. "They followed up on every number Dresden called or received calls from in the last six weeks. There's a ton of incoming calls from burner cells, which we're trying to track, and from Rikers, so that's a day trip at least for interviews. Then a bunch of other calls from some of his clients upstate—"

"But we've already talked to some of those skells and they loved them some David Dresden," Lourdes interrupts.

She's about to get ripped by them; she can feel it coming like a weather condition. Some obvious call she should have made. A name she should have recognized.

"Okay, check out what I found on the set of numbers that just came in." Bobby flicks at the corner of the printout he's given her, which is filled from top to bottom with digits and length-of-call timings. "Cluster in the middle of the page. Obvious landline. Anything jump out?"

Lourdes scans the page, the clot in her chest expanding. What kind of messed-up test is this, where she's supposed to recognize phone numbers at a glance? Would they do this to a new *guy*?

"There." She forces herself to slow down and read more carefully. "I see five calls in three days going back and forth to 212-384-1000. I've dialed that myself. What is it?"

"What'd I tell you?" Sullivan nudges Captain Mac, almost knocking the mug from his hand. "I told you: 'Give that girl half a chance and she'll knock us all for a loop.'"

"It's the main number for the FBI office in New York." B.B., who's heading out of his third marriage, gives Lourdes a smoky bedroom look. "And there's a lot of calls like that in the days right before he was killed. Interesting, no?"

"Yeah, but what does it prove?" Andy takes off his granny glasses. "He was about to start the lawsuit against the Bureau and probably had a bunch of other cases that involved them as well. He could have been calling to depose an agent, or arranging for a client to come in and cooperate . . ."

"Except the widow told us that Dresden had been threatened by an agent named Paul Kirkpatrick because of the mailman lawsuit," Lourdes points out.

"We talked to Kirkpatrick; he said it was hype," Andy says. "He was just referring to classifying matters of national security and Dresden was blowing it up to create a phony issue in the case."

"Talk to him again." Captain Mac puts a foot up on an empty chair, striving for a rum-bottle pirate pose while displaying the Nike swoosh on his black sweat-sock. "That's a lot of back-and-forth to someone you're just trying to shut down."

"Sir, can Sullivan and me take a run at him?" Lourdes asks. "Just to try a different approach?"

Instantly, she can feel the energy in the little room change. She's overstepped by about a foot and a half. Nice. When she's still basically here on parole. Andy Chen starts rubbing his glasses furiously with a handkerchief. B.B. opens his eyes and blows out his cheeks. Captain Mac takes his foot off the chair.

"Might be some wisdom to it," Sullivan says slowly, like he's trying to ignore a bad smell. "The widow just made the accusation directly to us, so we'd be coming in fresh. Plus we got the phone calls back and forth." He glances at Lourdes. "No disrespect to Andy and B.B., of course."

"Of course," says Lourdes, finally taking the hint that's what she should have led with.

"Okay, odd couple out, odder couple in." Captain McKenna claps his hands, signaling the meeting is over. "Sully, show her the ropes without strangling the agent. Robles, try not to shoot anyone in the nuts or insult any cab drivers along the way—or whatever the fuck you did before. Both of you: tact, diplomacy, and discretion. In other words: surprise me."

6

As soon as Natty steps into the waiting room area, he plunges into a state of full-on battleground paralysis.

A skinny boy on the couch looks up from playing with an iPhone, midmorning sun streaming through the picture window behind him. And all at once, Natty is out of the law office and back on the stairs in Sadr City with the sound of falling snow in his head.

Here, he reminds himself: Not there. Now, not then. *Siudo.* The kid's not even Iraqi, let alone Arab. He's African or Caribbean, blue-black skin contrasting with white earbuds, Dr. Seuss-meets-Rastaman knit cap with yellow-and-green stripes. Laces on his sneakers. The only thing remotely the same is the fact that he's wearing a jersey. But it's yellow, not white, and it says "ROYAL" on the front. One of Dad's typical no-load no-pay loser clients. Probably just ROR'd for selling weed or purse snatching on Albany Avenue. He shares sofa space with a shrunken Indian lady in a sari and nose ring, a mumbling urban scarecrow of ambiguous ethnicity and gender in a straw porkpie hat, and a doughy whey-faced white guy with a rose vine and a Rolling Stones tongue tattooed around the sides of his bald head.

My peeps, Dad called them. Exactly the kind of defendants Natty couldn't stand to look at when he was visiting his father's old scrappy little solo-practitioner office over on Montague a block and a half from the courthouse, with the rec room paneling on the walls, the suspicious stains on the carpet, and the overfed pigeons staring through dusty windows.

The new Dresden & Grimaldi office is on the twelfth floor of a recently completed Atlantic Avenue office building, looking out on New

York Harbor, the Brooklyn Bridge, and a Jurassic Park of looming construction cranes in the mid-distance that are changing the borough where he was born into one he no longer recognizes.

"Hey, what can I do for you?"

The receptionist is different as well. Instead of Estelle, the cranky half-deaf red-haired old bat who his father kept on out of respect to her late husband, the crooked union organizer, there is a stylish young Asian woman, with a black licorice curtain of hair on one side of her head and a close shave on the other.

"Uh, I have an appointment to see Mr. Grimaldi," he says, shoulders cramped and waist pinched in the blazer and corduroy pants taken from Dad's closet. "I may be a little early."

A half hour, to be exact. He's gotten in the habit of showing up way ahead of time so he can scope out the locations and avoid panic attacks like the one he just had.

"You must be Natty." She half rises. "I'm Jen. So awesome to finally meet you. I loved your father *soo* much."

"Yeah, I definitely hear that a lot. Now."

Her smile yields a small provocative gap between her front teeth, but somehow he can't quite make himself smile back. What's wrong? She's flirting, but he doesn't know where to look.

"Ben's in with a client," she says. "But I'll buzz." She hits a button and softly sings, "He's he-ere," into her headset like the little girl in *Poltergeist*.

"Go ahead." She points down a corridor. "Straight down, hang a left past the picture of Ebbets Field and the door to your dad's office."

He nods and heads down the surprisingly wide hallway, carpet fibers quietly moaning under every step. A tall young black dude in bright yellow spandex wheels a shiny road bike toward him and lowers his shades to give Natty the once-over as he passes a little too close. Natty has no idea how to judge his own presence these days. Sometimes he seems too big for the space he's occupying; sometimes he's invisible. He can't even remember how it used to be.

Just past the framed stadium photo at the end of the corridor, he sees a half-open door on the right with Dad's name on it. A pair of memories stab him like scissors through the eyes: the sleepy satisfied smile on

Dad's face when Natty said he was going to law school (*"Who knows? Maybe one day it'll be Dresden, Dresden & Grimaldi."*) and then how a pall fell over him when Natty added he was going to become a prosecutor.

"Heading to the dark side, eh?"

He pushes open the door. Dad's old oak desk sits in the middle of the empty room, a ghost ship adrift on a sea-blue carpet. All his papers have been cleared away and there are uncharacteristically orderly chest-high stacks of cardboard boxes lined against walls. Even at the best of times, Dad's work areas were riot zones. His photos are still around, though. There's Bob Marley on the *Natty Dread* album cover next to John and Yoko in the nude, and the poster of Muhammad Ali, standing over Sonny Liston with his fist cocked, the underdog lording it over the fallen champ. An image Mom banished from the house as "a celebration of hetero-normative violence"—exactly what Natty cherished about it. Now it rests against the wall, under the ghostly outline of the space where it used to hang. But what truly tears into Natty is a smaller picture on the credenza, among the awards from the ACLU and the Center for Constitutional Rights. A photo of himself in full camo and helmet, sitting on the front of a tank, canvas tents and desert in the background, an M4 cradled in his arms.

He picks it up, knowing from the slight smirk it must have been from early in the first tour. When he was still sending home photos and emails to clue the folks in about how the world really worked, far from the courthouses and coffee klatches where what you said was more important than what you did. Letting Mom and Dad know they couldn't keep their little boy from playing with guns anymore. But then he remembers the line he put at the end of every email: "I'm still okay. With Love and Rockets from Baghdad, Mighty Natty Dread."

He weighs the frame in his hand, with warring impulses to either hug it to his chest and start crying, or fling it against the wall and hear the glass shatter.

"There he is."

Ben is in the doorway, behind him. "You're here this early, you might as well come in," he says. "Someone you ought to meet."

The door across the hall is wide open, the corner room inside filled with light from the north and the east. Natty steps in and finds two Middle Eastern men waiting.

His pulse skyrockets as if he just breached the doorway of a weapons cache and ran straight into two Kalashnikovs pointed at his head.

"Natty, I don't think you've met Ibrahim Saddik or his son Hamid." Ben clears his throat, pulling him back into the moment. "Guys, this is David's son."

Natty blinks, trying to get his bearings again. Okay, these are nominally friendlies. Ibrahim the mailman he recognizes from Dad's press conferences on TV. Slightly stooped as he leans on a cane, balding and paunchy in a waist-length brown imitation-leather jacket, an open-collared white shirt with a coffee stain between the buttons, rumpled brown pants, and scuffed-up loafers. Easy to picture him trudging down Eighth Avenue with his mail cart and a pith helmet on a hot August afternoon, stopping by the mosque to press his forehead to the prayer mat after his last drop-off of the day and then hitting the corner deli to buy lottery tickets, just in case piety wasn't enough.

The son, Hamid, is another story. A big belligerent-looking refrigerator in a dishdasha—or, as Staff Sergeant J. R. Cuddy called it, "a man-dress"—with a white skullcap, a scholar's wire spectacles, and a frizzy black half-beard. He reminds Natty of those village clerics who'd nod and listen thoughtfully when you talked about bringing in water treatment facilities and then would order their followers to mortar your Crusader ass as soon as your back was turned.

"How's it going?" Natty shakes Ibrahim's hand and notes how Hamid hangs back, taking inventory.

"I was just talking with Ibrahim and his son about the case." Ben plants himself on a corner of his desk, with a poster over his shoulder that shows a finger pointing and the words "SOMEONE TALKED." "I was telling them how important it is to keep the pressure on."

"Sure." Natty nods, trying to suss out why Ben didn't make him wait outside until this meeting was over.

"I saw you speak at your father's funeral," Ibrahim says in a shaky, high-pitched voice with a slight Egyptian accent. "I meant to introduce myself afterward, but there were too many people."

"Yeah, it was hectic." Natty sneaks a glance at Ben.

"Your father was a very honest man." Ibrahim raises a trembling finger. "I liked him very much."

"You're kind to say so."

"I came to him five years ago after they finally let me out of these terrible places where they torture me but never charge me. I had tried to get my old job back at the post office, but I can't lift my arm higher than this." He raises his elbow to halfway up his rib cage. "And these so-called interrogators damaged my knee so I have trouble walking. Do you know I'm only forty-seven years old?"

He looks about sixty-five. Natty gives the Headshake of Collective White People Guilt, even as the SSGT Cuddy in his head keeps spitting tobacco and telling him never trust a hajji.

"These Macedonian animals that the FBI turned me over to—they beat me every day, they played the loud music, they waterboarded me seventeen times. They left me in a cell without food or water for four days, so I almost died from dehydration. But what's worse than all the physical injuries?" He taps a finger against the side of his head. "What they did in here. I have nightmares all the time. Even when I'm wide awake and my eyes are open. The psychiatrists call it the post-traumatic stress disorder. Your father said you know soldiers who have this . . ."

Natty accidentally chomps on the sore spot in his mouth again. "Yeah, kind of." Did Dad pimp out his problems to bond with a client?

"Every other lawyer I go to says, 'Ibrahim, this is very sad, but it's almost impossible to sue the federal government.'" The mailman shows a broken-toothed smile. "They say, 'The FBI made an honest mistake. Just accept the apology and move on.' But this I cannot do." He touches a fist to his chest. "I am a proud man. I am an educated man. My great-grandfather was a judge in Upper Egypt. The memory of justice lives in my heart. So I went to see your father and this is when I learned he was an honest man."

"Yeah?" Natty eyes Ben, not sure whether to stay or go. "Why's that?"

"He shows me this office next door with the pictures of Clarence Darrow and Che Guevara, your Muhammad Ali, and your Bob Marley. He tells me he admires men who fight for justice. Even soldiers like yourself."

"He included *me* on that list?" Natty pings a look from Ibrahim to Ben, sure he's getting jerked around.

"Yes. He says he hates the war personally but you fight for what you believe."

"News to me," Natty grumbles under his breath.

"Then he asks me, 'Ibrahim, what do you want to see happen now?' And I say, 'Mr. David, I would like to see the bad men who did this to me punished.' And your father shakes his head and says, 'Ibrahim, this is not going to happen. What is the second thing you would like?' I said, 'Mr. David, I want no one else to suffer as I have.' And he tells me, 'Ibrahim, this is not going to happen in a civil suit. No one will ever be held to account.' And I say, 'Mr. David, how can this be in America? How can someone just kidnap you off the street, take you away so your family doesn't know what happened, then give you to people who hurt you so that you are never the same? How can you say this is okay when you are a man who believes in justice?' And then he says, justice is a dream. And he loves dreamers. But he's not one himself anymore."

"*My father* said that?" Natty's voice cracks. "That's a direct quote?"

It doesn't sound like the old man. "Imagine" and the "I Have a Dream" speech were the "Mary Had a Little Lamb" and "Jack and Jill" of Natty's childhood.

"Yes." Ibrahim nods. "He says, 'The people who did these bad things to you will never suffer. They will sleep peacefully in their own beds and die fat, happy, and old. This is how it will be. Anyone who says otherwise is lying.' And I am like this . . ." Ibrahim lets his shoulders slump. "But then he pats me and says, 'Ibrahim, if you cannot have justice, what do you want?' And I say, 'Could I at least get some money?' Then your father does this." He rubs his hands together, while doing a decent imitation of Dad's Scrooge McDuck shtick. "He says, 'Ibrahim, *now you are talking.*'"

Ben laughs. "You said he was honest."

"Except for one thing." Ibrahim shakes a gnarled finger, missing half its nail. "I think Mr. David lies when he says he's not a dreamer anymore. Otherwise he would not have fought so long for me, for so little reward."

"And we're going to finish what he started." Ben comes over and puts a firm hand on Natty's shoulder. "I was just telling Ibrahim and Hamid that the firm is very committed to continuing this fight."

"There an alternative?"

"A number of attorneys have approached Ibrahim since your father died." Ben's hand slips halfway down Natty's back.

"Vultures." Natty straightens his shoulders.

"Yes, so this is why I'm here." Ibrahim holds out his shaky hands. "I don't know what to do. These other lawyers—they say, 'Mr. Benjamin Grimaldi is a very good defense lawyer, but he has no experience in civil litigation. Please, let us take care of you.'"

"My father didn't have much experience with this kind of litigation either," Natty points out, remembering the conversation with Mom about other lawyers trying to horn in.

"But he worked around the clock to get up to speed," Ben says, the pressure of his touch subtle but persistent on Natty's spine. "Which is why it's essential that we keep the momentum going now that we've got the federal tort claim accepted and the way cleared to sue . . ."

Natty watches Ibrahim lean heavily on his cane again, trying to regain his balance. He wants to keep going with the firm, is Natty's read, but he can't quite get comfortable. The Rat Pack swagger that endeared Ben to his wise-guy clients doesn't play as well with a Muslim former detainee. Dad's soft-spoken tolerance and world-weary sympathy were no doubt a better fit.

"I'm sure David mentioned that Natty followed in his footsteps in becoming a lawyer," Ben says, a little too smoothly. "So you can be assured there will be continuity in how we handle the case. You're still in good hands."

"So would you be working with Mr. Ben on my case?" Ibrahim's eyes shine hopefully.

"Ah . . ." Ben's palm is still on his back and his father's jacket is too tight on his shoulders.

Is this why Ben asked him to come in? To keep the client from walking away? The image comes to him of a puppeteer with his hand stuck up a hollow body. Is it just a coincidence that his mother sent him to ask about a job and now Ben is invoking his father's memory to keep the case? Fire ants of doubt crawl over him. Maybe the people he loves are just using him. Maybe no one is what they pretend to be.

But wait, that can't be right. He was the one who showed up early today. Ben invited him in because he was standing right outside while he was meeting with Dad's former clients. It would've been weird if he kept Natty out. Wouldn't it?

"We hadn't talked about me getting involved *specifically*," Natty starts to say.

"Nathaniel is an excellent lawyer in his own right," Ben interrupts, his arms crossed, biceps bulging in his tailored shirt. "And he brings a wealth of his own experience."

"Your father did speak to you about my case, though, yes?" Ibrahim nods at Natty, eager for confirmation.

"Well, in a general way . . ."

Now Natty's not sure what to think. He had an appointment to talk about his own problems, but now it's turning into something else. Is it good or bad luck, or another reason entirely that he can't recognize yet? The people in Iraq were always saying *"Insh'allah"*—God willing—about everything. As if the hand of the Divine was behind every power outage, every burst water pipe, every wheel that came off a donkey cart. They used the expression as often as American soldiers said "fuck."

So maybe things are working out as they're supposed to. Except, honestly, Natty hardly knows anything about the case. Dad barely talked about it in the one or two tense conversations a month they had after Natty moved to Florida. Most of Natty's information is what anyone else could get from Google. But Ben's hand is patting him on the back now. Don't fight the funk. Go with the flow.

"Perhaps it would be good not to change then." Ibrahim looks at his son. "The horse is in the water already."

Hamid has been standing there the last few minutes glowering and putting out an aura of devout belligerence. "Begging your pardon." He turns to Natty, his accent more Shore Parkway than Tahrir Square. "Did I hear correctly that you were in the military?"

"I was in the army." Natty puts his shoulders back and his chest out. "That a problem?"

"So you fought Muslims and now you're trying to help one?"

A second silence, more weighted than the first one, falls over the room. A slant of refracted light comes through the window, catching a revolution of dust motes slowly turning in the air.

"Different circumstances," Natty says. "Different times."

Hamid continues staring at him, as if he can see through the dust motes and past the trappings of the well-appointed law office, all the way back to a dim stairway and an empty sneaker on a second-floor landing.

"Trust me, we want Nathaniel going through the door with us." Ben flashes a salesman's grin.

Natty holds Hamid's stare for a few more seconds, sustaining the contest until Hamid looks away. Not so much conceding as deliberately withdrawing.

"*Insh'allah*, maybe it's for the best to stay then." Ibrahim bows his head. "God willing, everything will work out."

"I'm sure it's what David would have wanted." Ben gives Natty a final triumphant slap on the back. "Right, kid?"

"Absolutely."

As Ben finally moves his hand, Natty notices he can still feel the damp pressure of a palm print through the layers of fabric.

7

Lourdes and Sullivan have been kept waiting through lunch hour outside Paul Kirkpatrick's office, her stomach audibly mulching the remains of the kale shake she tried for breakfast, while various FBI agents hustle in and out with salad and soup containers, wafting faint odors of split pea and Manhattan clam chowder. Finally, at about quarter to two, a tall male agent with the thinning white-blond hair and the peeling sunburn of an aging lifeguard exits without looking at them and a husky broad-shouldered man sticks his head out.

"You folks still here?" he says. "Might as well come on in."

Lourdes catches herself doing the duck lips again as Kirkpatrick waves them in like a high school football coach inviting the second-stringers to a late practice.

The office looks like a set for a network TV show, a little too strenuous about pushing the symbols of the U.S. government and a little short on evidence of actual boring scut work getting done.

There's a federal seal on the wall behind a big battleship of a desk, next to eight-by-eleven photos of the POTUS and the director of the Bureau. Naturally, there's a big American flag on a gold pole in the corner, reflecting light from windows with sky-blue curtains, which look out at the Freedom Tower trying to needle its way through the clouds as it rises from the site of the Trade Center. And just in case anyone missed the point, there's a "9/11—Never Forget" poster above a leather couch, a picture of George W. with a bullhorn amid the smoldering remains of the twin towers, and a huge collection of baseball caps with the emblems of law enforcement agencies from every state in the union. Those terrorists better not mess with Cedar Falls, Iowa. Or Senoia, Georgia.

Kirkpatrick, in his mid-fifties, wears a white shirt with the sleeves cuff-linked and a bright red tie. He's almost Sullivan's height, maybe six foot three, 220 pounds, hair slicked back with gel and skillful combwork. But unlike Sullivan, he has pale blue eyes that project a kind of needy attention-seeking masculinity that Lourdes usually associates with steroid-addled gym rats and country music stars.

She notices there are pictures of him with a little tow-haired kid on the table behind him, but no wife in any of the images and no ring on the agent's finger.

"You folks are here to talk about David Dresden," Kirkpatrick says with a forceful tug on his tie. "Isn't that right?"

"It is," says Sullivan, not taking off the black overcoat he kept on while they were in the overheated outer office.

"Have a seat." Kirkpatrick points to the leather couch. "This shouldn't take long."

"We just have a few questions." Lourdes sits down first, noting the presumption in the subject setting the time limit for the interview.

She's dismayed as she sinks in deeper than expected, her flats coming off the rug and the air whooshing out of the cushions. Whoa, she thinks. Keep that girl away from the cuchifritos.

Sullivan sits on an arm of the sofa, hands clasped on his lap, the overcoat spreading in a stately fashion like a priest's cassock.

"Sorry you had to make the trip." Kirkpatrick perches against the side of his desk, maybe angling for cover. "I tried to tell you on the phone that I can't say much beyond what I already told your fellow detectives. I know we try to operate in the spirit of cooperation between our agencies, but we're still officially engaged in a civil suit with Mr. Dresden's law firm. Though I expect that will be dismissed any day now."

"I thought you already lost a motion to dismiss," Sullivan says quietly.

"Temporary setback, liberal New York judges." A broad smile spreads across the agent's face as he puts one buttock down on his desk, crosses his arms, and swings his left leg as if feeling carefree. "Our lawyers are onto at least a half dozen errors in the ruling."

"We just wanted to ask about your personal interactions with Mr. Dresden." Lourdes tries to rock forward and regain her balance on the couch.

"Look, I completely understand the position you're in." Kirkpatrick maintains a steely smile. "You have a high-profile victim who was murdered in a public park. But you have to understand *my* position. There's a limit to how much I can tell you."

"Yes, you said about the lawsuit . . ."

"Not just that. This mailman case involves classified matters of national security that I can't get into and Dresden was bombarding us with these FOIA requests . . ."

"We know all that." Lourdes tries to squeeze a couple of dimples into a girlish smile. "We're more looking at the personality conflicts."

"I'm not sure I follow." The agent looks to Sullivan, as if there's some code they're supposed to share as men.

"We've spoken to Dresden's widow." Sullivan passes his hand through the air like a croupier cutting off betting. "She says you threatened her husband . . ."

"I told your friends from the precinct, that's a bunch of garbage." Kirkpatrick frowns. "I never threatened anybody. I've been with the Bureau nearly thirty years. I worked on Ruby Ridge, Oklahoma City, Waco, the Cole investigation, the Trade Center, and dozens of other cases that never made the media. If I rattled that easily, you think I would've gotten those assignments?"

Lourdes finds herself looking at him and marveling at how big his head is. She'd once heard a group of older detectives discussing a rumor that J. Edgar Hoover would not hire an agent who wore less than a size 7 hat, decreeing, "I will not have pinheads in this agency." She wonders if this supervisor is at least a size 8.

"You never threatened Dresden with physical harm?" Sullivan interrupts. "Not even when it got heated?"

A kind of surprised, boyish hurt comes through the piercing blue eyes.

"Can we go off the record here, just for a minute?" Kirkpatrick lowers his voice. "I know there have been a lot of sentimental tributes, but the truth is that David Dresden was a really bad guy. Okay?"

Lourdes looks over at Sullivan to see if he's going to concur. He's just sitting there, still as a monument, waiting for the pigeons to land.

"Everyone's carrying on like he was some kind of saint, but he represented terrorists and kidnappers and drug dealers and murderers," Kirkpatrick says. "The scum of the earth. The Bin Ladens and Baghdadis of the world never had a better friend. The people you and me and this young lady here are out fighting to keep off the streets. He had clients who are still plotting to this day how to kill innocent Americans. And this poor supposedly innocent Mr. Saddik was one of them. He was trying to smuggle in bomb parts that would have killed thousands of people in Grand Central and on the George Washington Bridge. And that's not going to happen on my watch."

"Is this all justifying why you threatened him?" Lourdes asks.

"*I never threatened him,*" Kirkpatrick says loudly, and then looks bewildered. "Listen, Dresden was trying to use this case to find out where we got our information about a terrorist plot. He wanted to expose people who risked their lives to help the United States stay safe. What he did is he tried to put the name of a registered informant in the court record. And did I let him know I wasn't happy about that? Yes, I did."

"So you think he had it coming?" Lourdes asks.

From the corner of her eye, she sees Sullivan put a hand over his midsection and frown. She's shown too much too soon. Pulled out a machete when a surgical scalpel was needed.

"No, I did not," Kirkpatrick says, more evenly. "Look, David Dresden helped dangerous people get out to commit more crimes. Instead of wasting my time and your own, maybe you should be looking at whether one of them turned on him."

"No one's accusing you of doing anything improper," Sullivan says, using his voice as a balm. "We just need to cover all our bases. You understand, don't you?"

"Of course." Kirkpatrick nods. "I'd be asking the same questions if I was where you are."

The voice is conciliatory, Lourdes notes, but his knuckles are wrapped around the edge of his desk.

"So maybe you can just help explain this," Sullivan says.

He moves the folds of his overcoat, revealing the manila file he brought. He flips it open, takes out the phone records, and crosses the room to hand them to the agent.

"You see where we circled a cluster of calls back and forth between Dresden and this office at a time when this Saddik case seems to be heating up," Sullivan says. "Since we've been looking at the court records and it appears that the Bureau had been blocking every single request that Dresden made during the discovery process, we were surprised by the number of calls made during this period and their duration. It appears he was having longer conversations with somebody here."

"We were hoping you could put some light on that," Lourdes says.

This time, Sullivan gives her a tiny sideways nod.

"This meeting is over." Kirkpatrick stands up.

"Really?" Lourdes looks at Sullivan, the change in tone so swift that she wonders if she spaced out for a second.

The agent moves to the door. "From now on, all requests should go through our counsel's office."

"You want to give us a clue what's going on?" Lourdes says.

"It seems you people have your own agenda." The agent turns to Sullivan as he holds the door open. "Which is a shame. I thought we were all on the same side here."

"Somehow I doubt that." Sullivan gives him a faint ghost of a smile as he walks out. "Thanks for your time."

8

"What's with the bike messengers?" Natty looks out into the hall as Ibrahim and his son depart and the messenger he saw earlier wheels into one of the side offices. "I must have got here just in time for the *Flashdance* revival. *What a feeling!*"

"Your father's thing." Ben closes the door. "Ever since he filed the tort claim, he got all bent out of shape worrying about the FBI and the NSA reading his emails and listening in on phone calls, so he decided it was better to have the physical documents ferried around. It's crazy expensive, but I think the real reason was he wanted to give former clients a job and a paystub for their parole officers. His 'Give a Skell a Skill' program."

"Sounds like Dad."

The old-fashioned altruism of it was embarrassing and, *okay*, touching. His father was the Great Sentimentalist of the Left. Not just taking in clients' kids, but forever boring the pants off Natty and Mom with stories about seeing Dylan at Forest Hills, marching on the Pentagon with Abbie, trying cases with Kunstler and Kuby, boozing with Hunter S. Thompson the night the author set himself ablaze with flaming Bacardi shots at Elaine's, and, of course, the legendary (in Dad's estimation) adventure of sneaking into Cuba in '95 and smuggling out a couple of dozen Cohibas for Ben and himself.

It was a wonder, to some, how the two of them could ever be friends. Dad with his scraggly hair and spongy gut, the rumpled suits he wore to court, and sideways wisecrack delivery he'd use to zing judges and opposing counsel with pieces of obscure case law. As opposed to Ben with his declamatory style, brash and bull-like in his Italian threads, his bald head sticking up like a boxing glove from his buttoned collar, always the loudest voice in the courtroom. Lebowski and Sluggo, some people called them. The son of a union organizer and the son of a cop. What did they even talk about?

The simple answer was, they killed each other. Literally made themselves laugh to the point that more than once Natty had walked in to see them clutching their stomachs and gasping like a landed fish. They joked about things almost no one else thought were funny. Myron Cohen routines. Lundy's waiters. Dumbest clients. And most of all, shared memories of Midwood High School, where they met back in '66. Warp and weft had put them on opposite sides a few times over the years. Ben up to his neck in the rice paddies with the Fifth Marines in Nam while Dad was with the hairy puke protestors getting clobbered at the Hard Hat Riot on Wall Street. The two of them ended up at Brooklyn Law at the same time. Then split up after graduation when Dad went to Legal Aid and Ben went to the Brooklyn DA's office. But fifteen years ago when Ben got divorced for the second time and realized he needed to make some real money, Dad, with an established private practice, welcomed his old friend with open arms. Wise-ass sharp-elbowed Brooklyn Boys up from the street, wielding their law licenses like trash lids, the last gang in town.

"So the mailman case," Natty says.

"Obviously, other firms are interested," Ben says. "You know why they say sharks don't attack lawyers swimming in the ocean?"

"Professional courtesy." One of those things Ben and his father said to each other more often than "hello."

"Apparently even that's gone now." Ben sits and gives a long sigh. "You'd think they'd have the decency to wait until your father's at least a week in the ground. But maybe I'm just getting soft-hearted in my old age."

"I want to ask you something, Ben. And please don't get up on your hind legs."

"Ask me anything, Natty. I've always been open with you."

"Did you have me stick my head in just now to keep the mailman from going with another firm?"

Ben cricks his neck, with an audible wrestler's snap. "You think I'd use you like that?"

"Well . . ." Natty fingers a worn patch on one of his father's lapels. "I don't mean to make it sound like an accusation. You're a lawyer and a lawyer does make deals . . ."

He realizes he's afraid to put it more bluntly. Two tours with the army, but he doesn't want to risk losing the affection of the one mentor he has left.

"Come on." Ben sticks his jaw out. "You're the one who came in early. What was I supposed to do? Ignore you while your father's most important client is in the office?"

"Maybe not."

"But let me be honest." Ben puts his hands flat on the desk. "Did I see an opportunity when I knew you were here? Probably yes. Ibrahim and that pain-in-the-ass son aren't a hundred percent comfortable with me yet. So is it wrong to put them at ease by giving them a greater sense of continuity? You tell me."

Natty stops rubbing the lapel and looks down to see his father's pant cuffs hovering an inch and a half above his own unpolished shoe tops. "Okay. I get it."

"But you look like you have something else to say." Ben levels his stare.

Natty undoes his collar button and loosens his father's tie. "I could do more."

"What, with Ibrahim? You did enough. You introduced yourself as David's son, so now he feels better. I think he's going to stay."

"I'm not just a greeter, though."

"You're an expert in suing the federal government all of a sudden? Funny. I thought your only experience was prosecuting nickel bag dealers and Medicaid fraud in Orlando."

"You don't have any experience with Bivens actions either."

"True dat." Ben lowers himself into the leather chair behind his desk and rocks back, steepling his fingers and giving Natty a long look through slitted eyes. "But do you seriously want me to surrender the case to another firm?"

There's a knock at the door, but Ben ignores it. A buzz from his desk phone gets no attention either. Natty knows his measure is being taken. Pounds of resistance per square inch.

"Nathaniel, what is it that you want?"

"I'll tell you what I *don't* want." Natty exhales. "I don't want to feel like I'm just being used to keep the case, because of who my father was."

"You're not." Ben puts his feet up on the desk, a slight bulge under one cuff where the ankle holster is. "But realistically, what else do you have to offer?"

"That's a tough question."

"Look, I know you need a job. Your mother called last night and suggested I throw some work at you."

"She did?" Natty grimaces.

"But there's a limit to what you can practically do here with your experience."

"It's my father's case, Ben."

"Right. And you spent your whole life fighting him. But this is not the way to make up for it." Ben puts a finger up, anticipating an objection. "Listen, I know you feel bad about how you two left things. But this is high-stakes litigation. Your father gave a press conference in front of the courthouse, where he said he was going to ask for twelve million. This man Ibrahim almost died three times while he was in custody."

"Ben, I need a job," Natty says.

There it is. Plain as a beggar's outstretched cup.

"Ah, Christ." The feet come off the desk and the leather chair squeaks forward. "Look, I know money is tight for you and your mom . . ."

"Dad didn't do a lot to prepare."

"Yeah, well, who does?" Ben says, leaning back again, fist under his chin. "But here's the problem—or *one* of the problems. You've got a case of your own that you're fighting."

"I thought we were getting that diverted to Veterans Court. You left a message the probie's out of his coma . . ."

"It's still not a slam dunk. The victim's family's still hot to see you on Rikers. Which means you need to start focusing on showing contrition and going to your treatment sessions."

"What am I supposed to do the rest of the time? Sit around picking at scabs?" Natty grinds his back teeth, remembering group therapy at the facility in Orlando, where they had Mickey and Goofy stickers on the wall of a room that was used for family sessions as well. "I'm a worker.

I want to work. I'm stuck in the city because I'm on bail, and I passed the bar in New York before I moved to Florida. Use me."

"I can't pay you." Ben's eyes stray over Natty's shoulder.

"Why not? Nothing in my bail conditions says I can't earn a salary."

"No, I mean I *can't*. The firm is in the red."

"What?"

"We're broke. I don't know how else to say it."

"How can that be? You've got these big new offices, bike messengers and paralegals, you just put up my bail . . ."

"And I'm two hundred grand into my credit line with the bank to pay for all that." Ben holds out his open palms. "Plus three ex-wives eating me alive with alimony, two grown daughters with no jobs and no husbands, who want money but won't even speak to me, and a monthly mortgage on my townhouse that's not getting any smaller."

Only now does Natty notice there are no pictures of Ben's two daughters, Claudia and Emma, high-strung, high-maintenance twenty-somethings he's been long estranged from. Each born from a different mother, wives one and two from what Ben called his "Murderer's Row." The third was a forty-something former lingerie model named Tiffany (really), who relieved Ben of half the assets he had left after his previous divorces.

"And let me tell you something else, Natty, in case you haven't noticed." Ben rolls back his chair. "There is no big money in being a criminal defense lawyer anymore."

"Come on."

"John Gotti is dead. There's no more Super Flys. No one is giving out million-dollar retainers anymore. The only real money is in white-collar defense work. And neither your father or me ever got accepted to the Harvard Club. Not that we ever wanted to be. But now we're paying for it."

"So you need this mailman case as much as Dad did?"

"It would be good to see justice done. But I'm not going to lie, Natty: the money wouldn't hurt either."

"I could work until you could afford to pay me."

"I don't even know where I'd put you," Ben mutters, as if talking to himself.

"Put me in a broom closet. I don't care. I just want to be part of something. I'll read transcripts, I'll find docket numbers, I'll help track down witnesses. I did searches for high-value targets in Iraq with people trying to blow us up all the time. How hard can it be to work on something that's at least half local?"

"And you're really not going to let up until I say yes, are you?"

"What do you think?"

"I know the answer." Ben tips back. "I remember the Knights of Columbus."

When he was sixteen, and his classmates at St. Ann's were going to raves on Randall's Island or acquiring fake IDs to get into clubs, Natty finally managed to get into a full-fledged Golden Gloves event at a Knights of Columbus Hall in Mineola. Fighting near the top of the bill in the 175-pound division against some jacked-up future Olympian who landed four solid body shots in the first thirty seconds that would have put a horse on its side. But with Ben yelling, "Don't quit, champ," Natty clenched and held on for three rounds until the bitter end. Then he let Ben drive him to the ER at Methodist Hospital, where x-rays showed three broken ribs.

"You're an army veteran who'd be helping someone from the Middle East sue the United States government for acts allegedly committed to save American lives. That won't bother you?"

"You worried about the static between me and Ibrahim's son?" Natty waves like he's tossing paper in the trash. "We'll work past it."

"There's something else." Ben takes a deep breath. "I don't want to be responsible for anything happening to you."

"What are you talking about?"

"I'm serious. This thing with your father is very disturbing. No suspects, no evidence. Whoever did it was very careful."

"Are you saying that's to do with this case?" Natty's eyebrows go up. "You actually believe someone from the federal government followed my father to Prospect Park, shot him, and took his car because of a lawsuit?"

"Twelve mill is a lot of money."

"Ben? This is *you* talking?"

His parents were always supposed to be the wild and woolly paranoids, detecting racism in taxi drivers passing them and government surveillance at the donut shop, while Ben Grimm remained grounded and solid as the orange rock-beast from the Fantastic Four who inspired his nickname. Patiently sipping his after-dinner grappa and grumbling, "Guys, come on," while Dad was stretching his Mr. Fantastic elastic conspiracy theories, Mom was bursting into righteous flames like the Human Torch, and Natty yearned for the power of invisibility.

"I know it sounds nuts." Ben rests his elbows on his desk. "But your father always said paranoids and broken clocks get it right occasionally."

"You seriously believe the feds would come after me or my mother?"

"All I know is you'll be safer if you stay out of it."

"Please, Ben. I need this."

The plaintiveness in his own voice is embarrassing. An army commendation medal, a Purple Heart, a Combat Infantryman Badge, and he sounds like a little kid at the screen door, trying to get in out of the rain.

"I'm a good lawyer," Natty says. "I just need a chance to prove it."

"Okay: sell me." Ben slouches in his chair again, the side of his face resting on his hand, King Lear hearing out the Fool. "Why is it so important to you to be involved?"

"I'm a little lost, okay?" Natty flaps his arms. "You want me to say it? There it is. Everything is fubar."

"You think a civil case is going to fix that?"

"Dad always said I could learn a lot from you."

"He did?"

"He said there wasn't a better courtroom performer around."

Though sometimes the description was appended to the word *showboat* and a mild headshake. *Fireworks are nice, knowing the law is better.*

"I maybe had the edge at trial," Ben says, not lifting his cheek from his hand. "But David was better behind closed doors."

Why is this so raw and hard to ask for? He could probably hit the pavement and find some other kind of temp work, reading contracts or volunteering at the VA. But he needs to be closer to home now, a creature in more familiar surroundings.

"So you're just asking me to help you until you get back on your feet?" Ben asks.

"You're doing a lot already on the assault case, and I can't afford to pay you. Maybe we could say I'm working some of it off . . ."

"Shut up already. You're family. End of discussion." Ben gives a soft grunt, like the admission cost him. "You know, my girls don't want anything to do with me these days, because of their mothers."

"They'll probably come around some day and bring you a raft of grandsons."

Though honestly Ben's daughters always struck him as being as single-minded and unrelentingly vengeful as Islamic fundamentalists.

"Look at me and Dad," Natty says. "If he was still alive, I'd take back half the things I said . . ."

The words turn to ash on his tongue, worthless as burnt paper at this point.

"*If* we do this . . . And I'm still at 'if.'" Ben puts his laced hands on top of his shaved head. "You don't make court appearances, you don't sign your name. Your role is support and research. You go through boxes, make phone calls, and follow up on David's Freedom of Information Act requests. As long as you're hanging around, you might as well help me get up to speed. But only if you keep up with all the appointments for your own case."

Natty nods, deciding now is not the time to discuss how much he'd get paid in the long run, or to belatedly bring up the business the detectives raised about going through the case files.

"You won't regret it," he says.

"I don't know about that." Ben gets up to shake his hand. "But at least I can keep an eye on you and make sure you don't get into any more trouble."

9

Come on, ring already, ring. Put a crown on my checker. Give me a few more moves. Lourdes keeps eying her iPhone, trying to limit the number of times she looks up to see if the chief of detectives is still in the office talking to Captain McKenna.

She licks her lower lip and sneaks a quick glance as the clock hits 11:13 a.m. on the screen, a full four minutes since last time, and when she looks back up, the two white men are watching her like old eagles eying a field mouse from an oak tree branch.

She drops her gaze again, pretending to read a text and resisting the urge to play her skeeball app or shop for bras online while she's waiting on the callback from Nathaniel Dresden's cell phone carrier.

Four other detectives are working the day tour at the Seventy-Eighth Precinct, all of them more practiced at keeping their heads down when the brass is rattling and the glare is harsh. Beautiful Bobby is leaning back at the desk in front of her, the back of his shirt collar slightly frayed. He must not be back together with his wife; what woman would let her man leave the house like that? When she was going out with Mitchell Vogliano, her skinny little Italian from the DA's office, she'd stay up to iron shirts for his court appearances, even if she'd come off working four days in a row. But here's B.B. chatting away with patrol about cars getting broken into on Bergen Street, like he hasn't got a care in the world. *Compartmentalization.* That's her new crossword puzzle clue for getting all the pieces.

Just over Bobby's shoulder, Chief Gunther is giving her a stony Mount Rushmore gaze, his hairline not so much receding as failing to keep pace and cover the apparent expansion of his head circumference. She can't help it. Bosses terrify her. Having the gun dry-click twice against her dome didn't cost her sleep the way a rip from an administrator could. A cross word and she turns into a little girl getting scolded by the principal. She lowers her eyes again and sees she missed a call from her mother. Somehow the phone didn't buzz or ring, like it knew she was handling all she could this morning.

The chief stalks out of the captain's office, walking straight past her desk without a word, and the captain crooks a finger through the glass, a longshoreman's hook pulling her up out of her seat.

"Close the door," he says as she comes in.

"*Que pasa?*" She puts her back against the door as it shuts, blocking the squad's view. "Am I in trouble again?"

He has one of his little Yankee Clippers halfway into a beer growler on his desk with its masts pulled down, the work probably interrupted by the chief's unexpected visit.

"Let's talk about where we are," the captain begins. "Have we discussed Kevin Sullivan?"

"Not specifically, I don't think."

"Kevin Sullivan is a great detective." He pauses and raises his eyes to the ceiling. "Correction: Kevin Sullivan is a great *fucking* detective. I worked with him five years at the seven-seven."

"Do or Die Bed-Stuy."

"Those were the days, my friend. And let me tell you, the man rocked the house. Cleared at least half a dozen Page One homicides while he was there. Just walked into a crime scene and saw something no one else noticed, or got skells to confess things they had no business telling anyone."

"But there's a problem now because . . ."

"There's a problem now because he's getting too old to give a shit what anyone else thinks." He wrenches around to reach into the confines of his tweed jacket and scratch the small of his back. "Chief Gunther wasn't here to give me an attaboy."

"The FBI pitching a bitch?" Lourdes squeaks and shifts her weight to do a little fake innocent ballerina tiptoe.

"Like you didn't know."

"Captain, we didn't do anything wrong. We went over there like you asked, we asked our questions respectfully, and the agent threw us out of his office as soon as we started getting into those phone calls from our vic."

"Whatever it was, the FBI complained to the U.S. attorney." The captain starts fiddling with getting the little ship into the bottle again. "The U.S. attorney complained to the Brooklyn DA. And the DA complained to the police commissioner, and the commissioner asked the chief of detectives to pay me a visit." He pauses from trying to push the prow through the bottleneck. "Do you understand the physics at work here, detective?"

"Sir, we were totally professional. The agent was not being forthcoming. I don't know how else we were supposed to handle the situation."

The captain has taken on the anxious look of an elderly tourist trying to read a subway map. "Look, I know you're in a tough spot. You've just come up for air again, and then you get hit with your first big case."

"Yes, sir."

"And I know you're scared of screwing up after what happened with Heinz."

Though even now she's not sure what she was supposed to have done while Heinz was yelling at the cab driver and telling him to go back where he came from ("fucking towelhead"), oblivious to the hipster passenger filming them from the backseat. Was she supposed to dress down a senior officer in public? Yeah, that would have endeared her to everyone on the job. They'd still show up if she got shot, but the next time she needed to switch vacation days with somebody? Later, *amiga*.

"I'm just doing the job, sir."

"Robles, I'm trying to help you out here. There are people who thought I shouldn't take you back into the squad after what happened with Heinz."

"I know that."

"I could have said I don't want you. We're taking you back in a high-profile neighborhood. And let's face it, you didn't have a ton of experience to begin with. But I've worked with your aunt back in the day and she talked to me about how much this job means to you."

Aunt Soledad, coming through for her again. *Mi tia*, the sergeant from Brooklyn Narcotics and vice president of the local Hispanic Soci-

ety chapter. Always looking out for her sister's daughter from the projects. Got Lourdes out of trouble for her one dumb-ass arrest, jumping
turnstiles when she was late for first period, freshman year, Bishop Ford
High School. Then helped steer her toward a patrol assignment within
walking distance to the apartment in Sunset Park, where Lourdes's mother
and sister moved from the Whitman Houses.

"You probably feel like you owe Sully because he lobbied to keep you
on this case as well," the captain says.

"He did?"

The first she's heard of this. Does that mean someone's actively lob-
bying to get her taken off? She looks back through the glass at the squad
room.

"So I get it. I know the kind of pressure you must be feeling," the
captain says.

Like, seriously? Like this middle-aged white man can understand
what pressure is? Like he has any clue about what it's like being the first
one in her family to graduate college and the second one to hold a steady
municipal job? Like he can understand trying to make your bones as a
detective when you've got a father doing life in prison, a mother in and
out of rehab, a sister off the psych ward at Bellevue, and an older brother
you barely knew in an urn on the mantelpiece that you used to touch
and say "good night, Georgie" to until you were eight? Like he could
possibly comprehend the intense step-by-step concentration it takes every
day not to fall off the high wire?

"Really, I empathize," the captain says. "You think that you need to
defer to a more experienced investigator. But you're also worried because
you were with a senior detective who blew up on you before. Right?"

"If I can speak honestly, sir, Sullivan seems a lot more stable than
my previous partner."

Heinz was a numbskull juicer from Rockaway who spent all his time
either at the gym or on the phone screaming at his ex-wife's lawyer. He
allegedly tested negative for steroids every time he pissed in a cup, which
revealed either significant flaws in the system or a frightening natural
temperament for someone legally empowered to carry a firearm and use
it at his own discretion.

"And Sullivan *is* more stable, like ninety percent of the time." The captain sets the schooner aside and blows into the bottle to clear away obstructions. "But anybody who's good at this kind of work has to be a little off the beam. You have to be, otherwise you'd be thinking about normal things on your day off. You'd be playing golf or coaching Little League or . . ."

"Putting ships into bottles."

"There you go." He starts untangling the tiny riggings again. "But you know what Sully used to do when his tour was over? He'd put on the shittiest, bummiest clothes he could find, walk home through the nastiest part of Prospect Park, where he was sure he'd get jumped by a wolf pack, and then he'd grab a couple of them and beat their balls off while the others ran away." The masts slant back and the ship starts to slide in. "We'd hear about it at the ER afterward. The kids described exactly what Sully was wearing. But they never wanted to press charges."

"What's up with *that?*" Lourdes asks, aware of the other detectives timing how long she's been in here, getting her inventory taken.

"Who knows? The man's an enigma inside an enigma. I've sat in cars with Cochise for twelve hours straight and never had a clue what he was thinking. So I'd be very careful about following him off the reservation."

"Okay, but what are we going to do about this guy Kirkpatrick at the FBI?" she says. "He's fucking with us big-time . . ." She looks over her shoulder and sees B.B. and Andy coming toward the office. "I mean, he's impeding our progress."

"It's all right, you don't have to watch your language with me. But you need to tread lightly with Sullivan—and the feds. There's all kinds of agendas we can't be aware of."

B.B. and Andy enter with files and purposeful looks.

"What up?" The captain finally puts the bottle on his desk, the ship still only halfway in.

"We followed up on what Sullivan was saying and ran the son's name through the NCIC database." Andy hands Captain Mac his folder. "Nathaniel had at least one previous contact with the police, down in Florida. An altercation in a supermarket parking lot. Bashed up a sporting goods salesman for knocking down his girlfriend's daughter. Got the charges dropped, but had to go into counseling. I'm guessing with some help from his job with the prosecutor's office. Sounds like anger management was on the program."

"Hey, your boyfriend Nathaniel's got a temper as well." The captain sideswipes Lourdes with a glance. "You really have a type."

"He's too young and buff for me, captain. I like 'em old and gray, like you guys." She makes a claw at B.B. "Gimme some of them love handles to grab onto."

"Oh, snap." Bobby dances back, laughing. "I'm a be too hot and bothered to work the rest of the day now."

"A-right, settle down," she says, reining them all in before it goes too far.

A little joking was good to show you could play with the boys. A little too much, flies start getting unzipped and harassment forms have to be filled out.

"We still believing he beat the probie up in self-defense?" Lourdes asks.

"We found a couple more witnesses who thought they saw the probie throw the first punch, but two self-defense claims in two separate assault cases?" Andy stoops his shoulders. "Lightning doesn't usually strike twice."

"Okay . . ." The captain pages through the folder, the atlas map of veins in his nose starting to darken. "But are we thinking there's some connection with his father's murder?"

"That's the other shoe." B.B. places his folder on the captain's desk. "Remember how Sullivan said that Natty's mother answered when you asked where he was before the killing?"

"Yes, I was there," Lourdes reminds them. "Sullivan wasn't the only one who noticed."

"Might be a reason the mother jumped in." B.B. smoothes the sides of his pompadour like a teen idol. "Natty was in town before the murder. And forgot to tell us about it."

10

His left knee going up and down like a pile driver, Natty sits in the therapist's office at Brooklyn Veterans' Services that afternoon, answering questions in a dull voice while staring at dark stems in a clear vase. Reminding himself these are just flowers. Not a .357 Magnum revolver suspended in a pitcher of frozen water.

"Look, I don't mean to be rude, miss . . ."

"It's Stacy," says his court-appointed counselor, Stacy Willen, apple-cheeked and soft-chinned, with an upturned nose, iron-straight brown hair parted down the middle, and a little too much blue eyeshadow over her light gray eyes.

"I don't mean to be rude, *Stacy*. But I've got a lot going on right now, in terms of work. I'm in the middle of a major lawsuit. Can we pick up the pace a little?"

"Well, Nathaniel, that kind of depends on you and what you're willing to put into these sessions. I was told you asked for the diversion program because you wanted to battle your issues head-on."

He leans back to tuck in his shirt and tries to sneak a look at the time on the cell phone sticking halfway out of his pants pocket, wincing, as Stacy locks him down with an affectless stare.

The meeting room is set up with three threadbare couches at kitty-corner angles and a kind of studious informality to accommodate group therapy sessions for people who'd rather leap out of a plane or jump on an IED than talk to a psychologist. The bright blue wall behind Stacy has posters that say "Support Our Troops at Home" and "These Colors Don't Run," with a light scuff mark below where it appears someone recently kicked it with a size 11 boot. Pamphlets for twelve-step programs and "Living With PTSD" are stacked on the wooden coffee table. There's a papier-mâché soldier's helmet next to them, sides wrapped in yellow DO NOT ENTER crime scene tape and barbed wire, top covering split open to expose flames on one side and a map of the Middle East on the other.

"Okay." Natty slaps his thighs, ready to giddy-up and get'er done. "I told you that I don't smoke weed anymore. I haven't snorted cocaine in years. And I'm ready to get the drinking under control . . ."

"Though you did black out recently and beat a firefighter into a state of unconsciousness." Stacy balances a notepad on her lap. "How many AA meetings have you been to recently?"

"If I start going again regularly, how many times do I need to see you?"

"At least twice a week. Some people come five times a week. It depends."

"Any of them have jobs?"

"Of course." She draws back her head, producing a small roll under her chin.

A pair of calf-high black leather boots with stiletto heels are mostly buried under a long gray peasant skirt with a faux-Mexican design around the hem. A chunky Santa Fe turquoise necklace and bracelet combo are worn with a puffy white blouse that looks like it came from a suburban-mall Dress Barn. Not a city girl, Natty thinks. More like the runner-up to the valedictorian in some shitty upstate high school. Probably with a graduate degree from one of the state universities. Trying to make it downstate on sixty thou a year or less. Maybe living with a roommate or two, in Cobble Hill or Ditmas Park. Attractive, if not exactly pretty. Not so much the type men chased as the type they were glad to come home to.

"We try to work around everyone's schedules," Stacy says. "You mentioned you're working on a lawsuit. You're an attorney?"

"Last time I checked, I was."

"And your father was a well-known lawyer who died recently?"

"He was murdered. It's been all over the media. I'm sure you've seen that."

"I'm asking you about it personally."

"Is that something we really need to discuss?"

"It's *therapy*, Nathaniel." A pale childlike hand with hard-bitten fingernails toys with the pleats of her skirt. "No one is forcing you to be here."

"I was told it was this or jail time. So much for no one putting a gun to my head."

"Interesting choice of words."

He looks over at the flowers on the windowsill. Just stems in a vase, dude. Not a .357 in a frozen pitcher. Slowly defrosting on his kitchen counter.

"Okay—we're doing this." He exhales, resigned. "The court sent over my service records?"

She reaches for the file that's been sitting on the couch behind her. "You were a second lieutenant in the Tenth Mountain Division?"

"Check."

"What was your job?"

"Intelligence officer attached to a unit with the First Brigade Combat Team."

"You were in Iraq?"

"Better believe it."

She stops fussing with her skirt. "I'm curious why you joined up in the first place."

"Why do you want to know? A lot of people signed up after 9/11."

"Not with your background."

"So you do know about my father."

"Are you going to tell me it's not relevant to what happened to you?"

He braces for the usual litany: Why would the son of a left-wing activist and a *Village Voice* writer join the military when he had the grades to go to law school? And then why volunteer for the infantry when he'd passed OCS and had been through intelligence training?

"My father had nothing to do with my signing up," he says. "I love my country, and I wanted to protect it after it was attacked."

"So you went over while your father was arguing on behalf of flag-burners and Gitmo detainees in front of the Supreme Court?"

"Why does any of that matter? I thought we were talking about *my* case."

"You were involved in a serious assault less than a week after your father's funeral." Stacy parts the curtains of her hair with two index fingers. "You're telling me there's no connection?"

He makes a show of pulling out his cell phone to check the time and sees he has a text from Detective Lourdes Robles, asking him to stop by the Seventy-Eighth Precinct.

"My father had nothing to do with me going in the army." He sticks the phone back in his pants pocket, arching his hips to make room. "That's such a typical therapist way of looking at it. Some people just want to serve."

"And a lot sign up because they don't see where they had any other choices."

"It's called 'public service.'" He hears the automatic defensiveness in his own voice. "Societies used to honor their warriors. Now they need deep psychoanalysis?"

"Skilled at evasion, aren't you?"

"Army sent me to school for it."

A year and a half at Fort Huachuca and Fort Irwin. Hundreds of hours in the classroom and the field. Studying linguistic tics and body movements. Likely reading some of the same texts Stacy got in her grad programs. But she probably didn't go through any other special programs. The role-playing where they shot at you or pretended to be locals serving you vinegar in place of tea, watching if you could swallow instead of getting up to offend them. Or the SERE training. Survival, Evasion, Resistance, Escape. Or, as it was known more informally, Torture School. Where they stripped you down, beat you up, and hosed you off to see what would be required to break you. Simulating the conditions of an interrogation to see if you could take it as well as you dished it out. Strapped to chairs and kept up for days, under blinding white lights and battered with questions no one in their right mind would ever want to answer. It'll be a cold day before Stacy gets anything out of him.

"You've been in this kind of therapy before?" She crosses her leather boots at the ankles and they make sounds like tiny ropes tightening.

"Do I seem like I have?"

"I can tell the judge you're not interested in doing this, Nathaniel."

"Okay, yes. I've been in therapy." He locks his hands over his stomach. "I was in a Warriors in Transition program in Florida."

"Okay." She makes a note. "Now we're getting somewhere. What was it for?"

"PTSD."

"How was that treated?"

"With copious amounts of weed and alcohol."

Not even a smile out of Stacy. Figures. If she's been doing this a week, she's heard this routine a hundred times already.

"Did they give you prolonged exposure therapy?" she asks.

"Where we talk about the same things over and over until they stop meaning anything?"

"Obviously you're familiar with the concept."

"Yes. I've gotten to that point where things stop meaning anything. I didn't find it all that helpful."

The corner of her mouth twitches, almost appreciating the joke. "Did you just volunteer for this program or was that court mandated as well?"

"The latter," he concedes with another look at the flower stems in the vase.

"Because you were arrested?"

"Only for a minor assault. In which I wasn't necessarily the instigator."

"Not 'necessarily'?"

"It's done." He pictures Tanya's face boiling with tears again, feels heat rising from the parking lot asphalt. "The case was adjudicated. The file's closed. Everyone's moved on."

"Yet, amazingly, here you are again—after beating the daylights out of someone at a bar."

He snorts, amused in spite of himself by the mock innocence of her wide eyes and the flattened sarcasm in her voice.

"There was another unfortunate misunderstanding, which wound up with someone getting badly hurt," he says. "But I've drafted a letter of contrition that I'm about to send to my victim in the hope I'll be forgiven."

He notices how her little oval face lights up and flushes when he uses the F word. *Forgiven.* Like it's something real, of measurable value. Not just a sanctimonious diversion tactic. Forgive me for I have sinned. Now get off my fucking back.

"So what happened at the bar anyway?" she asks.

"I don't know. I blacked out." He rearranges himself in his seat, leg over leg, arm over arm. "I thought you were up on all this from the court file."

"As best you can recollect. In your own words."

"Why do the details matter? I'm here."

"Details always matter." She sits up, with her pen poised. "If you're a lawyer, you already know that."

"Oh boy . . ."

He looks at the flaming skull on the coffee table. Alas, Yorick, old buddy, you know how it is. You start off talking about why you needed a drink, and next thing you know you're talking about your father and the war, and nothing good can come from that.

"I just needed to get out of the house," he says simply. "So I went to this bar . . ."

"Why?"

"Uh, maybe for a drink?" He gives her his slack-jawed retard impression.

"What was going on right before this?"

"Nothing much." He shrugs. "Quiet house, four walls. I'm staying with my mom . . ."

No way he's going to talk about the fight he'd had on the phone with Tanya, right after he told her they needed to stop seeing each other. Because that would entail explaining how he'd started to be afraid of himself.

"And this is how long after your father died?" Stacy asks.

"Four days. I was just looking to blow off steam, hear people's voices, catch a few innings of the game."

"And this bar just happened to be called Rescue One?" She stops writing.

"It's a name. That's all it is." He waves his hand, noticing a scab forming where the tooth was lodged. "It's a couple of blocks from my mother's. I just didn't feel like going farther."

"Sounds like you were in a bad space. Were you under a lot of stress?"

"You miss the part where my father got killed?"

She focuses on her penmanship, taking it in stride. "I'm asking, did that bring up other things you'd already been stressing about?"

"Having your old man murdered isn't enough?"

"Not everybody engages in the grieving process by getting into a fight with a room full of firemen. But I'm sure we're all missing out on something."

He feigns a yawn. "Yeah, okay. Whatever. Probably wasn't the best choice I could have made."

"Was there anybody you could've called instead?"

Don't look at the vase again, he tells himself. Don't picture the gun in the freezer. Don't think about the hotline operator, who talked in the same kind of bright neutral cadence as Stacy, as she told him that he should find a steel or a plastic pitcher, fill it with water and then plunk the .357 in it.

"I felt more like drinking than talking," he says. "And most of my friends aren't around."

"That's surprising," she interrupts. "You're a veteran in the New York City area. You'd think there'd be people you could've called."

"Yeah . . . no. Maybe."

Ron Kendrick ran his father's Camaro over a guardrail in Houston, at 120 miles an hour. Jose Estep put a Sig Sauer in his mouth behind a Wal-Mart in San Diego. And the last Natty heard of Cuddy, his staff sergeant was back in southern New Jersey. Like two hours away. And with Dad's car still missing, he doesn't have wheels. A thousand reasons not to make that drive and face that particular ghost.

"I guess I just couldn't think of anybody, spur of the moment," he says.

"But have you talked to any of your guys since you've been back?" She drops her chin, making that soft little roll again.

"Of course," he snaps. "Who else am I supposed to talk to?"

Not his father, who'd at least been honest enough to say he didn't want to know. Or his mother. Or any of his old girlfriends. Or even his mixed martial arts buddies from the gym. People thought they wanted to hear what it was like in a war, but they didn't. All his friends from Cornell didn't have a clue. They said, "Thank you for your service," but it was about as sincere and personal as telling a girl, "Hey, baby, nice rack." As soon as you got into describing the reality, their eyes receded and started to shift, their body language all torque and torsion as if they were as miserable in listening as you were in being there. And then the inevitable

squirming, sneaking glances at watches and cell phones as they tried to figure out how long they had to wait until they politely said goodbye and left.

"But you do have friends you could have called." She uncrosses her
legs and leans over her notepad.

"*Yes.* What do I look like, a freak?"

Though the fact was, he'd always been kind of a loner. Always out of
step with whatever he was supposed to be. Drawing "Support Operation
Desert Storm" posters when the rest of the third grade was learning "We
Shall Overcome" and "This Land Is Your Land." Into *Band of Brothers*
when other kids were into Power Rangers. Hanging out after school at
the army-navy surplus store on Flatbush when other kids were going for
math tutoring or piano lessons. Sorta-friends came and went, but he'd
never had real buds until he went overseas and needed people like Cuddy
and Borat just to get from one end of a day to the other.

"Then why didn't you call any of the people you'd served with?" she
asks. "A lot of the people who've been in the service form the strongest
bonds of their life with their fellow soldiers."

"It was late, okay?" He makes a fist on his jiggling knee. "Why do you
keep harping on it? It's not that complicated. I was at my mom's, I needed
some air, I went to a bar, somebody maybe spilled a drink, somebody said
something about it, a punch got thrown, and then it was off to the races.
Happens every night in every city, in every part of the world."

"Except you chose to be alone when you're in your hometown, among
so many people. And you blacked out from drinking before you got in
this fight."

"So what?"

"You have some training of your own. Don't you think it sounds like
you're practicing avoidance?" She leans toward him farther, strain lines
in her cheeks showing.

Very slowly and deliberately he looks down to where her blouse has
drooped open, exposing not so much cleavage as the rim of a maidenly
white bra. Then he stares at her face and faintly smiles. Nice rack. Putting her back in her place. At a safe distance, behind the wire, where she
can't get at him.

"I bet they taught you that in your PTSD clinic. I bet you think that sounds 'open-ended' and 'non-threatening.'" He crooks his fingers into quotation marks. "I bet you wrote a paper about veterans and avoidance strategies for your masters of social work program. I bet your professors found you *very* empathetic."

"Your father's death clearly stirred up a lot for you."

"Yeah, that's brilliant. It must be great to not know what the fuck you're talking about. Where did you get your degree, the Teletubbies School of Obtuse Psychotherapy?"

"Actually, Nathaniel, four members of my family served in the military." Faint purple splotches are visible on her cheeks and on her chin, as blood rushes to her face. "My brother was in Iraq with the Tenth Mountain Division as well."

"Then you should know better than to keep needling me."

"You experience this as 'needling'?"

"My fucking father was murdered. How many times do you need to hear that?"

"And instead of picking up the phone and calling up any of your friends, like other veterans do, you went out on your own and got so shit-faced you didn't know where you were or who you were fighting or what you were fighting for."

"Big fucking deal."

"You must have been pretty pent-up."

"I made a mistake. *Okay?* I'm not the first, and I'm sure I won't be the last."

"I'm going to go out on a limb." She sits up, hugging the pad to her chest. "And say you probably had a lot of conflicts with your father that led to you joining the army in the first place. And now you're realizing that you're never going to be able to resolve them."

He looks over her shoulder at the light refracted through the clear vessel on the sill. The water turning to ice, as the vase becomes the pitcher on his counter again. No rushing the thaw. The hotline operator told him to put the .357 in a metal or a plastic pitcher filled with water before he put it in the freezer overnight. Because metal and plastic can't go in the microwave. The only way to get to the gun was to set the pitcher on the counter and wait for the ice to melt. The sun through the glass and the tick of the clock. Time to think things over.

"Nathaniel?" she says.

"What?"

"You've been sitting here for a few minutes, not saying anything. You all right?"

He pulls out the cell phone to check the time and sees the message from the detective is still waiting.

"We almost done?" He puts the phone face-down on his leg. "Because I really gotta get back to the office."

"You're going to be a tough nut to crack, aren't you?"

"What's so great about cracking? What's wrong with keeping it together?"

"That what you call getting into a fight with three firemen?" She smiles, sweet as a cheerleader with an assault rifle. "Because that doesn't sound like keeping it together. That sounds like PTSD."

"Bunch of sob sister bullshit. I'm *fine*. In fact, most people who come back are fine. PTSD's been hyped, so all the wimps and whiners who didn't sign up can feel better and pretend to pity the poor veterans."

"So you reject that diagnosis."

The phone slides off his leg as his knee keeps jiggling. Vibrations reminding him of the staircase banister. Right before the shadow moved in the triangle of light on the second floor landing. Don't worry, Dad. You'll never have to know what I did over there.

"I know you must think I'm an asshole," Natty says. "But I just don't want to get a label that's going to haunt me. I need to be able to practice."

"And be a lawyer, like your father was?"

"You know, you guys are unbelievable." He stands up. "You think everything is about the same things."

She raises her head, brown hair dripping over a chunky necklace. "That's not answering the question. Where are you working anyway?"

"At my father's old office." He clears his throat, busted. "Just a temporary arrangement."

"I'll see you here the day after tomorrow, five o'clock sharp." Stacy takes an appointment card out of her skirt pocket. "We've got a lot to cover."

11

Would I do him?

Lourdes finds herself making a spontaneous sex evaluation as she watches Nathaniel Dresden—or "Natty" as the mother calls him—come trudging up the stairs to the squad room. A couple of variables moved around: maybe. She can't help it sometimes. She'll automatically size a man up and run him through her system, dividing the doable and the arrestable. Trying to avoid overlap in the two categories, though she's had a couple of questionable calls the last few years.

Natty has cleaned up nicely for his visit, putting on a jacket and tie with a pressed shirt and shined shoes. The semi-brute she met with a bandage on his hand the other day is not quite erased, but appropriately civilized with his close-cropped hair and his smooth-shaven face.

"Thanks for coming in on short notice." She holds the door open for him. "Helps move things along."

"We all want the same result. Right?"

She guides him through the length of the room, past the currently vacant holding cell. Andy Chen, who'd helped process the arrest after the Rescue One fight, has made himself scarce to avoid arousing Natty's suspicion, and Captain Mac has yielded his office so they don't have to use the interrogation room.

"You need anything before we get started?" Lourdes sits on a corner of the desk as Sullivan comes in and closes the door behind them, still wearing that big black overcoat. "Coffee? Water? Soda?"

"I'm good." Natty lowers himself into the chair with uneven legs that Sullivan had dragged in earlier.

"I know it's been frustrating for you." Lourdes lets her flat's heel dangle off the end of her foot, as if this is all just going to be easy and flirty.

"Not just for me." Natty rocks in the chair, discovering it's not quite stable. "For my mother as well. And everyone else who knew my father."

"That's why we needed you to stop by and help us figure out a few things. Hopefully we can pick up the pace a little."

She sees Sullivan lean against a wall with his arms crossed, obdurate and unreadable. You could look at that face a year and never have a clue what was behind it. Doing his human predator drone routine. Why does it feel like he's watching her as closely as he's watching their subject?

"Did you have a chance to speak to Mr. Grimaldi about seeing your father's files?" he asks.

"I'm afraid not." Natty checks his pockets, probably looking for a matchbook to slip under the chair leg. "There was a lot of other business going on at the office. Especially with figuring out what to do about this FBI case. Not a great time to open the files."

"Right."

She looks over at Sullivan again, wondering when he's going to jump in. Is he just testing her to see how long she can go without making a mistake?

"In your messages, you said there were some things I could help you with immediately?" Natty prompts, looking at the file at her side.

"Yes, of course." She smiles. "I almost forgot you're a lawyer too. Prosecutor, right? You're thinking like we do."

"So where are you in the investigation?"

"We're following up on all leads, recanvassing the park and the rest of the neighborhood for witnesses who might've been missed. We're checking street cameras and E-ZPass records to see if your father's car turns up. And we're tracking down everyone we can find who's been arrested for car theft or violence near the park."

"So basically you have nothing?"

Natty looks from Lourdes to Sullivan, as if searching for a better place to dock his disappointment.

"We're making some progress." Lourdes hands Natty the first file. "But there are other details you can help us with. Like these phone records of your father's from the weeks before he was killed. Do you recognize any of these numbers?"

She watches how Natty's face changes as he opens the folder and scans down the page, his finger moving slowly down the margin, and the resemblance to his mother gradually emerging in the beady-eyed squint of his concentration.

"Not offhand," he says. "But I'd like to look at these more closely. Can I make copies?"

"I'm sure you can access your father's accounts as easily as we could." Sullivan finally speaks up, in a voice full of gravel and tar. "Probably more."

"Yeah, I could." Natty's chair makes a grumping sound as he tries to adjust his angle. "I just thought we were trying to move things along."

"We noticed that a number of these calls are to the FBI office in Manhattan." Lourdes points to the papers on his lap. "Any idea why your father would be calling them so much?"

Natty holds her stare for a beat with his light green eyes. "Obviously, there could be a number of logical explanations." His voice trails off as he studies the page more closely. "Though there do seem to be an awful lot of those calls toward the end."

"He never mentioned to you why he would be calling them so frequently when they were adversaries in this mailman case?" she asks.

"No, not specifically." Natty shakes his head. "But it wouldn't be unusual if he was requesting access to documents and witnesses."

"Did you speak to him in depth about that case?" Sullivan asks.

At least five things happen on Natty's face within a half second, none obvious. His mouth shrinks, his brow retracts, his eyes get small, his cheek bulges, the cleft in his chin goes up and down before he goes back to the expression he had. But Lourdes can still feel the waves of alternating current coming off him.

"No." Natty shrugs. "Not really."

"Did you speak to him frequently in general?" Sullivan asks, hands in the pockets of the overcoat.

Lourdes wonders if leaving the coat on is strategy or eccentricity. Could be he thinks hanging it up will suggest an extended interrogation and the need for an attorney. Or he could be as weird as Captain Mac said and into wearing the thing constantly like some kind of talisman.

"I don't know what you'd term 'frequently.'"

"How often would you say you spoke to him?" Sullivan asks. "Say in an average week."

"I don't know." Natty looks down at the file again. "Probably not a lot."

"You guys weren't close?" Lourdes thrusts her lower lip out, half admiring his containment.

"Why does that matter now?" Natty asks.

"We're just looking at everything in your father's life and not making any assumptions," Sullivan says, each word sturdy as a brick. "Did you two have a falling out at some point?"

"Not really." Natty stretches and half closes one eye with a look of wry caution.

"So why can't you tell us how often you spoke?" Lourdes slides off the desk as Sullivan comes over to join her, presenting a united front. "We know you probably didn't see eye to eye on some things, since you were in the war and he was against it."

"Where is this going?" Natty closes the folder and looks back and forth between them. "You know how often I called my father, if you have all his phone records."

"We also have *your* phone records," Sullivan says.

"You pulled my records? Why?"

"Nathaniel, come on."

Plain black words from a red-faced man. Sullivan just puts them out there and cuts the sound, so they hang suspended between him and the victim's son.

"You're not seriously looking at me." Natty turns to Lourdes with an incredulous smile. "Are you?"

With a lot of effort, she mirrors what she sees Sullivan doing, which is nothing. Don't smile back reassuringly. Don't cross your ankles. Don't clear your throat awkwardly or bat your lashes girlishly to give him a second to collect his thoughts. She just follows Sullivan's lead and lets it be.

"On what basis did you pull my phone records, detective?" Natty addresses Sullivan directly.

"Nathaniel, nothing that we've done here should surprise you." Sullivan bows his head and looks up reproachfully. "And since you're a prosecutor yourself, you should understand why these steps are necessary. You're a close relative of a recent murder victim, a close relative who himself was just arrested for a felony assault."

"Less than a week after my father was killed. You think you'd be at your best?"

"You also have a prior history of violence." Sullivan reaches for the file he'd had waiting on the captain's desk. "We have an arrest report for a parking lot fight in Florida. And we ran your parents' home address on President Street through the system and saw patrol responded at least four times to disturbances reported at that location since 1993. Sounds like there was a lot of fighting going on in that house."

"No, no, no . . ." Natty starts shaking his head. "This is not really happening."

"Maybe your dad wasn't so into peace and love at home," Lourdes says, trying to give him an opening.

"It's not what you think it is." Natty sets his jaw. "You're misinterpreting what's here."

"Okay, then what is it?" Lourdes says.

Natty tilts back in his seat, so the front two legs are a quarter inch off the linoleum floor. "None of those fights were between him and me."

"Then who were they between?" Lourdes eyes Sullivan.

"This is crazy." Natty blinks at the ceiling like he's getting eyedrops. "Okay, look, my parents had all these foster kids coming and going out of the house when I was a kid, and a lot of them were all screwed up because they were kids of my father's clients. Sometimes when things got out of hand, my mother had to call 9-1-1. But that was all."

"Sucks for you," Lourdes says. "Right? You must have resented your father for letting that happen."

"I took care of myself."

"You're saying you never fought with your father?" Lourdes asks.

"Everyone fights with their father. Didn't you?"

She falls silent, a sting in the corner of her eye. Like he just casually read her signs and backhanded her across the room without moving a muscle. Not your typical mope. This was some high-level psychological jujitsu he'd pulled on her.

"Here's the other thing." Sullivan picks up the second file that was sitting on the captain's desk. "You weren't quite a hundred percent honest with us when we talked to you before, were you?"

"What are you referring to?"

"When you said you weren't in town when your father was killed."

"I wasn't. I was in Florida."

"Were you?" Sullivan stands up and drops the file in Natty's lap. "Because according to this, you were in New York a few days before he was shot."

Natty looks down at the folder, the waves of electrical resistance ramping up to 500 ohms in a matter of seconds.

"The cell tower pings put you in at least a half dozen locations around the Tri-state," Sullivan says. "Including a call a few blocks from your dad's office. You want to tell us what that's about?"

Natty keeps staring at the folder, the red marks on his knuckles more visible to Lourdes as he makes his hand into a fist.

"I don't see why it's anybody's business," he says.

"You don't?" Sullivan arches his black eyebrows, a few white threads poking through the double thickets. "You give us misleading information when we're trying to investigate your dad's murder, and you don't think that matters?"

"I didn't give you misleading information," Natty says. "You asked a question and my mother answered it."

"You didn't correct her, though, did you?" Lourdes says.

"When you followed up, I just shook my head." Natty shrugs. "Maybe you assume more than you realize."

Here we go. Lourdes curls her lip at Sullivan. Now Natty sounds like a lawyer, parsing his words and playing games.

"Why didn't you just tell us the truth?" she says.

"I *did*." He lurches forward in his seat. "I was back in Florida by the time my father was killed. I'd been in New York a few days earlier. One thing has nothing to do with the other."

"You sure about that?" Sullivan says.

"Of course, I'm sure. Do I need to show you the airline ticket?"

"You could." Lourdes pushes off the desk, standing less than a foot from him. "But it would also help if you could turn over the rest of your records."

"Why? Am I a suspect?"

"Not necessarily," Sullivan says. "But would you mind telling us what you were doing here?"

"I had business meetings."

"Could you be more specific?" Lourdes tries to follow Natty's elusive gaze. "Just so we could confirm."

"No, I could not. It's none of your concern. And it has nothing to do with what happened to my father. It was a private matter, which I have no reason to discuss with you."

Lourdes finds herself edging closer to Natty, so his forward knee is almost touching the inside of her thigh. She's heard older detectives say there's nothing like the moment when you know your suspect is about to give it up. That when your man finally cracks, it's as good as sex. Now she finally knows what they mean.

"Let me just ask you," she says, trying to measure her own breath against his. "Are you sure you were back in Florida when your father died?"

"What do you mean, am I 'sure'?" He looks to Sullivan as if there's some relief available there. "You think I can't tell where I was?"

"But you didn't seem to know where you were the other night." Lourdes glances toward the door wistfully. "I understand that your defense in the fireman assault is that you blacked out and don't remember the fight. Is it possible something like that happened earlier with your father?"

All the air seems to go out of the room. She's gone a step too far again, a step too fast, and tripped the wire. She hears a sniff and sees a hand up in her peripheral vision. Then she turns and sees Sullivan taking the folder back from Natty and giving her a barely perceptible headshake.

"I think you guys are going a hundred miles an hour in the wrong direction." Natty rises. "And I can't tell if it's because you're blind or you're covering something up."

Oh my God, Lourdes thinks. My man is a serious player. If he wasn't a suspect, she'd be macking on him and putting out her man-trap right this second. And probably regretting it for years afterward.

"Thanks for coming in." Sullivan puts out his hand. "Let's keep talking."

12

Flick. Hiss. Flick. Hiss.

Natty is lying on the bed in his old room, feet hanging off the end of the mattress, looking up at the ceiling, as he makes phone calls and plays with one of his father's old Bic lighters. Found in a kitchen drawer next to rusty knives and forks and a roach clip. A potential incendiary device threatening to detonate a string of memories. His thumb rolls back and forth over the flint wheel, then comes off and presses the red button separately. Flick, hiss, without the ignition to make the flame shoot up.

He's been making calls for like two, three hours since dinner ended with Mom. Commandeering Dad's old laptop and guessing the password to look up the cell phone accounts the detectives mentioned at the precinct. *Nattydreadtakingover.* Of course. What Dad used to say when he let Natty slide behind the wheel for a driving lesson. Only took two tries to figure that out. Had to be some combination of that nickname and a reggae reference. Which should induce a general state of irie, knowing that the old man was always thinking of him, even when they were outwardly estranged. But that just adds another pressure plate to the minefield he's trying to get through.

After the ambush interview at the precinct, he'd walked home in a half shell-shocked state, the placid streets of Park Slope suddenly as menacing as Tikrit and Ramadi. As if there were snipers lurking behind the barbershop windows and clerks with remote detonators in the cell phone stores. Trying to get the hiss out of his head, he'd changed into his gym clothes and worked out at the Y for two hours on his mother's pass; two hundred fifty push-ups, two hundred crunches, full circuits on the cable

weights and free weights, and fifty laps on the inside track. And somehow managed to get through dinner without blowing a fuse in front of
Mom. But as soon as the table was cleared and the dishes were washed,
he was up in the room, sitting on a bed that was too small for him even
when he was a teenager, making calls to every unidentified number Dad
connected with in the two weeks before the murder. Flick, hiss. Stay busy.
Do anything, except stop and think about where things stand.

He puts the lighter on his chest, scans halfway down the screen on
his lap, and punches in the next number.

"Uh, hello, this is Nathaniel Dresden . . ." His voice goes up like a
Valley Girl's after the robotic voicemail greeting. "I don't know who I'm
leaving this message for or if you already talked to the police, but I'm
David Dresden's son. And I'm just calling because I'm trying to piece
some things together. So if you could get back to me . . ."

He leaves his contact info, punches out, and scrolls down to the next
number. Then pauses to play with the lighter again. Rolling the wheel two,
three times without striking a spark. Then presses the butane button for
the hiss. The sound of escape. Or running out of gas.

So far he's reached a court reporter who Dad owed $486 for a tran-
script ordered last month, the Brooklyn Law School alumni fund-raising
drive, the spaced-out common-law wife of a low-level heroin dealer called
Chewbacca currently residing on Rikers and in sore need of a new lawyer,
four disconnected numbers, and at least nine other numbers with robo-
voicemail set up to take incoming messages but no identifying details.
And of course, the FBI main switchboard number in New York with the
recording of a disgruntled middle-aged white man who sounds like he's
spent his whole life waiting for elevators.

The cursor blinks, waiting for his next move. He should be going to
sleep, starting with a clean slate in the morning. But he knows if he closes
the computer and turns the light off, he'll just lie in the dark, grinding
his teeth. And then maybe wind up sleeping under the box spring again
tonight, bracing for incoming mortar rounds. Or wake up thrashing and
yelling from nightmares. Like Ron Kendrick did before he went over the
guardrail.

You don't have to do this.

Yes, I do.

It's a fucking hornets' nest between his ears. Below his window, he hears the drag and drone of the neighbors hauling out their garbage and recycle barrels for the morning sanitation men. The arthritic creak of joists alerts him to his mother padding up the stairs from getting her midnight tea, reminding him of his father trudging up after a long day in court, probably weighed down by all the moral equivalencies he was carrying, occasionally stopping on the landing and sticking his head in to say, "How's it going, sport?" And Natty, with N.W.A. and Megadeth blasting on his headphones, a "Peace Sells . . . But Who's Buying?" poster replacing the "War Is Not Healthy for Children and Other Living Things" his parents preferred, barely looking up from *World of Warcraft* to mutter, "Just chilling."

Not that it was always bad between them. He used to love sitting next to Dad on the couch and hearing him pick out "Friend of the Devil" on the guitar while waiting for his chance to add his impetuous little yelp to Dad's sardonic croak on the chorus. Lying on their backs under the Prospect Park trees in October, Dad tossing a basketball straight up at the maples so that the brown leaves would rain down. Always getting his big long hands in the way to keep the ball from coming down and hitting his son in the face. Waiting at the bottom of Suicide Hill when Natty went sledding in February. Always there, long after Natty stopped needing the protection. My old man, the lawyer. He remembers how proud he was the first time he saw Dad in court. Getting a conviction overturned for an accused rapist named Malik Sanchez, who'd already done seven years upstate when Dad debunked the prosecution's DNA evidence. They'd just read *To Kill a Mockingbird* in school and he seemed like Atticus Finch. "My Jewish Gregory Peck," Mom said and gave him a deep kiss, mortifying Natty in the middle of Gargiulo's, where they'd gone for a celebratory dinner under the giant squid. A moment of joy mitigated a few weeks later when Malik was arrested for showing his dick to a bunch of schoolgirls on the F train. Another two-pronged memory useful for self-torture sessions.

He picks up the lighter and flicks it twice, letting the flame shoot up and die.

He wonders if Dad left some weed in the study. He was always toking up when Natty got up in the middle of the night for a glass of milk.

"Wanna get high and study for AP Chem, pal? Heh, heh." No, that was never good. Seeing Dad stoned didn't help either of them. Pot helped Dad focus on his cases, but it sometimes made Natty edgy and adversarial with the old man. They had more mellow conversations when they were drinking. The Macallan 18 is still in the cabinet downstairs where Mom put it after dinner. One little tribute drink couldn't hurt, could it? It's not like he's going to head out to a bar and wind up in a holding cell again. At least it wouldn't be as bad as some other options. Like continuing his little shock-and-awe secret mission. How long until that blew up on him? The police already knew he'd been in town just before Dad was killed. If they already had his cell records, it was just a matter of time until they got his computer and figured out what else he'd been up to.

Fuck it. He tosses the lighter aside. Can't keep making excuses or asking for absolution from someone who isn't alive. What's done is done. You have to find a way to live with it. *Siudo*. He needs to shut the laptop and turn his brain off. No more nosing around. And no more reading more glowing tributes to Dad on the Internet and reminding yourself about the kind of son you were. Which leaves you with dozens of jagged memories that can't be sanded down and put away comfortably now. No, I don't want to talk to you, Dad. I don't want to smoke weed with you. I don't want to play guitar with you. I don't want to come to court and watch you defend another scumbag.

Never were in a war, Dad. Were you? Got you there, don't I?

You never got to hear the muezzin's call from the minaret, where militants might be hiding with grenade launchers. You never smelled burning tires, saw the garbage bags in the middle of the road, heard sirens for incoming at the FOB or the monotonous rumble of the convoy rolling out into the desert, where Cuddy liked to say God just fucking ran out of ideas and spilled a lot of sand instead. Maybe I should feel sorry for you. Or maybe I should envy you because you never got hit with the concussion of sound that blows everything away for a few seconds and then brings it back diminished. You never were in the middle of a firefight on the roof of a cigarette factory, thousands of rounds going back and forth, because everyone was shooting at everything, the acoustics different when a bullet was coming right at you, the shooter's intent to kill you *specifically* as plain and clear as the buzz of a mosquito a quarter inch from your ear. You never felt cold air seeping out from the bottom of your stomach where someone stabbed you right beneath under your ceramic plate, or smelled camel guts spilling out in 110-degree desert heat because your guys went crazy once in a while and just had to let it out by strafing a humpback with machine-gun fire. You never saw your best friend literally cut in half, viscera hanging out where his junk used to be as he screams and begs you to finish him off, and then calls you a coward later for not keeping your promise. You don't get to have a never-ending loop in your head of a sneaker lying sideways on a landing just before you turn around and see the parents looking up at you.

His phone buzzes, a little vibro-shock to his nervous system. Little blue letters appear in a gray text bubble.

— YOU JUST CALLED?

He stares at the screen, the word "Unknown" at the top. Then starts mashing his thumbs at the little pop-up keyboard to reply.

— WHO IS THIS?
— YOU CALLED ME.
— THIS IS NATHANIEL DRESDEN. YOU CALLED MY FATHER.
— YES.
— SO WHO R U?
— HOW DO I REALLY KNOW YOU'RE DAVID'S SON?
— WHO ELSE WOULD I BE?
— HOW DID YOU GET MY NUMBER?
— FROM DAD'S RECORDS. I'D LIKE TO SPEAK TO YOU.
— NOT SURE.
— WHY NOT?

No reply. Just what he needs. A message from the ether that can't be traced back to its source. He scans all the other numbers he's called tonight, not sure which one to try back first.

Under his window, unsteady high heels clack like castanets on the sidewalk and the voices of whoo-hoo girls leaving the Fifth Avenue bars soar with wayward jubilation. In a few minutes there will be the inevitable clatter of aimless high school boys knocking lids off the garbage cans instead of having female company. And shortly after that, the sounds of cans clattering and bottles clinking will start, homeless people rummaging through the recycling.

He tries the previous two numbers that called his father's cell phone in the three hours before he died, but they're disconnected as well.

Not on you, Natty Dread. It's not on you. Except that it is.

Stop. Don't go through that door again. There's work to be done. The mailman case. Tons of files to review. Depositions. Freedom of Information Act requests. Reports from the Department of Justice's Inspector General's Office, the Armed Services Committee, and the Council of Europe. Some of them in cardboard boxes from Dad's study, most of them locked up behind a dead man's passwords in the cloud.

He stifles a yawn, not ready to face all that yet but scared to close his eyes, exhausted but restless, a hiss growing at the edge of his hearing. To NyQuil or not to NyQuil, that is the question. Not supposed to be drinking or drugging now, though he's thinking about that Macallan again. The impediment being that when Ben went to bat for him in Veterans Court, Natty promised to stay on the wagon.

Sex could maybe help take the edge off, but online porn is the last thing he needs to put on his computer if the feds are spying on him. The alternative of going out and trying to strike up a conversation with a real woman is more than he can contend with. Better to keep his hands to himself and limit the collateral damage.

He goes into the bathroom to wash his face and brush his teeth. That face in the mirror. The war still right there in the eyes; the mouth strained from keeping in all the words no one else needs to hear. He cups his hands under the faucet, but the cold water comes in a thin desultory drool. Great. When the only kind of pressure he wanted was water pressure. He turns the handle to the off position but the hiss continues. Similar to the butane coming from Dad's lighter when he pushed the red button. Only now it's louder, more like the white noise he heard after Cuddy's stun grenade went off.

He looks out the little bathroom window and sees the fire hydrant in front of the house is open and spewing into the street. Technically not his problem. Especially since the landlord, Mrs. Asterino, is selling the place out from under his mother.

But Boy Scout Natty Bumppo can't let it be. He goes back into the bedroom and dials 9-1-1.

"Dispatch, what's your emergency?"

"I'd like to report an open hydrant . . ."

"Hold, please . . ."

The wait-time music is Taylor Swift. *Shake, shake, shake it off.* This is the freedom he was fighting to defend? Within thirty seconds, he decides he can't take it anymore and he might as well try to fix it himself. After two tours of "nation building," dealing with water treatment plants and irrigation projects, he should, in theory, be able to get this part right.

He goes downstairs, slips on his sneakers, and opens the front door, an unseasonable chill waking him up as he steps onto the sidewalk.

Gallons are pouring into the gutter, sluicing down toward the Gowanus Canal. Someone's knocked over one of the brown plastic compost containers, spilling apple cores, eggshells, and brown lettuce by the curb. At the edge of the street light penumbra, the fire hydrant cap sits face-up by the curb, like someone left it there.

Just as he bends down to screw it on, he sees flitting in the shadows, shades of darkness separating from each other. He smells cheap bourbon and Listerine strips, sees the slant of black roofs against the starless light-polluted sky and white plastic bags caught in the branches, hears the grunt of heavy trucks down by the expressway, the city's unconscious moving while most of the citizenry sleeps. There's movement from the corner of his eye, something flying toward him with bad intent. Metal crunches into bone, bringing a rush of pain and adrenaline as the veil of civility drops, revealing once again that the world, even a few steps from his front door, is a savage and unforgiving place.

13

By ten to midnight, it looks like half the neighborhood and most of its municipal workforce is out on President Street. A fire truck with its light going is parked in front of the Dresden home, and two patrol cars are tucked behind it. An ambulance from Methodist Hospital idles close by. Neighbors in terrycloth bathrobes with sexless baggy pajamas underneath, furry Ugg boots, and untied New Balances stand in front of their stoops, gossiping and using their cell phones.

Lourdes and Sullivan watch from the Impala parked by the corner of Seventh Avenue as medics give Natty a new ice pack to put on the side of his head and his mother, Alice, gestures dramatically at the sergeant on the scene and then points accusingly at the firemen using wrenches to shut off the spurting hydrant.

"Okay, how does this figure into our murder?" Lourdes asks, getting antsy from Sullivan's long Apache silences.

"It might not." He doesn't look at her. "Two things could have absolutely no relation."

"Then what are we doing here?"

"Nothing is irrelevant. Until it is."

"Hmm, NYPD Zen. Thanks for clearing that up."

Seven hours into her tour, still waiting on her period, two weeks after breaking up with Mitchell and the day after the Chief of D's sent out an email blasting everyone about not properly filling out requests for overtime. *Que batingue!* She taps a fingernail against her front teeth as Natty sits down heavily on the front step and grimaces while his mother keeps ranting at the uniform officers.

"So why'd you go at him so hard before?" Lourdes says.

"Natty, at the station?"

"I thought it was all about building up trust and rapport before you hit 'em with the tomahawk."

"It is." Sullivan nods, the sage at the steering wheel. "But this is not your average skell. He's a lawyer, who is the son of a famous lawyer. If he wasn't expecting those questions about the cellphone, then he's dumber than he looks. And I don't think he is. So I figured get them out of the way first, so he's not on edge waiting for them. Then we can look each other in the eye, like we're all being honest and start to develop a trusting relationship. Then, if he lies, hit him with the broadaxe."

"Oh, you got levels, Papi, don't you?"

"Well . . ."

He flexes his fingers on the wheel, endearingly embarrassed and pleased with himself. Like a gawky choirboy surprising everyone on the dance floor by pulling off a credible merengue step.

The sergeant who'd been talking to Alice, Danny Kovaleski, breaks off and crosses the street to their car, leaving two patrol officers to deal with her.

"What do we say?" Lourdes rolls down her window.

"We say the lady is a pain in the ass, but the son's not talking much," says Danny K, a superciliously tall *Top Chef* fanatic who Lourdes went out with a few times and then dumped unceremoniously before she started seeing Mitchell.

Love 'Em and Leave 'Em Lourdes. That's her. The Quick Draw Mc-Graw of romance. Always the first to show a man the door. *Adiós, amigo!* And don't leave your dirty dishes in the sink.

"How bad is he hurt?" she asks.

"He's going to have a big lump over his eye tomorrow, but his arm got the worst of it." Danny ducks down to keep his head at window level. "He's lucky he got it up in time to block the weapon, so it just glanced off him. He said it looked like a steel seagull coming right at him."

"It was a wrench," Sullivan says flatly.

"How do you know?" Lourdes asks.

"It's probably just like the one they're using now."

Sullivan leans over so his shoulder lightly touches Lourdes as he points

across the street toward the two firefighters using a heavy tool to close
the hydrant valve in front of the Dresden place.

"You're guessing, or *you know*?" Lourdes says.

Sullivan shrugs. "I've been watching this whole time, and Natty hasn't
looked over at the firemen once, and they haven't looked at him either.
Seems . . . peculiar."

"He's not being tremendously helpful." Danny almost bangs his head
standing up. "Says it was too dark, so he can't give us a description of who
attacked him. Neighbors looking out the window think they saw two
white males in dark jackets, running down the street afterward. For whatever that's worth."

"You ask Nathaniel if there could have been two of them?"
Lourdes says.

"I'm telling you, he's not interested in cooperating." Danny looks
around square-jawed, playing the man in charge for the patrol officers who
might be watching. "He doesn't want to go to the hospital for an MRI
and he doesn't want to look at a photo array. My impression is he just
wants us to go away, but the mother won't let it go."

"And what's her story?" Lourdes asks.

"She thinks it was some kind of setup by the government or some
shit, but she didn't see anything herself. Pain in the ass."

"Thank you, sergeant." Sullivan nods.

"Hey, LRo, stop by and see us in patrol sometime," Danny says before he turns to trot back across the street. "Be nice to catch dinner. Or
whatever."

"Yeah, I hear you."

She half waves and rolls the window up, hoping Sullivan doesn't pick
up on that little note of romantic pleading in Danny's voice. But the detective is staring intently at flaws in the windshield and gently rocking
back and forth in the driver's seat, like some Borough Park Hasid in shul.

"So?" she says.

"So, what?" Sullivan adjusts the rearview mirror.

"So what do you think is going on here?"

"What do I think?" He checks the side mirrors and holds up a finger. "A: this was just a random attack. Which seems . . . unlikely."

"B?"

"It's payback by some of the firefighters for Natty putting their brother in the emergency room and he's decided to take his lumps quietly and keep his mouth shut."

Lourdes watches the firemen close up the valve and head over to their truck without sparing a glance for Natty, his mother, the medics, or the cops.

"And in exchange, they don't beef when he gets therapy treatment instead of jail time for breaking their friend's jaw?"

"That would be my guess." Sullivan nods. "But it's only a guess. Which means there's still other possibilities."

"Such as?"

"C." He puts out a third finger. "Maybe this does have something to do with the father's murder and the fact that Natty went dark for a few days before that."

"How?"

"If I knew, you think I'd be sitting here spitballing?" Sullivan turns up his palms. "There's one other long shot. And it may sound off-the-wall. Are you ready?"

"Hold on." Lourdes fastens her seatbelt and opens the glove compartment. "I'm just looking to see where I put my tinfoil hat."

Sullivan stares until she starts to squirm. Then the stone face cracks and a low, complicit chuckle spills out. After all the long pauses and grim looks, it feels as close and intimate as the bristle of his stubble against her ear.

"Look in the mirror," he says.

She adjusts the rearview, wondering when she got that extra fold of her skin over her eyes and why no one pointed it out to her. A downside of working with men. None of them would have the nerve to be that honest. But then if they did she'd never forgive them. So there's no winning.

"What am I looking for?"

Nothing but parked cars and empty street all the way up the slope to the park.

"You don't see a Time Warner cable truck?"

He jerks a thumb over his shoulder. A white van with the cable company insignia is idling a half block behind them.

"Yeah, so?"

"How often do you see those guys out in the middle of the night?" Sullivan asks.

"I'm sure they have emergencies sometimes."

"Handled by two people sitting in the front seat the whole time, not going anywhere? Like they've been watching the house?"

"Now you sound as loopy as the widow," Lourdes says.

"Do I?"

Sullivan gets out of the car, hikes back his jacket to feature the shield clipped to his belt so it's visible from two hundred yards away, and then starts to walk back toward the truck. Headlights go on, a turn signal flashes, and the van pulls away before he's taken five steps.

"What did I tell you?" He comes back to the Impala. "All is not as it seems."

"Who were those guys?"

"Watchers of the watchers." He gets in and slams the door. "Could be the feds. Could be IAB checking up. Could be Question Mark and the Mysterians. All I know, they're not here to help."

14

"Let the bodies hit the floor."
  "Let the bodies hit the floor."
  "Let the bodies hit the floor."

Natty hears the headbanger chant even before he walks into Ben's office the next morning, with his left arm in a sling and a cut over his eye. Ibrahim Saddik is rocking back and forth and declaiming the words of a '90s heavy metal song like he's undergoing an exorcism, his eyes pinched tight and his mouth locked in a pained grimace.

"For as long as I live, I will never forget this terrible music," Ibrahim says, gradually opening his eyes and gripping his armrests. "Every day they blasted it into my cell at unbelievable volumes, right before they started torturing me. Just thinking about it, my arms ache and the soles of my feet hurt. A few months ago, I was in a pizza store with Hamid when they play it. I swear I almost passed out."

"And I used to love Metallica." His son Hamid, big and bearded in his skullcap and dishdasha, pats his father's shoulder. "I went home and made a fire to melt all their CDs."

"Except that song is by Drowning Pool." Natty takes a seat by the bookcase.

Ben and the two Middle Easterners stare at him, the radius bone in his elbow throbbing where he blocked the fireman's wrench and the cut over his eye stinging where the deflected blow glanced off him. The x-rays at the Methodist Hospital ER said nothing was broken inside, as far as they could tell.

"Just saying." Natty ignores Hamid's malevolent stare. "Drowning Pool isn't Metallica."

"What happened to you?" Ben asks.

"Had a little problem with a fire hydrant." Natty tries to shrug. "But it's all good now."

"Yeah, I heard about that," Ben cocks an eyebrow, underplaying the drama. "Glad you got it worked out."

The probie's family must have called and accepted the deal this morning. Figuring if Natty could take last night's beating with grace and keep his mouth shut, they could swallow an alternative to a prison sentence. So they were even, for the time being.

"Anyway." Natty readjusts the sling. "What'd I miss here?"

"Ibrahim was just getting us up to speed on the facts of the case." Ben points at the daunting pile of cardboard evidence boxes piled against the wall. "The government just laid a massive document dump on us and I've been up all night reading, but it's always good to hear the story in the client's own words."

"One day I come to work, to start my mail route, and these two FBI agents are there, speaking to my supervisor, Mr. Walid," Ibrahim says, only too eager to restart his tale of woe. "They say they need me to come in and help them with an investigation. 'It's okay, Ibrahim! It won't take long!'"

"Who says this?" Natty asks.

"Mr. Special Agent Paul Kirkpatrick. Then it's more than five years until I see my family again."

His dark eyes are already brimming as his son puts an arm around his shoulders and says something that sounds like, "It's okay, Daddy," in Arabic.

"But as you say, 'it's by the boards.'" Ibrahim sits up, trying to force back the tears. "Ibrahim is still alive. They don't break me. Even though they waterboarded me, hung me by my arms for hours, and beat my head against the wall, and made me listen to this terrible music for days and days . . ."

You got off easy, Natty thinks. Nobody put jumper cables on your nuts or a hot-comb up your ass. He heard all the horror stories from earlier in the war at Torture School. Along with a stiff warning not to violate the Geneva Convention himself, because the army wouldn't back him up. Not that it made a difference when they were looking for Ahmar.

"So when was this?" Natty tries to grab a pen and pad off a side table.

"April the fourteenth, two thousand and six," Ibrahim says with a slight spray between the gaps in his shattered teeth. "I remember this precisely because it was right before taxes were due and I knew the sacks would be very heavy that day. And because once they rendition me to these Macedonian animals and put me in this cell to begin torturing me, I could not keep track of the time anymore."

Sound familiar?

Did I raise my voice? Sure. Crank up "Master of Puppets" and "Ride the Lightning" once in a while? Believe it, papa-san. Interview subjects who hadn't got enough sleep? Well, I wasn't getting that much shut-eye myself. Explicit threats of bodily harm or harm to family members? Depends what you call "explicit." The occasional upending of a chair and face slap? How would you have felt if one of your friends got killed because of an order you had to pass on?

He was a good man, Borat. Played bass in one of those outlawed Iraqi metal bands. Dreamed of coming to America and playing at Ozzfest. Talked about all the groupies he'd get and have to lie to his wife about. No one had the heart to tell him a dude who looked like a notary public at a Bay Ridge pharmacy wasn't going to get any rock-and-roll pussy, no way no how.

So when he was executed in front of his family, everybody and everything was fair game, short of getting yourself court-martialed. Every trick and mental manipulation available was used. Including an excursion to Waterworld. A cloth over the nose and a gallon of water to simulate drowning. Of course, the hajji under heavy manners, Crazy Eddie the double-dealing shop owner, would've said anything to make the torture stop. So he gave up an address in Sadr City.

"I'm sorry. Can we go back a minute?" Natty grimaces as his elbow hits the armrest. "Why *exactly* did the agents say they wanted to talk to you in the first place?"

Hamid rubs his father's back and gives Natty a goatish glare with his goggly glasses and half-beard.

"It's okay." Ibrahim sniffs and nods. "This Joanna Kirkpatrick says they have evidence that someone in my post office branch is collecting funds to support terrorism and helping to smuggle bomb parts through the detectors."

"*Joanna* Kirkpatrick?" Natty holds up his good arm. "I thought we were talking about an agent *Paul* Kirkpatrick."

"Evidently there's a husband and wife working out of the same office." Ben massages his temples. "For all the other stupid bureaucratic rules, agents are allowed to be married to each other and work in the same building. I guess the FBI thinks it cuts down on paperwork when they need to get security clearances."

"Anyway." Natty turns back to Ibrahim. "They brought you in for questioning without a lawyer?"

"They said I wouldn't need one. But then they start getting angry. Especially this Paul. He calls me a liar. He starts banging the table and screaming. He's a big man with blue eyes and a loud voice. He tells me I'm not going home until I tell him the truth. He says I know about plans for terrorism. That I'm helping bring in bomb parts. And I am trying to be like, 'Hey, man, this is crazy. I love America.' But the more I say this, the angrier he gets. Even Miss Joanna has to leave the room. I thought he was going to kill me."

Natty makes a note. If this is, in fact, the same agent who threatened his father, they might have some psychological issues they can explore in a court case.

"Did he literally lay hands on you?" Ben asks.

"No. The torture doesn't begin until I get to Macedonia and Guantanamo. And then the people who do it are wearing masks . . ."

Natty drops his pen. It hadn't occurred to him that interrogators might still be allowed to wear masks in Gitmo while they were outlawed for interpreters in Iraq.

"Hang on." He picks it up again, recalibrating. "Why did they focus on you in the first place?"

"My father didn't do anything wrong." Hamid glowers.

"They didn't just pick his name out of a hat either," Natty says. "He must have done something to get their attention."

He can see why his father fell in love with this case. It has the Holy Grail elements he looked for but could so seldom find in one place: the innocent victim, the false accusation, the vast government conspiracy, and, above all, the David versus Goliath long odds.

"My father has never been arrested in his life," Hamid says. "Never went to a protest. Never spoke out. He's worked for the post office for twenty-five years. He even made us wear those stupid t-shirts with the slogan—'Neither rain, nor sleet, nor gloom of night.' And this is how the government that he worked for treats him?"

"Please, Hamid." His father rests a hand on his shoulder. "It's a fair question. I discussed it with Nathaniel's father as well."

"And?" Ben arches his eyebrows, making steplike ridges up to the grand dome of his scalp.

"We talked about a supervisor at my post office branch named Walid al-Masri." Ibrahim wipes at a corner of his eye. "Mr. Dresden took notes about this. Everyone calls this man Wally. He's from Jordan. He owed me a great deal of money. He borrows ten thousand from me to open a falafel restaurant near Bay Ridge Parkway. Instead he goes and gambles it away at the Foxwoods Casino. I got so mad that I threatened to call the police. Three weeks later, this Paul and Joanna ask to speak to me."

"So you believe he was the one who sicced the dogs on you?" Ben swivels in his chair.

"It's very possible." Ibrahim nods. "Wally is a postal employee, like myself. He works for the federal government. I know he helps these same agents on a mail fraud case a few years before I got in trouble. I think maybe he called them again when he felt threatened by me."

"We should check that out." Ben glances at Natty. "Can you handle it?"

Natty stares back. Remembering that "Who Let the Dogs Out?" song from a few years back. They listened to it in the Humvee sometimes, when they were looking for high-value targets. Like the one in Sadr City. Which turned out to be the address of a Dr. Muhammad Ramzi. A surgeon at Baghdad Hospital. Husband of Maya. Father of Abeer and Khalil. The former of whom Natty was following on Facebook and was going to Rutgers in New Jersey. The latter of whom was accidentally killed during a raid by army forces following up on a false lead, which was provided under duress by Crazy Eddie, who, it turned out, owed the surgeon the Iraqi equivalent of $500.

"Yeah, all over it." Natty squirms in his chair, trying to turn a page of his notepad.

"Anaa mabatheqsh feh," Hamid mutters under his breath.

"How's that?" Natty squints at him. "You don't trust me?"

"You speak Arabic?" Ibrahim puts an arm in front of his son, as if to keep him from going through a windshield.

"Enough to understand what he just said." Natty edges forward, presenting his uninjured shoulder to show he could handle the other man with one arm. "Are you and me having a problem?"

Hamid glares back, belligerent and owlish. From the get, there's been hostility between them, the kind of instinctive dislike that makes one young man purse his lips as soon as the other starts talking.

"Is it really necessary for him to be here?" Hamid asks Ben.

"I was about to ask the same about you, my brother." Natty raises his sling in a mock salute.

"You are not my brother."

"And you're not a lawyer or a witness or a translator. So I don't know what you think you're contributing here . . ."

"Forgive us." Ibrahim keeps his arm in front of his son. "Hamid is still bitter because of what happened to me, but I have tried to tell him we are in good hands here. Mr. David Dresden was my friend. He worked on this case for years without being paid. If Nathaniel is his son, I trust him as well." He cups a hand and presses it to his heart. "I speak with all sincerity."

"Okay, fellas, let's try and work this out." Ben looks back and forth between Natty and Hamid, like a ref giving rules before a fight. "The clock is running. Even with the court delays, there's a statute of limitations on a Bivens action and we've got a high burden of proof to meet to show the FBI agents *deliberately* violated Ibrahim's rights in their official capacity. We'll need to file Freedom of Information Act requests to see all their personnel records and whether we can establish any relationship between them and this Wally from the post office."

"I think your father already filed some of those requests." Ibrahim nods at the cardboard boxes. "He said the FBI was trying to find excuses to ignore them."

"Shocking, isn't it?" Ben rocks back in his chair. "Look, the fact of the matter is that the government will do anything in its power to make this case go away. We all have to be careful about what we do and say now, and who we say it in front of."

"I agree," Hamid says, still giving Natty his fatwa stare. "That's why I think some people shouldn't be here."

"Hey, I just want to get along with everybody." Natty smiles back at him.

"Really?" Hamid strokes his half-beard, still scowling. "Then why is your arm in a sling, my brother?"

15

As Sullivan pulls up at the traffic cone and Lourdes jumps out on the passenger side, she sees the Benz dangling from a tow truck hook outside the salvage yard, a half dozen crime scene techs arguing with a half dozen white guys in FBI windbreakers, and a red-and-brown rooster doing a funky head-bobbing strut past the scene on Linden Boulevard, ignoring the human squabble and the screaming of jets trailing in and out of Kennedy Airport a few miles away.

A sergeant from the NYPD Queens auto theft squad is standing in the middle of the blocked-off two-way street, facing a live poultry shop across from the junkyard while yelling into his cell phone.

"I told him, *'I do not give a fuck.'* I do not. I said, 'I'll call the inspector. I'll call the borough commander. I'll call the fucking PC's office and ask the commissioner to call the White House if he has to. This shit is not proper chain of command.' I'm getting gelded in my own stable. And no, don't tell me to calm down. I am totally calm."

He holds up a finger and gives Sully and Lourdes a quick embarrassed smile before the fever of outrage seizes him again. "Five minutes later, I get a call from the special agent in charge of the New York office for the FBI. He says, 'Stand down, Sergeant Negroni. Our investigation supersedes yours.' Like, go play in traffic. You believe this shit?"

A hunched, aggrieved man with a tuft of hair sticking up in the middle of his scalp like a samurai's topknot, he lets out a deep breath. "Anyway, I better stop or they'll put me in the loony bin. Love you, ma. Talk to you later."

"Sergeant, what's up?" Lourdes waits for him to pocket the cell. "We just got a call that your guys found the Dresden car."

"We did." Negroni grimaces as he bends back in a working man's version of a yoga stretch, hand to the small of his arched back with knees slightly bent. "One of our snitches, works at this yard, called it in. Said some skell he knows drove it in with different plates and phony documents, looking to make a quick sale. We ran right over, called you guys on the way. A half hour later—boom—here comes the FBI. They say it's part of a case they were already working on."

Sullivan sniffs and walks stiff-legged over to the tow truck fifteen yards away. The Mercedes hooked up to the back not only looks old enough to be the missing vehicle, it has what appears to be a bullet dent in the driver's side door. Immediately, one of the FBI agents they saw outside Paul Kirkpatrick's office—the aging lifeguard with the thinning hair and the sunburned nose—blocks Sullivan and puts his hands up.

"A case they were already working on?" Lourdes glances back at Sergeant Negroni. "Que pasa? This is *our* victim's car."

"You're preaching to the Pope." The sergeant shrugs. "Nobody's telling me anything. Personally, I'd like to drive the thing back to our garage and leave these fucks in the dust. We already got the Benz hooked to an NYPD tow truck. But there's a lot of palace intrigue going on."

"Yeah?"

"Yeah, pardon my political incorrectness, miss, but it's the Big Balls Fiesta. We won't give up the car, so they're arresting my man Thor over there, who's a material witness."

Lourdes looks over and sees two FBI agents coming out of the salvage yard with a worker between them, rear-cuffed and grease-smudged. A stout middle-aged man in a black knit cap with tiny black eyes, a face the color of an ill-used Pink Pearl eraser, and a Viking's long gray beard.

"That's your CI who called this in?" Lourdes asks.

"Thor, the King of Catalytic Converters. We caught him with six stolen ones last fall and he's been asking for a little rhythm ever since. He's looking at seven years so we registered him as an informant. This other idiot drives in with the Benz, Thor drops a dime to us. Then all of a sudden the FBI shows up and arrests him for lying to an agent and receiving stolen property."

"Wait, what?" Lourdes wipes the air. "How did the feds even hear about this so quickly?"

"Beats me. Thor's our snitch, not theirs. We put the car's info into the federal and state systems when it was reported missing. But we didn't alert the FBI we were doing a raid. Best I can figure, either it was off the scanner or they have their own informant who works in the yard and he called his handler at the same time Thor was calling us. No honor among thieves, right?"

Lourdes surveys the terrain. There are police vans and patrol cars cordoning off all the side streets. A helicopter has started to circle in the sooty sky. A bunch of unmarked Escalades with tinted windows are double-parked in front of the tow truck. Only a matter of time until the media shows up. The FBI agents put Thor in the back of the first one as Sullivan stands in front of the vehicle, going chest to chest with the supervisor, the shriek of a rising jet drowning out their voices until Lourdes, hustling over, is just a couple of feet away.

"I don't know you," Sullivan is saying in an implacable voice, even as his face and shirt start to rumple. "And I don't know anything about this alleged federal investigation."

"Agent Douglas Bryce." The aging lifeguard grins at Lourdes. "I'm trying to explain to your partner here that we want to cooperate with the police, but this is our case and I am directing you to release this vehicle to the FBI."

"I see." Lourdes tries a girlish smile. "Maybe I'm being naive because I'm not so experienced, but how does a Brooklyn homicide get to be an FBI case?"

"Right now, I can't speak to that." Bryce looks down his peeling nose at her, the Prince of the Surf ready to blow the whistle and call in the swimmers. "We have to limit the circle."

At close range, Lourdes can see the driver's side window of the Mercedes is gone and bits of broken glass are gummed in a smear of blood on the passenger seat. An NYPD crime scene tech comes over to take a picture and an FBI agent puts out his arm to try to obstruct him.

"But isn't this a little silly?" Lourdes asks, the lilt of sweetness fading from her voice. "I thought we were all Team America these days."

Bryce nods. "I have great relationships with many of your colleagues. But this happens to be a very sensitive investigation that could be hurt by local cops leaking details."

"Total nonsense," Sullivan says like a schoolmaster about to discipline an unruly student. "As far as I'm concerned, this is still our case and still our crime scene. And no one higher up on the food chain has told me otherwise."

"I have a call in to the U.S. attorney's office." Bryce hitches up his pants. "They're going to speak to someone at One Police Plaza and we'll get this straightened out. Trust me, folks. You don't want to die on this hill."

"Oh no, he di-idn't." Lourdes shakes her head.

"Pardon me." Sullivan walks off to have a word with the tow truck driver.

The engine starts and the truck pulls away, dragging the Mercedes and leaving the uniformed cops nearby creasing themselves laughing and high-fiving while the FBI agents look on, helpless and aghast.

"You have just made another serious mistake, my friend." Bryce looks like he's about to keel over from sunstroke as Sullivan returns.

"I'm sorry." Sullivan sticks a finger in his own ear. "You say something I needed to hear?"

Up until this second, Lourdes hasn't been quite sure what to make of the old man. Despite her captain's warning, she's still half-figured Sullivan as a dinosaur, a once-fearsome presence about to take his place on the fossil pile. But now he's snapping and snarling like a pitbull at the junkyard gate, off the leash and ready to tear ass.

"You have a witness we want." Sullivan points at the SUV, where Thor sits handcuffed. "And now we have a car you want. So the only question is: can this relationship be saved?"

Fifteen minutes later, the Impala is bombing past the tree-shaded malls of Eastern Parkway, heading back to the Seventy-Eighth Precinct.

"That was dope," Lourdes says.

Sullivan taps two fingers on the wheel, humming along with that "they're not gonna catch the midnight rider" song that all the old white cops love on the radio. The sun pokes between branches and a pudgy kid in a skullcap and side curls keeps pace with them on a longhorn BMX bike, fringes of his prayer shawl flying straight behind him. Satellite dishes sprout on either side of the boulevard, upturned ears straining to receive messages about the Moshiach from the rooftops and terraces of steel-and-glass Chabad schools and brick homes getting renovated by Southeast Asian workmen.

"Think there's gonna be fallout?" she asks.

"I only have a few months left until mandatory retirement. What are they going to do? Put *me* in a VIPER room?"

Her heart does a little triple-time pump at the thought of going back to that cinder-block room with stacks of little blurry monitors. The Place Where the Broken Toys Go. In the basements of projects even skeevier than the ones she grew up in. Word was, there was a camera watching her in the room the whole eight-hour tour, so the bosses would know if she was sleeping on duty. All because she kept her mouth shut when she should have spoken up.

Sullivan floors the pedal and spins the wheel, going all *French Connection* around the Jews, switching lanes suddenly and threading his way between an Acura and an Infiniti, as the neighborhood starts to get a little more Caribbean—jerk chicken shacks and storefront Pentecostal churches salting in among the yeshivas.

"Whoa, daddy, slow down." Lourdes is getting thrown around in the passenger seat, as the red needle on the dashboard flicks toward sixty mph and Hasids, hipsters, and Rastamen crossing Utica Avenue scatter to avoid getting mowed down.

"You want me to let you out?" he asks.

"No," she says. "If I'm in, I'm in. I'd just like to know whazz up."

"Whazz up is we got a prominent defense lawyer murdered while he was suing the federal government." Sullivan checks his rearview. "Then we got phone records indicating multiple calls to the FBI's New York office right before he died. Then we've got a supervisor refusing to answer questions and complaining to our job about us. And now we've got the feds swooping in where they've got no clear jurisdiction. If you don't think that's mad grimy, you should give back that little shield."

"'*Mad grimy*'?" She throws back her head and laughs. "Where you learn to talk like that? That's some old school street knowledge you're dropping."

"What can I tell you, *chica*? I've been at this a while."

She checks her makeup in the side-view mirror, knowing it should bother her when he calls her "chica." Belittling 1970s sexist jive. But somehow she likes it. He's starting to loosen up around her, letting her into his bizarre little Irish-Apache tribe.

"So what do you think they're up to?" she asks. "You still think that was them in the cable truck on President Street last night?"

"All I'm sure about is they're scared of losing control of this. It could be that they really were running their own investigation into Dresden when he got killed. But that raises the question of why the FBI would be checking up on him when he just happens to be suing them at the same time."

"Uh-oh. That ain't kosher."

"Even worse if it turns out that he was murdered when they supposedly had him under surveillance."

"And how does the son being so squirrelly with us figure into it?"

"It may not. Maybe there's an innocent explanation for him not wanting to tell us why he was here before his dad was killed."

"I'm not getting 'innocent' off him," she says.

"We don't know what we don't know. He looked like he'd been through something even before the old man was killed."

Afternoon sun strobes wildly through the dogwoods and cherry blossoms, leaving bursts and stripes on the back of her eyelids when she blinks.

"The game's getting deep," she says.

"Still not too late to ask off. I know you're trying to get back to where you were. And you don't need another partner blowing up on you."

"I'm not going anywhere." She stares at the pockmarked side of his face, thinking he must have gone a lot of years without love looking like that. "But let me ask you something. Why did you stick your neck out so far just now?"

"To get at Thor? He knows who brought the victim's car in. That makes him an essential witness for us."

"Yeah, I know that. I'm a girl but I'm not that stupid, Sullivan."

She side-glances him, making sure he can handle the give-and-take. But he's impassive at the wheel as they go by the spaceship entrance and the dancing fountains of the Brooklyn Museum.

"What I'm saying is, you put a lot of weight on the scale to try and leverage that," she presses on. "A lot of guys your age wouldn't care enough to put up with the grief we're gonna get from the feds."

"Just being a stubborn old mule." He starts punching different stations into the radio tuner.

"You said you knew him." She shifts around to face him as they go into the curve near the Botanic Garden.

"Who?"

"Dresden. The vic. When we were at the widow's house, you said you knew him."

The light turns red and stops them at the Plaza Street intersection, where the symphonics of the borough start to merge. Crown Heights, Prospect Heights, and Park Slope coming together at the terminus. The archway of Grand Army Plaza looms ahead, banged-up livery cabs and U-Hauls swinging around, with traffic feeding in from Vanderbilt and Flatbush Avenue. West Indian nannies push wailing white babies in full-on stroller rebellion toward the library main branch with its Pharaonic façade and the victory columns at the Prospect Park green market entrance on the left. Union Temple looking a little stooped and sooty on the right next to the glassy postmodern ice cube of $2 million condos on the corner.

"Everyone knew him," Sullivan says. "He was a defense lawyer for as long as I've been a cop. If there was ever a bigger pain in the ass, I don't know who it was."

"So he had you up on the stand, for cross-examination?"

"Yeah, a few times." Sullivan scratches the back of his ear, as if he's more interested in the weather report. "What's the difference?"

"You said you knew him. Like personally."

"Where are you going with this, Robles?"

"I'm thinking there's something you haven't told me yet."

"Like what? I was the one who popped him?"

She crosses her arms and leans back against the door. "I don't know. But like you said, I got in trouble because of a partner before, so now I'm nervous. And you're holding out on me. I was watching you when the widow went on about how a cop could've done this. You looked serious, hombre."

His foot pumps up and down on the brake, the only part of him that's moving as he waits for the endless red light to change.

"All right," he says finally. "Let's not make a soap opera out of it. About twelve years ago, I was testifying against one of Dresden's clients in an Asian gang murder case. Scumbags killed a cooperator and his girl-friend down by Bush Terminal. Shot them both and then the leader says—and you'll have to excuse my language—'You know what? We really should've fucked her first. She was a nice-looking girl.'"

"Aii . . ."

"Yeah, that was something." His hands turn white on the wheel, a physical reaction to cursing. "Anyway, I'm burying his guy on the stand, and something came up where I had to be excused early. Dresden helped me out with it."

"You've come this far, chief. Might as well tell me the rest."

Sullivan puts back his shoulders and takes two deep breaths like he's about to go off a diving board. "I had a sick kid who had to go to the hospital in a rush."

"Yours?"

"Dresden found out about it and called ahead for a specialist he knew, so we could get in to see him right away." He pauses, sucks in one side of his mouth. "He said, 'Work is work, but babies is babies.' I never forgot that. But don't think I went easy on him after that. I was back up on the stand the next day. And his client got twenty-five-to-life."

"And what happened to your kid?"

"Christ, Robles, what're you trying to do, write my life story?"

"I just wanted to know how it all worked out in the end."

The light changes and Sullivan tears into the traffic crescent, slam-ming Lourdes against her seat with maximum g-force.

"Let's just put this one down," he says. "I always pay my bills."

"I'm still with you, daddy. Just give me a little more of a heads-up next time. Chica gets kinda nervous when she don't know where we're going."

16

Natty stares at the little boy holding a stack of menus by the cash register. Stay in the moment, bro. You are at the Cadman Plaza diner on Court Street. Six thousand miles from Sadr City. That Arabic-sounding music you hear is Britney Spears's "Toxic" on the radio. That smell is burning bacon on the kitchen grill, not human flesh in a blown-up car. And those are court officers, not Iraqi police, sitting at the counter, droopy mushroom-cap asses on stools, guns hanging off their belts.

Smoke wafts from the kitchen. A couple of young kids share a black-and-white cookie. An old manager with tufts of gray hair coming out of his ears and a big Greek Orthodox cross around his neck spikes checks on a crooked rusting nail. But Natty finds himself starting to breathe hard, palms getting sweaty, unable to break off from looking at this small boy with black hair and brown eyes.

The kid glances at the manager and then at Natty, getting creeped out by how this dude in shades, with his arm in a sling, is staring at him, respiration coming in increasingly intense heaves through his nose. Other people are starting to notice as well. An NYPD sergeant is watching from the end of the counter. The manager pauses from spiking the checks.

"Can I help you?" the boy says.

Natty licks his lips, eyes the "Please Wait To Be Seated" sign, and then forces himself to look at the child's feet. Converse high-tops, with the laces tied. Here, not there. It's all good. For now.

"Yeah, I'd like a table for two. Near the back, please."

He follows the boy, forcing himself to take slow, evenly spaced breaths as he removes his Ray-Bans and looks around. Naproxen is helping the bruised arm, but now a vein in his neck is throbbing. The text message he got an hour ago suggested meeting here at two o'clock, but again he's arrived early, to get himself situated and calmed down.

Not that this is unfamiliar terrain; he must have eaten here a half dozen times back when he came to watch Dad in action at the courthouses across the plaza. But now everything must be examined and assessed as a potential threat. A Britney Spears song. A snatch of a muezzin's call from a passing cab on Atlantic Avenue. A white garbage bag lying unattended in the middle of the street. A woman wearing a full black burka. Exhaust fumes from an idling diesel truck.

The boy puts him at a two-top table in the back, near a booth of Court Street lawyers, prunish faces and lumpish bodies in Men's Wearhouse suits, haggling over a bill. He takes the seat facing the door, so he can see the whole restaurant, and angles his chair away from the windows as if a few inches are going to protect him from flying glass shards if the Krasdale tractor trailer parked outside happens to go off.

Good thing the lunch rush is over, so he doesn't have to freak out about being in a crowd either. The malls in Florida were the worst, but subways in the city are a challenge as well. He wonders how long he can really stay in New York. Sometimes a drink helps. It's a risk, since he's near Veterans Court, where he agreed to go on the wagon, but no way he can get through this without some liquid assistance. He flags down one of the dissolutely thick-browed waiters, who dress like second-rate knife jugglers in black vests and white shirts, and orders himself a scotch and soda, thinking he has just enough time to belt it down and even himself out before his appointment arrives. A half-hearted tribute to Dad, who probably sat here belting down a couple himself with the sunset slicing through the strings of the Brooklyn Bridge after a long day trying to salvage a bit of freedom for his miscreants.

"Nathaniel?"

He wrenches his arm, trying to pull it out of the sling and reach for his gun. The M4, which he hasn't carried since 2008.

The woman standing over him matches the general description she gave in her text message: Not young, not old. Not thin, not fat. Just sort of regular. If she was inclined to be more descriptive, she could have said something about an oval face with a pixieish haircut, close-set eyes, a smoker's cheeks, and rosebud lips that combine to make her look like a cross between a parochial school administrator and a thoroughly disenchanted Tinkerbell.

"Marygrace Kelly." She sets down a bulky attaché case and sticks out a weathered hand with short nails and clear polish. "Your father liked to call me 'MG.'"

"He did?" Natty shuts one eye, trying to imagine his father being on nickname terms with a dour woman in a buffalo-brown pants suit.

"I recognized you as soon as I walked in." She settles into a seat across the table, straightening her lapels with a forceful tug. "We met a few times when you were little."

"Really? What were the occasions?"

"I used to be very friendly with David." She looks down at the leather-bound medieval-looking menu that seems a compendium of every meal in history. "But I'm not surprised you don't remember. Anyway, lots to talk about. Do you want to order first?"

"I'm not hungry."

"I'm famished, but I'm on a diet." She contrives a twinkle-eyed smile for the waiter. "I'll just have half a cantaloupe and a cup of Lipton tea with lemon and honey on the side."

Natty watches the twin glimmers die down to fine hard points of attention as the waiter leaves.

"If you were such a good friend of his, how come I don't remember you from the funeral?" He tries to get his elbow up on the table, still having trouble getting used to the sling.

"I had to be in court that day. I've been feeling guilty about not sending a card ever since . . ."

"'In court'?" He turns sidesaddle to get his balance. "What do you do?"

"I'm with the U.S. attorney for the Eastern District."

Someone lowers a window shade and in the altering of light everything in Natty's field of vision seems to become slightly more three-dimensional and angular.

"You're a federal prosecutor?"

"Civil division," she says quickly. "I never tried cases against your father."

"Though your office is part of the Justice Department, as is the FBI." Natty slides his elbow forward. "And my father had just filed a lawsuit against the Bureau."

"I wasn't involved in that." Her mouth closes, tight as the clasp on a velvet purse. "Mostly I do white-collar cases. Securities fraud."

The waiter comes over with a tray and a saturnine look. He carefully sets down her cup and saucer with a dried-up wedge of lemon on the side, and then slams the scotch-and-soda down in front of Natty.

"Don't mind me." MG brightens. "I'd join you if I didn't have to go back to the office."

Natty moves the glass off to the side like a rook on a chessboard. "So I'm a little confused about what's going on here. We had our text exchange last night because your number was one of the ones listed on Dad's phone bill. I saw that he'd phoned you half a dozen times in the week before he died."

"Yes. David and I went through periods when we didn't talk for months at a time. And then other times we'd be on the phone practically every day. It's like that with old friends. It never mattered that he was a defense lawyer and I was a prosecutor."

"But I saw that the number he was calling you on was a no-name cell."

"Yes, it's my private number." She tears open a Lipton packet. "Given the kind of work I do at the office, I like to keep things separate."

"So you texted me back on one number last night and then texted me to set up this appointment on a different number today. You said it wasn't safe otherwise. What did you mean by that?"

"Probably just an excess of caution." She dips the bag into the cup. "Most of the work I do involves prosecuting financial firms for security violations. A lot of money is at stake. I wouldn't be surprised if some of these companies hired private investigators to spy on me."

"You sound almost as paranoid as Dad."

"He wasn't always wrong." She drops the tab on the string and lets the tea steep. "But now *I'm* curious: the police gave you access to David's phone records?"

"I looked them up myself. I'm not entirely happy with how they're handling the investigation."

"I see. Your father mentioned that you'd been a prosecutor yourself. I thought that was very telling."

He watches steam rise from the surface of her cup as she raises the bag and squeezes it out, surprised she doesn't burn her fingers.

"Perhaps you've forgotten my original question about why you were calling Dad so much right before he died."

"David and I were trying to make plans for a lunch date. But things kept coming up, so we had to keep rescheduling."

"Six calls. Each at least five minutes long. That's a lot for just rescheduling."

"My, aren't you the persistent one?" She sets the teabag aside.

"Was it about the mailman case?" He starts to reach for his drink and then stops himself.

"I believe I already told you that I wasn't involved, didn't I?"

The eyes keep feigning the stardust smile as she blows into her cup.

"And even if this was about an ongoing investigation, you know it's not something I could talk about."

"I said 'an ongoing case,' you said 'an ongoing investigation.' We both know there's a difference."

She doesn't look up as the waiter returns with her melon, instead maintaining a serene implacable gaze that now makes him think less of Tinkerbell and more of Margaret Thatcher ordering tanks into Kuwait.

"Your father was right." She uses a spoon to scoop a few stray seeds from the cantaloupe. "You did learn the art of interrogation in the army."

"He told you about that?"

She stoops her shoulders, in lieu of answering. Who is this woman anyway? He can't quite figure the basis of the relationship. But then again his father's dirty secret was that he couldn't help liking most people he worked with, even the ones on the "Dark Side." Even when Mom would rag on him mercilessly for having a sandwich with a prosecutor or a drink with a detective, like collegiality was a form of selling out, he'd shrug haplessly and say, "What're you going to do, hate everybody all the time?" Sometimes fiery political rhetoric was just professional wrestling to him: a lot of posturing and bellowing, but not all the blood on the canvas was real. But did that mean everyone he was friendly with was a friend?

The little boy in the tied sneakers comes over, bringing a plastic bear full of honey.

"What else did you talk about, if it wasn't that case?" Natty finds he can't meet the boy's eye as he nods thanks.

"We talked about lots of things." MG digs into her melon's crater. "I knew your father more than thirty-five years."

"Did you? How did you meet?"

"Law school. He was my first study partner."

"Then why all this sudden urgency?"

"It wasn't so sudden." She carves conscientiously at the side of her fruit. "David and I used to talk all the time. Especially before he met your mother."

Natty watches her raise the spoon to her mouth, trying to picture his father's existence before he was born. Before he had a wife. Before he had press conferences on courthouses steps and raw-throated screaming matches with right-wing lunatics on TV talk shows. Before he had a reputation for getting scumbags out of trouble. Before he had enough of a public profile to make people who didn't know him send him business envelopes with pieces of excrement and misspelled death threats inside. Before he had an identity as anything other than David Dresden, a skinny kid from Midwood High School with a big nose, oversized glasses, and a motormouth.

Then Natty reverse-ages this Marygrace thirty-five years and ten thousand cigarettes younger, the pixie cut bloomed into Farrah Fawcett feathers, her fair complexion not yet hardened and covered with heavy makeup, the flesh underneath still supple and pink. And all at once, he knows at some gut level, this was his father's girlfriend. A whole alternative history sits on her side of the table. One in which Dad married a prosecutor instead of the daughter of social justice warriors. A purebred white girl. Who wouldn't have given him a mixed-up mutt of a son, who in turn would rebel against his father's rebellion by joining the army.

"We were talking about a lot of things." She makes a face. "People we've known. Ideas we used to have. When we started out, I was at the Brooklyn DA's office and he was with the public defender. But somehow it felt like there was some common cause. You know, I'm not sure if this melon is ripe enough."

Sappy horseshit, Natty thinks, readjusting the sling, restless with his own regrets. She didn't just agree to meet with him for the sake of old times. You could always tell when someone was lying in normal interrogation when they got all misty-eyed and nostalgic. One thing you could say about waterboarding: no one sounded wistful when they thought they were about to drown.

"You started out at the Brooklyn DA's office?" he says, circling back to pin her down.

"Yes, I went from local to federal. I never went into law to get rich." She looks under the table with a practiced grin. "And I've got the shoes to prove it."

"So if you began at the same time as Dad, then you must know Ben Grimaldi as well."

"Yes, I do know Ben," she says, no longer smiling. "We started in the same year. I sat behind him for almost every lecture the first six months."

"So you were friends with him too?"

She surrounds the teacup with both hands. "Ben is a big personality," she says. "When he jumps in the pool, he tends to displace a lot of water."

"I'm gonna take that as a no."

She pours milk into her tea and swirls it around, frowning at the diluted result. "One thing I always found intriguing about Ben. He always liked to brag that he never lost a case."

"Why is that 'intriguing'?" Natty asks with a twinge of annoyance.

"Everybody loses sometimes. Evidence gets mishandled. Witnesses go missing. Juries ignore the judge's instructions. Tell me something: does Ben still say that now that he's a defense lawyer?"

"I haven't heard it." Natty starts to reach for his drink. "Why?"

"I just don't see how it's possible for an honest lawyer to win every single case." MG blinks twice with the mocking innocence of a third-grade teacher asking her class who shot a spitball when her back was turned. "Do you?"

"What are you implying?"

"Just making an observation."

He stops with the glass halfway to his mouth, suddenly self-conscious about drinking. If someone from Veterans Court happens to be here, he'll be screwed for violating the terms of his agreement. But fuck it, this is how he's *choosing* to deal. The only people watching are MG and the boy with the menus.

"You do know Ben Grimaldi is taking over the mailman case from my father." He takes a defiant gulp. "Don't you?"

"No, I *didn't* know that." She takes a Kleenex out of her bag to blow her nose, even though there's a perfectly fine paper napkin on the table. "I'm not sure why it's relevant."

"Even though you're a prosecutor with the office that's trying to get the case dismissed?"

"It's an enormous office. I'm not even on the same floor as the people involved."

"I find the timing of all this very suspicious." The scotch is burning in the pit of his stomach and sending fumes up to his head.

"Why? What do you think is happening here, Nathaniel?"

"You keep saying things are 'telling' and 'intriguing.'" He crooks his fingers in contempt. "What I think is *telling* is that thirty-five years after law school, you turn up in my father's life when he's suing people you work with. Then he ends up getting killed."

"What are you suggesting?" All the sparkle is gone from her eyes.

"It seems awfully convenient the way you pop up right before Dad's murder and start talking smack about Ben now that he's taken over the case."

"You're forgetting one very salient detail." She squirts honey into her tea. "You tracked *me* down, not the other way around. You asked for this meeting."

He bangs his elbow against the side of the table. "That could just be part of the setup."

"*Setup?*"

"You left a trail of crumbs for Dad, and I picked up on them."

"For God's sake, what do I look like, Mata Hari?" She picks up the plastic bear she just used and shakes it at him. "This bear is more of a honeypot than I am."

He realizes that the drink has hit harder than expected on an empty stomach, leaving him slightly disoriented by his own logic.

"Let me ask you something." She puts the bear aside. "Am I the only one your father was calling repeatedly right before he was killed?"

"Who else are you thinking of?"

She lowers her voice. "He was also calling the FBI, wasn't he?"

"And how do you happen to know that?" He leans halfway across the table to hear her, almost knocking over a water glass with his sling.

"Because I was the one who told him to." She looks away, her voice as smooth and quiet as the hum of a new dryer.

"Why?"

"Because he was scared," she says.

"Of what?"

The boy in the sneakers is staring at him once more. He realizes he's been talking too loud. Fortunately, the diner has mostly emptied out, leaving only the abandoned fruit cups and crumpled napkins to witness his outburst.

Her eyes go back and forth. "Nathaniel, I don't think you're ready to hear the rest of this."

"The rest of what?"

"Your father used to say, 'You can never tell people the truth until they're ready to hear it.' And you don't seem there yet."

"So that's it?" He nudges the rest of his drink away, his mood starting to darken again. "You're just going to lead me on and let it drop? What are you, a tease?"

She hoists her bag up onto her lap with a heavy sigh.

"I think I made a mistake in agreeing to come meet with you. It's too soon."

"Too soon for what?"

She gives him one of those pitying looks that drove him out of counseling. The kind that suggested someone who sat in an office all day knew more about the basic facts of life than a vet who'd seen a good friend's viscera dangling from the bottom of his torso.

"You must think I'm a moron," he says.

"Not at all."

"Then why are you trying to play me?"

"I'm not." She starts to reach for his good arm. "Look, Nathaniel, you've been through a lot already and it's not about to get any easier—"

"Yes, thank you for your service." He draws back with a fuck-off grin. "What's the joke?"

"It's what people say when they want to shine you on."

"I don't think I can eat any more of this. It's too hard." She sticks her spoon in the melon and leaves it there like a shovel. "I know you may not believe it, but I cared about your father, deeply. What happened to him was wrong. I'd like to help you."

"You know what I think?" Natty says. "I think this is just a pack of lies you're trying to sell me. The government wants this mailman case to go away. And now that my father's gone and Ben's picked up his sword, you're trying to run him down as well. So forgive me if I don't jump up and throw my arms around you in gratitude for being a loyal friend."

She stands up, opens up her bag, and takes out a twenty. "We should meet again when you're in a better frame of mind," she says, sliding the bill under the metal napkin dispenser. "There's someone you need to speak to."

"You're leaving me too much." He looks down.

"It's fine," she says, turning to go. "You'll get me next time."

She walks out, leaving the boy with the menus staring at Natty again.

17

Thor Nystrom is sitting in the interrogation room with his lawyer as Lourdes walks in carrying a cockroach-brown accordion file and singing, "You have fucked up," to the tune of "Ride of the Valkyries." She slaps the file down and starts pulling out pictures of David Dresden at the crime scene, throwing a lusty Brünhilde trill for emphasis every few lines. Thor stares at the photos, his attorney Leslie Benjamin whispering in his ear, as he starts yanking more furiously on his long beard, hand over hand, like it's a rope he's using to try to pull himself out of a sandpit.

"So you're the King of Catalytic Converters, huh?" Lourdes takes a seat across the table with an impressed huff.

Sullivan comes trudging in, with his elephant tread and bloodhound orbs, and makes his own kind of thunder with the door slam. Four hours of arguing with the FBI to get an interview with a witness who should have been theirs to begin with. But misdirection and trickiness are the orders of the day. After the raid at the auto graveyard, the FBI took Thor to their offices and the NYPD kept Dresden's Benz in their garage while the U.S. attorney called the Brooklyn DA, who in turned called the PC, who then called back the director in Washington, and then they all jerked each others' chains until an arrangement could be reached to give the FBI the Mercedes in exchange for ferrying Thor and his lawyer over to the Seventy-Eighth Precinct.

"I just want to stress that my client has been cooperative at every phase of this investigation," says Leslie Benjamin, all hyperthyroid eyes on a stalk-like neck and fluttering sparrow hands. "He made full statements to the FBI agents he spoke to this morning, so anything he would tell you is already in their 302s . . ."

"Yes, thanks for that." Lourdes glances over at the one-way glass. "But we prefer to do our own interviews."

Douglas Bryce and other FBI agents are right outside, watching and taking notes. And offering no clue about what their interest is in what is technically still a local homicide investigation.

"So who brought this car into your yard?" Lourdes asks.

"Like I told the agents," Thor says in a pinched nasal voice at odds with his troll-on-steroids physique. "I never seen this dude before but when I seen the bullet mark in the door I called it in. But what do I get for being a good citizen? I get fucked. Totally. *Again*. Every day is No Justice for Thor Day."

"Okay, Mr. Nystrom." Sullivan opens the file he's brought in. "Here's where it all goes pear-shaped. You wouldn't have taken this Mercedes onto your lot and risked your scrap processors' license unless you knew who was bringing it to you. Am I right?"

Leslie Benjamin holds up a tortured-looking digit. "As soon as the car was brought in, Thor recognized it was going to be an issue and he called it in to his friend Sergeant Negroni at auto theft . . ."

"The problem is that another employee at the yard was calling his case agent at the FBI at the same time." Sullivan takes Thor's rap sheet out of the folder and puts it on top of the photos of Dresden's corpse. "So here we are."

"Fucking Mohammad," Thor mumbles. "I didn't even know he'd gotten arrested."

It turned out that Mohammad McIntyre, a Bangladeshi-Irishman who ran the compressor at the yard, had gotten locked up for trying to sell a military tank with a mounted 50-cal. machine gun on the Internet last year. What were the odds that there would be two different people facing state and federal charges working at the same salvage yard? Not bad, it turned out. Though without a doubt, most salvage yard workers were upstanding citizens with proper paid-up permits, there were also a fair number of parolees, many of whom had been forced out of the once-lucrative chop shop business by technological advances that put computers in even the cruddiest domestic models and rendered the dark arts of hot-wiring and repurposing stolen parts nearly obsolete.

"You had the Mercedes on your lot two hours before you called it in." Sullivan taps a picture of the Benz at the yard. "*Por que*, bro?"

Thor makes two fists and stretches, showing a vast tundra of white belly as his sweatshirt rises. "The dude who brought it in had all the paperwork together, including title and registration for the vehicle. He even had an insurance card with a fake name."

Lourdes and Sullivan exchange a look. A fake title for a car that's more than ten years old?

"I'm still thinking this was someone you must have known who brought the car in." Sullivan rubs his finger in the groove between his nose and his mouth. "Otherwise, why take a chance when you're already working off charges for selling all those catalytic converters?"

Thor and his lawyer start whispering behind their hands.

"Okay." Leslie Benjamin sits back, a little out of breath, as if she'd just been manhandled. "I'm starting to get a sense that this is part of an even more major case to both you and the FBI than we were led to believe. Whoever stole this vehicle went to serious lengths to disguise its origins: switching out the license plates, obtaining a fake title, trying to alter the VIN. My client's cooperation obviously has value to you. Can we get him a Queen for a Day?"

"A few kind words on his behalf to the DA?" Sullivan studies the back of his own hand. "What's he got to offer?"

"What if, just hypothetically, this individual who brought in the Mercedes turned out to be someone my client did business with in the past?"

"So this dude's—what?—a guy you used to steal cars with?" Sullivan asks.

"I used to shoot smack with him." Thor drops his beard toward his chest, the fur matting out on his chest. "Back behind the leaf."

"'Behind the leaf'?"

Lourdes eyes Sullivan, wondering if this is old school slang for places junkies stick themselves. The one thing she's always been squeamish about, because of Georgie.

"He's talking about The Leif," Sullivan says. "It's a bar in Bay Ridge. Named after Leif Erikson, the Viking. Nice place, now that they reopened.

The old Norwegian seamen used to hang out there before the neighborhood went Arab."

This city, Lourdes thinks. *This borough.* You could live here all your life, drive around every block five times, and not have a clue about what went on inside the houses.

"You got a name for my man from The Leif?" Sullivan asks.

"I never knew his real name." Thor shrugs. "Everybody called him 'Science.' Though he wasn't much of a scholar, if you know how I'm saying."

"Describe him," Sullivan says.

"Big fella." Thor, at least an extra-large himself, holds his arms out to indicate someone even more spherical. "Black—but not like engine-filter black. More of rusted brown undercarriage tone . . ."

Lourdes glances at Sullivan again; okay, everybody's got their own way of describing things.

"A black guy hung out at a Norwegian seamen's bar?" she says.

"He sold drugs outside." Thor pets his beard with a faraway look. "But yeah, I think he liked hanging out and talking about fish. He always said his main thing was he wanted to be a marine biologist. Kind of sad. Kid from the PJs who'd never been out on the water . . ."

Lourdes hears a thump against the glass. Probably Captain McKenna smacking it in frustration, knowing he could have finally put one of his bottled ships to good use in the interrogation room. Or maybe it was just a mad scramble of FBI agents and detectives pushing each other out of the way to get to the computers and start searching the databases for anyone with a nickname like Science.

"Why didn't you dime him out as soon as he drove the Benz onto your lot?" she asks.

"Tell you the truth, I didn't notice the bullet mark right away. See, what happened . . . I dropped a sledge hammer on my foot last winter, and broke one of my metatarsals," Thor looks down at his boot diffidently.

"The Thunder God dropped his hammer?" Lourdes tries to look sympathetic.

"I'm named after the explorer." Thor turns to Sullivan. "Thor Heyerdahl? *Kon-Tiki?* Hello?"

"Anyway," Sullivan says.

"Anyway, that started me in on the painkillers. Then when the Oxy got too expensive, I switched back to the heroin because it was cheaper. Ten dollars for a stamp bag versus thirty dollars a pill—what're you gonna do?"

"So you were into Science for a favor because he was selling to you?" Lourdes asks, eager to get off the needle-talk.

"I think he was chipping again too." Thor slouches. "He brought the Benz in this morning and asked if I could get him fifteen hundred fast, without a lot of questions. He said it was for some special ed school for his daughter, but come on. His pupils were like the size of pinpricks. He was like, 'How much can I get for this shit?' And once I saw the bullet hole, I was like, 'Um, twenty-five years.'"

"But all his paperwork was together?" Sullivan asks.

"Yeah. Totally. Best I've ever seen."

For once, Lourdes knows what Sullivan might be thinking. What they're hearing doesn't add up. Someone reckless enough to shoot a famous defense lawyer and take his car to a scrapyard for $1,500 isn't likely to be sharp enough to come up with fake license plates and phony documents that quickly.

"So we good?" Thor asks.

"We're better than good—we on *fire*," Lourdes says. "Like thunder gods."

18

Things are a little different this time: Stacy Willen, in a jewel-tone blouse and dark slacks, has her hair tied back, presenting her ingenuous farm girl features without mystery or eye shadow. The soldier's helmet has been moved to the side table near Natty's elbow, the fire in the left hemisphere visible when he tries to turn his eyes and avoid Stacy's unnervingly steady gaze. And the flower vase on the sill, which kept turning into the gun in the water pitcher, has been replaced by a ficus plant. Which keeps threatening to morph into a palm tree outside Ramadi, with black smoke wafting through the fronds.

"You want me to repeat what I just said?" she asks.

Natty fidgets on the opposite couch, arm out of the sling because he's sick of the restricted movement, tongue burning from the little bottle of mouthwash he swirled around so she wouldn't know he'd had a drink before the session.

"Yeah." He grins, three Naproxen barely making a dent in the soreness of his arm and the cut still stinging over his eye. "Hit me again, why don't you?"

"I said I was going over your intake form again and noticed you left a blank where it asks if you've been married." She now has a clipboard on her lap, which she keeps double-checking.

"I'm on my own right now."

"Another evasive answer." She mimes making a check mark.

"Okay. Never married."

"You're thirty-three. What about long-term relationships?"

Is there some further provocation in the way she has the ballpoint poised over the clipboard at a forty-five degree angle?

"Got out of one a few months ago," he says.

"The same time as your arrest in Florida?" Her buttery brow curdles. "Coincidence?"

"Pretty much but things were maybe winding down anyway," he says, pretending to be more interested in the "These Colors Don't Run" poster. "You know how it is."

"Not really. How long had the relationship lasted?"

"I want to say—like—a little less than a year and a half?"

"And were there problems before that incident?"

He puts his right hand up to his brow to rub it and shield his face, managing to aggravate the cut over his eye.

"Do we really . . ." He starts to put his elbows on his knees, and then grimaces, having forgotten he's supposed to limit his movement.

He still feels bad about that one. Tanya from the Disney World marketing division and her daughter Ariel, named after the mermaid. He was going to help them escape from the paved-over swamp of their lives. The parasite relatives, the abusive ex-husband, the bug-infested condo that she couldn't afford on an administrative assistant's salary. The decorated veteran with a private school education and a solid job at the prosecutor's office was going to rescue them. Instead he turned out to be just another exploding man.

"Were there domestic dispute calls to the police?" Stacy asks.

"Never." He shakes his head. "I never laid a hand on her or her daughter."

"Then what was the problem?"

"I guess I just didn't trust myself, past a certain point."

The fear that he'd do something terrible never went away, and in fact kept getting worse and worse. At night, he made Tanya sleep upside down next to him, with her feet by his head, because he was afraid he'd wake up choking her, like the SPC 7 who killed his wife back at Fort Drum two months after the deployment ended. When they made love, they either had to do it in total darkness or with him from behind, because he couldn't deal with her looking right at him.

But the worst was how he flinched every time Ariel tried to sit on his lap when he read to her or tried to put an arm around him as they were watching television together. Monsters didn't deserve the warm touch of a child's hand or a woman's loving gaze. They needed to be isolated out in the woods or left on an ice floe, where they could avoid hurting anyone else, while alternately consoling and torturing themselves with the knowledge that they'd once been part of the human race.

"Anyway," he says, "the arrest was because I roughed up a guy who knocked over her daughter in a parking lot, and that's that. Why keep looking back?"

"Because that's probably where the answers are." Stacy puts the clipboard sideways and tucks her pen into the metal clip at the top. "Have you given any more thought into when you might have started having these violent incidents during blackouts?"

"How would I remember if I blacked out?" He tries to enlist her in a laugh.

She remains unsmiling, in the forward position, conspicuously not writing. Good strategy for getting people to talk, he learned from interrogation school. Acting like it's not just about the job.

"Were you injured during the war?" she asks.

"Never severely."

"How many times?"

"Twice." He shrugs, setting off another twinge in his shoulder. "Three times, you want to get technical."

"What happened?" She starts taking notes again.

"First one I don't even count. I got winged during a big firefight near the old cigarette factory in Sadr City. In-and-out wound. Didn't hit anything. I was out of the field hospital in less than a week. Never got evacuated to Ramstein or anything. Just packed me up and turned me loose again."

"Second?"

"I got stabbed just below the body armor when we were in some shitty mudbrick house, looking for a weapons cache in a little village outside Mosul." His hand drops to his navel. "There wasn't supposed to be anybody there. Some asshole insurgent came out from behind a door and stuck a shiv in just beneath the ceramic plate."

"That sounds rather . . . traumatic," she says carefully.

"There was a lot of blood but he missed the major organs by like an eighth of an inch. My guys put about a hundred rounds into him, but I didn't see it because I was passing out from losing blood and air coming in where it's not supposed to."

"Is that when the blackouts started?"

"No. My head was fine. And they did such a good job sewing me up that you can barely see the scar. I got a tat that says 'Infidel' over it. Wanna see?"

He starts to pull out his shirttail, not so much to flirt as to throw her off her game. The gray eyes don't blink for a half minute.

"You didn't get sent home after that?" she asks.

He crunches his brow, chagrined by the memory of deciding not to tell his parents. Half because he didn't want to scare them. Half because he didn't want to hear any version of "I told you so" from his father.

"No, of course not. I wasn't hurt that badly. And I was a second lieutenant. How would it have looked to my guys if I quit then?"

She rests the butt of her pen against her pursed lips. "So interesting the way you call them 'your guys,' " she says.

"Why is that 'interesting'?" he asks, reminded uncomfortably of the way MG riled him earlier.

"You were an intelligence officer. I thought that meant you were supposed to spend a lot of time in front of a computer, analyzing data and writing reports."

"That's not what I signed up for."

"So instead you're out there in the field, acting like an infantry platoon leader?"

"Only because we were looking for HVTs and I had the intel. It wasn't just trying to be a big swinging dick."

"Really? Sounds like you had a lot to prove."

"Oh, Stacy." He gives her another squinty screw-you grin. "It's not all about suffering and trauma. Some of us are over there because we want to be."

"Tell me about that," she says, halfway between a taunt and a serious question.

"I wanted to be in the United States Army." He finds himself flexing like she just asked him to make a muscle for her. "I wanted to carry a gun. I wanted to wear a uniform. I wanted to be part of something bigger than just me. And you know what? Some of it was fucking awesome."

"'Awesome.' Really?"

"Four months into my first tour, we were in a convoy going through some shitty little town near the Sea of Najaf. I see this kid slide a pizza into the road and then nod at this older guy off to the side, holding up a cell phone."

"The detonator?"

"Yeah, right." He nods, a little surprised that she's gotten ahead of him before he remembers she has a brother in the service. "Anyway, I took my carbine and I shot that asshole before the snipers even had a bead on him." He uses his good arm to demonstrate. "You think I felt guilty about that? Fuck no. I felt *epic*. *Hooah*. He wanted to kill us and Natty Dread drilled that sucker right through the gut from twenty-five yards. Didn't kill him, but he'll remember me every time he tries to take a shit. That night, we drank smuggled Chivas in shampoo bottles to celebrate. And laughed our asses off when the other kid showed up, asking for his pizza box back. Best night ever."

He waits for her to look annoyed, or dismissive, or nonplussed. Something. Or maybe just use the excuse of glancing down at her clipboard. But instead she merely holds his gaze, without retreating, curious as an anthropologist spotting an ape in the thicket.

"And these are the same guys you didn't call when you went out drinking on your own after your father died?"

"Jesus Christ, are you ever going to quit with that?"

"You said you were in it for the camaraderie and now you're avoiding them."

"People move on."

"There's a lot we're still not talking about, Nathaniel."

He tries to change his seat position, putting pressure on his bruised arm. "I'm here, aren't I?"

Her eyes finally lower to the clipboard again. "And what about the third injury?"

"Different convoy, different day. We got hit by an IED outside Ramadi."

"You got hit by an improvised explosive device?"

"Yes, ma'am."

"What happened?"

"It blew up under the vehicle and flipped us. We went off the road into a ditch. It was part of an ambush. I hit my head and cracked some ribs. No big deal. Some of the other guys didn't make it. It wasn't a good day."

He finds himself staring at the ficus plant again. Its leaves turn back into a desert palm by the side of the road, its fronds splayed out like hands beseeching the pale sun for mercy as it glares down on the black smoke sacrifice of the overturned Humvee and the scattered body parts.

"Nathaniel?" Stacy's voice tugs him back.

"Yeah, I'm here." He forces a smile. "It's all good."

"You said some of your guys didn't make it?"

"Two of my guys died. And my staff sergeant lost both his legs. Above the knee."

"How high up?"

"Pretty much up to his waist. You want to hear about that too?"

"We're talking about you," she says, a little tongue showing in the corner of her mouth as she writes more industriously.

"Staff Sergeant J. R. Cuddy," he says. "Twenty-one years old. Good old boy from Maryland by way of South Jersey. He got engaged right before he went overseas. His wife and him were going to have a kid soon as he got out. He talked about how great the first night was going to be. Atlantic City, hotel suite, champagne, and baby-making. But then he got blown up. And even though they had a chance to save his spunk at Ramstein, they threw it out—his sperm. All of it. Regulations. Then when he came back, his girl married someone else while he was at Walter Reed. So . . ." He feels a dot of blood forming above his eye as he scowls. "I'd say I'm pretty lucky, by comparison."

"But you have survivor's guilt?"

"Not me. *Siudo.*"

"What does that mean?" She starts to chew the end of her pen, then catches herself.

"Ask your brother."

"I'm asking you."

"Suck it up, drive on. You never heard that?"

"You're bleeding," she says.

He presses his fingers to the cut and grumbles when he sees a couple of red dots. "Must've hit myself with the medicine cabinet door."

"Is that how you hurt your arm as well? Or are we not going to talk about that either?"

"I just aggravated an old injury that I got from riding in a Humvee. But you're aggravating me more."

"You're not drinking or doing drugs?"

"You want to piss test me, give me a goddamn cup." He drops his hand near his fly. "I'm good to go."

She goes back to note-taking, a little more studiously now. "You mentioned you had a head injury from this IED explosion. Did you ever have an MRI?"

"I don't have traumatic brain injury." He focuses on the little fold under her chin, trying to make her self-conscious enough not to probe further. "If that's what you're getting at."

"What makes you so sure?"

"Can't practice law with TBI."

"I see. And how soon after this explosion did you start having blackouts?"

"Actually, I might have had one before," he mutters.

"Before the incident with the IED?"

"Yeah . . ."

"Would you care to elaborate?"

"Nothing to it. I had an argument with one of the fobbits at the PX about policy in regard to interpreters and masks. He said something about dogs. The next thing I knew my staff sergeant was pulling me back, saying, 'Let it go, LT. Let it go. It's not on you.'"

"What was 'not on you'?" She looks up, her hair starting to come loose from its bun.

"Huh?"

"You said your friend referred to something not being 'on you.' Was there an earlier incident that was connected to this issue of interpreters and masks?"

"Don't be stupid . . . ," he starts to say, then puts a hand up. "Sorry. I think I meant the opposite."

"It's all right." She reaches back to fix her hair, presenting her features plainly again. "I can take it."

"That's no excuse. You're just doing your job."

"And maybe getting close to striking a nerve?"

He takes out his cell phone and checks to see if he has messages from the calls and emails he made before leaving the office. It turned out his father had sent five Freedom of Information of Act requests to see the personnel files for Ibrahim's case agents and had been getting excuses for more than a year.

"I just don't see the point," he says. "Whatever happened happened. Until they perfect the time machine, I'm moving forward."

"And walking in here with a cut over your eye and your arm so messed up you can't move it without cringing."

"Who's cringing?"

She turns sideways on the couch and cocks out a hip like she's leaning over a pool table for a trick shot. "Are you familiar with the term 'moral injury,' Nathaniel?"

"What's your point?"

"Something's eating you. And it was there before your father died. And it's not going to get better until you deal with it."

"I gotta go," he says. "This case is a bear."

"Staying busy only helps so much."

"Spoken like someone who bills by the hour."

"Actually I get paid whether you stay or not. There's the door." She points to where the receptionist, a beefy Vietnam-era black dude with a leather vest over his POW t-shirt, is peering in through a tiny window. "You want to abort the treatment plan and take your chances going back to court, that's up to you. But whatever you're avoiding will still be there. And I'm thinking you're going to be safer facing it in here than you will be out on the street. Unless you think getting into brawls with firemen and going to jail is working out for you."

"I ain't afraid of no ghosts," he says, looking at the flaming head again.

"See you Monday morning," she says. "This is progress."

19

"Detective Sullivan, you going around with younger women these days?"

Ben Grimaldi doesn't stand up from behind his desk as Lourdes and Sullivan pause in the doorway, letting a couple of bike messengers, who appear to be packing anacondas in their spandex crotches, sidle out past them.

"You're moving up in the world, counselor." Sullivan's pockmarks deepen as he surveys the office. "I remember when they had you in a room about the size of a phone booth at the DA's."

"You said we needed to have a conversation right away?" Benny G. gives Lourdes the confident smile of a man who can leave a waitress a twenty-dollar tip without acting like he's entitled to squeeze her ass afterward.

"There's been some developments in the case," Sullivan says. "You told the other detectives you wanted to be kept apprised."

Lourdes notices Sullivan and Grimaldi don't look at each other when they talk. She wonders why Cochise didn't clue her in about having knocked heads with the lawyer in the past. The last time she was in a room with this much tension was right before she shot through Tyrell Humphries's nut-sack.

"This have anything to do with the story I saw on the news?" Ben glances at the flat-screen TV in the corner. "You guys found a Mercedes at a scrapyard by the airport?"

Lourdes hears Sullivan cracking his knuckles. It would have been nice to have kept that quiet a few more hours, but it was inevitable that somebody with a cell phone camera would have put it on the web after seeing all the trucks and police cars around Thor's place.

"So is it David's car?" Ben asks, still looking at Lourdes.

"It appears to be." Sullivan looks at the "Someone Talked" poster behind the desk.

"Well, *that's* a break, isn't it?" Ben nods at Lourdes.

"May we sit down?" she asks, trying to make this discussion a little more normal.

With a kind of reluctant magnanimity, Ben shrugs at two empty chairs. "Were there any prints or DNA to be had in the vehicle?"

"A little soon to tell." Lourdes lowers herself into one of them, while Sullivan remains standing. "We're working with the FBI's lab on putting together a profile on one or both of the shooters."

"So who brought the car in?" Ben asks. "That's the $64,000 Question."

"We're checking it out." Lourdes hands him the file she brought in. "We have a nickname, 'Science.'"

"Sounds like a Five Percenter name." Ben finally deigns to glance at Sullivan. "Or a wannabe. They're a Black Muslim splinter group, miss. Got started long before your time."

Lourdes twirls a strand of hair around her finger, pretending to be complimented. But anyone who'd been conscious in a New York City public school or a police precinct in the last fifty years knew the Five Percenter Nation, or the Nation of Gods and Earths, was a movement that started in the sixties and which allegedly believed the Black Man was Allah and the White Man was the Devil. A lot of them had names like Divine Mercy and Justice Overall. Over the years, a number had broken off into street gangs, using crackpot theology to justify criminal behavior. In practice, though, the majority had gotten tired of being so celestial and had turned into a regular decent ungodly people holding civil service jobs, raising families, and eventually collecting municipal pensions.

"We're thinking this individual's not necessarily part of the Nation," she says. "Apparently this was a street guy who had an interest in marine biology."

"Unusual profile." Ben loosens his purple tie, unbuttons his collar, furrows his brow, and hums an opera tune as he swivels and starts to read.

"We've found several dozen people in the system with similar aliases," she says.

"Yes, of course," Ben says. "But how does that bring you here?"

"At least two were represented by this firm, at some point," Sullivan says.

He has closed the door and started moving around the office, making a point of touching every single thing in it at least once. Almost like a ritual to let the occupant know that even though he's not currently in a police station, he's no longer completely in control of his own environment.

"Really?" Ben bunches up his mouth, trying not to react. "That's odd."

"Isn't it?" Sullivan walks along the wall, dragging his fingertips across every plaque, civic citation, and framed headline. Then he crosses behind the desk and stands behind Ben's chair, almost daring the lawyer to stop reading and turn around. Lourdes starts to get unnerved herself as Sullivan pauses at the credenza and picks up the picture of Ben and David Dresden together.

"I don't recognize these names." Ben rubs his jaw, acting as perplexed as an immigrant facing his first customs officer. "Melvin Ferguson. Shawn Davidson. They either had cases before I joined the firm or were represented by David or his associate Steven Beldock." He closes the file and hands it back to Lourdes. "And Steven, as I'm sure Detective Sullivan remembers, died from a brain aneurysm a couple of years ago."

"Maybe that's what happens when a lawyer develops a conscience." Sullivan leans over Ben's shoulder.

"What's that, detective?" Ben asks, refusing to look back.

"We'd like to see whatever files you have on those cases," Lourdes says cheerily, striving to keep this halfway collegial.

"I've already turned over anything that could possibly be deemed relevant to David's murder to the administrative judge for review . . ." Ben clasps his hands behind his head and leans back in his chair, as if encouraging worship at the shrine of his deltoids.

"We've heard that before . . ." Sullivan steps back.

"We believe time is of the essence," Lourdes speaks over him, starting to get tired of playing nice. "If this Science knows we've got the car, he's going to be on the run. And since we've kept up our end by keeping you apprised, we were hoping for a little more cooperation on your end."

"And you'll get it, as soon as you produce a warrant for the rest of these files," Ben says. "I'm just surprised someone as experienced as Detective Sullivan would come over here without one."

Now Sullivan isn't looking at her either. Okay, she didn't expect this meeting to be flowers and chocolates. They're detectives at a defense lawyer's office. But she'd heard that Benny G. was the kind of full-on, no-holds-barred, exterminate-the-brutes prosecutor most cops loved. She would've expected at least the patina of mutual respect. Especially since Sullivan said that he owed it to Dresden to see that this got done right.

"We would limit the scope of our review—" Lourdes argues.

"It doesn't matter." Ben puts his hands up. "I would lose the trust of every client who's ever contacted this firm. And despite my longstanding acquaintance with Detective Sullivan, I have no faith in your partners at the FBI. Especially when this firm is in the middle of a lawsuit against the Bureau. I'd be out of business by the morning."

She watches Sullivan start ambling around the room again, not asking questions, but making his presence felt like a basketball player moving without the ball or an actor claiming the stage without dialogue.

"Listen," Ben says, "I'm as eager as you are to see David's killers brought to justice."

"Then can you tell us, did Mr. Dresden ever mention being threatened by former clients who were unhappy with their sentences?" Lourdes asks, changing tack and trying to establish a rapport on softer issues before circling back to the files again.

"No. As I told your talented colleagues Detectives Borrelli and Chen, most of the people David represented loved him as much as I did. Their families invited him to christenings and *quinceañeras* all the time. Even when he was doing radio and television appearances up the wazoo, he followed up on every lead and pursued every appeal to the last brief. The clients didn't hold it against him when they went to prison for life; they sent him Christmas cards every year. Because he was a wonderful man. As you know yourself, Detective Sullivan."

This time Lourdes has no trouble interpreting Sully's expression. He looks like he just got a broken beer bottle waved in his face.

"I do indeed, counselor," he says, with leathery restraint. "Which is why we're going all out on this case. And why we'd like to see some fuller cooperation than we've been getting from this office. Because we now have a potential link between the firm and Mr. Dresden's murder."

"I'd say a very tenuous link." Ben tips back in his chair again.

"You know what?" Sullivan moves in front of him. "I think we need to review not just all of David Dresden's files, but your files as well."

"Really? You're going to bust my balls because you don't get what you want when you want it?"

"For your own protection." Sullivan shrugs. "You were Mr. Dresden's co-counsel on several recent cases, so your life could be in danger. Maybe they shot the wrong attorney."

"Hmm, let me consider if I have enough malpractice insurance to cover the cost of all my clients suing me at once for giving up their files." Ben assumes the pose of the *Thinker* statue. "Ah . . . no."

"Way to look out for your friend, Benny G.," Sullivan says.

"You know what? I resent that, Detective Sullivan." Ben pushes up on his armrests. "And by the way, no one calls me that anymore."

"That's not what I heard . . ."

Lourdes finds herself doing semi-conscious girlish things, fluffing her hair, looking at her nails, sighing audibly, to assert herself as a calming feminine presence.

"You know, you could make this a lot easier on all of us, Mr. Grimaldi," she says. "Because we're just going to have to come back with a subpoena for those records."

"And you can be sure I will fight that, miss," Ben says. "The last thing David would have wanted would be the police trampling on the rights of his clients."

"Even if it concerned his own murder?" Lourdes asks.

"Especially in that case," Ben replies. "David was all about demanding fairness from the system. And I'm on his side in that."

"Coney Island," Sullivan says.

"What did you say, detective?"

"You heard me."

Lourdes tries to catch Sullivan's eye, to figure out what to make of that. But he's gone to some place deep inside himself—pressing his lips together, sticking them out, and then nodding to himself, as if he's churning internally and going over the conversation word by word.

"We're not going away," Sullivan says.

"Okay, you guys need to get out of here now," Ben says. "I've got serious catching up to do on David's cases. And I've given you all the cooperation I can. Especially under these circumstances."

"And which circumstances are those?" Sullivan leans over the front of the desk and starts picking up the pens one by one, putting each down at a slightly askew angle.

"I'm sure Alice has told you about her suspicions about the police or the FBI being involved in David's murder." Ben straightens them and then puts his level glare on Sullivan. "Maybe there's something to that."

"I think we're both old enough to know better, counselor," Sullivan says.

"I don't know anything of the kind," Ben answers. "Show yourselves out, please."

"We'll be back." Sullivan lightly taps Lourdes on the shoulder.

"Good luck with your new partner, Detective Robles." Ben gives Lourdes a wave and then shakes his head at Sullivan. "Men this age— hard to know what to do with us."

20

Dad had a study on the garden-level floor, a converted laundry room just off the kitchen, where he'd somehow managed to jam in a rolltop desk, four file cabinets, two bookcases, a Garrard turntable with tinny speakers, and a frumpy reefer-scented sofa. He liked to sit here and try to show his son how to play "Don't Think Twice" and "Redemption Song" on the old Gibson acoustic guitar with a Woody Guthrie sticker on the pick-guard that said "This Machine Kills Fascists."

But with his big clumsy fingers, Natty could never master that nimble C, G, A minor progression for the Dylan song or even the G, E minor, E minor seventh broad strokes for the Marley one. He'd try each a half dozen times with Dad patiently coaching, and then storm out in frustration to blast *Reign in Blood* and *Me Against the World* upstairs. Now it's eleven o'clock at night and he's sitting on the couch, surrounded by Dad's old file cabinets and laptop and a Coors bottle open by his feet, police and ambulance sirens speeding by outside, the sounds of confusion and despair, wailing down toward the Gowanus Canal.

He wishes he could open up the guitar case and lose himself in strumming, but his arm is throbbing again and his brain is on overdrive again. Moral injury. Stupid fucking idea. Who cared about your parents' precious little "Free to Be You and Me" organic composting values after your favorite interpreter has had his head cut off in front of his family, after you've heard a seven-year-old gurgling for his last breath, after you've seen your staff sergeant's lower body pinned and crushed to pulp under a Humvee?

It shocked him, how unprepared he was for war. The world wasn't about consensus-building or respecting cultural differences or any of the other useless lessons he'd learned from Beansprouts Nursery School or the Park Slope Food Co-Op. It was about never-ending hatred and vicious sectarianism. It was about power and retribution. He should have been raised like a Spartan to deal with it. Taught to be a gladiator from the time he could hold a sword. Schooled in endurance and self-denial. Fuck moral injury. Fuck Therapist Stacy. Fuck Ibrahim's son Hamid and his accusing stare. Fuck Daddy's ghost saying, "I tried to warn you," in a hundred different ways. Fuck everyone who didn't go over and do what he did. Let the chips fall. Let the bodies hit the floor. Suck it up and drive on.

He looks under the desk and sees Dad's old briefcase. The battered Saddleback bag with the shoulder strap and tarnished buckles, made from cracked chestnut-brown boot leather. Nothing politically correct about it, the only halfway badass item his father had in his arsenal, his Indiana Jones bag.

Growing up, Natty had always wanted one like it, running to bring the case to Dad at the door as he was heading off to work and then rushing to take it from him as soon as he got home, breathing its natural oil smell, running his uncallused fingers over a weathered pigskin exterior that felt like it was made in equal parts from a 1930 football, Jack Dempsey's boxing gloves, and Clint Eastwood's face.

He'd had fantasies of inheriting it someday, since a new bag would need decades to get that rugged broken-in look. Until the day Stephen Carbone, his worst enemy at P.S. 51, brought in a copy of the *New York Post* to discuss at Current Events class. The one with the headline of "DRESDEN WINS FREEDOM FOR COP-KILLER."

That night, Natty looked inside the bag and found it overstuffed with tendentious arguments on behalf of one Lockwood "Junior" Woodley, accused of pushing a patrolman named Edward Ridgeway off a rooftop in Bedford-Stuyvesant. An officer who took three days to die, according to the *Post* story that Stephen Carbone read out loud during the Current Events homeroom period. Right before Natty lunged at Stephen in the schoolyard. And then got jumped on and righteously stomped by five of Stephen's friends.

The smell of the bag reminds him of the assistant principal's office, where he sat with a bloody nose beside his mother, hearing that he was going to be suspended for the week. He didn't come down from his bedroom to greet his father after work that night. Just lay on the bed, under his Han Solo poster, pretending he couldn't hear Dad calling him to dinner. Then steadfastly ignored his father as he stood in the doorway, waiting *to talk*. Natty realizes now that was when he began to push the old man away, disassociating himself from wretched causes and lonely stands. Step by step, he'd declared his independence in what must have been the worst way imaginable for Dad. Acting like his disloyalty was a virtue, a higher calling. Always finding a way to say, "I'm not like you" or "I'm better than you." Never dreaming there would come a day when he couldn't take it all back.

So what now, Natty Dread? What if you can't suck it up and drive on? What if there's never any "Redemption Song"?

He sold the .357 in Florida after he took it out of the freezer. And he can't bear the thought of Mom finding him hanging from the chin-up bar or having to ID the birthmark on his thigh at the morgue because he'd shot himself in the face.

No, dawg. You can't go out of the picture right after she's lost the old man. You're in this for a while longer.

He looks deeper inside the saddlebag and finds a blue folder marked "Ibrahim Saddik, 2008." Inside are printouts from *New York Times* articles about detainees at Guantanamo Bay, photocopies of a Council of Europe investigation into torture at Black Sites in Macedonia and Egypt, and a heavily redacted inspector general's report on the Department of Defense with entire pages blacked out. Then there's a page of his father's chicken-scratch handwriting. No need for cyber-encryption; almost no one else could read this code. The only reason Natty can decipher it is because his father tried to teach him penmanship in first grade—probably half the reason the school threatened to leave him back a year.

"Get Wally 209. Send FOIA requests for Kirkpatrick 302s, 472s, 209s, and 292s."

He reaches for the half-empty Coors bottle by his feet, trying to wring some meaning from the words. Dad reminding himself to make Freedom of Information requests about Paul Kirkpatrick, the FBI agent who'd been running the Ibrahim investigation until the mailman was renditioned to the military's Black Site. Most of the form numbers are vaguely familiar to Natty from his own work with the state attorney in Orlando. A 302 is a summary of an agent's interview notes. Fair enough. A 472 is a consent form for a wiretap. A 209 is a record of a contact with an unofficial criminal informant, which, according to Ibrahim, could have been his post office supervisor, Walid "Wally" al-Masri, who owed him money. But what's an FD 292?

He pulls out his iPhone and plugs the term into the Google search engine. A Wikipedia list of FBI forms loads. Halfway down it says, "An FD-292 form is used by FBI agents to notify the agency that they're getting married or divorced." So fucking what?

"What are you doing in here?" His mother stands in the doorway in her green silk Chinese bathrobe and black slippers, more sirens wailing in the background.

"Just trying to catch up to where Dad was in the mailman case." He sets the folder aside and reaches for his beer with a renewed stab of pain in his elbow.

"How is it going?"

"If it was easy to sue the FBI, a lot of other people would've done it sooner."

"Tell me something I don't know." She waves a hand. "But I was asking how are *you* doing?"

"Livin' the dream, Mama."

"You stopped shaving." She puts her fingers to her chin. "You going to grow a beard like your father's?"

"Hadn't thought about it. Think he'd be amused?"

"He always tried to be amused by you, Natty. Even when he knew you were hating on him."

"Thanks for reminding me."

He takes a long swig off the Coors. Dad's least favorite brand. Right-wing stalwarts. Natty started ordering it just to annoy the old man. But now he has to admit that it's just fermented ox piss.

"Wasn't all bad times, though," she says. "Was it?"

"No. I guess not."

He remembers all the leaves coming down from the trees in the park.

Then Dad raking them into piles for Natty to jump in. And then Natty would duck his head down and disappear beneath the papery heaps while Dad would pretend to look for him. Right before neighborhood dogs scurried over to sniff and lift their legs.

"I was a little shit sometimes," he says.

He remembers now that he never got to tell Dad about the constitutional law professors at Duke who practically fell to their knees when he grudgingly admitted, yes, he was related to that Dresden up north.

"He'd be glad to see you in his study," she says.

"Think so?"

"He always thought you'd end up on the same side again."

"Isn't that what they call wishful thinking?"

She moves past him into the study, opens one of the file cabinets, and pulls out an old yellowing folder marked "Feel Good Inc." in black Magic Marker.

"When he was down about what he was doing, he liked to look at this." She hands it to him. "He said it helped him remember that maybe he'd done some things he felt good about in his life."

"Like arguing in front of the Supreme Court two times wasn't worthwhile?"

"In case you haven't figured this out yet, Natty, you don't get a lot of big wins when you're a grown-up. Most of the people David represented had made some serious mistakes. He knew they all deserved the best defense, but it wore him down sometimes. Everyone needs a little solace once in a while."

Natty pages through the file. There's citations from the American Civil Liberties Union and the Center for Constitutional Rights. Wedding pictures from the dawn of the Reagan era, Mom in a mortifying short skirt and suede boots and Dad in a semi-psychedelic tie on the steps of City Hall. And then, unexpected, a shot of Natty with his helmet off, playing soccer with the local kids in Tikrit.

"I forgot I even sent this," Natty mutters. "I can't even remember who took it."

"David loved that picture. He said, 'That boy is my heart.'"

"Never said that to me."

"Maybe because you didn't let him say it." She sits down beside him, resting her head on his shoulder. "You were always kind of edgy around him."

"He was a tough father to have sometimes." He shifts, feeling the pressure on his bad arm. "I hated his clients, and all their little psycho kids who came to stay at the house."

"Your father had a lot of different sides. I'm sorry you didn't get to see more of them."

"So who is Marygrace Kelly?" he asks abruptly.

"Why do you want to know about *her*?"

"She got in touch with me, wanting to talk about Dad."

"Just out of the blue?" She stiffens.

"I'd been doing some poking around, calling different numbers on his bill trying to see if there's something the police might have missed. She happened to hit me back."

"David had been calling her?" She separates herself and leans away from him. "Recently?"

"A few times." He looks after her. "About some kind of situation he was scared about. Do you know what it was?"

"The only thing he was nervous about was this mailman case. So I don't know why he'd still be dealing with that . . . prissy, uptight . . . pain in my butt." Her face hardens with a kind of urgent displeasure. "Did you speak to her?"

"I did. She said to say hello."

"I never liked that woman and I never trusted that woman." She crosses her arms. "And it's not just because I thought she was trying to steal my man. She's a goddamn snake. In fact, I called her the Kool-Aid Queen because she always bought into the government line. Watch yourself around her. What did she want to talk about?"

"I think she just wanted to make contact, because she couldn't make it to the funeral."

"She wasn't *invited* to the funeral." She narrows her eyes. "Because I didn't want her there. She is no friend to our family."

"What exactly did she do, Mom?"

"*Huh.*"

She gives that abrupt bark of a laugh that's reserved for certain

white women who go above and beyond her standards of tolerable
haughtiness.

"I'm not going to get into it. But let's just say, I wouldn't trust her
dumpy Marymount ass any further than I could throw it. She say anything about the mailman case?"

"No. Not that much."

She holds up a finger and looks away, as if she's too overcome with
unladylike emotions to speak.

"You just stay away from her," she says. "She was no friend of mine
and she was no friend of your father's. It's just too bad he couldn't see
that until it was too late."

"Too late for what?"

"Just stay away from her," she says. "Your father is dead, but his case
isn't. And she's on the other side."

She stands up and starts fussing with the belt over her bathrobe.

"All right, that's it," she says. "I'm going to bed. Tell me if you hear
from that so-called friend of your father's again."

"Peace, Mama."

"Peace out, Natty Dread. Good night." She comes over, kisses him
on top of the head, and then lightly caresses his stubbly cheek. "Nice. I
always wanted you to grow your hair out. Reminds me of David."

She heads upstairs, each step registering as a heavy-hearted thump
over his head.

It ain't no use. Don't think twice. Stuff happens. You can't rewind
the clock. Or raise the dead. No redemption songs here. Peace is an unnatural state. He swallows the rest of the beer and leaves it next to the
two other empty bottles on the shag rug.

Then he opens the Feel Good Inc. folder again, looking for a little
solace of his own. He turns past the pictures of himself and finds a photo
of his mother, in a straw hat and sunglasses on a sailboat. Maybe a summer in Wellfleet. Mom playing the movie star, a little glamorous and un-
knowable. An old 45 record in its white paper sleeve. *Mendocino* by Sir
Douglas Quintet. And then a Ziploc bag of weed. Another bag has mush-
rooms. Probably something primo he was holding back for a special
occasion or a gift from a client he was particularly fond of. More photos:
Natty and his father on bikes at the Jersey shore, with Mom in her

sunglasses and plastic bib having lobster on City Island in the Bronx, the three of them coming home from what looks like a sun-dappled afternoon at the Prospect Park Zoo, Natty a toddler aloft and joyful in his father's arms.

Natty realizes this might not just be a happiness folder, but a place where his father filed away his contradictions and pretended they all belonged together.

No pictures of Ben, strangely. Natty wonders if he was the photographer for some of the shots. And then the last photo in the file. A yellowing Polaroid. Dad, younger than Natty is now, clean-shaven, short-haired, and barely able to meet the camera lens with his gaze. The background looks like one of the old Brooklyn Law School buildings in the Heights. Dad's soft uncovered chin tucked down, almost hiding a clandestine smile that Natty doesn't recognize. Plainly the grin of a young man who has just gotten laid for the first time. By his side is a vaguely familiar young woman with auburn hair, well-tended lashes, and a look of fragile promise in her eyes. Marygrace. The only tension between them is in their arms; they're holding hands like they're bracing for a tidal wave that's about to pull them apart.

Natty closes the folder. More sirens are coming from different directions, coming together somewhere down near the Gowanus Canal, as if they're all rushing to the same place for consolation.

21

Science has dropped.

He lies at the foot of an aluminum slide at the Thomas Greene Playground on Third Avenue, a.k.a. The Pit. It's a few minutes after one in the morning. Face-down with two entry wounds in his back and his head turned to the side. He's surprisingly hefty for a heroin addict. A Biggie Smalls–looking dude in a hoodie and baggy jeans, except unlike Biggie, he didn't *own* his fat or wear it easily. Even in death, he looks like he's burdened by it, the expression on his face slightly embarrassed, as if this large lumpish frame doesn't fairly represent the soul of the man within.

Lourdes exchanges faint nods and waves of recognition at the same crime scene techs and homicide detectives she saw at the Dresden crime scene less than two weeks ago. More than likely, it's the same police helicopter circling as well, searchlight strafing the tenement roofs of Gowanus and Boerum Hill, with the occasional water tower painted bright folk art colors or redesigned as an event space.

Uniform officers are canvassing the projects on the west side of the playground and the newly renovated brownstones to the east. Andy Chen is talking to the duty captain on the scene and B.B. is standing just outside the yellow tape, taking notes.

"Well, this sucks." Lourdes sticks her hands into the pockets of her raincoat, feeling a light damp mist on her face as she comes up. "How come no one called me until like fifteen minutes ago?"

"Get off your Mustang, Sally." B.B. barely looks up. "There's other detectives working this job. The world doesn't need you to save it before your next tour begins."

"*My case*, B.B." She jabs a freshly reconditioned fingernail nail at him. "I'm the primary. You knew I was looking for this dude."

"For Chrissakes, Robles, everyone was. It was a citywide search. But no one realized it was Shawn Davidson until his mother showed up and started yelling his nickname."

Lourdes turns to see where B.B. is pointing. A big busty lady is shrieking outside the yellow tape; flabby-armed in a hot-pink "You Can't Touch This" t-shirt, hair tied back and brow bulging out like an onion dome, as she starts to collapse and beat her fists on the chest of a tall young uniform officer, who's trying to hold her up while looking around in terror for someone to hand her off to. For a moment, Lourdes almost feels sorrier for this clueless pasty-faced child of the suburbs, who has no idea how to handle all this raw ghetto-mom grief pounding on him.

"Siiiiennnnce. Sieennce. Why they kill my baby?" She falls against him, then starts to punch him dead-center of his chest. "Tell me why. *Why . . .* "

Pretty much the only thing in the world that can literally make Lourdes cringe. That sound that comes from deep inside a mother when she knows the child she carried is dead.

"Hate this shit," she hisses, trying to get to a state of brusque professional detachment. "Notifications ever get easier?"

"Nope." B.B. tugs on his collar. "But tell you what. If your kid doesn't hang around a playground middle of the night, doing what he's not supposed to do, then maybe he won't get shot five times."

"Our boy took *five* rounds?" Lourdes looks over at the body. "Damn. What else do we know?"

"*Stoogats.*" Bobby fans his fingers out from under his chin. "Not a lot of potential witnesses, since it's mostly warehouses and open lots around here."

Lourdes looks around. It's one of those areas where the frayed edge of old industrialized Brooklyn meets the border of the new aggressively overvalued artisanal borough. Corrugated aluminum fencing, truck repair yards, and brake shops butting converted family-friendly loft spaces, glass blower studios, jewelry design centers, and house-made ice cream shops selling seven-dollar sugar cones along the sulfurous banks of the Gowanus.

"People down the streets heard raised voices and gunshots," B.B. goes on. "They called 9-1-1, and patrol found the victim bleeding out by the jungle gym, with no pulse, gaping wounds to the lower back and the back of the head. He was probably dead before he hit the ground."

"How did his mother get here so fast?" Lourdes watches the young patrol officer try to lower the grief-stricken mom onto a bench and then look around for a supervisor.

"Schermerhorn Houses are just across the way." B.B. gestures toward Nevins Street. "Apparently, Shawn was staying with her and got a call asking him to come out and meet someone. Told his moms he'd be back in like *twenny* minutes."

Lourdes watches the crime scene techs get down on their hands and knees to start looking under the see-saws and raised wooden-plank platforms.

"So does the mom know who he was meeting?" Lourdes asks.

"If she does, she's not saying." B.B. tilts his head. "According to her, he was just a poor misunderstood boy who wanted a microscope and a fish tank. Like everybody who gets killed out on the street stealing cars and selling drugs."

"We didn't find a phone, did we?"

"Not yet. No gun either."

"Ain't easy, B.B., is it?"

"Hey, I could use a little easy right about now."

The mother is doubled up on the bench, howling inconsolably and hugging her knees. Everyone is giving her wide berth, like this much sadness is something you can catch. A large man in a black coat ducks under the yellow tape to approach her, the Grim Reaper offering condolences. Science's mother stares at Kevin Sullivan, opens her eyes wide, and lets out a scream that gets three more lights turned on across the street. Instead of retreating, Sullivan calmly sits down next to her on the bench and puts an arm around her.

"Okay, well here we go," B.B. sighs. "If she's got anything to say, Sully will get it out of her."

"He's that good. Huh?"

"He da man. But keep a little distance with him, LRo."

"Why's that?"

The mother has suddenly stopped screaming. Instead she's leaning against Sullivan, her broad face pressed into his collarbone, her big body quivering, as he puts a comforting arm around her and moves his lips like he's reciting a mourner's prayer.

"Just a word to the wise. He's keeping you on the case. But you're still vulnerable because of the Heinz thing."

"Shit. I know that, B.B. That's why I keep trying to come back strong."

"Maybe a little too strong. There's more fallout from that Mexican standoff with the *federales* at the auto yard." Bobby touches the side of his hair with the darting vanity of a man aware he's losing his looks.

"Yeah, what about it? They took the witness, so Sullivan hulked out on them and we towed the car back to the NYPD garage until they were willing to make a trade for Thor. But now it's settled. It's all I love you, you love me, right?"

"Someone is bitching again?"

"After you left, the Chief of D's came back in to talk to the captain."

"Chief Gunther came back to our house?"

Red light from an arriving squad car washes over her.

"Himself," Bobby says. "And the Skipper was pretty much reaching for the Prozac by the time he left. It seems the FBI complained to the U.S. attorney about what happened at the scrapyard. Then the U.S. attorney bitched to the Brooklyn DA . . ."

"And the DA bitched to the police commissioner." Lourdes nods, finishing the thought for him. "And the PC got into it with the Chief of D's."

"And so on." Bobby makes a circle with his finger. "It seems Sullivan provoked some consternation."

"So now what happens?"

"I don't know. But it's serious stakes. Big-name lawyer shot by the park. Feds showing up without explaining themselves. Witnesses getting killed before we can talk to them. The gods are not happy."

A set of paparazzi flashes go off around the body, the corpse an instant celebrity to the crime scene techs taking his picture. Everyone in life is supposed to have their fifteen minutes. With most victims, Lourdes thinks, it's probably more like fifteen days. A little over two weeks when you added up all the investigative hours, paperwork, and court time accumulated living it, eating it, dreaming it over the weeks and months when all your other cases and the rest of your life were happening.

"Anybody saying why the feds care that much?" she asks.

"Just that they have their own separate investigation going. For all we know, they may have agents who are already here."

She hears a grunt of brakes and sees a Con Ed truck come around the block and pull up by the corner of the *Daily News* garage, disgorging two workers in yellow helmets. Then she notices a couple more middle-aged white guys than you'd expect to see among the lookie-loos hanging out behind the barricades this time of night. It's true the neighborhood is changing, and they could just be landed gentry taking an interest in the effect of crime on their property values. But in her experience, white people usually prefer to gawk at their laptops at this hour of night.

"So what are we supposed to do about the gods not being happy if we don't even know what they want?" Lourdes nudges B.B.

"Above all our pay grades." He shrugs. "But they must be placated. A sacrifice might be necessary."

"The fuck you say?"

"Look, Robles, this is a good job for people like us." He puts his mouth close to her ear, no flirtation in his voice. "Keep your head down and you could be making six figures with overtime in a couple of years. You'll be out by the time you're my age with a fat pension and your mortgage paid off. If they come for you, protect ya neck. Don't worry about anybody else."

Lourdes looks over and sees Science's mother still clinging to Sullivan with both arms while his big rough hand keeps patting her back, her pink t-shirt expanding and contracting like a wad of bubble gum with her sobs.

"I'm not throwing anyone under a bus, B.B."

"Better to learn to duck then, because once they bury Science, that bus may be coming for you."

Lourdes looks over at the victim as the white sheet covers him, and for some reason a wave of delayed sadness hits her. The marine biologist who never made it to sea. The black kid who hung out at the old Norwegian seamen's bar, wanting to hear whaling stories. Some people, she realizes, never figure out where they're supposed to be.

22

Natty stops on the threshold, strong midday sun reflecting off the conference table and almost blinding him as he tries to discern the extra, unexpected presence in the room.

"I asked Doug Bryce from the FBI office in Manhattan to join us," Marygrace Kelly says. "I hope you don't mind."

"Why would I mind?" Natty shields his eyes. "Just because Dad was suing the FBI when he was killed?"

He leans against the doorjamb, his newly unslung arm pulsing with pain at his side. They're still in downtown Brooklyn, just across from the Cadman Plaza diner, at the office of the U.S. attorney for the Eastern District. But all at once the room feels as unstable as Iraq. Like there could be explosives beneath the mound of egg salad sandwiches on a platter by the window. Or the sunburned middle-aged man sitting at the head of the conference table could be planning to strap Natty down for waterboarding.

"You can leave at any time." Doug Bryce points to a chair on a diagonal from his seat. "But I think you'll want to hear this."

"What I think is I should call Ben Grimaldi right now." Natty starts peeling the security sticker off his jacket. "This feels like you guys trying an end run around the mailman case."

"It's not. It has to do with your father's murder." Bryce points to a stack of files in the middle of the table. "But if you'd prefer to leave without hearing the evidence, that's your choice."

Natty studies how the files are not quite evenly stacked, but have their corners fanned out suggestively in the way a magician proffers a deck of cards to the gullible.

"You're under no obligation to stay." MG pats an empty chair at her side, like a schoolgirl eager for a study partner. "But you were asking why your father was calling the FBI so often right before he died. Doug has some answers for you."

Natty steps in and closes the door behind him. "What's this about?"

Scudding clouds outside the picture windows redirect the sun's glare and momentarily turn MG and the agent into a pair of darkened silhouettes with the green Astroturf field of Cadman Plaza Park behind them.

"Nathan—" Doug Bryce touches the end of his peeling nose self-consciously. "You mind if I call you that?"

"Call me Nathaniel."

"Nathaniel, please sit down." Bryce gestures again. "There are certain things I can discuss with you today, and certain things I can't discuss. What I can tell you is this: at the time he was killed, your father was assisting us with an ongoing investigation."

"You're trying to tell me that my father was helping the FBI at the same time that he was suing it?" Natty takes two more steps into the room, still not committed to staying.

"I know that sounds like a conflict," MG says in a perky, bureaucratic preamble voice.

"With all due respect, MG, but how fucking stupid do you think I am?" Natty plops down into the seat, to get eye level with her. "You're trying to tell me that *my father*—Mr. ACLU Human Rights Watch Pinup Boy—would risk his law license *and* his livelihood to become a federal cooperator?"

"That's not how he was looking at it," she says.

"You know what?" Natty thrusts his chin out. "I think you must not have known him as well as you say you did. Because my father didn't hate anybody—*except cooperators*."

"He also liked to say John Wayne was just an actor." She smiles into her curled fingers, like she's making a private joke.

"Meaning . . . ?"

"In his own way, your father was as into theatrics as Ben Grimaldi." She exhales and sits up, as if ready to be more ingenuous. "A lot of what he said was just for show. The reality is David liked to rail publicly against the sellouts of the world, but he could cut a deal with the best of them. He represented many cooperators."

"Oh, so you knew him better than I did?" Natty puts an elbow up on the table, two-alarm pain pulsing where the fireman's wrench struck it.

"I knew him differently."

"I thought you said you were in the civil division, handling white-collar cases." Natty slides the elbow off with a grunt. "Was that just a lie to get me in here?"

"No, Nathaniel." She tilts up her face, serene and pure of purpose as a yoga instructor. "I *am* with the civil division. But your father came to me, very upset, with an urgent concern he had and I put him in touch with Doug, who I'd worked with on a money-laundering case. I thought they'd work well together."

Natty knuckles the underside of his growing stubble. Now he knows why Dad had a beard; it helped mask your response when people were trying to put one over on you.

"And what was this case my father was allegedly helping you with?" he asks Doug Bryce.

The agent stops touching his nose. MG looks out the window. Plainly there was some serious discussion between them right before he came in the room. Now they remind Natty of a couple trying to socialize after an argument.

"I know that you're an attorney yourself with a background in military intelligence, so we're not going to try to pull the wool over your eyes," Bryce says. "But I think you might want to take a look at these."

He pushes the stack of files at Natty and then sits back, his features obscured by the harshness of the sun coming in over his shoulder.

"What are they?"

Natty takes the first folder off the stack and opens the cover. There's an indictment from Kings County Supreme Court on top, with a federal indictment filed in New Jersey beneath it, and then a thicker pile of court transcripts.

"It's a set of cases that we've compiled from New York, New Jersey, and Connecticut by using resources that the NYPD doesn't have," Bryce says. "At least four murders over the last seven years. From at least four different jurisdictions. In the top file, you'll see that your father was the lawyer for a Mr. Kenneth Holloway, also known as 'Kenny' or 'KK.' Mr. Holloway was a cooperating witness in a state drug case who was murdered a few months ago by the same type of gun that killed your father later. A .45 with hollow points. We're trying to get the ballistics report from the NYPD to see if it's an even more exact match."

"Okay, so what does that prove?" Natty's eyes move down the page, as he becomes aware of a soft buzz of static at the edge of his hearing. "A cooperator gets killed in a drug case. Happens all the time. And a .45 is pretty standard issue in that world."

"Then check out the other three cases." Bryce gets up to stand behind Natty. "In each, the murder victim was also an informant who was scheduled to testify in a major criminal case."

Natty flips back through the pages, seeing references to a case in Newark, another in Westchester, and a third in Bridgeport, Connecticut, the buzz of static getting louder.

"So what?" He shrugs, his eyes not leaving the text just yet. "Cooperating witnesses getting killed. It's dog bites man over and over. If they were informants, they probably weren't Boy Scouts to begin with. They were criminals who got caught and decided to cooperate to avoid long sentences themselves. So they decided to rat on their friends and they got killed for it. As they said in Iraq: stuff happens. But what does it have to do with my father?"

"You're missing the common element." Bryce reaches over his shoulder. "The lawyer for the main defendant in each of the four cases where the informant was killed? Ben Grimaldi."

Natty stares at Bryce until the agent lifts his finger from the page. The static is no longer just in his head. It's become a prickling sensation in his veins. Like his blood is fizzing.

"Don't take our word," Bryce says. "It's all public record. Look it up independently. In the case from last year, Mr. Grimaldi was representing a defendant named Shakneela Wilkins in the KSB, Kash Sex Blood, gang case and your father was representing his codefendant Kenny Holloway. Then Mr. Holloway decided to testify against Mr. Wilkins and their mutual boss Jamar Mack. A week after he signed his cooperation agreement, Mr. Holloway was shot to death crossing Troy Avenue in Crown Heights with his stepfather."

Natty tries to force himself to keep reading, even as the fizzing is causing air pockets to form in his blood stream. Some of these names sound vaguely familiar. Kenny. Jamar. Shakneela. Maybe because Dad talked about people like this as if they meant as much to him as his own family.

"Okay, but it says right here this dude, Kenny Holloway, was a mid-level drug dealer himself." Natty focuses on the page again. "He got arrested and agreed to roll on his friends to save his own sorry ass. Then he caught a bullet for it. Snitches get stitches, or worse. Happens all the time. Doesn't it?"

His own voice is becoming distant to him, his fingertips numb as they touch the paper, the words swimming under his eyes.

"Your father told us that he believed that Mr. Grimaldi's client, Shakneela Wilkins, was responsible for Mr. Holloway's murder," Bryce says. "He believed Mr. Grimaldi advised Shakneela Wilkins to eliminate the witness before Mr. Holloway could testify."

"*Bullshit.*"

Doug Bryce pats the end of his nose. MG fingers the front of her white blouse and then her pearls as if it's requiring some conscious effort not to complete the sign of the cross. But neither of them speaks.

"You're not accusing my father's best friend of murder, are you?" Natty says. "Is that seriously what you're trying to get me to believe?"

"Look up the court records and media stories on your own." Bryce goes back to his seat. "The same thing happened to cooperating witnesses in at least three other cases where Mr. Grimaldi represented a codefendant who would have suffered from their testimony. And there's one new detail to add."

"What's that?"

Bryce pushes over a fax of a local report. "There was a murder in Gowanus the other night which may be connected to your father's car turning up. An individual named Shawn Davidson was found dead in a playground off Third Avenue. He may have had ties to associates of Mr. Grimaldi as well."

"That's why Ben never loses," MG adds quietly. "The witnesses against his clients get killed."

They all stop talking for a few seconds. Natty hears birds, but the windows are soundproofed. He sees a couple of sparrows on bare branches just outside the glass, and realizes the noises are only inside his head.

"This is the biggest bunch of crap I ever heard," he says. "And believe me, I heard a lot of crap over in Iraq. Why would Ben even care that much? They're just clients. Win or lose, he gets paid either way."

"Your father believed Mr. Grimaldi may have shared larger interests with these clients," Doug Bryce says quietly. "And that's why he felt the need to protect them."

" 'Larger interests'?"

"Your dad was starting to suspect that Mr. Grimaldi had an illegal side business that he was running with some of the criminals he represented."

Natty turns and watches a shadow grow long over the Justice Department seal on the wall, while a yellowish rectangle of light beside it stretches, becoming the size of a doorway, and darkens a half-filled water glass that's been sitting at the other end of the table as if another guest was expected.

"And Dad just came to you and told you all this while he was in the middle of suing the FBI?" Natty leans back his chair, trying to project an air of control and equanimity. "You expect me to swallow that he just decided to rat on his best friend when he was trying the biggest case of his career?"

"The discussions were still in the preliminary stages," MG says. "David had not yet signed an official cooperation agreement. But it was clear where we were heading."

"But why on earth would my father turn on Ben?"

"When all was said and done, David was still basically an honorable man," she says. "He was very angry when he figured out what Ben was doing. And he learned about it just as the mailman case was finally coming together. It put him in a terrible position. To be honest, he was talking about handing the mailman case off to another firm when he was killed."

"Fuck this." Natty slaps the table, unsure why he's not up and heading out the door already.

"When you're talking about witnesses being murdered, it undermines the integrity of the process," Bryce says. "I'm sure your father wanted no part of that. But again, draw your own conclusions. All we ask is that you not tell Mr. Grimaldi about this meeting. Not just for the sake of our case, but for your own safety."

Mentally, Natty knows this is probably all lies and manipulation, intended to help the government's case. But somehow his body is responding like he's back in combat. Respiration increasing, muscles tensing, sweat on the back of his neck.

"And this supposed criminal operation was being run out of the law firm where my father was partners with Ben?"

"Apparently." Bryce steeples his fingers.

"That's absurd." Natty closes the file and pushes it away. "My dad might have been a lot of things, but naive he wasn't."

"We don't think your father was complicit in any of these illegal activities," Bryce says. "In fact, we think he took action after he learned about them. Mr. Grimaldi was no doubt very good at covering his tracks. Remember: he is not only a skilled defense lawyer, he's a former prosecutor. He's smart enough to hide what he's up to. Even, for a long time, from someone as close to him and perceptive as your father."

"But you still haven't explained why Ben would get mixed up in any of that."

"It's no secret that he has serious money troubles," MG says. "But to be honest, I think he was always capable of it. I don't think he was always scrupulous as a prosecutor either. And your father had a blind spot when it came to Ben. A lot of people did. They saw someone who liked to win. And everybody likes to be with a winner."

"Wait a second." Natty massages his temples with growing force. "You're not really suggesting Ben had something to do with my father's murder as well, are you?"

"I'm not suggesting anything," Bryce says. "I'm just giving you facts."

"And what do you want me to do with these so-called facts?"

Bryce shrugs. "It's very difficult for us to get probable cause for a warrant to search the premises because of attorney-client privilege. You mentioned to MG that you were working at the firm."

"So you want to use me to help you get your probable cause by spying on Ben and report back to you?" Natty finally gets to his feet. "You guys have got some nerve."

"We believe that the criminal operation at the law firm is ongoing," Bryce says. "Your father was killed before he could expose it. So whatever Mr. Grimaldi was doing before, he's still doing. He considers himself invulnerable, so other people may still be at risk."

"And this just happens to be going on while Ben is taking over the mailman case. Isn't that convenient?"

"We understand your suspicion," MG says softly. "But you saw your father's phone records. You know he was in touch with me and calling the Bureau in the weeks before he died. Look at these documents and ask yourself why else he would have been calling."

Bryce pretends to look busy, studying the files. "If you're content to let sleeping dogs lie, go right ahead. I couldn't."

"You know, if you were just asking me to undo everything my dad stood for in his life, that would be bad enough." Natty stops with a hand on the doorknob. "But you're also asking me to turn on someone who's been like a second father to me."

"Then maybe it's time to grow up," Bryce says.

23

As soon as Lourdes comes clomping up the stairs to the fourth floor, feeling every minute of two a.m. in her shoes, she can hear the ruckus and tell there's trouble at home again.

She undoes the lock, smells cigarette smoke, and hears that cassette tape of her mother singing "Con El Diablo En El Cuerpo" from her '74 Fania Records audition. Her aunt Soledad is in the living room with her shoulder to the bathroom door, hand dangling loose near her size 40 waistband, like she's about to draw her gun.

"Leave me alone!" Lourdes hears Mami call from inside the bathroom, where she's no doubt got the boom box up on the toilet again and a Winston smoldering in defiance of her oxygen tank.

"*Ándale, Rosita. Para que sirve.*" Soledad gives Lourdes a first responder's weary headshake. "You don't open up, we'll have to call 9-1-1 and take the door down."

"No, no, don't do that, mi tia." Lourdes's sister Ysabel waddles from the shadows in her XXL Alex Rodriguez nightshirt. "We won't be able to get the super to put the door back on and then I won't be able to use the toilet because I can't go when people are looking at me."

Soledad stands back, drops her arms to her sides, and shuts her eyes to contain herself. A big tough lady in a Hawaiian shirt and a butch crew cut, built like Jackie Gleason in the old *Honeymooners* episodes she taught Lourdes to love. She's put up with a decade and a half of discrimination and harassment as an overweight Hispanic lesbian in the police department and made it to sergeant in Brooklyn Narcotics without losing her mind or eating her gun, but *caramba*, no one can push your buttons like flesh and blood.

"Déjame en paz!" Lourdes's mother calls out. "Let me be! I just need time to think."

"Why?" Lourdes nudges her sister out of the way. "There too much action out here? You haven't left the damn house in two weeks."

Soledad puts a hamlike hand on her shoulder, to calm her. Mi tia. The family champion. The woman who raised her when Papi was upstate, Georgie was dead, Mami was strung out, and Ysabel was bouncing from one special needs program to another. Soledad helped Lourdes learn to cook for herself and get into a decent parochial school while showing her how to fill out the paperwork to retain their Section 8 housing and keep the SSI taps open. And when Lourdes announced she wanted to be a cop, after getting a degree in accounting from Brooklyn College, Soledad gave her just the one stern obligatory lecture about the easier choices a pretty girl could make before making the calls to get Lourdes moved up the list and steered into a unit in Brownsville where she could start collaring up and earning a rep in a hurry.

"How long she been in this time?" Lourdes asks.

"What, like, two, three hours?" Her aunt looks over at Ysabel and shrugs. "The party never stops."

Lourdes's sister creeps back to the living room, where she was probably bouncing on her purple isokinetics ball-chair, surrounded by her botanica candles and the shrine to their brother, updating her Match .com profile when Mami decided to play her audition tape and lock herself in again.

"She's been in the bathroom since like eleven and Izzy calls you instead of me?" Lourdes turns on her aunt. "What's up *with that*?"

"I'm working steady days and you're in the middle of a major-ass homicide investigation." Soledad shrugs. "Easy decision."

"I don't even get a text?"

"Rosie locks herself in the can every other week." Soledad shrugs. "This is your first big case. I'm not gonna let you get distracted with a bunch of family nonsense. Especially when there'll be some other crisis next week."

"Yeah, but I thought you were in a van, ghosting heroin buys over on Mother Gaston Boulevard all day. Do you need this?"

"Come on, let's get you something from the fridge." Soledad lays a softer hand on the back of Lourdes's neck. "Your mother's not going anywhere. Your sister says there's at least two more hours of oxygen in her tank. We can wait her out again."

Her aunt trudges into the kitchen ahead of Lourdes and flicks on the lights, the 60-watt gleam in the middle of the night bouncing off the newly waxed linoleum floors and wiped-down Lowe's cabinets where Georgie's urn now resides.

"Check it out." Lourdes whistles and does the hot-stuff rag with her hand. "Who called the maid in?"

"I made Izzy help me." Soledad opens the refrigerator. "I'm like, 'Your older sister is out all night, trying to clean up the streets. You can get off your rump and clean up the house.' You want a kale shake?"

"I'd like a margarita and a massage. And a *Murder, She Wrote* rerun I can fall asleep in front of."

"How's your big lawyer case going anyway?" Soledad fishes a couple of Pacificos out of the refrigerator and butt-shuts the door with an exhausted slam.

"Like you always say, if it was just like TV, we'd all be Miss Fucking Marple."

"How's my man Terry McKenna treating you? He breaking your shoes?"

"The captain? He's okay."

"That man turned me into an *avowed* lesbian." Soledad pops the lids off both bottles. "He got naked while I was at the Christmas party one year at O'Connor's, and I was, like, 'I'm not looking at nothing like that again.' I started arm-wrestling him and saying the loser has to start putting clothes *on*. So who are you partnered with? "

"An older guy, Kevin Sullivan."

"Sully from Brooklyn South Homicide?"

"You know him?"

"Damn, he was an old-timer when *I* came on the job." Soledad takes a swig, standing up, then hands Lourdes the other beer. "And that was— what?—more than fifteen years ago."

"He's got a lot of history, that's for sure." Lourdes tilts the bottle, not sure how far into it she wants to get. "Kinda hard to figure, though."

"Yeah, I heard he went crazy for a while."

"Really?"

"Yeah, but that could just be jealous talk." Soledad clucks her tongue. "He say anything about your father to you?"

"Why?" Lourdes puts her beer down, suddenly chilled. "Was he one of the detectives on Papi's case?"

"I don't know that specifically, but it was kind of a big deal at the time. Everyone in the Brooklyn detective squads would have talked about it. I wouldn't be surprised if he had a role."

"Shit . . ."

"Look"—Soledad squeezes her arm—"if he hasn't said anything yet, I'm sure you're good."

"Robles *is* a pretty common name." Lourdes turns the bottle around, trying to reassure herself. "He might not have made the connection."

"Sure."

"But I'd hate to think he was one of the people who broke the door down that night and . . ."

They both stop talking at the same time. Both still thinking about the night ESU came with a battering ram to take the door at the old apartment at the Whitman Houses. With a warrant to arrest Raffi Robles for second-degree murder. The so-called community leader who started off as a crusader against the dealers who sold his first-born Georgie the heroin that killed him and then turned out to be a dealer himself. Almost twenty-five years ago now. Soledad happened to be staying in the apartment that night. Taken in by her crazy older sister and her family because her own mother, Lourdes's *abuela*, had kicked her out of the apartment for bringing girls home in the middle of the school day. At least two dozen officers came flooding in wearing Kevlar vests and helmets with visors, aiming high-powered rifles and screaming, "Hands where I can see them!" and "Get the fuck down!"

Lourdes, eight years old at the time, came out of the bedroom that she shared with Izzy to find Mami howling inconsolably in Soledad's arms and Papi spread-eagled on the floor with an officer's boot on his neck and a muzzle in his ear.

For some reason, the sergeant on the scene, maybe trying to keep the kids cool, had turned to Lourdes and asked, "So, little girl, what do you want to do when you grow up?"

Lourdes looked at the guns, her father on the floor, and said: "I wanna be a cop."

"Anyway, it was a long time ago." Lourdes starts picking the label off the bottle.

"True that." Her aunt sits heavily at the breakfast table by the window overlooking Forty-Fifth Street. "You'd let me know if anybody was giving you a hard time, right?"

"You've done enough for me, mi tia. Don't you think a big girl should make her own way in this department?"

They haven't talked about it much directly, but Lourdes knows Soledad went out on a limb to get her beloved niece back to the seven-eight squad. Which cost her dearly in terms of accrued credits she was saving up at the favor bank for a move of her own.

"Still a man's world, *chiquita*, till you prove yourself," Soledad says. "And you've already got enough baggage."

"I'm managing."

"What's the problem now?" Soledad flares her nostrils, picking up the stink of an issue right away. "Am I gonna have to arm wrestle Terry Mac in the nude again?"

"No, it's not him. Feds are nosing around. No one knows why."

"Uh-oh."

"You saw how they took charge of the vehicle at the auto yard in Queens?" Lourdes allows herself a slightly longer sip off the beer. "Lately they've been skulking around some of the other sets we've been on too. The vic was suing the FBI when he was killed and his widow thinks the Bureau was tapping the phones and reading the emails when it happened. And meantime, the FBI is pissed because we forced them to share a witness."

"Ay-yi-yi . . ." Soledad throws her head back. "You letting Sully take most of the heat?"

"He's *making* some of that heat himself. But that's all right. He's a damn good cop."

"My advice? Stick to your business and put your head down."

"That's what everyone keeps telling me." Lourdes sits across from her, scowling. "But I got in trouble for keeping my mouth shut in the first place while Heinz was blowing himself up. And number two: look who's talking about putting her head down? Soon as you were out of the academy, you were taking guns off the street . . ."

"I'm a stud, honey." Soledad grabs Lourdes by both cheeks. "I had a face like yours, I'd never had to work that hard. Do you need your fat old tia to get you out of a trick bag?"

"No way." Lourdes rubs the sides of her face as Soledad lets go. "You're not using up another favor for me."

Knowing damn well that Soledad getting deeper into her niece's mess won't help anyway.

"Let me tell you something, baby girl," Soledad says. "You come a long way back. The Erik Heinzes and Kevin Sullivans of the world can afford to make mistakes because they got bosses who look like them looking out for them. You have a brother who OD'd, a mother who won't come out of the bathroom, a sister who thinks she's going to marry A-Rod, and a father doing life in state prison."

"I know . . ."

"Just the fact that you're working a regular job and not going into rehab makes you a superstar." Soledad raps her knuckles on the table for emphasis. "*Escúchame*, baby. I'm telling you straight. You don't have to prove nothing to nobody. Surviving is enough. Don't put yourself on the line. I don't want to end up having to pry *you* out of the bathroom."

"Yeah, like that's really going to happen . . ."

Her aunt's eyes stray over her shoulder. Lourdes turns and sees Mami in the doorway, stooped over with rattails of gray and red hair, a cannula up her nose connected to the oxygen tank at her side, and the cigarette burned down to the filter in her right hand.

"I decided to come out on my own," she rasps.

"Great." Lourdes looks at Soledad, as if to say, *How did I come from this?* "What got you out?"

"Your sister just asked me if it was okay to use your picture in her Match.com profile. I figured someone ought to let you know."

24

"Spread your fingers," Ben says. *"Wider."*

Natty leans against the ropes in the boxing ring as Ben starts to wrap the red fabric around his hands. He hesitates when he gets a close look at Natty's knuckles.

"Jesus," he says. "You got scar tissue on these. This all from the bar fight with the firemen?"

"No, it's older." Natty starts to close his fists and pull them back, embarrassed. "Listen, Ben, I should be able to do this myself."

"Shut up." Ben holds his wrist firmly. "Let me help you. Okay? Put your hand flat, like I showed you."

Ben, wearing black Nike workout pants with a white stripe and a red-and-white Everlast muscle shirt, furrows his brow as Natty gives him the left hand back, palm-down, arm still sore as Ben weaves the doubled-up fabric delicately over the knuckles. He waits for Ben to repeat his father's "you don't have to do this," knowing the injury from the other night can't have healed completely. But Ben just keeps wrapping and humming "Finiculi, Finiculà" as if he never noticed the sling Natty was wearing before.

It's an hour after work, sunset glaring through the windows of Landau's Gym under the Manhattan Bridge, slants of amber light and shadows crossing the half dozen rings being used by ghetto contenders, Wall Street traders trying to get their macho on, fierce female kickboxers, two large Orthodox Jews throwing bombs at each other with beards and fringes of tzitzis flying under their t-shirts, and a pair of gimpy professional wrestlers stuffed into spandex singlets and moving between the ropes gingerly like aging Broadway showgirls as they practice their theatrical violence.

Ben paid the $60 entry fee to get Natty into the gym, a smelly, acne-floored old pugilists' emporium where they used to go when Natty was attending a school with no contact sports. With his two preadolescent daughters already hating on him, Ben relished the chance to impart the sweet science. Stick and move. Keep your elbows down and your guard up. Cut the ring off. Mind your footwork. Don't present too much of a target.

"Madonna." Ben gives a little laugh. "You got piano player hands, like your dad."

"I thought you said it's not what you got, it's what you do with it." Natty flexes his left hand into a fist, smiling through the pain shooting up his arm.

"You need big gorilla mitts like I have." Ben shows his palms. "But at least you got hair on your knuckles. Guys like us never have to worry about anyone saying we have girly hands."

Natty can't remember his father ever setting foot in Landau's. After the schoolyard brawl with Stephen Carbone, he started training for the Golden Gloves with Ben on Saturday mornings while his afternoons with Dad became more strained and obligatory: homework sessions, aborted guitar lessons, and the occasional leisurely drive upstate, where they found they had less and less to say to each other. Especially after Natty realized the old man defended cop killers. Every mile marker on the highway a reminder of how he wanted to distance himself.

"This may feel a little tight at first." Ben brings the wrap under Natty's palm. "But at least it'll keep you from injuring yourself again. I-ight?"

Natty nods, watching one of the pro wrestlers use the ropes to climb atop a turnbuckle in the corner and perch there like a mangy overstuffed jungle cat. On a signal, he flings himself down toward his opponent, who neatly sidesteps him at the last split second. Let the bodies hit the floor. The resounding boom makes Natty flinch, like a mortar round hitting.

Then the fallen wrestler gets up, fist-bumps his partner, and starts to practice the move again. All for show.

"You should get back into coming here," Ben says, threading the wrap between Natty's fingers. "You could use an outlet. Keep you out of bar fights."

"Word."

By any sane standard, Natty shouldn't even be trying to lift the arm. But the thirteen-year-old is still part of him, desperate to show Ben there's no quit in him.

"So how's the case?" Ben asks.

"Which one?"

The more walrus-like of the two wrestlers tries a flying dropkick on his opponent, and his heavy form slams the canvas as he misses and a bell rings to signal a break between rounds.

"Uh, Ibrahim, *the mailman*. You working on some other multimillion-dollar tort claim without telling me? You came in late this morning and were out for a long lunch yesterday." Ben draws the fabric over the webbing where Natty had found the probie's tooth lodged. "What's doing?"

"Just following up on a couple of things Dad was looking into."

"Could you be any more vague, counselor?"

Go slowly here. Natty keeps thinking he should lay the cards out and tell Ben about his meetings with MG and the FBI agent, but somehow he hasn't done it yet.

"You know, just trying to read the notes Dad left." Natty tries to make a fist with his right hand. "And following up on the Freedom of Information Act requests that he filed."

Maybe there's a simple explanation. His first reaction could be right. This could be a setup. It's in the government's interest to undercut Ben when he's taking over a twelve-million-dollar case. The documents in the conference room looked authentic. But so had the evidence of WMDs.

"Find anything we can use?" Ben finishes the wrap, knitting Natty's bones and sinews together like a cat's cradle.

"Getting there." Natty cocks back his fist. "May take some time to develop."

"Time is what we don't have. Along with money and resources. I meant to tell you that I just spoke to Judge Gomez's clerk about extending the period for discovery since the government's been dragging their feet about declassifying some of these files."

"And?"

"The judge won't give us any rhythm. The motion for summary judgment hearing is scheduled for Wednesday next week."

"Are you fucking with me, Ben? We only just got this case."

"Tell me about it." Ben picks up one of the sixteen-ounce boxing gloves lying at his feet. "I'm still trying to get the timeline and narrative of events memorized. The upside is that the judge is allowing us to put this Agent Paul Kirkpatrick on the stand so we can grill him about information your father wasn't given access to in discovery. The downside is we need more heavy artillery to hit him with."

"You think if I found anything relevant, I wouldn't tell you right away?"

Ben holds the left glove open for Natty to slide his hand in. *"Push,"* he says. "We're not playing patty-cake."

Worn old leather, clammy with other fighters' sweat, encloses itself around his hand. Snug and comfortable. This is how it's supposed to be. There's no way that any of the things they were saying about Ben can be true. The man is family, Natty thinks. One of the basic building blocks of your life. As familiar as your first blanket. You could spell his name before you could recite the alphabet. He put you on his shoulders to watch the Thanksgiving Day Parade while your own father was chasing after one of those foster kids with scrambled eggs for brains who'd gotten lost in the crowd. When you learned to walk like a man, it was Ben's stride you were imitating.

"We need specific details to pin him down," Ben says. "Times, dates, inconsistencies . . ."

"I'm working on it, boss."

"Pick up the pace. We gotta get up to speed on this rat, Wally al-Masri, who worked at the post office with Ibrahim."

"Do we know if he was working off charges of his own when he started informing?"

"That's what I need you to help find out. Get your act together, Natty Dread. What are you doing, sitting around eating bonbons?"

He fastens the Velcro tab on Natty's glove and gives it a savage testing tug. Another lightning bolt of pain shoots up Natty's arm and into his head, as he pictures the Velcro sneaker at the top of the stairs.

"Barely a week to reinvent the wheel. I can see why no one's ever won a case like this before." Ben fakes a punch to Natty's jaw. "Come on. Let's start moving. All this agita is starting to get to me."

Natty tries to force a smile as he watches Ben reach down and don a pair of Everlast practice pads that were lying on the canvas. The gloves on his hands suddenly feel heavy and stiff, not fitting quite as easily as they did a few seconds ago. He'd looked up two of the cases Bryce showed him before coming to the gym. Drug trials in Newark and Bridgeport, where Ben had clients. And witnesses happened to be killed before testifying. But that was the game. If you play, you can lose.

"Show me what you got, champ." Ben holds the pads up. "Let's see if you remember anything I taught you."

"I'm warning you, I'm rusty." Natty starts to move around the ring, front foot, back foot. "Don't expect too much."

"Close your mouth and open your eyes. Jab, jab, jab. *Cross.*"

Natty plants himself and throws the combo, the punches coming straight from the shoulder and delivering a machine-gun *rat-a-tat* as they land, his left elbow screaming bloody murder every time he extends it. Referred pain goes around his body like gossip.

"You call those punches?" Ben rubs the pads together and holds them up again. "You hit like my aunt Elena's cat after they cut his balls off."

"I've mostly been doing BJJ in Florida."

"BJJ? Blow Jobs for Jews?"

"Brazilian jujitsu, boss."

Ben flares out bull nostrils as he lowers his head. "You're in Brooklyn now, son. Get your hands up."

Natty raises his gloves in front of his chin as he warily circles Ben. Four cases, four jurisdictions. Two confirmed, two more to check.

"Look down at your feet," Ben says, following him around the ring. "Why are you so squared off? How're you going to keep your balance with that stance? That how I taught you to stand?"

He pops Natty on both shoulders with the pads, knocking him back a foot and a half.

"Establish your base, Gentleman Jim." He swings a mitt at Natty's chin. "*Fortissimo.* Use the body jab to set up the left hook. Remember that rope-a-dope trick I showed you?"

"Which one?"

"Stand your ground but lean forward a little with your upper body." He holds the pads up like heart defibrillators. "Remember: Your opponent cannot afford to look at where your feet are. If he miscalculates when he lunges, he's going to be off-balance and you can just . . ."

The mitt swats Natty hard on the cheek, distracting him from the pain in his arm temporarily. His back grazes the ropes as he rears back. Don't present a full target. Show him the false lead. Use your head. Throw the fake. Make him come to you this time.

"So who's MG?" Natty turns sideways.

"Who?"

"You were asking what I found in Dad's file cabinets. I saw there was an old picture and a letter from some woman named MG. Sounded like she knew Dad pretty well."

The pads lower an inch and a half, revealing remote contempt in Ben's eyes and a defiant thrusting chin.

"Marygrace Kelly," he says. "I called her Machine Gun Kelly. Flat-faced Irish cunt."

"Whoa . . ."

Of course, he's heard Ben be crude before, but "cunt" is new.

"Was this an old letter?" Ben raises the pads again, angling them more like gladiator shields.

"I don't know." Natty feints with his right. "I'd guess it was from within the last couple of years."

"What did it say?"

"Nothing much. 'Thinking of you, thinking of old times.' That kind of thing."

He watches how Ben moves with him, keeping the pads up defensively. Nothing's been proven, Natty reminds himself. Criminals killed each other all the time. Just like governments lied all the time.

"She talk about any of your father's cases?" Ben asks.

"Not directly. She said something about how they'd come a long way from where they'd started. Who is she?"

"Prissy little mother superior–type I knew from the DA's office. She's with the U.S. attorney now, civil division."

"She involved with the mailman case?"

"Maybe not officially, but—come on—these people all work together. The U.S. attorney's office is part of the Justice Department."

"But Dad stayed friends with her?"

The question slows Ben more than any of the punches so far. His guard comes down a little more, and his back foot drags.

"Your father had certain feelings that may have clouded his judgment," he says, squaring up more evenly. "I always tried to tell him that woman was no friend of ours."

" 'Friend of ours'?"

"Yeah, what's so funny?"

"Just that expression. You always told me, when somebody was a 'friend of mine,' they were a real friend. If it was a 'friend of ours,' they were organized crime."

"Don't be stupid." He swats Natty on the bad arm. "Marygrace Kelly is the enemy."

The pain and sharpness of the words land with equal force, a flash-bang that puts him right back to the Knight of Columbus Hall and the first body shot that cracked his ribs.

"Hey . . ." He sucks wind. "Easy on that wing, dude."

"No mercy, Natty Dread. You gotta play hurt sometimes."

Ben starts to move in on him more aggressively, his face grinning between the red vinyl pads. Ben Grimm. Somehow he seems even more imposing and muscle-upholstered in his sixties. One of those rare men who become harder and more implacable with age. Natty wonders if he's gone in for TRT—testosterone replacement therapy—like some of the old juicers from his Florida gym. Crusty sons of bitches who spent all their time getting pumped up by their trainers and chasing twenty-nine-year-old blondes with $4,000 boobs and $100 tans.

"I'd like to see that letter." Ben pushes Natty toward the corner.

"I threw it away."

"You threw it away?"

"I didn't want Mom to see it." Natty hunches his shoulders, impressed by the agility of his own lie. "I thought it might hurt her."

The pad comes flying at Natty's bad arm again and he dances back to avoid it.

"You shouldn't have thrown that letter away without showing it to me," Ben says, no longer smiling.

"I had no idea it was relevant. It just seemed like she was an old girl-friend and I didn't want Mom to find it, feel hurt."

"You still should have shown it to me. That nice old girlfriend might have been trying to hurt your father's case. And maybe your father while she was at it."

"Seriously?"

Natty tries to drive Ben back with two right hooks and a left upper-cut that costs something just to throw, the impact of his gloves hitting the pads like artillery shells echoing across the gym floor while moving Ben less than six inches.

"I don't know why else she would have been reaching out to him after all these years, unless it was about the mailman case." Ben resets his stance. "I find that very suspicious."

Marygrace was right; she was hardly your typical honeypot. She seemed more like someone who, given a couple of extra twists in her life, could have wound up working in a high school guidance counselor's office, making young men feel bad about themselves. When Dad razzed his mother about other women he could have had in his life, it was usually someone with a little more *flava:* Halle Berry, Chaka Khan, and, maybe just to be hip, Queen Bey herself.

"Think about it," Ben says. "Maybe your father wasn't just out to move the car the night he got shot. Maybe he was meeting someone."

"You think some dowdy federal prosecutor lured him into a hit?" Natty dances out of the corner, starting to feel the spring in his legs. "Does that really seem likely?"

"When did I say she was dowdy?"

"Just the way you were talking about her. You called her flat-faced."

Ben swings the left pad at Natty's face. Natty ducks and bobs up. The right pad clubs him on the ear, temporarily deafening him and mak-ing him wobble like a top losing centrifugal force.

"See what you did?" Ben stands back, beaming. "You went for the fake and you paid for it. Don't get played for a sucker."

"Now you tell me."

Natty grabs onto the top rope, trying to steady himself as his knees go rubbery.

"You sure you didn't meet with her?" Beads glisten on Ben's scalp. "Like at the funeral."

"Not that I remember." Natty hangs on, trying to blink away the bursting stars. "But I don't remember everyone I met."

"You'll tell me if you hear from her again. Right?"

"Of course. Whose side do you think I'm on?"

He makes a beckoning gesture for Ben to raise the pads again. But something has changed. One ear is still ringing and the sound in the other is muffled like another stun grenade just went off close by. His eyes have trouble focusing, distracted by floaters and flashes. The force of the blow was not what he'd expected. There was nothing instructive in it. It was meant to force him into submission, and put an end to questions like the one he'd just asked.

"Three jabs and the hook," Ben commands. "And don't crouch, like you're anticipating a takedown. This isn't high school wresting."

On a surge of adrenaline, Natty rapid-fires the punches, the left arm killing him, but each burst of pain containing a hidden reward. You can do this. You're the man now. His fists are hitting Ben's pads more solidly, driving him back a step with each blow.

"Come on. Bring it. Right-left, right-left, right-left, right-left. High-low-high. Work the body. Start slipping to the outside. And don't pick up your fucking elbow."

Natty unloads full force, shoulders like pistons, fury building up internal combustion, punching straight from the chest now, elbows down, every fist into pad a shot of dopamine into his brain. A guttural burr starts at the back of his throat and rises to a roar as he pours it on, ignoring the sensation of his left arm getting chainsawed off as he drives Ben back across the ring, forcing him to keep the pads up in front of his face, until he's in the opposite corner, breathing hard and covering up, his vulnerability making Natty more avid by the second.

"Natty, okay . . ."

Three times with the jab, then the uppercut, the undercut, the cross, and a satisfying right hook that Ben barely manages to deflect from breaking *his* ribs this time.

"I said 'okay,' champ. The bell rang."

"Hooah." Mighty Natty Dread rests, his bad arm limp at his side, the credit balance of agony he's built up overwhelming his system, promising consequences for hours to come. Ben is leaning against the ropes, still trying to catch his breath. Vulnerable for once. All the other fighters in the gym are staring, as if wondering why he's been beating up on a man old enough to be his father.

"Nice job." Ben says, gasping as Natty starts to back away. "Now get back to work and find us something for the hearing."

"I will."

Natty drops his hands and looks around for a water bottle. Then Ben slams a pad into his solar plexus, doubling him over.

"And don't let your guard down, okay?" Ben bends down to look Natty in the face. *"Minchia*, didn't I teach you anything?"

25

Lourdes had never noticed the place Sully picked for their dinner break: a narrow doorway between a charcuterie and a nail salon reeking of acetone four blocks from the precinct and three blocks from the Barclay Center. But as soon as she steps through the door, it's a time and space warp back to Havana before the Revolution, with menacing undertones of the house she just escaped from. There are brightly painted royal palms and rose-throated parrots on the walls, white cloths and red napkins on the tables, but the lusty woman singing over the big band on the stereo almost made her lose her appetite. For a few seconds, she thinks it's La Lupe, belting one of those hysterical boleros that Mami tried to record herself at the failed Fania audition. "I've got the devil in my body!" But then she hears the cry of *"Azucar!"* and relaxes, realizing it's Celia Cruz.

"Por favor." Sully looks up at a grave-faced waiter in a little white jacket and black bow tie. "Un lechon asado, un arroz con pollo, un Moros y Cristianos, plantanos maduros, dos aguas, dos café con leches."

The waiter looks at his pad, bows, and walks stiff-legged past the bartender polishing glasses and pictures of Lucy and Desi between bottles of Bacardi and Havana Club rum on the shelves toward the turret-like kitchen where garlicky clouds of yucca and plantains are drifting out.

"Your accent's not bad." Lourdes shakes out her napkin. "Where'd you pick it up?"

"My wife was Cuban." He looks down at his iPhone.

"How long were you married?" she asks, noting the past tense and the ring he's still wearing.

"We are not talking about this," he mutters, eyes on the screen as he tucks his orange-and-gray striped tie between the buttons of a checked blue-and-white shirt. "Do you read me?"

She studies the clash of his colors, thinking it had probably been years since a woman had been anywhere near his closet. Even a straight son, if he was still alive, would have saved the old man from some of these eye-watering selections.

"By the way, TARU finally got back to us about trying to match cell phone numbers within the radius of the Dresden and Science crime scenes," he says.

"And?"

"A palpable hit, m'lady. A 347 number."

"Lemme guess: burner cell."

"*Naturally*. So there's no name to go with it. But the good news is that the same number that was making calls going down Fifth Street from the park right after Dresden got shot was also making calls close to where Science got shot, going down Degraw and over on Bond."

"One call leading away from each crime scene?" Lourdes raises her eyebrows and spreads a napkin on her lap.

"Correct: multiple calls in rapid succession in each case, less than twenty seconds in duration. Two calls after Dresden, three calls after Science. All outgoing to other no-name cells."

"So it could be the shooter making calls after each homicide to say it's done?"

"That would be one theory. But the bad news is the pings stop as soon as the phone reaches the Gowanus Canal. No more calls after that."

"He tossed the phone in the water," Lourdes says.

"And probably tossed the gun in it too." Sullivan nods. "Ballistics confirms it was the same .45 in both homicides."

That's the end of that. No one is diving into the Gowanus to retrieve a body or a gun, unless it's the Toxic Avenger. The canal is a superfund site, one of the most polluted bodies of water in the United States, and arguably one of the last places in the world where something can be truly and irretrievably lost. More than a hundred years of runoff from the factories, tanneries, and oil depots along the banks had filled the soup with cement mercury, sulfur, battery acid, *E. coli*, gonorrhea, and various other volatile organic compounds that made the surface bubble and stink like a witches' brew. It was said by Harbor Patrol that if your best friend fell in, you'd pay your condolences, tip your hat, and walk away.

"Anyway, dead end." Sullivan tucks a napkin into his collar. "Let's eat and have another think."

The waiter brings their food and backs off quickly.

"Okay," Lourdes says, pouring on the hot sauce. "So what's Coney Island?"

Sullivan unfurls his silverware. "It's where the rides are."

"When you were getting into it with Benny G. at his office, you said 'Coney Island,' and he looked at you like you'd just shown him naked pictures of his children."

"Did he?"

"All right," she says. "Why you the one acting mad grimy now?"

"It's an old story, probably nothing to do with anything going on now."

"But—"

"But . . ."

Sullivan tucks in the corners of his eyes and looks away. For a half second, she can see what he must have been like as a young cop. Angry and immovable, already pockmarked but not quite permanently molded by the shape of his accumulated sadness.

"Summer of '92." He sighs, unfolding just a little. "Neptune Avenue. I was working out of the six-oh detective squad. We caught a murder with a pregnant seventeen-year-old found in a Dumpster outside Kennedy Fried Chicken. Grimaldi was the prosecutor for the Brooklyn DA's office."

"And?"

"He got a conviction on a semi-retarded handyman who was living at a rooming house around the corner and violating the terms of his probation for showing his little wonder to a bunch of day campers at Astroland."

"And you had a problem with Benny G. because . . . ?"

"I had a problem with Benny G. because I found two witnesses who put the handyman at a job site in Mount Vernon the night the girl disappeared." He busies himself dissecting his meat. "I gave the names and phone numbers to Grimaldi personally. But the defense never called them at trial."

"You think Benny G. didn't turn them over?"

"I *know* he didn't." His cheeks start to turn rosy. "Defense counsel wasn't a hamburger. And the witnesses were homeowners from Westchester. You'd have to be dumb as a catfish not to put alibis like that on the stand if you have them. It was exculpatory Brady material, pure and simple. And he buried it."

"I assume you didn't bring it up either." Lourdes lowers her face toward the steaming chicken and rice platter.

"*That's not my yob, man.*" Sullivan holds his knife up, knowing she'll let the old-school Freddie Prinze bit slide. "But I'll tell you something for nothing. That wasn't the only problem. Grimaldi had one eyewitness who claimed to see the handyman putting the body in the Dumpster. A crack whore called herself Chardonnay."

"Yeah, okay." Lourdes shrugs. "Who else do you find hanging around crime scenes? A bunch of after-school reading specialists?"

"Thing is, I asked around. Turns out Benny G. used her as a sole witness in at least three other cases. In one, she saw a murder under a streetlight on Utica Avenue that hadn't worked in a year. In the other, she supposedly followed a shooter home after she saw him stab another prostitute. And in a third, she supposedly saw a murder through a keyhole in a closet that turned out not to have one."

"But no one said anything?" Lourdes closes one eye.

"It was the Wild West Days." Sullivan keeps chewing and carving dutifully. "Twenty-two hundred murders a year. We were all just trying to hold the line. But Benny G. was something else."

"Don't hold back on me now, Papi." She grazes his shoe as she crosses her legs under the table. "We've come this far."

Sullivan puts down his knife and fork and wipes his mouth, as if preparing to make a formal declaration. A wave of heat hits her as the kitchen door opens behind him and a busboy comes out with a stack of clean plates.

"My problem with Benny G. is that he's all about winning, no matter what," Sullivan says. "I didn't trust him then and I don't trust him now."

"You think he's dirty?"

"If he is, he comes by it honestly." His hooded eyes follow the busboy as he lowers his voice. "His father was one of the dirtiest cops ever to walk a beat in Brooklyn."

"You knew him?"

"I knew *of* him. He was at least five years gone by the time I got on the job. But all the old-timers still remembered Two Bag Charlie from the seven-seven."

"Why'd they call him that?"

"Because he thought if he didn't have two garbage bags full of cash at the end of every week, someone was cheating him. He was part of the Frito Bandito Squad in Bed-Stuy. They wore bandit masks to rob the neighborhood drug dealers when they were off duty."

"Get out of town."

"Oh yeah, he was kicking it old-school. This was pre-Knapp, pre-Serpico days, when there was still a lot of that going around. But Two Bag Charlie was above and beyond in every category. He borrowed axes and ladders from the local firehouse so he could break into drug dealers' apartments. And if one of them had the nerve to call in the robbery, he'd show up as one of the responding officers so he could steal whatever he missed the first time."

"Wow, that's bold."

"Personally, Robles, I don't hate that many people. But Two Bag Charlie was the kind of cop who wouldn't work with an honest cop. Because he couldn't trust a man who didn't steal. Word was, Charlie Grimaldi let his first partner die after getting shot in the street because he thought the guy might have been talking to IAB."

"So you're thinking 'like father, like son'?"

"Let's just say I got my eye on him. Apple and the tree, you know."

Lourdes feels capsaicin sweat from her hot sauce popping beads from the top of her head and she wonders if there's a discreet way to dab it with her napkin after she's already used it to wipe her lips.

"Well, we can't try everybody for the sins of the father." She drinks a long sip of water. "Can we?"

"Who said we were?" Sullivan cuts into his meat. "Anyway, what were we talking about?"

"The cell phone and the gun disappearing."

"Yes, now I remember why we changed the subject."

He looks up and nods as the waiter brings a heaping platter of sweet fried plantains.

"I had an idea," says Lourdes. "You said there was a series of short calls made by someone going down Fifth Street, away from the park, right after the shooting and then heading toward the canal on Bond Street. Calls were close together."

"Yeah." Sullivan puts down his fork and picks up his iPhone, to double-check. "Less than ten seconds between each call. Like the signal kept dropping and they kept calling back. But the locations indicate they were moving quickly. Like they were driving away."

"*Right.*" Lourdes snaps her fingers, realizing what's she's been tripping on. "But you said 'away from the park' on Fifth and toward the Gowanus on Bond. That's the wrong way on both streets. And it sounds like they're covering too much distance too quickly for the calls to have been made by someone on foot."

"And even Shawn Davidson wouldn't be stupid enough to get caught driving the wrong way on a one-way street after shooting Dresden and spreading around the wrong shell casings." Sullivan nods, following her lead. "It could have been someone else using another mode of transportation to get away from the scene."

"I'm thinking about a bicycle," Lourdes says. "Aren't you?"

"We're going to make a detective out of you yet, Robles. Have a couple of plantains as a reward." He pushes the platter at her.

"You evil old man." She turns away in her chair, only half resisting. "You know I'm supposed to be a diet."

"As if you could be more perfect than you are."

26

A man on a walker starts angling toward Natty in the housing project courtyard. The clank of the aluminum frame and the squeak of rubber wheels audible even before the crooked figure rounds the blue benches in the middle of the Cypress Hills Houses in East New York. He's rolling a hair too fast for a normal cripple as the sun goes down and the government-quality floodlights flicker on. Coming straight at Natty, with what looks like increasingly hostile intent. With each clank, Natty finds himself battling memories of Bravo company losing two men to a guy on crutches who gimped up wearing a suicide vest beneath his dishdasha.

Natty freezes as he sees the man coming toward him is dark, thirtyish, with big shoulders. Too young and buff to be on a walker. Must be a setup. An ambush. Unless it isn't. Maybe the safest thing would be to charge the target, tackle him and pin his arms to his sides before he can hit a detonator. Or do nothing. Natty turns sideways, as the man starts to pass, not sure whether to run or attack.

But then the dude lowers his eyes as he wheels past, and Natty recognizes that particular thickening of the air that comes with shame, anger, and despair. My brother. Another wrong place wrong time story. A young man turned into an old man by a bullet in the back.

It's finally a decently warm spring night. Little kids are outside playing before dinner. They chase each other around an oxidized green metal pole, in the middle of a circumference of asphalt, which might have once been a tetherball court. Gap-toothed girls in pigtails trip across faded hopscotch squares that have probably been there since Jews lived in the projects. Boys just slightly taller than fire hydrants try to heave basketballs up at crooked orange hoops without nets. Middle-aged church people wearing bright hues of yellow, red, and green are having loud impromptu community board meetings around the concrete chessboards.

Natty watches the guy on the walker go up a ramp into the seven-story buildings that surround the courtyard, like filing cabinets for poor people. Stop being such a fucking pussy. Nothing wrong with you, outwardly. So move already. You know what you came here to do.

His records search from earlier in the day found Kenneth Holloway's family listed as living on the sixth floor of the building facing Fountain Avenue, where a public library branch used to be. Natty goes up and gives a curt nod to a bunch of teenagers clustered around the entrance, the girls slightly larger and scarier than the boys, eye-fucking him on the way in with his file folder.

"Don't you be looking at me like that, officer," one of them says, solid as a hockey goaltender in a bright-yellow hoodie as she raises her arms, inviting him to step to it. "I ain't doing shit."

"Have a nice night, guys."

"Fuckin' faggot" and kissing noises trail him into a hallway that looks like 1955: mustard-colored tile walls and metro-blue doors. Naturally, the elevators are all out of service. It's a Housing Authority building: the stairwell reverberant with ghosts of pre–World's Fair NYC; five generations' graffiti faintly visible under layers of white paint applied without primer; vague odors of paraffin, incense, oil soap, and Chinese food; the garage opera they used to call doo-wop floating down from the upper floors. "Heavenly shades of night are falling . . ."

He pauses on the landing, slightly winded, surprised at the challenge to his endurance. He used to be able to hump a hundred pounds in his pack in triple-digit desert heat easily. But at the gym, he was panting even before Ben caught him in the midsection. Something about civilian life has softened him up too much.

He pushes open the fire door and looks down the hallway. His eyes see cinder-block walls, blue doors, a halo from a bare bulb lighting the evening just outside the barred windows at the end of the corridor. But his mind is insisting that there's a blazing sun overhead, a row of mud-brick villas on either side of him, dust in the street, and a smell of burning shit from the waste pits in the wind.

He forces himself to start moving down the hall, hoping the flashback will fade the way it usually does. He runs the mantra: Here now, not there. Now, not then. The sound behind the first door is laughter from an *Everybody Hates Chris* rerun, not an imam chanting the Koran. The welcome mat in front of the door says "Come Back With A Warrant," not anything in Arabic. There's no grit from a sandstorm in his nose, no insane radio monkey chatter in his ears, no one watching him through the peepholes with an IED trigger in hand. Your balls are hanging loose and free, not sweat-stuck to your thighs from cramped hours riding in the Humvee, watching both sides of the road for hajjis with RPGs, the grenades rotating in slow motion as they come at you so you can see their indentations as plainly as the seams of a football.

Irie, Natty Dread. It's all good. You know where you are. In a housing project hallway, looking for a potential witness in your father's case, not searching for an HVT in Sadr City. No reason for your eyes to be burning or your hamstrings to be getting wound up like ropes on winches.

He presses the button for 6C twice and stands back from the door with a mild unthreatening smile of someone getting a photo taken for a driver's license. The TV that had been blaring inside gets turned down and voices go back and forth: a young woman sounding soft and inquisitive, an older man mean and intransigent. Footsteps pad up to the door, a rusty cover swings back from the peephole, and chains rattle tentatively.

"Hello?" the woman's voice says.

"Good evening, I'm sorry to show up unannounced. My name is Nathaniel Dresden." He digs a business card out of his pocket and holds it up so that his index finger covers his old job title at the prosecutor's office in Florida. "I'm a private attorney."

"How can I help you?"

"I was hoping I could come in and talk to someone about Kenneth Holloway."

"What he say?" The man has joined the woman behind the door, his voice gruff with phlegm, alcohol, and ragged suspicion.

"Sir, I said it's about Kenneth Holloway. My father, David, was his lawyer. I won't take much of your time, I promise."

There's fierce whispering behind the door, a sound like animal nails scrabbling on a wood floor, and then the chain jangles more deliberately.

A bolt shoots back and as the door opens, Natty finds himself turning sideways like he's part of a stack again.

A big-boned tan-brown woman wearing an orange headwrap, a denim workshirt, and blue jeans stands in the foyer with tired eyes under plush satiny lids.

A few feet behind her, a bent older man, darker and thinner, leans on a cane, an old Pittsburgh Pirates cap askew on an oblong head with a patchy graying riverboat-gambler's mustache and black-framed glasses with lenses so thick and poorly made that his eyes appear to be of radically different sizes.

"Kenneth was my younger brother." The woman stands aside, letting Natty pass. "This is our stepfather, Albert." She nods at the man behind her. "He was with Kenny when he got shot."

"Thank you for allowing me in." Natty says as she closes the door behind him and puts the chain back on. "I would have called ahead if I had a number."

"Who the fuck are you again?" The stepfather hobbles forward on the cane, courtly and menacing.

He is one of those ropy, eternally slender men of indeterminate age. A face and body ravaged by either hard work or hard drugs, or maybe both. He could just as easily be sixty-five as forty-five. His eyes stare expressionlessly and his lips tremble slightly, as if he's constantly on the verge of being overcome with violent emotion. Natty tries to put him at ease with a bigger smile. *My man. I understand more than you know.*

"My father was helping Kenneth with his state case," Natty begins. "I just had a couple of questions about that."

"I heard about what happened to your father." She touches his arm gently. "I'm Evening Empress Starshine, by the way, but everybody calls me Evie. We're sorry for your loss."

She gestures toward a small living room, cold public housing space warmed by immaculately maintained Goodwill furniture. There are lit candles on every flat surface, their citronella scents mingling with Lemon Pledge; plywood cabinets are painted to look like walnut with polished glass fronts; bright-colored homemade china pieces are carefully arranged inside like they just came out of the potter's kiln. Lego castles and ships sit atop board games in boxes, overseen by tribal masks on the walls;

slightly cheaper versions of his mother's beloved pan-African tchotchkes sit on the end tables; poinsettias and pussy willows rest in black and red ceramic urns. On a TV set, some cable sports channel shows an old game with a group of players in New York Knicks uniforms trying to maintain their dignity against the San Antonio Spurs. And everywhere else that Natty looks, there are photos of the same young man at different stages, presumably Kenny.

Here he is on the coffee table: a toothless terror on a tricycle, the handsome slim-faced young man beaming behind him barely recognizable as Albert, who is staring at Natty with quivering lips. Next to that, a picture of Kenny in a Cypress Hills All-Stars Little League uniform, maybe eleven years old, a lanky kid with an Afro exploding out from under his cap and a promising glimmer in his eyes. But in a photo beside the TV, the glimmer is gone. There's a baby in Kenny's muscular arms, a plump girl showing off a hot-chocolate-brown midriff at his side, and a couple of buddies behind him, upraised fingers splayed in what look to Natty's eye like blatant gang signs.

"I'm sorry about Kenny as well." Natty bows his head, a show of sympathy that seems as phony as "thank you for your service" even as he's doing it.

"You should be." Albert is six inches away, his finger shaking.

"Don't mind him." Evie waves for Natty to have a seat on the beige velour couch. "He hasn't been the same since that day my brother died."

"They shot my son right in front of me." A couple of white flecks of foam appear on Albert's lower lip. "They put a fucking hole in his melon . . ."

"*Eeeveee!*"

A child's voice calls from another room and Evie sags like she just finished one factory shift and heard she had to start another immediately. "That's Kenny's son, Tyrion," she says, as Albert sits down in a ragged old leather Barcalounger that looks like it was retrieved from a street corner and then carefully conditioned with linseed oil.

"Tyrion?"

"My brother loved *Game of Thrones*, so he named his child after the dwarf," she sighs. "I tried to tell him most don't stay that small forever, but Kenny was kind of hardheaded. His son's the same."

"Kenny was my son. *My* son." Albert strikes his chest with his fist. "Can't nobody tell me otherwise. I don't care about no DNA."

"Albert wasn't my brother's biological father." Evie shakes her head at Natty. "But he raised Kenny like his own."

"That was the child that *I* raised," Albert says, big eye and little eye blinking behind his glasses. "My son was lost to me. Then he was found. Then they killed his ass. And someone got to pay."

"Do you mind if I record this?" Natty pulls out his cell phone and starts poking around for the app. "I'm just trying to find out who's responsible for what happened to your son. I think the same person might have had my father murdered."

"I met his mother in the year 1994." Albert tilts his head back, with a slightly more mellow expression, speaking in a more formal voice like a streetwise church deacon. "Kenny was born in the year 1993. I married his mother in the year 1995. And she died in the year 1999. And after that, him and me was like peas in a pod."

"It's true." Evie nods. "Albert was the only father Kenny ever knew. Our so-called real father never gave a damn. Didn't even bother to show up at Mama's funeral. Used our public assistance money to buy himself a brand-new Hyundai. But Albert was just always there. He was very, very close with Kenny. The two of them had dinner together every Sunday night."

"Every damn Sunday," Albert affirms. "No matter what all else that boy was up to. I didn't care if he was running in the streets or shooting dope or robbing banks. I expected him on my doorstep at six o'clock every Sunday night, and he was always on time, and always respectful of his father. Because that's what I was."

"Yes, sir." Natty finally locates the record button and puts the phone on the coffee table in front of Albert.

"That boy never missed our dinner." A tear suddenly streaks down Albert's cheek. "Even when they had him on Rikers. He'd call at six o'clock and just ask me to talk about what we'd be eating if he was there. Roast beef and yellow rice. That was his favorite. And iced tea with five packs of sugar, because he always had a sweet tooth. I loved that child, even when he was doing wrong. Because I was the same when I was his age. I did six years for armed robbery in Attica before I turned my life around. I told him if I can do it, you can."

"Daddy, don't cry." Evie comes over to put an arm around him. "He's in a better place."

"Those low-down dirty lawyers killed him." Albert takes off his glasses. "That's what they did."

"How?" Natty glances up.

"Like you don't know."

Without the lenses, Albert looks like a completely different person. The babbling bespectacled old coot disappears, replaced by a mean and lean Mack Daddy with sculpted cheekbones and a hustler's switchblade glance. Someone you'd want to avoid pissing off if you were thinking of selling numbers or running a rival drug spot across the way.

"For real," Natty says. "What are you talking about?"

Albert takes out a white handkerchief, wipes his eyes, and puts his glasses back on again.

"The police arrested my brother for criminal sale of a controlled substance." Evie pats Albert's arm. "They had him on video making five sales to different undercovers. And it wasn't a first offense."

"And since it was first-degree, he was looking at eight years minimum?" Natty checks the arrest report in the file folder. "Did my father try to get it knocked down?"

"He told Kenny he had to make a deal." Evie lowers her voice.

"My son comes to me for Sunday dinner and says, 'Daddy, what should I do?'" Albert sniffs, trying to hold himself together. "'This lawyer is telling me I gotta snitch to stay out of prison.'"

"My father said he had to become an informant against the dealers he was working with?" Natty nudges the recorder forward.

"That lawyer said no one else was ever going to know." Albert wags his chin, staring ahead blankly again like he's confronting some monster no one else can see. "It was just going to be him, the police, and the prosecutors. They wasn't even gonna make Kenny testify. They were just going to take what he said and use it to arrest his friend Shakneela. And then they was gonna turn Shakneela against Mr. Jamar Mack, who was the big man selling that heroin and Oxycontin and whatever, and then they was probably gonna turn Jamar against his supplier and distributors, and so on . . ."

"Hang on . . ." Natty fingers an earlobe, half distracted. "Why do I know the name—Jamar Mack?"

"Everybody fucking knows Jamar Mack around here," Albert coughs. "But nobody can do anything to him, because they all too scared or too dead to testify."

"And my father encouraged Kenny to take the deal to become a co-operating witness against this Jamar?" Natty checks the recorder, trying to stay on point.

"Mr. David Dresden, Esquire, famous lawyer on the evening news, came to this motherfucking house for our motherfucking Sunday dinner, and he sat right at that goddamn table with my son and me, and he told us 'five years' probation, no mandatory, no Rockefeller time in state prison."

Albert points through half-open double doors into another room, where a heavily lacquered brown dinner table sits surrounded by four old wicker chairs under a yellow Chinese paper lantern.

"And my son said to me, 'Daddy, what do you think?' And I said, 'Son, you got your whole life ahead of you and Mr. Dresden seem like a smart man. You don't want to waste the best years of your life in prison, like I did. You got a little boy of your own. You need to be there for him.'"

"So you told him to take the deal and become a cooperating witness?" Natty says.

"I'm'a have that burden the rest of my life." Albert starts to cry again. "I thought it was the right thing. Kenny said, 'Daddy, I want to start living like you. I want to learn a trade. I want to stop doing what I've been doing in the streets and be there for Tyrion.' And I said, 'Son, that's all right. I wasn't very smart in school. And that's why I got in trouble. But then I got out and I learned to build things. I got into construction and roofing. And I can show you how to do that.' Because that's how it was in the old days with him and me. When he was little, he'd come on jobs with me and be my right hand. He'd take my tools out before I'd even think to ask for that. Those was the happiest days of my life. And I thought it was going to be like that again. My son was lost to me and then he was found. Do you know how I'm saying?"

"I believe that I do," Natty says with a catch in his throat.

He sees himself bringing his father's leather briefcase to the front door. When he was about waist-high to the old man. *Make sure you have all your arguments.*

"A week later, I had Kenny working with me at a jobsite, carrying my fabric and tar bucket, and this fat motherfucker with a do-rag over his face and gloves on his hands rides up to us on Troy Avenue and puts a fucking hole in his head." Tears are running freely and unashamedly down Albert's cheeks now. "I just felt the burn on the back of my neck and I turn around and my son is lying there with a hole you could roll a golf ball through and this fat piece of shit is stuffing a gun back in his pants. I said, 'Oh my God,' and I fell to my knees. It's the middle of the day, this motherfucker is riding away, a lady is screaming, and no one saw nothing."

"The detectives from Brooklyn South Homicide interviewed my father twice but he couldn't give them a good description," Evie says softly, as she rubs Albert's shoulders. "It just happened so fast."

"I know it was Shakneela, the way that sumofabitch be riding."

"Riding what?"

"He was on a bicycle," Albert says. "Yellow ten-speed or something. The police found it two blocks away, but they said they couldn't get any evidence off it. No fingerprints because he was wearing gloves. I'm like, 'Check the seat. What about ass DNA?' But those dumb crackers just laugh in my face."

Natty knuckles the bristles of his chin, trying to picture a fat man on a road bike. "You're sure he was on a bike?"

"Of course, I'm sure," Albert says. "Everybody who was involved with their crew was using no-name cell phones and bikes to distribute the drugs. That way there was no cars or license plates the police could track. I tried to tell those detectives, but they were like, 'Yeah, right.' Because you all are in on it."

"In on what?"

"Selling drugs. My son told me half those motherfuckers worked for the law firm, as paralegals and such."

"You telling me they were selling drugs out of the law firm?"

"Like you didn't know . . ."

Natty tries to slow the wheels and take this spoke by spoke. This isn't admissible, but it *is* plausible. Bicycles are all over the city now. If you happened to be running a criminal conspiracy out of a law firm—maybe selling drugs—why not have a little army of Lance Armstrongs distributing drugs? Without probable cause, it would be tough to stop-and-frisk them. They could claim any package they were carrying contained legal documents, protected by attorney-client privilege. *Your father's thing,* Ben claimed. Give a Skell a Skill.

"You think Kenny was killed because he'd agreed to become a cooperating witness?" Natty asks.

"What else?" Albert leans on his cane. "He wasn't selling drugs himself no more. The police said someone must've known he was thinking of snitching. But the only ones who'd been told were the other cops and the lawyers. So one of them must have talked."

"Daddy, we don't know that." Evie shakes her head and then fixes the wrap.

"The *heck* we don't." Albert raises his voice, doubling down on his consonants. "The case come to go to court, and the attorney for Shakneela is Mister Benjamin Grimaldi." His trembling finger finds Natty on the couch. "That's the partner of this fool's father. And Shakneela is under Jamar Mack. So you tell me who's responsible."

"And you think someone connected with Shakneela killed your son to keep him from testifying?" Natty looks from Albert to Evie to confirm.

"Motherfucker, what'd I just say?" Albert yells. "Two days before my son got killed, Jamar Mack himself come up to him on the street and call him a sellout. Before he sign the cooperation agreement. So how he know unless one of the lawyers tell him?"

"You don't think the police or the prosecutors could have tipped someone off accidentally?" Natty asks.

"There wasn't no fucking accident." Albert shakes his cane. "Kenny called your father right after Jamar threatened him. He hadn't even been in front of a grand jury."

"And what did my father say?"

" 'Kenny, I promise you that we're gonna get to the bottom of this.' "

Albert imitates the infamous slightly nasal David Dresden accent. "'I'm gonna talk to Ben.'"

"Those were his exact words: 'I'm gonna talk to Ben'? Did you hear him say that?"

"No. But Kenny told me as soon as he got off the phone."

Hearsay, like everything else that's been said. Persuasive but legally useless. The story makes sense. Dad would have almost certainly told his co-counsel and best friend that a client had decided to cooperate in a case they were both working on. And almost certainly would have known something was wrong when that client got killed. But "almost certainly" was worse than knowing nothing, because it made you twice as helpless.

"Did you speak to my father again after Kenny was killed?"

"Stopped taking my calls and didn't come to the funeral. He knew what he did. And he knew what I'd do if I saw him. He promised my boy he'd be all right. And then I had to watch my son get shot down like a goddamn dog in the street."

The child in the other room gives a sudden piercing shriek.

"Daddy, come on now." Evie tries to hug Albert. "Look what you're doing. Tyrion can hear you getting upset."

"Let me be." He pushes her away. "I ain't saying nothing else to no one."

"Sir?" Natty looks up. "I'm just trying to get to all the facts . . ."

Albert staggers off into the other room, ignoring him.

"Sorry, he gets like that." Evie looks at Natty. "It's bad for his hypertension. He's not over what happened."

"I understand."

"If he didn't have Tyrion, I don't know what he'd do. I'm at the hospital all day, so sometimes even I can't deal with him."

Natty nods, his mind refusing to let him stay in the room now. The china cabinet, pussy willows, and basketball players on television insisting on reminding him about the red sofas in the sitting room, the trophy on the mantle, and the sneakers on the landing again.

"Daddy, what do you think you're doing?"

Albert is standing in the doorway, with a gun in his hand.

"Sir." Natty rises. "I don't think you want to be holding that."

"How you know what it is I want?"

The hole at the end of the barrel is level with Natty's left eye. He tries to judge the depth and width of the aperture. A Magnum, for sure. Maybe even a .45.

"Daddy, don't you be acting the fool . . ."

Natty stares into the tiny black circle. It wavers and moves around as if searching for something in his face. A sign of fear or maybe remorse. A recognition that he'd been on the other side of a gun himself. Right before he exerted the pressure required to pull the trigger back and change the balance of the universe.

The hole has steadied. It hangs before him, looking straight into his eye, threatening to widen out into an abyss and swallow him entirely. He tries to remember if there was a moment of conscious decision on the stairs that day, a split-second when he could have done something different that didn't inevitably lead through the labyrinth of passageways to him being right here seven years later, looking at the same kind of hole from the other side.

"One way or the other." Albert turns the gun sideways, like the cold young gangster he once was. "You got to go . . ."

He pulls the trigger, punctuating the thought with a twelve-millimeter period.

27

Lourdes steers around the assembled squad cars and pulls up right behind the ambulance parked outside the Cypress Hills projects, where bright arcs of red, blue, and white light make it look like the plain brick buildings are suddenly throbbing with conflicting emotions. She sees a body on a stretcher being wheeled through the courtyard, EMTs jogging along beside it, taking notes and trying to keep the tubes from getting tangled. Sullivan trudges along, following behind the procession, head bowed, slow big steps, like the Grim Reaper bringing up the rear of the parade.

Then she spots Natty Dresden as he breaks off from talking to a couple of precinct detectives over by the tetherball court, not just alive and well, but noticeably more animated and lively than he usually is. Especially for someone who's reportedly just been shot at and missed by less than a foot.

"*Natty*, wait." She hears her own ghetto girl voice bounce off the housing project walls, shrill and intemperate; every male officer in hearing vicinity looks askance. "What's up?"

"I could ask you the same." He stops and looks back at her, annoyed by the nickname. "We're a long way from the Seventy-Eighth Precinct, aren't we?"

"One of the officers who responded to the report of shots fired is the cousin of Detective Chen from our precinct, and he called us right away."

"How 'bout that? It *is* a small world after all."

"You don't seem that freaked considering someone just threw a shot at you." She notices a small smile on his newly stubbly face right before he books a few steps ahead of her toward the Fountain Avenue side of the projects, probably heading for the subways.

"I was in Iraq. You kind of expect it after a while."

How fucked up is it that she understands? Maybe she *could* have gone out with him under other circumstances.

"You okay?" she asks. "What were you doing here in the first place?"

"Why don't you ask the other detectives?" He shrugs, hands in his pockets like they're just a couple taking a brisk evening stroll. "I just gave them a statement . . ."

"I'm asking you, all right?" She stops and raises her voice, tired of trying to keep pace. "I'm investigating your father's murder and you just got shot at in a city housing project. You seriously don't think I got questions about that?"

"Not my problem."

"Come on, yo. Your father gets killed. Then you get locked up for going loco with firemen in a bar. Then you get clobbered outside your house and won't talk about why. Now you're getting shot at? You're like a mobile disaster area."

He finally turns and hunches his shoulders, project lights hard on his back. "What can I tell you?" he says. "I'm unlucky."

"Or very lucky. The report I heard was the shot went right by your ear."

She hears Sullivan catching up with them before she sees him, his steps loud as a pile-driver even against the street noise, window music, and lookie-loos yelling across the courtyard.

"I told your fellow detectives it was just an accident," Natty says, going all official and lawyerly on her. "Mr. Holloway was speaking to me in a very excitable way, when he happened to knock a gun off the table. It hit the floor and went off. Fortunately, I was not hit. Unfortunately, Albert seemed to suffer from some kind of coronary event afterward and his stepdaughter had to call 9-1-1."

"And you just happened to be there why?" Lourdes asks.

"Mr. Holloway is a witness in a case my father was working on before he was killed. But you probably knew that already." Natty stops to look up at Sullivan. "Or you should have."

"Where you coming from on this, Natty?" Sullivan huffs, even more displeased than Lourdes about being forced to move too fast.

"You guys really don't know why I'm here?"

"Tell us," Lourdes says.

"You seriously didn't know my father represented a Kenny Holloway, who was shot to death in front of his stepfather Albert on Troy Avenue a few months ago?"

"I might have heard something about it but it wasn't my case." Sullivan does a fair impression of a stone-faced Easter Island figurehead. "What's the relevance?"

"Then I take it that you also didn't know about Kenny getting shot right before he was going to testify against Shakneela Wilkins?" Natty asks, his voice sharp as a rap on the knuckles.

Lourdes can hear the tiny arthritic crack as Sullivan straightens up to his full height. "Why don't you let us worry about what we know and don't know?" he says.

Natty laughs with an edge of contempt. "Exactly how far behind the curve are you guys anyway?"

"We're right here with you." Lourdes tosses her hair back casually, trying to ignore the knot forming in her stomach.

"Really?" Natty says. "Did you even know about the drugs getting distributed on bicycles or three other cases the FBI was looking at where witnesses were killed right before they testified?"

"Where?" Lourdes asks.

She knows before the syllable is out of her mouth that she's given away too much. She can feel the weight of Sullivan's disappointment fall over her like a wet fur blanket.

"Forget it." Natty waves a hand. "I'm not going to do your jobs for you."

"We don't need you to do our jobs," Lourdes says. "We need you to help us. That's all."

Natty looks over toward the old man on the stretcher getting wheeled toward the ambulance, with a young woman in a headwrap following close behind holding a child's hand.

"We'll be testing Albert's gun to see if it was the one used to kill your father," Sullivan says.

"It won't be." Natty shakes his head.

"What makes you so sure?" Lourdes glances over at Sullivan.

"Albert is upset and confused," Natty says. "But he didn't murder my old man."

"You want to tell us who you think did?" Sullivan puts his shoulders back, the stance of an officer expecting deference.

"I thought Detective Robles said you didn't need me to do your jobs for you." Natty looks him up and down, performing a kind of instant status update. "But if you change your minds, I'm ready to take over."

"I say you're better off working with us than against us." Sullivan moves closer to him, trying to use his natural height advantage.

"Could have fooled me." Natty motorboats his lips and looks up, unimpressed. "Anyway . . ."

Across the courtyard, the old man on the stretcher has been loaded into the ambulance, the doors have been shut, and the young woman with the headwrap and child waving forlornly in her arms is being steered away by the patrol officers.

"So what happens to Albert now?" Natty asks.

"Unfortunately, Mr. Holloway is under arrest for having an unregistered handgun," Sullivan says. "And since it's not his first offense in New York State, he could be going away for a long time."

"Poor guy," Natty says. "He just wanted someone to pay for what happened to his kid."

"You know what they say about revenge and two shovels," Sullivan says, hands behind his back. "Make sure you dig two graves. One for your victim and one for yourself."

"They say a lot of things." Natty turns and starts to amble away.

"Once in a while," Sullivan calls after him, "they turn out to be right."

28

When Natty gets home that night, his mother is up in the kitchen, drinking tea, smoking a joint, and listening to music on the old Sony boom box next to the toaster. A dry, drifty song with strummy guitars and an Englishman singing impassioned words in an ironic, detached voice.

"What is this?" He takes his jacket off and sets it on the back of a chair. "'Wild Is the Wind'?"

She makes a face as she holds the smoke in. "Used to sing it to you as a lullaby."

"But this isn't the Nina Simone version." He cocks an ear. "Who is this?"

"Bowie."

"You're listening to David Bowie?"

His mother, Miss Social Justice, daughter of an East Coast Black Panther, exemplar of Afro-power feminist activism, listening to the androgynous Thin White Duke version of the song instead of the one that the Great Nina, her fierce uncompromising personal musical heroine, did.

"What can I tell you?" she says. "Sometimes you can handle the Full Nina. Sometimes you can't. She can get a little intense. Especially with how I'm feeling nowadays."

"But Bowie? Since when do you listen to Bowie?"

"There's a lot about your old mama that you don't know." She exhales, filling the space between them with dissipating smoke dragons. "I had a life before I met your father. I used to go to Studio 54 and the Mudd

Club, dance my ass off all night long. It wasn't all 'Young, Gifted, and Black' and 'Power to the People' all the time. I liked to have fun. Which is something you could start doing."

"*You* are going to start telling me that I'm too serious?"

"Just saying. You could lighten up a little . . ."

She closes her eyes and sways her head in time with the music, threatening to become a younger, more sensual version of herself amid the cannabis clouds and the understatedly funky drumming.

"Where were you tonight anyway?" she asks. "I thought you were helping Ben with the mailman case."

"I was following up on a lead."

"You tell Ben where you were?"

"No, and I'd like you to keep what I'm about to say quiet." He sits down. "Did Dad ever mention a Kenny Holloway to you?"

She opens her eyes and wrinkles her nose, staring at the joint pinched between her fingers like she's not sure how it got there. "Why do you want to know?"

"So he *did* mention Kenny?"

"Yes, he certainly did." She places the joint on the side of a small plate and studies it, not sure if she's ready to stub it out. "Lost some sleep about it, as a matter of fact, thinking it was his fault for telling the boy to cooperate before Kenny got shot."

"So he did work with cooperators?"

"Wake up and smell the coffee, son—your daddy didn't always practice what he preached," she sighs. "But I told David he couldn't blame himself for what happened to that young man. Kenny made his choices before he ever walked into your father's office to sign that agreement."

"Did Dad have any idea who was responsible?"

She pushes back from the table, wrinkling her nose as if she just realized her kitchen was starting to smell like dead skunk. "I'm sure it was whoever rode up and shot that kid in the back of the head."

"Did Dad know who that was?"

"Look, Natty, David and I didn't sit around solving murders all night. That's what the police do. Why you asking me about all this anyway?"

"I'm just wondering if there could be a connection to what happened later on to Dad." Natty puts his elbows on the table, the pot starting to irritate his eyes. "Did he mention anything about witnesses getting killed in other cases?"

She reaches for the joint again with visible annoyance. "Where you getting all this from—the police?"

"Never mind where I'm getting it from."

"Well, someone is trying to turn your head."

"What can you tell me about Marygrace Kelly?" he asks.

"Is *she* the one feeding you this garbage?"

"How do you know it's garbage?"

"I know she's a goddamn lying bitch who wanted to steal back my man." She stares in a daze at the smoke rising from between her fingers and then shakes herself to more focused attention. "I already told you that," she says. "I don't trust that woman."

"You still haven't said why."

"If she's making you believe David was killed for any reason except that he was about to expose a government conspiracy—*which she is part of*—then what she's giving you is worse than garbage."

"Mom." He waves the smoke away and reaches for her hand. "There were other cases where witnesses were killed."

"What?"

"It's the truth. I looked it up on my own, to confirm what she told me. The firm was involved in at least two cases, in which cooperating witnesses were killed."

"And what does that prove?"

"There may be two others. *Four*, Mom. Four is a lot."

"With those people?" She shakes her head, not looking at him as she puts the joint back to her lips with her free hand. "They kill each other all the time. It's unfortunate that they're forced into these illegal trades by the racism of society . . ."

"*Mom* . . ." He squeezes her hand hard, forcing her to pay closer attention as the tempo picks up and Bowie's voice rises. "Ben was directly involved in all of those cases. His clients are the main suspects. And in at least one of those cases, the only ones who knew the victim was a cooperator were the prosecutor and Dad."

"No way, no how . . ."

"Dad never said anything about confronting Ben?"

She turns her head to the side, denying him a full-face view, even as her small delicate hand remains lodged between his two sweaty paws.

"It's not possible that Ben was involved." She sniffs. "He was your father's best friend."

"But did they have a falling out before Dad died?"

"David didn't tell me everything. He didn't need to. We didn't have that kind of a marriage . . ."

She goes quiet as Bowie's voice starts to wobble, a tiny suggestion of emotion where Nina would be starting to brew up a full-on tempest of a nervous breakdown in her version. His mother's fingers wiggle between his, testing their ability to escape.

"But there was a fight between them?" Natty won't let go.

"They had beefs, but I didn't think they meant anything. I know Ben feels guilty about them now. I think it's why he hired you."

"Did Dad tell you what they were about?"

"No. But I'm sure they weren't important. Ben and David always had the same priorities."

"Are you sure about that?"

Her pot is starting to make his throat itch and his eyes tear. Somewhere along the line, he lost the ability to enjoy getting high himself. And for some reason, right now, the fumes are more than just an irritant and a distraction.

"I don't know anything about these cases," she says quickly. "I have my own work. I write my articles. I have my poetry. I'm trying to raise money to make a documentary about my father—"

"Mom," he interrupts. "Did Dad ever say anything to you about letting another firm take over the mailman case?"

Her hand starts to go cold. All his life, she always seemed to stay at the exact same temperature, never needing a thermometer as she put her brow against his to test his fever, always able to take the chill from his bones with a hug when he came in from shoveling snow. Now he can feel the blood drain from her fingertips.

"That was just foolishness," she says absently. "I knew he didn't mean it."

"Did he say why he wanted to give it up?"

"Why would I want to involve myself that much? I'm not a lawyer."

"But this is important. Did he ever say anything about Ben running a side business out of the firm?"

"No." She pulls her hand away. "Why do you keep asking me these things?"

"I think it's possible that Ben knows more about what happened to Dad than he's letting on."

She stubs out her joint and frowns as she pushes her tea away. Still not able to look at him.

"I'm not listening to this," she says.

"So you know it could be true."

Which means he'll have to act. And then she'll stand to lose whatever she has left.

"You know why I can't take Nina sometimes?" She stands up. "Because it's *too damn much*. She gets too damn caught up in the drama and wrings you out. Sometimes you just want a tune you can sing along with. Is that so wrong?"

"You know I might be right," he says. "Don't you?"

"I'm going to bed." She kisses the top of his head. "Nina barely made seventy, but I'm planning to stick around longer. See you in the morning."

29

Dawn finds Lourdes and Sullivan heading north on the New York State Thruway, redbrick housing projects and poorly maintained tenements giving way to suburbs and strip malls, and then rolling farmland and rusting silos.

She remembers herself on the stuffy Adirondacks buses with Mami and Ysabel. Getting picked up by the old New York Coliseum near Columbus Circle in the middle of the night, with all the other made-up ladies and screaming babies going to see their men upstate. With stops in Hudson, Fishkill, Coxsackie, and Attica. Daylight revealing the first real cows and horses she'd ever seen in the sprouting grass, as if nature was just getting invented as they sped along the highway. Passing out from Dramamine to keep from throwing up during the endless journey with the family members of other convicts, hollering across the aisles and blaming each other for some supposedly sweet pure beloved son or husband being up in this terrible place. The crushing boredom wrestling with the embarrassment and the smell of gas fumes on the thruway.

Then the endless lines to get through the metal detectors and the guards waving the wands in front of your face, like this was some kind of sick Harry Potter–type school for criminals. And then the agonizing hours in the visiting room, listening to Mami coo over Papi's exercise yard muscles, his beautiful black ponytail, and the ugly-ass tats with his children's names he got from some cretinous *prison-artist* on his tier. Both her parents acting like they truly loved each other and were dying to be together again, when all Lourdes remembered was hiding in the bedroom with Ysabel trying to stay lost in her Encyclopedia Brown when the two of them were howling and clawing at each other in the kitchen for spending cash they didn't have.

She wonders if her father's still here as Sullivan steers them up to the sixty-foot-high walls of the Clinton Correctional Facility just before ten o'clock, that same Aerosmith song that was playing on the city radio station somehow playing up here as well. *Sweet Emotion.* Fifteen years since she last saw him. In the largest prison in New York State. Well, they get moved around a lot within the system. Might be downstate, by now, if he's behaved himself. She resists the urge to ask about him after they leave their phones in the car, sign in, check their guns with the corrections officers who are still all grim-mouthed and tight-assed after a pair of recent escapes. Then they get brought to the private room to wait for Shakneela Wilkins to be brought out.

She sits quietly beside Sullivan in the little cinder-block room with one wooden table and the window in the door for the guards to see in. Contemplative as the little straight-A student she used to be, determined to prove she wasn't some filthy ill-mannered child from the PJs. She clasps her hands in front of her, one thumb on top of the other, trying to stay focused on the job they're here to do.

After Natty dropped that bomb on them about the FBI looking into other cases where witnesses were killed, they tried to reach out to the Bureau and follow up. The message they got back through Captain McKenna this morning was succinct: "Doug Bryce says you can take Thor's hammer and sit on it." Predictable. So what else could they do, besides snatch up the loose ends and try to weave them into the tattered case they already had?

When Shakneela arrives, he turns out to be a six-foot-nine crybaby wearing a black do-rag, a green uniform, and a razor scar under his eye. He starts listing his ailments and complaints as soon as he limps in and sits down across the table from them.

"Diabetes," he says. "Epididymitis. Bursitis. Sinus infections. And now they tell me I got gout. You believe that shit?"

"What's epididymitis?" Lourdes looks at Sullivan.

"Man thing," he murmurs.

She's decided there should be a two-minute rule for people who want to whine about their ailments. If it's something like cancer or leprosy, *okay.*

Those are exceptions. But for commonplace aches and pains, so not happening. One of the few things she remembers clearly about her father living at home was him spending three hours lifting weights in front of the TV and then sniffling in egregious self-pity when Mami wouldn't give him a back rub.

"Gout!" Shakneela raises his foot up, wooly white athletic sock in a black shower sandal.

Lourdes is distracted for a second, seeing a prisoner in a ponytail like her father's go past the window with a guard, followed closely by a little girl in pigtails carrying a book and holding her mother's hand. On their way to a family reunion in the visitors' room down the corridor.

"You know what gout is?" Shakneela raises his voice, trying to draw her attention back.

He puts the foot, which is just a little smaller than a full Wonder Bread loaf, on the empty chair beside him.

"It's the worst pain man has ever experienced," Shakneela says. "It attack the joint and won't let go. Feel like a bull shark be biting down on my big toe. I swear even wearing a sock is too much pressure. I got tears in my eyes sometime getting dressed . . ."

Oh Lord, don't take it off and make me look at that thing. Lourdes stares back at him.

"I cannot even believe how much control my toe has over the rest of me," Shakneela says, his eyes damp and imploring. "My big toe has become the emperor of my body. I can't walk, I can't sleep, I can't focus my mind . . ."

"Sounds hard." Lourdes looks at Sullivan, to see how much they should indulge. "You usually think it's like something English noblemen get from too much beef and brandy."

"My problem's uric crystals." Shakneela's white sock wiggles like a wounded bunny. "I got too much of them backed up in my system."

Kidney stones were her father's thing once he got sentenced. Doubling over and crying out, *"Aiii, Mami!"* in constant misery, ruining everybody else's time in the visiting room. People who'd spent most of the day getting upstate and couldn't have a normal conversation with their jailed loved ones because of his caterwauling. Lourdes always made sure she had two good mysteries to bury her face in as she sat by the candy machines, pretending not to know him until she had to come over for the goodbye hug. Bad enough to have a father doing murder time plus Rockefeller time for all the drugs they found in the house when they came to arrest him, but then the El Jefe of Myrtle Avenue had to go and turn into the Bitch of Dannemora, the biggest complainer in the system.

"The medical staff up here don't care." Shakneela shakes his head. "They say Advil is 'well-tolerated.' But I'm like 'well-tolerated' *by who*?"

"We can talk about getting you better attention, but we need a little assistance from you first." Sullivan looks up from his watch, having reached the edge of his own tolerance. "We want to talk about Shawn Davidson."

"Who?"

Lourdes lays the mug shots and rap sheets on the table. "You grew up across the hall from him at Schermerhorn Houses and got arrested with him in 2008," she says. "And he called the number for a cell phone that was bought with your credit card on the night he was killed in Brooklyn. So can we try again?"

"Oh, *Fiscal Science*." Shakneela spins the photos around. "Why didn't you say his name right the first time?"

Lourdes shares half a smirk with Sullivan.

"I don't know what you all think I can tell you." The prisoner looks at his foot glumly. "I was in here when my brother Science caught the bullet. Seven years for shuffling plastic. That seem right?"

"Identity theft first-degree is a D felony," Lourdes reminds him. "And it sounded like the state had you on a lot of other things. Your lawyer did a good job, getting the charges knocked down."

"Benny G., that's my boy." Shakneela nods. "The DA try to make out like I'm part of some big-ass Murder Incorporated drug conspiracy racketeering case when all I was trying to do was help out a few people in the neighborhood who had some problems with their credit ratings. You know how that is, sister, don't you?"

Lourdes smiles, humoring him, knowing full well that a lot of the major Brooklyn drug dealers had segued into running identity theft scams, using cashiers and customer service reps to steal credit numbers the way they used to use couriers and pitchers to sling crack and heroin.

"Helped that Kenneth Holloway didn't end up testifying against you as well, didn't it?" Sullivan says. "So you didn't have to roll on Jamar Mack."

Shakneela stiffens as if an old Manhattan yellow pages book just dropped on his bad toe.

"I didn't have nothing to do with what happened to Kenny," he says. "Brooklyn South Homicide talked to me for three hours with my lawyer present and they never charged me. I wasn't anywhere near Brownsville when Kenny got dropped. Fact, they got witnesses who put me shopping at Burlington Coat Factory at the Atlantic Mall when he was crossing the street with his stepfather."

"Yes, we know." Sullivan absently taps his ring finger. "Clerks at the same store that you were getting the stolen credit card numbers from."

"Asked and answered then!" Shakneela gingerly touches his toe and then draws his hand back like it's on fire. "Why you living in the past, old man?"

"Seven years is the max you can get for a D felony." Sullivan fiddles with the wedding band and the cop ring he wears above it, so the NYPD emblem is facing the inmate. "It doesn't have to be that way."

"What you got in mind?" Shakneela asks, studying the Indian and the colonizer.

"A cooperation letter from the DA could help get you out in two and a third," Sullivan says. "Or even sooner if they decide to further reduce the charges. And in the meantime, we can get you transferred to a prison with better medical facilities."

"I'm'a need that if I start cooperating with you all." Shakneela wags his chin dolefully.

"We're not talking about anybody in here." Lourdes scoots her chair forward, so her knee is almost touching his.

"Then who do you wanna talk about?"

Lourdes turns to Sullivan, deferring.

"What about if 'No Kenny, No Case' wasn't your idea?" Sullivan leans in, his voice no louder than a whisper of paper from the gutter.

"Yeah, what about it?" Shakneela abruptly takes his foot off the chair.

"We know about witnesses getting killed in three of Benny G.'s other cases." Lourdes slides over the file she's been holding. "Other people are talking."

"About *what?*"

She looks down under the table and sees Shakneela has his ankles crossed, his supposedly injured foot jiggling nervously, big toe pressed down into his sandal, all the pressure on the joint he was complaining about so bitterly a few minutes ago.

Most of existence is about prioritizing pain, Lourdes thinks. Figuring out what you can and can't live with. She remembers Papi talking about the pain of not seeing his family while he was up here. Before one of the female COs tipped off Mami that another lady with two daughters had been to see Raffi here last week. His family from Newark, it turned out. Who didn't mean as much to him, he insisted when Mami finally confronted him. Because he'd started that family earlier, and left them to be with Mami and their two beautiful daughters. So he must love them more. Right?

"Seems Mr. Grimaldi has a pattern of being involved with clients who are acquitted when witnesses fail to testify." She bears in on Shakneela, trying to use her old anger for a current advantage.

"And you want me to put Kenny's murder on myself to help you make your case?" Shakneela throws his hands up. "That's your plan? Woman, is you fucking crazy?"

"Cooperation in a case involving a well-known member of the bar would carry a lot of weight," Sullivan says. "I've heard of people getting out from under nineteen murders by cooperating. You have a lot less to be concerned with."

"You want me to be a witness in a case about witnesses getting murdered?" Shakneela tilts his head and then looks down at Sullivan's ring again.

"You're that afraid of your own lawyer?" Lourdes thrusts out her jaw.

"That's who you're after? My lawyer?"

"You can't be *that* surprised."

"You want me to turn on Benny G.?"

"It's not like he'd be out on the street waiting for you if you got out sooner yourself," Lourdes says. "Or even like he'd have family waiting. He's got daughters and they don't even speak to him."

The girl with the pigtails and the book comes marching past the door again in the other direction, as if her meeting with the ponytailed guy in the visiting room went badly.

"Yeah, but Benny G. has represented a lot of people who are still in the system." Shakneela leans forward, keeping his voice down. "He can reach way in if he wants to get to you. I'm afraid of Jamar Mack. But I'm scared *to death* of Ben Grimaldi."

"Come on, Shakalack," Lourdes says. "Man up."

The guard who'd been standing with his back to the door window looks over his shoulder at Lourdes. She realizes her volume must have jumped unexpectedly.

"Who's going to do favors for a lawyer who's been locked up and lost his license?" she asks.

"I'd give it some real thought if I was you." Sullivan gets up, granite-jawed and gimlet-eyed. "And I wouldn't talk much to Mr. Grimaldi about our visit. Your sentence isn't going to get shorter and that foot's not going to get better on its own."

"Like you care." Shakneela touches the toe with tender pity.

"Amazing what one little joint can screw up." Lourdes rises.

She walks out without a wave or a look back, same way she'd leave her father when she exited the visiting room.

30

As wan morning sunlight sifts its way through the woods of Gloucester County, New Jersey, Natty stands behind his old staff sergeant, J. R. Cuddy.

"Hey, sarge, isn't it a little early for hunting season?"

"Yes, sir," Cuddy says in his laconic drawl. "But we have an unusual situation of what you call your basic feral pigs eating up all the seedlings in this area."

They're in a clearing by a stream. Crushed Red Bull cans and torn-up brown-purple pods of skunk cabbage are strewn on the banks, along with half-eaten ramps, yellow forsythia leaves, and ripped-open Subway sandwich bags. A cell phone tower looms over swaying pines, discarded Bud Light empties, and storm-felled oaks. The trees left standing still look a little hungover from the hard winter: sagging dogwoods just starting to bloom, weeping willows barely moving in the breeze.

"Feral pigs?" Natty says.

"Some people call them 'wild boar,' but that seems kind of . . . I don't know . . . *overdramatic?*" Cuddy tongues a wad of tobacco deeper behind his lip. "Any event, we probably won't run into them. But if we do? They have been known to charge and some of them weigh like two fifty, three hundred, with tusks like little fuckin' scimitars. And they do run in packs of fifty, a hundred. So you might want to book if that happens, LT."

"And what are *you* going to do?"

With a light touch on the joystick, Cuddy swivels the all-terrain wheelchair to face him. A one-man tank, with six-inch rubber track on each side and compartments for ammo and beer. Cuddy is held into the

chair by vinyl straps. A rebel army forage cap sits on his pumpkin-shaped
head, a camo shirt is stretched over his weight-lifter's torso, and a Bushmaster AR-15 lies across the empty space where his lap would have been.

"Don't worry 'bout me, LT," he says, patting the stock. "I should be
able to keep them pinned down while you haul ass this time. The least I
can do. Right?"

Natty rubs the back of his neck, already regretting how he set this
up. He should've softened the ground up first. Should've called as soon
as he got back to the northeast for Dad's funeral. Certainly long before
he needed a favor from a man who'd lost pretty much everything below
the navel. But now fucking Cuddy can smell the desperation on him.

Natty had hoped to handle this quickly and quietly, zooming by
Cuddy's house early in the rented car to ply him with Dunkin' Donuts
coffee and crullers. But the sergeant, sensing the rawness of his need, had
of course drawn the whole thing out, insisting on giving his old second
lieutenant the full nickel tour of the place, a one-story wonder built with
financial help from an actor who'd won an Oscar playing a paraplegic
vet. The place was set up beautifully for Cuddy and his parents, who'd
come to live with him. Handrails along every wall, waist-high sinks, cabinets that went up and down with the touch of a button, and easy-to-reach
racks for Cuddy's growing collection of rifles and handguns.

"There's an argument that says maybe I should've brought the hunting dog instead of leaving him tied up at the house," Cuddy continues in
his I-95 South drawl, enjoying Natty's restlessness. "The downside is, some
of your Bluetick coonhounds have what you'd call a tendency to over-
estimate their abilities. Especially when it comes to taking down a larger
animal. They'll charge in, get themselves torn to shreds, and you end up
over them, laying down suppressive fire so the other pigs don't join the
attack."

Natty puts his hands in his back pockets, arching his back. Man, he's
really going to make me work for this.

"Thing is, the boars, if you will, don't have any business here." Cuddy
squeezes the rifle's handgrip. "They're not native to the area. Like us
in Iraq."

"You're not really comparing us to pigs, Staff Sergeant, are you?"

"I'm not into metaphor, LT. I'm just talking about things that don't belong." Cuddy spits. "Theory is, some rich fool brought them to his farm when they were cute little piglets, then let them go because he couldn't manage them. And when these hogs go wild, they grow hair, turn black as bears, and sprout those fuckin' evil tusks. Pull up the grass, foul the pools, scare off the other animals. Ruins the whole fuckin' eco-system. Gets to where you got no choice, except to start killing them."

"If we don't fight them here, we'll have to fight them at home," Natty says in his best Texas accent.

Cuddy takes a flask out of his shirt pocket, unscrews the cap, pours what is no doubt Jameson Irish whiskey into his beer can and takes a deep chug as if daring Natty to give him shit about drinking in the morning with an assault weapon in his hands.

"But I'm guessing you didn't come all the way out here to talk about feral pigs, LT." Cuddy puts down his Budweiser and raises the Bushmaster.

"I need a gun, sergeant."

A rustling in the grass a hundred yards away produces only a scurrying black squirrel.

"You taking up hunting, Natty Dread?" Cuddy lowers the rifle and sets it sideways across the armrests.

"Thinking about it."

Up until last night, Natty had been able to rationalize the coincidences. Most of the witness murders could have just been criminals killing criminals. But the hit on Kenny Holloway was different. Dad had talked Kenny into cooperating. And had called the FBI repeatedly after Kenny was gunned down. Something had been bothering him.

After Mom went to bed last night, Natty called up the other cases on the laptop and found the two witnesses murdered right before testifying in Connecticut and New Jersey. Four out of four. Each case on its own unremarkable. The geographic spread just enough to keep the pattern from being obvious. No reason for police in different jurisdictions to be talking to each other about them. But now that his father is dead, the connection seems obvious. Ben is the only common element in all five killings.

But some portion of Natty's heart still cannot accept it. This is *Ben*. Not just your father's friend, but someone who made you what you are. Which means that if you kill him, you're not just killing part of your past. You're killing part of yourself. And maybe not even the worst part.

But to ignore this set of facts would be never-ending torture. A slow and steady drip filling up the passages until you can no longer breathe. A gradual drowning.

"Were you looking to borrow an assault rifle?" Cuddy asks, tucking a new wad of tobacco under his lip.

"You told me you had a Glock 17, a Remington 700, and a Smith & Wesson .38 revolver back at the house, didn't you?"

"Uh-huh." Cuddy moves the chaw around inside his mouth. "I've been hunting and collecting guns since I was six. My daddy bought me my first rifle in Maryland when I was nine. That's part of growing up in the country. But I'm guessing your daddy wasn't the type to take you to a lot of gun shows. Was he?"

"No, he was not."

"Then let's just cut to the chase, hoss. You want this gun for protection or you planning to go shoot up a shopping mall?"

Natty doesn't laugh. A northern breeze carries the smells of beast shit and pesticides from the farm down the road.

"Better if I don't get into the specifics, Staff Sergeant. I have a situation."

If it *is* true, he wonders whether Ben lost any sleep about killing a friend ahead of time. Mom said there had been arguments. Had he tried to talk Dad out of going to the feds? And was he suffering for it now? Waking up with night sweats? Having panic attacks and palpitations? Dealing with flashbacks that seemed to get longer every time? Or was it all just business, cut-and-dried?

"Permission to speak freely?" Cuddy pushes back the bill of his cap.

"We're not in the army anymore. And you didn't exactly hold back when we were."

"That's right." The chair makes a whinging sound as Cuddy pushes the joystick to turn. "I always told you I'd call bullshit on you when I needed to."

"I remember."

"That was our deal right from the get-go when you came in, Mr. Butter Bar Second Lieutenant Artisanal Lesbo Cornell University, Warrior Leader Course, Army Intelligence School pussy who'd never heard a shot fired in his whole sorry panty-waist vegan life, and I was just an ignorant gearhead who barely graduated high school and happened to know five times more about combat than you ever will."

Cuddy spews out a shot-glass's worth of tobacco juice, reminding Natty that he failed to cultivate the chewing habit in the army because it made him want to vomit.

"Always said you saved my ass more than once, Cuddy."

"And you saved mine." Cuddy smirks. "Or at any rate, what's left of it."

"I thought we were done with this, Staff Sergeant."

"Not yet. I got something to say. Because you promised me, Natty Dread. We had a deal. As soon as we heard the hajjis were angling explosives toward our balls, we said if one of us got his junk blown off, the other would finish him. Did you forget that?"

"No." Natty looks up at an eagle on the cell tower. "I didn't forget."

"Then what the fuck, LT?"

Sometimes it feels like he was the one who lost his lower half. One minute they'd been in the Humvee with Rayfield and Willingham, talking about football and getting laid, and the next he was in the dirt with oil smoke in his eyes, his M4 ten feet away, and half of his staff sergeant beside him and the rest of Cuddy under the overturned truck.

It was as if they'd driven into the middle of the sun and wound up on the other side of the universe. All normal laws of time and space were suspended. Everything seeming to happen too slow and too fast at the same time. His left shoulder was dislocated. Blood was dripping into his eye. His eardrums, damaged in Sadr City, seemed permanently blown out now. He saw an arm close at his side and it took a second to realize it wasn't his. He was still alive. But why? The ground around him appeared to be carbonated. Little holes appearing in quick succession. As his brain settled, he realized it was .762 rounds from insurgents' guns chewing up the dirt around him, getting closer and closer both to his own body and the upper half of Cuddy, screaming beside him.

In his mind's eye, Natty can still see himself scrambling to grab his rifle as the Humvee wheels spin and smoke rises into the palm trees. Rayfield's shredded torso barely in his field of vision, just enough so that

Natty could briefly register the mildly astonished expression on his life-less face. But then AK-47 muzzle flashes from the tree line demanded his attention. He remembers his own surprise at being able to fire back. He'd thought he'd never be able to touch a trigger again after Sadr City. He'd glanced at Cuddy. His mind not quite able to encompass the reality of his friend getting half crushed, or the fact that it was not him under the overturned Humvee instead.

Portions of the rest are lost to him now. But he remembers he was grateful that no one pointed out how he'd pissed in his pants by the time the convoy circled back and the hajjis melted away. And he has a vivid recall of joining the six joes working together to put out the engine fire and lift the vehicle off Cuddy, while the medic readied the aortic ab-dominal tourniquet and muttered something about blood pressure plum-meting. What he wishes he could forget, though, is the look on Cuddy's face, when they raised the Humvee, and the staff sergeant, for some reason still not in shock, managed to say, *"Fuck you, Natty Dread. You promised me."*

"Bet you're good and proud of yourself, aren't you?" Cuddy spits again, this time closer to Natty's feet. "You still wear all those pretty rib-bons when you walk around the house?"

"I did save your life, Staff Sergeant. That's not nothing."

"Yeah, and they gave me a Purple Heart too. So that makes us even. Right?"

"It's not like I forgot."

"It's not like you came to see me before you needed something either."

Natty hears buzzing and swats the side of his neck. Too early in the season for mosquitoes. Might just be a delayed reaction to getting shot at last night. Or some other repressed memory. But then again, maybe every-thing about being out here is based on a false perception. Maybe he's wrong about Ben. Maybe there are no feral pigs. Maybe Cuddy just lured him away from the house to pay Natty back for breaking his promise. *Honest, sheriff, it was just a hunting accident.*

"Sorry I didn't come sooner," Natty says. "It's hard for me to be around people I knew over there. It shouldn't be that way. I didn't go through anything like you did."

"Yeah, well."

Cuddy looks up at the sun burning through the clouds and then over at a trembling in the underbrush.

"It's all right." He flares his nostrils as the rotten meat scent of the skunk cabbage rises again. "I know you got troubles of your own, LT."

"You're dealing better than I am, looks like."

"I got my good days and my bad days." Cuddy tilts the chair up with a slight push on the joystick. "You?"

"I killed a seven-year-old boy, Cuddy. That never changes."

There. Never said it quite so plainly to another human being before. The wind moves over the grass. A piece of the Subway bag tumbles into the stream and makes a series of concentric ripples across the surface. But the rest of the world remains unchanged.

"What's that got to do with anything?" Cuddy asks.

"I still think about that. Don't you?"

"I remember when you tried to take a swing at Captain Paultz at the PX after it happened."

"I did?"

"When he said, 'Don't feel bad, Dresden. That's one less future terrorist to worry about.'"

"Asshole."

Cuddy shifts his tobacco wad from one side of his cheek to the other. "I think he was trying to make you feel better."

"Jesus . . ." Natty bends at the waist, starting to sweat and get short of breath.

"You all right?"

"I was just thinking about that kid and how soon after that our Humvee got blown up."

"What are you talking about?" Cuddy picks his beer up again. "One thing don't have nothing to do with the other."

"Really believe that?" Natty straightens up, trying to remember how to breathe.

"Why not?" Cuddy swigs and belches. "You think I lost my junk because of some fuckin' Divine Justice Program?"

"I was the one who shot him, Cuddy. It should've been me instead of you under that truck."

"Dawg, why you thinking like that? That IED rattle your brains?"

"Maybe. I don't know. It sure feels that way sometimes."

He realizes now that there was a half-second last night when Albert's gun clicked and he knew he was about to be shot, and something in him was a little relieved.

"Fuck that." Cuddy crushes the can and puts it back in its holder. "Shit happens. That's all it was, all it is. Just bad fuckin' luck. Bad luck that kid happened to be upstairs when we were looking for Fuckface Ahmar. And bad luck we happened to drive over the IED. Nothing more, nothing less. No one's balancing the books."

"I've been thinking a lot about getting in touch with the family," Natty says quietly.

"Well, that's even crazier."

"They're here, you know. They live in America now."

"Are you fucking kidding me, LT? How did that happen?"

"They got a special visa through the State Department. They had family who were already living in the States who petitioned their congress-man and senator in New Jersey."

"They manage that, with all the people trying to get here? We couldn't even get Borat's family here."

"The father was a surgeon and a professor at University of Baghdad. And the family's got special status, because of what happened with us."

"All right." Cuddy sighs. "Good for them. Glad they got something out of that fucked-up situation. But is that really what you came out here to talk to me about?"

"You say it's not all connected, but it feels like it is." Natty shuts his eyes. "Look: I found out the dad's working at a Rite Aid in Jersey City and the daughter's going to Rutgers. I tracked them down on the Internet."

"Wait a second. You're *stalking* these people?"

"Just shut the fuck up." Natty clenches his fists, the words coming out in a rush now. "I flew into town after I lost my job in Florida and started tracking them because I wanted to talk to them about what hap-pened. I felt like my life was falling apart because I hadn't made things right. But then I lost my nerve and went back to Florida. And like a week later, my father was killed."

"And you think it's all part of the same thing?"

Natty pauses, watching dragonflies hover above unnatural ruts filled with standing rainwater. "It feels like I had my chance to make amends and then I blew it."

"I still think you're seeing connections that aren't there," Cuddy wipes his brow. "But for whatever it's worth, sorry about your dad. I saw it on the news. That time, *I* should've called you . . ."

"I think I know who did it," Natty interrupts.

Cuddy lets that sit a while, with more tobacco than it seems possible to keep in one mouth at the same time.

"Is that why you need the gun?"

"The less you know, the better," Natty says.

"If you're that sure who killed your father, why don't you just tell the police?"

"The guy who did it is sneaky. He's a lawyer. They'll never get him."

"Damn, LT." Cuddy leans over and lets some of the tobacco juice dribble out the corner of his mouth. "So do you want me to help you get rid of the body?"

Natty looks at the wheelchair and hears himself start to laugh in that down-and-dirty soldier's way that normal people can never understand.

"Seriously," Cuddy says. "Have you really thought this through?"

Natty scratches the undergrowth of the beard he's growing in semi-conscious tribute to his father. He can see himself vacillating for weeks, months, years while Ben cashes in and keeps calling him "son." What if this *was* just about money? Ben's share of the mailman case stands to be $4 million. And who knew whether he was profiting additionally from the other four murders? Somehow the thought makes him want to throw up. Because if it was just about money, it means Natty rejected his own father in favor of something even worse than a lie. And the only redemption is to do what he swore he'd never do after the war, and take another life.

"Can't leave it up to anyone else, Staff Sergeant," he says.

"Listen up, Natty Dread." Cuddy stops the chair and picks up the rifle. "Life is just one fucking thing after another. Things are what they are and not how you want them to be. I'm never gonna be able to go for another walk in the woods. I'm never gonna have a kid. And I'm never gonna make love to a woman again."

"Jesus, Cuddy." Natty wipes the corner of his eye. "You really know how to sugarcoat it, don't you?"

"Who am I gonna take it out on, LT? The hajjis? Myself?"

Natty looks at the rifle, thinking he'd have the muzzle under his own chin if he was in Cuddy's seat right now.

"Fuck it," Cuddy says. "I let all that shit go a long time ago. Because all I have is *this*. Okay? The sun on my face, the wind in the trees, and this fucking gun in my hands, so maybe I can kill something I can eat. And that's enough. I'm not going to lie to myself and pretend there's ever going to be more than that. I'll take what I have."

"Then I envy you."

Cuddy shrugs. "Leave it alone, LT. Let these people who lost their kid live their lives. And let the police deal with this cocksucker who killed your old man. Suck it up, drive on. Don't throw your fucking life away."

"No can do, Sergeant."

"Then if I can't talk you out of it, can I tell you one thing?" Cuddy pats the rifle. "Don't be fucking sloppy."

"Who said I was going to be sloppy?"

"Listen to me. What did the hajjis do? They watched us. They went to school on us. They learned our strengths and weaknesses. And then they used them against us. Like that piece of shit who sent us to the wrong house. Be the player this time, not the played. Think like a gangsta. Don't let him see you coming. Get his guard down. You know how they usually catch these feral pigs?"

"No."

"They set up a Judas Pig. They catch one hog and put a radio collar on him. Then he leads the hunters to where the rest are hiding. So you're smarter than a pig, aren't you?"

Natty snorts. "That mean you're gonna give me a gun?"

"You going to keep after me until I do?"

"I promise it won't come back on you."

"Yeah, I know all about your promises." Cuddy shakes his head, without looking up. "Your call, LT. You *did* save my life."

"Thank you, Cuddy."

"All right, shut up now."

Cuddy puts a finger to his lips, then straightens his torso, which is twice as thick and muscular as it was in Iraq. There must be a chin-up bar at the house. He lifts the AR-15 again, looks down the barrel, and becomes unnaturally still. Seconds pass, then a half minute. A lone sparrow sings. A twig snaps and the air around the cell tower hums. Then a large black boar charges from the underbrush, heading straight toward them, all shiny eyes, muscular sides, and bristling black fur. The rifle cracks twice. The pig keeps coming, then slows down as if it just remembered something it left in the bush. Then it falls like an overturned ottoman, blinking uncomprehendingly. Cuddy finishes him off with a shot to the head.

"Good eye, Staff Sergeant."

"Thanks, Natty Dread." Cuddy lowers the gun. "Now you gonna help me get this fucker back to the house or have you turned into some kind of goddamn cripple?"

31

Once they're well on the road back to the city, Lourdes tells Sullivan that she just remembered a CI at nearby Great Meadows Correctional who she needs to check in with on another case. And with a blessed minimum of suspicion, he agrees to hang loose for a few hours and make some calls at a local state police barracks while she goes to visit inmate 917.3872.

Wanting to keep her business on the down-low, she doesn't ID herself as a cop at the front or ask for a special room. Just signs in and parks herself at a table in the visitors' area, like any other family member. Across the room, an old gray-haired white couple are holding hands with a little whey-faced Jesus-haired dirthead. A Chinese lady plays Scrabble with an elderly prisoner who looks like he's had half his bones removed.

Lourdes stands up as they lead her father in. He more or less looks the same, even though his body is a little broader in the green overalls, his ponytail is streaked gray now, and his features are distinctly knobbier and less plausibly those of the Dominican aristocracy he once claimed to be descended from. In fact, now that he's in his late sixties, he looks more like what he really is: an aging Hispanic drug dealer who still thinks he's got everyone fooled.

"Lordy-Lourdes, I knew you'd come." He kisses her cheek briefly, not ticking the guards off with too much contact. "Eventually."

"Taking care of yourself." She looks him up and down. "As usual."

"I know why you're here." He slaps his annoyingly flat belly and sits down.

"Why do you think I'm here?"

"You heard about the letters I been writing to the Innocence Project, about getting my case reopened . . ."

"No . . ."

"I can get you copies," he says. "I got letters from three other inmates who know who really shot Tony Vargas . . ."

"I'll bet you do . . ."

She should have expected as much. Anyone who's been in the system long enough can get hooked up with crimeys willing to trade alibis and recantation stories.

"I've been saying it for years," Papi continues, getting up a good head of steam. "I was framed by a bunch of criminals who were threatened by someone trying to do the right thing for the community . . ."

She tries to be subtle about showing him the growing vacancy behind her eyes. Fifteen years since they last saw each other, though they've talked on the phone from time to time. She had to use the NYS Inmate Look-Up to find out which facility he was in now. Naturally, she'd pulled his case file as soon as she became a detective. And saw the state had two different eyewitnesses nailing him for firing a .38 at his crack rival Loco Tony Vargas outside the Walt Whitman Houses.

"But maybe you didn't come to talk about my case," Papi says.

"Nope." She sits back, arms across her chest. "You used to be up in Clinton Correctional. Right?"

"How are things in Dannemora?" he sings, which wasn't even a funny bit the first four times she heard it.

"We went to see a new inmate named Shakneela Wilkins."

"I don't know him . . ."

"*I know* you don't. I said he was new. *Didn't I?*" She hates herself for being bitchy with him. "Anyway, we need some help from him on another case. I was thinking you might know someone who might know someone who could reach out . . ."

"No." He starts wagging his chin.

"No, you won't help?"

"No, that's not why you came to see me either. You came because every little girl needs to see her daddy once in a while. Even if she thinks she doesn't."

"Yeah, keep telling yourself that."

What'd she expect to get from him anyway? Information? Reassurance? Might as well try to talk to a cat about coding.

"How you doing anyway?" He pitches forward in his chair, stretching his arms out like he wants her to admire his fresh new tattoos. "How's your mother and sister?"

"Fine. No thanks to you."

"You know what I think, Lourdes? I think you need to get another man in the family," he says. "At least until I get out. I've been reading a lot about the matriarchy while I've been in here, and I believe women must be strong. But man is still necessary for the good of the household . . ."

She can see now why people mistook him for a community leader. Papi always did talk a good game, and if she's honest she can admit that sometimes she loved to hear him riff about whatever obscure subject happened to catch his interest. For a while, it was Cervantes's life in prison, then it was the history of the Moors in Spain, and, just before he got locked up, it was botany in the Dominican Republic. But then she realized that fed into his figuring out how to make money off growing cocoa.

"Some example, weren't you?" she says. "Man of *two* houses."

"Doesn't mean I'm wrong," he says, taking her point and setting it firmly aside. "So are you seeing anyone yourself?"

"*Pfft.* Think I'd tell you if I was?"

"Sometimes I think you blame me because of what happened with your brother."

She puts her hand up. "I'm not talking about that."

"He got into drugs without me. I know you were too young to understand when he died but . . ."

"I said *we are not talking about that*. Okay?" She looks around, realizing she's been getting loud. "What's done is done."

"Okay." He shrugs. "So what are you reading these days?"

She shakes her head, not quite believing she's going to let him slide that easily again but doing it anyway.

"Nothing much," she mutters. "It's been crazy at work."

"You gotta check out *Gone Girl*. I took it out of the prison library. You'll love it."

"How do you know what I'll love?"

"It's got a lot to say about men and women with trust issues."

Someone's been watching too many daytime advice shows in here, she thinks. All the inmate families are deep in their own dramas. The old white lady hugging Jesus Hair Grandson like she knows she'll never see him again. The Chinese man flipping over the Scrabble board and watching his wife bend over and pick up the tiles. Lourdes makes a show of heaving her chest impatiently.

"It's like the books I used to give you when you were young," Papi says. "Remember? It's not just about who done it, but the why."

"Oh, Raffi, that's *so* insightful—"

She duck-faces him, making sure he knows he's being mocked. He mirrors the expression back, reminding her with a jolt who she got it from in the first place.

"You should send me a book sometime," he says. "I've read everything they have here. Doesn't have to be a mystery. I'll read anything. I miss talking to you about books. And everything else."

"I don't remember us talking all that much."

She stands up and the chair she'd been sitting in tips over. The guard at the station rises, ready to hit the alarm. Lourdes puts her hands up a little too authoritatively, letting everyone in the room know she's a cop. Making her father, in turn, look like a snitch.

"Anyway, Lordy-Lourdes." He puts his hands flat on the table. "I'll ask around about your Shakneela. But I know you were just looking for an excuse to see that your papi is all right. Don't worry about my kidney stones. They're all right too."

"What do you know anyway?"

"Love you, baby." He stands up, kisses her again on the cheek, and signals he's ready to go back to his cell. "Tell that big-mouth aunt of yours I said yo."

32

"My brotha, where you at?" Ben's voice crackles over the cell phone.

"On my way to therapy."

Two hours after his visit with Cuddy, Natty is still in the parking lot of a Rite Aid superstore in Jersey City, with a fuming sky pressing down, an open pint of Tennessee Fire between his knees, and a loaded Glock 17 in Dad's leather satchel, which is stowed under the passenger seat.

"Uh, Natty, did you forget that we're supposed to be getting ready for a summary judgment hearing?"

"No, I haven't forgotten." Natty takes a smooth pull on the bottle, taking care not to slur his words.

He looks from the Rite Aid entrance to the front of the Jersey City Islamic Society, directly across the street, a converted auto body garage situated between a barber and a deli that sells New Jersey Mega Millions tickets.

"You know that I'm going to have this FBI special agent Kirkpatrick up on the stand in three days," Ben says, his voice getting heavy and deliberate. "I need ammunition."

"Don't worry, you'll get ammunition."

The gun in the bag is a Generation Four model, nine-millimeter, recoil-operated, locked breech, semi-automatic, mostly plastic. It can't be more than two pounds, even with a seventeen-round clip inside. But it feels like it's making the whole rented car sag. The undercarriage is almost scraping the parking lot asphalt. As if the weight of his ambivalence is becoming more cumbersome and unbearable by the second. *What am I supposed to do? Turn the gun on him or myself?*

"I have to tell you, Natty, this is making me very uncomfortable."

"What is?"

Natty puts on shades to watch the congregants starting to stream in from the sidewalk. Mothers in hijabs pushing strollers and dragging toddlers from the day care center up the street, bearded men in denim shirts and dishdashas coming from the taxi stand and the smoke shop in the other direction. But no one from the Rite Aid yet.

"We're coming up on the most important court proceeding of my career, and I don't have all of your father's materials," Ben says. "You want to see me stroll up to the witness box with just my dick in my hands? Where's the FOIA material about Wally?"

"Who?"

"Jesus Christ, Natty. Get your head out of your ass. Walid al-Masri? Mr. Wally? The informant Ibrahim was telling us about? The supervisor from the post office? You remember now?"

"I'm working on it—trying to find Dad's passwords and encryption keys . . ."

"Pick up the pace, son. We're dying here."

Maybe not fast enough. Natty screws the top back on the Tennessee Fire.

"We know this Walid al-Masri was arrested twice before he turned rat, but was allowed to keep his job at the post office," Ben says. "Now he's disappeared completely. If we don't get the full records of how he was handled, we've got no case. And all David's work goes down the drain."

"Ben, trust me. Nothing is more important to me than finishing what Dad started."

"I hope that's true, Natty," Ben says, his voice starting to fade under static interference. "That's why I put you on this."

His degree of uncertainty about Ben's guilt wavers somewhere between twenty-five and fifty percent every few minutes. The rub is why would Ben let his victim's son hang around and get this close to him? Not only taking Natty on as an unpaid employee, but giving him a role in a major case and a little office at the firm. Wouldn't it have been smarter to keep this potential threat at arm's length, at least? Especially if your victim's son was a veteran who'd been recently arrested for felony assault? And someone who'd have the means to get his hands on a gun, like the one in the bag. Would it be arrogance? A death wish? Perversity? Or maybe it's as simple and straightforward as what Ben said about hiring him. "At least I can keep an eye on you and make sure you don't get into any more trouble."

Or maybe none of the above. Maybe he's just getting played again. This time by the FBI.

"What time are you going to be back at the office?" Ben says. "I'd like to go over some of these requests for 302s and 292s that your father made. There's something specific he wanted to know about Agent Paul Kirkpatrick's marital status."

"No later than three-thirty." Natty angles his Ray-Bans and sticks the bottle in the glove compartment.

"That's two and a half hours, my son. You sure you're just doing talk therapy with this Stacy? Is she really hot or something?"

Natty is distracted, watching the sun glint dully off the doors of the Rite Aid as they swing open. But still no sign of the gray-haired man in the blue pharmacist's smock or his daughter wearing the black headscarf.

"She's all right," he says. "She thinks we're getting somewhere."

The call for midday prayers goes out, the recorded muezzin voice issuing from a loudspeaker at the front of the mosque. It starts slowly like a man talking to himself in a lonely cell and then begins to ascend and steady itself, like a B-17 bomber rising through the clouds. "*Allahu akbar, Ash-hadu al-la ilaha illa llah, Ash-hadu anna Muhammadan-rasulu . . .*"

"What the hell is that?" Ben says. "I thought you said you were on your way to therapy."

"I am."

Natty sits up too quickly, knocking his head on the sun visor and jarring his shades crooked. People outside the Islamic Center are staring and pointing.

"Then where are you?"

A couple of the large men are heading over. His heart stutters and restarts, as if he's back at the checkpoint near Nisour Square.

"I'm on at Atlantic Avenue," Natty bluffs, pulling names from memory. "Near the Al-Farooq mosque. I heard Walid al-Masri still went to services here. I figured I'd stop by, see if I could catch a glimpse of him."

"Atlantic Avenue?" Ben's voice goes up. "That's a long way from your appointment, isn't it?"

"It's on the way," Natty says, hoping Ben doesn't pull up a map on his computer and check.

"Get a move on, Lieutenant. You're on the clock."

"At least you know I'm not back in the bar. Right?"

The line goes dead and he drops the phone on his lap, falls back against his seat, closes his eyes, and exhales.

You have completely lost your mind, Natty Dread. What are you doing here?

When he left Cuddy and the dead boar at the house, he had a definite Plan A. Drive back to Brooklyn, ask Ben to meet him late at the office, shoot him when no one was around, get rid of the gun, and then stonewall when the police showed up to ask questions.

But before he was even halfway up the Jersey Turnpike, he started to second-guess himself. How could he even dream of getting away with it? The police would ask where he'd been and what he'd done earlier in the day. They'd get his car rental and cell phone records immediately. They'd talk to Cuddy, trace the gun, and start asking questions about his stake in the mailman case. And the ultimate sick irony would be if they thought he killed Ben just to get a bigger share of the award. Thereby undoing everything his father stood for. Not only destroying his case, but putting his only child in prison while leaving his wife utterly destitute.

But Plan B is almost as hard to stomach: Do nothing. Forget the gun residing in Dad's old briefcase. Just shut up and live your life like a sucker. Gather the little crumbs that Ben lets spill on the floor and try to build a house out of them. Pretend your father's murderer is not just getting away unpunished, but *rewarded* from the old man's hard labor. Reaping millions while you stand by in a state of impotent rage. Act like it doesn't matter. Just do your little job, get a bunch of new prescriptions to numb yourself, and try to find another girl who'll put up with a half-dead zombie boyfriend until you drop from a brain hemorrhage or a premature heart attack from being so bottled up.

Of course, there's a Plan C. Polish off the pint and finish what you started in Florida, before you lost your nerve and called the hotline. Get the Glock out of the bag, put that barrel under your chin, and click—problem solved. No more pictures of dead kids in your head, no more torturing yourself over what a shitty son you were. No more flashbacks, nightmares, panic attacks, lashing out, numbness, or constant sense of a tidal wave about to smash down and atomize you into a billion tiny little pieces.

With any luck, Dr. Muhammad Ramzi and his daughter Abeer will come out of the Rite Aid where they work and see that the soldier who killed the first-born son in their family is now dead. But then that means writing a detailed note for the police on the dashboard, explaining who he is and why he's left such an unholy mess for others to clean up. He opens the glove compartment to look for a pen and paper, but finds only the rental agreement and the half-empty pint. Maybe he'd be better off getting caught driving drunk with a loaded gun coming out of the Lincoln Tunnel. At least in prison, his choices would be simpler.

He unscrews the top and takes another drink, which seems to further dissuade the bearded mosque men from approaching. As if federal agents can't be drinking this flagrantly on the job. He checks that it's 1:01 p.m. on the dashboard clock, picks up the cell phone and punches in Stacy's number as the muezzin calls out, *"Hayya 'ala-s-sala! Hayya 'ala-l-falah . . ."* Come to prayer, come to success. Borat broke it down for them, before he got his head cut off.

"Hello?"

"Oh, hey." He fumbles to put the cap back on the bottle. "It's Nathaniel Dresden. I thought this would go straight to voicemail."

"Where are you?"

"Um." He looks around, his brain too overloaded to come up with yet another excuse. "I'm not going to be able to make it to our appointment."

She doesn't say anything, as the call to prayer goes on. *"Hayya 'ala khayr al 'amal."* The best time for the best of deeds has come, according to Borat.

"You agreed to make every appointment, Nathaniel. If I start to let you slide . . ."

"I'm fucked up, Stacy."

"Well . . . okay. I think that's why you're supposed to be in therapy."

"No. I mean, I fucked up before, now I'm fucked up. I mean *right now*. I'm drunk off my ass in the middle of the workday and I'm not even in New York State."

"I'm sorry, Nathaniel," she says gently. "It sounds like there's a Muslim prayer going on in the background. Where did you say you were?"

"You really want to know?"

"I do."

"I killed this little kid in Iraq. Then I found out his family are here in America. So I tracked them down to a Rite Aid in New Jersey where the father and the sister work."

"You're there now?"

"Yes." He puts the bottle back in the glove compartment.

"All right," Stacy says evenly, as if this is a scenario she deals with every day. "And what are you going to do to them?"

"I was thinking of blowing my brains out in front of them."

"And what do you think that will accomplish?" Her voice is still calm, but he can hear her tapping keys frantically in the background.

"I don't know." He pulls his father's satchel out from under the passenger seat. "I just feel like I have to do something."

"Why?" she says. "You didn't kill their child on purpose. Did you?"

"No. But there are some things you can't come back from. That you shouldn't come back from."

"Assuming it's a just world."

"What?"

She pauses for a moment to collect her thoughts. "The way we drive ourselves crazy is by thinking the world's supposed to be just."

"I thought people in your business weren't supposed to use the word 'crazy.'"

"Well, I don't know what other term to use for what you're describing. There'd be something wrong with you if that didn't drive you crazy."

The front doors of Rite Aid open, catching the swinging reflection of the afternoon sun, and Dr. Ramzi steps out in his blue pharmacist coat with his daughter holding his arm, black hijab trailing behind her.

"I think you're just trying to make work for yourself and hold on to a job," Natty says.

"Why don't you let me worry about why I do what I do?"

"I just want to be free. That's all."

He pulls the zipper on the satchel halfway and looks at the grip of the pistol, which Cuddy thoughtfully wrapped up in a greasy old Skid Row band t-shirt.

You know, you don't have to do this.

"So you're there, outside the family's store now?" Stacy asks.

"Yeah. I'm looking right at them."

Dr. Ramzi moves more slowly than he did the last time Natty saw him here, a month ago. His daughter, who works at the same Rite Aid two days a week when she's not at Rutgers—according to her social media—walks a bit behind him, rubbing his back.

"So tell me something, Natty. What makes you so much better than them?"

"What? Who said I was?"

"They can keep going on after what they've been through and you can't? Is it because your pain is so much greater than theirs?"

"You don't have to put it like that," he says.

"I'm giving it to you straight. You're being an asshole."

He watches father and daughter stop in the middle of the parking lot. Abeer hands Dr. Ramzi something. He pops it in his mouth, puts his head back, and closes his eyes. Accepting the blessing of whatever natural light can make it through the Jersey smog onto his face. Then he swallows and keeps walking.

"Do you have to report me?" Natty asks.

"For?"

"Missing my appointment, relapsing with alcohol, crossing state lines . . ."

"I'd rather have you come in tomorrow," she says.

Natty realizes Abeer is looking right at him from twenty-five yards away and he slouches down low in his seat.

"You're gonna cut me a break?"

"You can call it cutting you a break, or not letting you off the hook."

"Why would you do that?"

Dr. Ramzi and his daughter continue past the SUVs and sedans, Abeer throwing an uneasy look in Natty's direction as he ducks behind the wheel again, her father staggering on into swirling dust devils of parking lot grit, candy wrappers, and discount flyers.

"Let's say I'm curious," Stacy answers. "But don't push me."

Dr. Ramzi and Abeer have stopped in front of the mosque entrance and are speaking to a couple of security guards, jumbo boys in gallabiyas with big brown calluses on their foreheads from pressing their brows to rough prayer mats.

An oil truck passes the parking lot, going over a heavy plate covering a construction trench and setting off an enormous boom.

"What was that?" Stacy says, sounding scared for the first time. "Nathaniel, are you still there?"

"Yeah, it's all good. Just background noise."

He finds himself stuck between the edge of the seat and the steering wheel from ducking down in terror.

"Think I'd kill myself while I was on the phone with you?" He takes a breath, trying to squeeze back up into his seat. "That what happens with your other patients? God, your life must suck."

"Just get in here," she says. "Before I change my mind."

"Thank you."

Just before she hangs up, he hears her give a quiet groan that sounds oddly familiar—because it's the sound that every woman in his life eventually makes. Then he takes the satchel onto his lap and pulls the zipper shut.

33

The bar is, Lourdes reckons, maybe one of the whitest places on earth. Three different dartboards on the wood-paneled walls, golf on two different TV screens over the bar, "Hurt So Good" blaring from the jukebox, and the Budweiser emblem covering most of the mirror behind the bar, so the men on the stools don't have to look at their own reflections.

Everywhere she looks, there are still-life studies in throttled white-man frustration and disappointment: off-duty corrections officers with pressure-cooker bodies and iron grips on brown bottles; rain-ruined gnomes in road crew reflector vests gently nursing their beers; strip-mall electronics salesmen in skinny ties seeking solace in cheap watery scotches. The door opens and more human tumbleweeds roll in from the damp upstate night. They wear biker vests with rock band t-shirts underneath, red bandanas without gay implications, and John Deere ballcaps. They high-five, call each other "bro," then look away with gritted teeth and dime-slot eyes like they can't stand the sight of one another. They let their jeans ride down and show the cracks of their asses when they sprawl forward over the counter; they say, "Lemme tell you something," as they joust with their pointed fingers; they howl over jokes that stopped being funny years ago; then they probably go home and act bewildered about why their wives are mad all the time.

Not only is Lourdes the only person of color in the place, she's one of three women, and the bartender with her big meaty arms and pug nose looks like she's barely in the sisterhood.

"Jaysus, what a dump." Sullivan comes back to the booth with their drinks, a spray bottle and a rag on a tray. "I had to tell her twice what goes into your Cosmopolitan and then beg her for a clean cloth to wipe the table down. You sure you're all right to stay?"

"We're here."

Since picking him up at the barracks, they'd been crawling through traffic, barely making it to Poughkeepsie before deciding to pull off and get dinner at a place called Hannigan's.

"We are." He sets her drink beside his Guinness and commences mopping. "But we don't have to put up with any old thing."

"Burger and fries, how bad can they screw it up?"

She takes a sip and shrugs; first time she's had a cocktail in a jam jar but at least there's real vodka in it. Nine hours on the road today, plus the visits at the two different prisons. Her lips are chapped, her blouse has coffee stains, and her hair is stiff and wiry. She doesn't know how Sullivan can even stand to be seen with her. But there he is, sweeping crumbs into his cupped palm and scrubbing away the mug circles like he's preparing the table for Lady Diana. She's had serious boyfriends for years who'd never think about pulling out a chair.

"Well trained, aren't you?" she says.

"Bachelor habits."

"But you weren't always a bachelor, were you?"

"You a cop or something?"

"Still wearing that ring, aren't you?"

"And we're still not talking about that." He keeps wiping, the rag getting balled up in his hand.

She has a vision of him at home. A man alone, deep into his habits. Living with old oak furniture and teacups his wife bought the first year they were married. Looking in the mirror maybe once a day, using a little too much Grecian Formula, vacuuming on his days off. Lots of history books but no cable television. Just a radio on the counter to listen to 1010 WINS news and the occasional ballgame. A bottle of sherry and a bottle of Four Roses in the cupboard that he gets into maybe two or three times a month. Lonely but dignified. Keeping the place so clean and orderly that if he died and got carried out tomorrow, someone could move in next week without a problem.

"I like how careful you are," she says. "Most men don't bother with the edges."

"There was an old lady lived upstairs from us in Windsor Terrace when I was growing up, who used to give me five dollars to come help her straighten up twice a week." Sullivan keeps his head down. "Mostly she just liked the company, I think, but she got me regulated. My wife used to say that was most of the reason she married me. I was the first man she met who knew how to dust."

Ah, so he does want to talk. "I'm sure you had other good points."

"Well, I don't know . . ."

He finishes wiping and lifts his beer, draining half of it in one gulp, his Adam's apple going up and down like the pump-action on a shotgun.

"What was she like, your wife?"

"Christ, Robles." He sets the Guinness down firmly. "How am I ever going to teach you to be a great detective? Don't you know you've got to relax your subject and get him comfortable before you start asking the hard questions?"

"Sorry, hombre. I thought you was comfortable."

He contemplates the gradual descent of sud trails inside the glass. "I'm a shy old man."

"I feel you." She sets her drink down. "People start to get into my business, I'm like, 'Hang on. Why you so interested?' There's usually an angle."

"So what's *your* angle, Robles?"

"Whatchoo mean?"

"Why do you want to know so much about where I'm coming from? A girl your age. Don't you have better things to think about?"

She holds up her hand and pretends to study her nails. "I don't know." She waits until he looks away to study the side of his face. "You got— what—forty years on the job. Maybe I want to pick up some tricks before you go."

"You weren't just asking about the job."

"Okay." She puts her palm flat on the table. "Maybe I'm just interested. We're spending a lot of time together. I like to know what makes people tick. That's why I got into this. I can't be the only one."

"So what makes you tick?" he asks.

"Huh?"

"You got real quiet, once we got close to the prison. And then didn't say anything for close to an hour after we left. Then suddenly you remember there's a snitch you want to see at Great Meadow?"

"Okay." She sniffs and looks for a cocktail napkin to blow her nose. "You got me."

"Who was it?"

"My father." She cricks her neck and fluffs her hair self-consciously in the mirror. "He's in, like, forever."

"Murder?"

"And drugs," she says, giving it up more easily than she ever thought she could. "Ever hear of Raffi Robles?"

He looks away and whistles. "That's your father?"

"Fifteen years since I last saw him."

He puts both hands around his mug, courteously lowering his eyes and giving her time.

"He used to be my hero when I was growing up," she says finally. "He was like the big man in the projects. They had him on *CBS News* one time for being an activist. Chasing all the dealers out of the stairwells and the courtyard when everything stank from crack, and people were shooting grandmothers and pimping out their kids for money. Kept a tire iron by the front door. You know how I'm saying?"

"I do." Sullivan nods. "I remember."

"I wanted to be like him, not my moms—who was acting crazy and strung out because I had a brother who died from a heroin overdose when I was two. Mr. Rock-Solid Barrio Community Leader, everybody coming to him for advice on the benches outside like King Solomon. I used to try to lift his dumbbells and wear his fake-ass alligator loafers when he wasn't around. He was the one got me into reading books and watching police shows."

"And then?"

"And then one night, the police came to our crib, locked him up. And then my aunt took me aside and told me he was a drug dealer. Like the one sold my brother the drugs that killed him. So that was that. I made up my mind that I'm never gonna look up to anybody again. I'd rather find out the truth than get hung up by a lie all my life. Let me be the handkerchief, instead of the teardrop. *Comprende?*"

"So how was it, seeing him after all this time?"

"I don't know why I was hoping he'd be different. Maybe because I am."

He finishes his beer and sits there nodding at the empty glass.

"Nicely done," he says.

"What?"

"You opened up to me, so I'd open up to you."

"You asked me a question, and I answered it."

"Whatever works," he says. "Never admit what you're up to."

He looks toward the bar and makes a little circle with his finger for the bartender to bring them another round.

"My wife was kind of like you, you want to know the truth." He takes a long meditative breath. "Christina Aguayo. Taught sixth and seventh grade English at St. Agnes in the Bronx. She was thinking of becoming a nun when I met her."

"And you made her forget her vows, you devil." She uncrosses her legs under the table, brushing his shin with the tip of her shoe. "I know how you work. You ain't *shy*. You *sly*, old man."

He starts to turn even redder. "She was the best I'll ever do, I'll tell you that much."

The bartender brings them another round and takes back the tray and cleaning rag. Lourdes studies Sullivan's gnawed-looking ear as he turns to say thanks. How can this be happening to her? The kind of men she's usually attracted to are either suave ghetto boys who go to the gym every day or slightly geeky white boys with glasses and college degrees. This craggy throwback is even older than her father. And she'll be damned before she admits she has some kind of daddy fixation.

"Anyway, the case," she says. "You made some calls from the barracks?"

"Nicely done. Divert me for a while." He shuts one eye and points his finger. "Here's what I'm putting together. Kenny Holloway gets killed to keep him from testifying against Shakneela Wilkins, who is Ben Grimaldi's client and Jamar Mack's underling." He folds over a cocktail napkin, takes out a pen, and starts sketching a tree of association. "Then David Dresden gets murdered because he was thinking of turning on Ben. And Shawn 'Science' Davidson gets killed because he fucked up after committing the murder and tried to sell Dresden's Benz at the junkyard."

"But why does Benny G. go to all that trouble of having witnesses killed in the first place? He's a lawyer. He gets paid win or lose."

"How should I know? He just has to win all the time."

"And risk going to prison like his clients?"

"What can I tell you, Robles?" He shrugs and drinks. "Man is both mysterious and simple. Sometimes we do things and we don't know why. We just do them."

"That why you used to go walking in the park?"

"Pardon me?"

Their burgers finally arrive and she realizes she's already drunk. Out on a ledge and not sure how to get down. The COs and road crew guys at the bar are staring at them and saying things out the sides of their mouths. The bartender, who seems to be the only person actually working at this place, goes back behind the counter and points at their booth. She says something and the men explode in hoarse laughter and high-fives.

"Never mind." Lourdes starts to remove her pattie from the stale-looking bun.

"No, you just said something. What was it?"

"Nothing. It was stupid. Let it go."

"Come on, Robles, you went to all this trouble to open up to me, you're looking to get something in return." He cocks back the corner of his mouth, halfway between a smile and a grimace. "You asked me about walking in the park."

She feels a subtle tightening in her chest and a dropping sensation in the pit of her stomach. This is what it must be like to be questioned by him.

"What'd you hear?"

"Just a dumb rumor."

This is how conspiracies unravel. First he's going to hear what she knows and that knowledge will drive a wedge between them. Then to get past it, he's going to demand to know who told her, and once she gives up the captain she's dead in the squad.

"Ante up, detective," he says. "You're still holding too many cards."

"I heard you used to beat up kids in the park."

"Says who?"

"Everybody," she bluffs. "I heard it was after your wife and son passed."

"Yes, that much is true."

"So what was up with that?" She picks up her fork and then puts it down. "You lose your damn mind?"

"I don't rightly know." He shakes his head, like he's trying to figure out how to lift a heavy stone. "I've never tried to put it into words before. I'm not sure that I really can."

"Try."

"I think I was trying to get a statement. Out of God."

"What the fuck did you just say?"

The gnomes at the bar swivel on their stools to see what's made her squawk so loud. She covers her mouth, embarrassed, but doesn't stop staring at him.

"See . . ." He exhales. "When I was growing up, I never questioned authority. I just did whatever I was asked to do. I listened to my parents, then to the priests, then to the teachers, and then to my bosses. I was brought up to never complain or expect things to be different than the way they were. Then I met my wife, and it threw me in the deep end. It was like giving a blind man sight and putting a rainbow in front of him. All the yelling and the screaming, and the food, and the language and the music, *Moros y Cristianos* and Machito, and the, uh, *privileges* of married life . . ."

"Okay, I hear you . . ."

"All of a sudden, I didn't know who I was anymore. She had me wearing Borsalinos and smoking Cohibas. Can you imagine? I started drinking Cuba Libres, instead of Guinness. I even took salsa dance lessons for her. Then she gave me a son and I was over the moon. I was loving my life. And I never knew it could be like that. It felt indecent almost. Terrifying, really."

"*Terrifying?*"

"Because I was always afraid of losing them. And then I did. My boy, Christopher, had a blood disease. Then my wife went a year and a half after. They called it a coronary event. But I know what it was. She put everything she had into that child. When he went, she had nothing left. Not even for me. After that, I was just marking time until I could be together with the two of them in heaven."

"Why'd you start going in the park then?"

He turns his hands over, showing her the rough arcs and latitudes of his palms. "Maybe I just wanted to die. But I was brought up that suicides don't go to heaven, so I couldn't just eat my gun. So maybe getting someone else to do it for me was the next best thing."

"You're still here, though." She pokes at the heart of the right palm with the tip of a painted fingernail, just to see if she can get a reaction.

"Damn kids couldn't fight to save their lives. They'd push me around, and do some punching and kicking. It barely felt like the punishment I deserved."

"For *what?*"

His hand flexes slightly as she pulls her finger away, the reanimation of lifeless flesh. "For having joy and losing it after God gave it to me. I was interested in why he would do that."

"My man, I'm Catholic too, but you taking it to a whole other level. That is some crazy bidness, Papi."

"Am I scaring you?"

"Not really." She touches the middle of his palm again, this time with the flesh of the finger instead of just the nail. "More like wanting to know why you decided to live after all that."

"Who knows? Maybe survival instinct kicked in." He closes his hand just as she pulls her finger away. "Or maybe I figured that if the good Lord was truly done with me, he would have sent someone more capable to finish me off. In any case, here we are. Doing what we need to do. And I guess the fact he's still letting me do it is as much of a statement as I'm likely to get in this life. "

"So is that over now? You still doing that shit?"

"I only enter the park for work. I don't even go for strolls."

She puts her finger back in his hand and leaves it there.

"I'm'a tell you something right now, chief." She leans across the table. "Next time you feel like walking home through the park in the middle of the night, you ask me to go with you. Okay?"

34

Just before closing time, Natty marches through the front doors of the Barnes & Noble on Court Street, the Glock in his father's satchel failing to set off the alarm system at the front. His bad arm is aching again and his jaw feels sore from grinding his teeth all day. His eyes flick past the stacks of children's books, discounted religious bestsellers, and Godiva chocolate boxes near the registers, hypervigilant to the threat of—what?—insurgents lurking in the celebrity bio section.

He rides the elevator to the second floor and finds MG Kelly in the self-help row, her pixie haircut looking a little shaggy, makeup freshly troweled on.

"What's on your mind?" she murmurs, not looking up from the book in her hands.

He tilts down to check the cover. *Smart Women, Foolish Choices*.

"I was thinking about our last conversation." He keeps his voice low, as a closing time announcement interrupts "Hungry Like the Wolf" on the PA.

"Say more."

"You're still looking for cooperation, right?"

"If we're still talking about what's going on at your office." She licks a finger and turns a page. "Are we?"

He finds himself slightly unnerved by the insouciance of her quick pink tongue as it goes back in her mouth. His brain flashing on a series of unwelcome associations to this woman and his father.

"You need someone on the inside," he says. "But meantime I need something from you."

"Why do *you* need anything? I thought we were on the same page about this."

She puts a finger in the book and peers down the end of the aisle, to make sure no one is listening. But the closest person is a security guard sitting on the Storytime stage twenty yards away, reading one of the *Fifty Shades of Grey* books.

"We're trying to do right by your father," she says, her whisper turning harsh. "Now you want something else out of the bargain?"

"I still don't know if I can trust you. How do I know this isn't a false flag operation to undermine Ben when he's taking the mailman case to court?"

"False flag? *Nathaniel*." A series of small vertical lines appear above her upper lip, tiny cracks in her porcelain complexion. "You seem like a very intelligent young man. I'm sure you looked up the cases we cited on your own. No need to connect the dots for you about Ben's involvement in what happened to David."

"I still have a lot of questions . . ."

"As do we. About what's going on inside that office. And you're the only one who can help us answer them."

"I need something first . . ."

He sees from the rapid semaphore of her blinking that he's spoken too insistently.

"I need a show of good faith," he lowers his voice and unclenches the fist he hadn't realized he'd made. "I've been through my father's papers. He submitted at least five Freedom of Information Act requests to the Bureau that were never answered. He asked for Agent Kirkpatrick's 302s, 472s, 209s, and 292s. There's a reason why my father wanted to know about the agent's marital status."

The cracks above MG's lip spread out. "Obviously, I have nothing to do with the mailman case. It's a totally separate matter from the investigation into what happened with these witnesses in Ben's cases."

"Then that's what I want you to prove to me."

"How? Do you have a polygraph in your father's shoulder bag?"

He shifts the strap, the gun making a knocking sound as it shifts inside the bag. "Use your contacts at the FBI to get the information."

"Are you nuts?" Her mouth falls opens. "You want me to act against the interests of the federal government when Ben's firm has a case against them?"

"You keep saying these are separate matters. And you claim that you cared about my father."

"I could lose my job." Her eyes get small and her nose gets pug-like. "You know that, don't you?"

"I'm not asking for anything that we're not legally entitled to."

Keep the lid on, LT. His bones are throbbing from the strain of holding the tension in. He should be attacking someone with a rifle now or a flamethrower or calling strikes with Hellfire missiles. He should be running down a hill with his bayonet affixed and bloody murderous rage in his eyes. *Yeah, get some, Judge Dread.* Instead of talking in muted strategic tones around *The 7 Habits of Highly Effective People* and *Chicken Soup for the Soul.* But no. Natty Dread needs to keep his finger off the trigger this time, play it cool, pick his spots. Be the player this time, not the played.

"If you keep stalling, I'm going to know you're just one of them." He pretends to be more concerned about tucking his shirt into his pants than he is about continuing the conversation. "Not my father's friend."

"I don't even know why David would have cared about an agent's marital status." MG puts the book on the shelf. "How is that in any way relevant to a Bivens action?"

"Let me worry about that. I'll need copies of everything before the end of business tomorrow. The summary judgment hearing is on Friday. But I bet you knew that already."

"And that's your price for cooperating against your father's murderer?" She sighs as if she's just discovered crushed beer cans under her bed. "I don't remember David ever strong-arming me this way."

"Don't talk to me about my father anymore." Natty hikes up the bag as the PA advises customers to make their final selections before the store closes. "I hear from you by tomorrow, I'll consider helping the Bureau on its other case. If I don't, I'll know where I stand."

35

The next morning, the smell of burnt coffee turns Lourdes's stomach as she walks through the homicide squad. Sullivan has been avoiding her since she showed up, keeping his head down while he mumbles into the phone, not offering the seat next to his desk, so she has to wander around like a nomad among the senior detectives at an unfamiliar office.

"Anyway." He follows her into the squad's break room, all business, to hand her a file. "Jamar Mack."

"What about him?"

She notices he's still not looking at her. Figures he'd be what the old-timers call hinky after last night in the bar.

"Remember how we were talking about him with Shakneela in prison yesterday?"

"I remember a bunch of things."

"I decided to give him a harder look." He straightens up, his eyes aimed at least two inches above her head. "Made some calls to Narcotics before you got in. Spoke to some colleagues of your aunt's. She speaks very highly of you, by the way . . ."

"Yeah, okay . . ." She stands on tiptoe, forcing him to meet her gaze. "But we're talking about Jamar Mack, not me. Right?"

"*Right*. Jamar. Enterprising fellow. Grew up in the Schermerhorn Houses. Ma and pa both addicts. Pa went away for beating on ma over and over. She can't care for anybody, so the kid grows up in shelters, brothers and sisters all addicts and dealers . . ."

"Yeah, yeah . . ." She nods. Okay, this is good. We're letting it go. Back to being regular partners again.

"Jamar first appeared in court as a witness in a case where a Housing cop killed a twelve-year-old for waving an alleged toy gun around." Sullivan eyes the folder she's holding, rattling the words off in that fake-neutral monotone cops use to get through unfavorable facts. "Then he spent six months in a Division for Youth facility . . ."

"Wait." She holds a finger up. "He's a juvenile witness in a case against a cop, and then *he* winds up getting arrested? Doesn't that seem, uh, kind of suspicious on our end?"

"We're not out to right the wrongs of the past, Robles."

"Okay, but how do we even know about his juvie record?"

"I pulled everything I could on him and found it in a presentence investigation for probation after a later adult arrest. Jamar brought it up himself, to say how he'd changed."

She mimes turning a crank. "And we care because . . ."

"We care because you were right."

"Oh-ho!" She fans herself with the file. "What was I right about?"

"That later arrest for distributing drugs. Which he did on a BMX bike, riding from housing project to housing project."

"So what? Am I missing something here?"

"Don't you get it?" He snatches the file back. "When you were tracking the phone calls going too fast away from the park on a one-way street. You said it couldn't have been a car or someone on foot. Must have been a bike, right?"

"I said, could be." She nods.

"And you remember what Nathaniel Dresden said the other night about the FBI looking into people selling drugs off bikes?"

"Yeah . . ."

He holds the file up like he's about to swat her. But they've passed the point where they can fool around and play grab-ass like other cops.

"Did it occur to you that might have something to do with the bicycle messengers we noticed at the law firm?" he says.

"Oh, snap . . ."

"I knew there was a reason we kept you around, Robles." Sullivan sticks the file under her arm. "Nice work."

36

Go, little dots, go.

Natty is sitting in the little converted supply closet of an office where Ben's assigned him, Office Max chair tilting forward as he watches two tiny blue specks wend their way across the Google map of Brooklyn on his laptop screen. The two bicycle messengers from the firm are unaware that they are each carrying GPS devices that Natty stuffed inside 8-by-11 business envelopes and placed in their bags along with the other innocuous-looking packages that have the names of other law firms on them.

He clicks a key to enlarge the map, and his eyeballs seem to enlarge proportionally, taking in every line and color. He can see that one guy is headed to the Louis H. Pink housing projects near Linden Boulevard in East New York. The other is headed toward the Sunrise Podiatry and Nephrology Medical Clinic on Kings Highway. Both more likely distribution spots for drugs than the other law firms where they were supposedly heading with labeled legal documents.

He enlarges the map again and taps an arrow, above it all and in control, almost like he's tracking them with a drone. This is the most calm and centered he's felt in weeks, maybe months; the hunter this time, instead of the hunted. The messenger at the Pink Houses stops first. The speed of the dot suggests he's off his bike and on foot now, heading into one of the buildings. Slowing down. Must be winded now, Natty thinks. Alone and vulnerable. Unaware he's being watched, but maybe still uneasy. Natty looks for the button to take a screenshot, just as the rider at the nephrology clinic slows down as well.

The door opens and Ben steps in, shirtsleeves rolled up and mouth a hard bottom line.

"What's up?" Natty starts to shut the laptop.

Ben pops him hard on both shoulders with open palms, almost knocking the chair out from under him.

"You did it, you son of a bitch." He grabs Natty by the shirt collar. "Didn't you?"

"What'd I do?"

From the corner of his eye, Natty sees the dots on the screen pulsing, calling attention to themselves. Plain evidence, if any is needed, that he planted the devices that are probably about to be found.

"And went behind my back to do it." Ben shakes him, the shirt material starting to choke Natty. "Didn't you?"

"Just tell me what I did, Ben."

He reaches for the satchel beneath the desk, his fingertips an inch short of the zipper.

"I just got an email from the government." Ben lets go of the collar and squeezes Natty's cheeks, pooch-style, with one hand. "Providing material from all the Freedom of Information Act requests your father was making for months. They gave up the prior arrest record for the informant Wally al-Masri, the notes from Ibrahim's interrogations, and the complete personnel file for Agent Paul Kirkpatrick and his ex-wife, Joanna Kirkpatrick, including their divorce papers."

"They did?" Natty finally pulls free, his jaw sore. "All of it?"

"I just want to know one thing. How did you do it? We've been asking for these documents since the case started."

Natty shrugs. "You always said, the art of persistence is a lawyer's greatest weapon."

"I said that?"

Ben glances at the open laptop and studies the map.

"Why you looking at this?"

"Just double-checking some of Ibrahim's mail routes to prove Wally al-Masri couldn't have been with him all the times he says he was."

Not bad, Natty congratulates himself, fixing his collar. Especially considering how fast he came out with the lie. But then Ben's look lingers on the map.

"Anyway, we got the docs—" Natty slaps him on the arm, trying to distract him. "Good shit. Right?"

"Yes, they're helpful." Ben looks at where Natty smacked his arm. "But don't get a swelled head. It doesn't make my case a slam dunk, by any means."

"Yeah, I know . . ."

"I mean, the government is not just going to wave the white flag when there's twelve million on the line."

"You asked for ammo. I gave you ammo." Natty shrugs again, letting the "my case" go for now.

"It's not just about the bullets." Ben looks back at the laptop, just as the screen goes dark from inactivity. "It's how you aim them."

"I would've said it's about the shooter."

Ben reaches down to finger the tie that Natty's wearing, one of Dad's old polyknit paisley wonders. "You didn't get these files from Marygrace, did you?"

"No way." Natty tries to pull away, a little like a dog on a leash. "Why do you ask?"

"Because if you did, I'd be very leery that it's fruit from the poisoned tree." Ben flips the fat end of the tie over Natty's shoulder. "She'd do anything to sabotage our case."

"Nothing to do with her." Natty smoothes the tie down. "I just kept calling the clerk's office until I got to someone who sounded friendly. Might take her out after the case is over. But you don't need to know all the sordid details. Do you?"

"Just enough to win, big guy."

"I think Dad would have enough," Natty says, unable to resist. "At this point."

"Ouch." Ben's ears redden a little. "Was that a diss?"

"Just saying: It's on you now."

"Love you, kid." Ben gives him a pat on the cheek that feels more like a light slap. "But remember who's letting you stick around."

37

As Natty Dresden stomps into the squadroom at the Seventy-Eighth Precinct an hour and a half later, Lourdes starts brushing back her hair and tucking in her blouse like her date has just shown up.

"This better be important." He blows past her desk. "I'm not supposed to be out of my office for even a minute now."

Sullivan is already waiting in the captain's office with the show-and-tell display of files and photos laid out on the desk.

"I don't think you'd be happy if we delayed talking to you about what we just found." Lourdes follows Natty in and closes the door. "You're the one who accused us of being behind the curve."

"Why would I think that?" Natty asks. "Just because I was at Kenny Holloway's house before you'd ever heard of him?"

She likes the scruffy beard he's still growing that makes him look more like pictures of his dead dad. And she doesn't mind his little sardonic commentary either. But maybe that's just some weird female thing, where the more dismissive a man is, the more she thinks she has to work to prove herself.

"You pull me in like it's an emergency when we're due in federal court tomorrow?" Natty throws his hands up. "What's the scam?"

"What can you tell us about Jamar Mack?" Lourdes asks.

"What can *I* tell *you*?" Natty does a double-take, from her to Sullivan and then back again. "About the guy who set up Kenny's murder?"

"You know him," Sullivan says.

"I know him?" Natty puts a hand on his chest, like he's about to recite the Pledge of Allegiance. "You're trying to tie me into my own father's murder again? That's what this is?"

Lourdes points to the empty chair in front of the captain's desk. "You remember when you sat in that seat and said the old domestic disturbance calls at your home address weren't about you fighting with your dad, but the foster kids staying at the house?"

"I do."

Sullivan picks up a folder full of papers, most of them probably still warm from the copying machine, and hands it to Natty. "You didn't tell us one of them was Jamar Mack."

Natty's legs slowly bend as he starts to read and lower himself into the chair, not looking where he's planting himself.

"What am I looking at?" he asks, landing just on the edge.

"Court papers, arrest reports, and newspaper clippings," Sullivan says. "All concerning a Jamar Mack, a.k.a. James McGillen."

"You've totally lost me here," Natty says, the snark gone from his voice. "What does this have to do with my dad?"

"The other name rings a bell, doesn't it?" Sullivan says.

Natty lifts a page out of the folder and holds it about three inches from his face as he reads. "'Lawyer David Dresden argued that James Mc-Gillen, fourteen, should be tried as a juvenile, not an adult for pushing another boy in front of an oncoming IRT train.'"

"Obviously, a troubled young man." Sullivan nods. "That was not James's first contact with law enforcement. He'd been a witness in a police shooting and had seen family members arrested on numerous occasions. So you can see why he'd be acting out. Plus there may have been other arrests when he was a juvenile, but those records would still be sealed."

"Do you remember him?" Lourdes asks, still not quite shaking the "there but for the grace of Soledad" vibe about the whole business.

"Should I?" Natty asks.

"I'd think so." Sullivan says. "Your family took him in as a foster child for six weeks after he got out of detention at Crossroads and his folks couldn't step up. It's all in the presentence reports and bail applications."

"This is James the Jealous?" Natty asks, his voice going high in boy-ish alarm. "That's who this is?"

"It took us a while to figure out that James and Jamar were the same person, since he changed his name legally when he was eighteen," Sullivan says. "We wouldn't have even known, except his fingerprints were already in the system. And his arrest as a juvenile made the newspapers."

Lourdes looks over Natty's shoulder. He's stopped on a Xerox of a *Daily News* clip about a later arrest: Jamar Mack coming out of court in a blazer and glasses after beating a multi-count racketeering case, looking very much like a promising scholarship student except for a lazy left eye that gives his otherwise open and sunny face a knowing prematurely cynical look.

"Remember him now?" she asks.

"Yeah, I remember," Natty says, nodding. "My parents had to throw him out because he was always stealing my shit."

This time she doesn't need to bounce a look straight to Sullivan. They've finally found the rhythm.

"But this makes even less fucking sense than before." Natty smacks the clip. "Why would James or Jamar, or whatever the fuck he's called, be tied up in my father's murder if my father helped him? It says right here in the *Daily News* that Dad got this subway murder case moved to Family Court, so James wouldn't get tried as an adult and sent upstate. He owed my father his life."

"Check out the prosecutor that made the deal happen," Lourdes says. "That's who he really owes."

As she leans over his chair to put her finger next to the offending paragraph, her upper thigh grazes the back of his shoulder. She can feel the weight of knowledge entering him as he reads, the legs of the chair groaning as he shifts, maybe finally leaning toward being on the same side as them.

"Benny G. cut him the break," she says. "Maybe you can tell us what's been going on in that office where you've been working."

He becomes unnervingly still. It's almost like waiting for a chemical reaction in a test tube. Then his shoulder presses harder against her leg and he stands, banging the chair against her knee.

"Excuse me," he says. "But I've got other places to be now."

He exits without giving them a chance to follow up, leaving the folder face-down on the seat and the photocopies spilling across the floor like the aftermath of a small semi-contained explosion.

38

The sight of the two aluminum road bikes chained together with a Kryptonite lock by the construction site causes Natty's adrenaline levels to spike immediately. This is definitely where the messengers he'd been tracking stopped after hitting Pink Houses and the nephrology clinic. A three-story townhouse getting renovated on Junius Street in Brownsville. With a rusting green Dumpster and a sign that says "J. S. Mack Contracting" out front. And the steady woodpecker knock of sledgehammers and the bone-conduction grind of a buzzsaw coming from within.

The tools pause for a few seconds and he hears voices arguing inside the house, through the billowing blue plastic covers where the windows should be. Naturally, it's insane for him to come here, straight from the Seventy-Eighth Precinct, at four in the afternoon, the day before the mailman case is finally set to begin. If he really wanted to honor his old man, he'd be back at the office, helping Ben prepare for the hearing and craft his questions for the witness Dad worked so hard to get on the stand. Instead of showing up without ceremony, wearing one of his father's patch-elbowed jackets that's barely roomy enough to cover Cuddy's Glock 17 as it sits tucked into the back of his waistband.

Be a fine thing if Detectives Robles and Sullivan followed him from the precinct to this address, which a cursory Google search off his cell phone revealed was also—not coincidentally—permitted for renovation by a home improvement company registered to a Jamar Stephon Mack. The cops had obviously given him the full download about Jamar in the hope that Natty would drop everything else, go back to the law firm, and start gathering evidence to help them with their investigation. Not take up arms and sail off into a sea of troubles of his own making.

The ring of the buzzsaw is still in the air as he slips through the half-opened front door and finds four men standing in what used to be a living room just off the foyer, a high-ceilinged space with parquet floors, engulfed in a sepia haze of sawdust and falling plaster. There's a stepladder by a fireplace, a large table saw in the middle of the room, and a spackle-encrusted Casio boom box in the corner playing the cheesy '90s dance-floor epic "What Is Love?"

Two of the men are Spandex-clad messengers he recognizes from the firm's hallways. Rosencrantz and Guildenstern. Another looks Chinese and holds two of the bulk-sized envelopes that Natty saw in the messengers' satchels. The fourth man wears a dust mask, a red do-rag, and a pair of expensive designer glasses.

"Can I help you?" Jamar Mack raises a brow over a lazy eye.

"I wondered if I could have a word about some of the work you're doing." Natty looks around, trying to sound semi-official, like a buildings inspector.

"You from the city?"

Natty pulls on the sides of his jacket, making sure the gun stays covered. "I'm a lawyer. I live in the area. Maybe we can discuss this privately."

"Y'all get out of here a few minutes." Jamar tugs down his mask, unveiling a thin mustache and a sturdy chin. "Get me a Diet Sunkist soda from the deli down the block. I know they got that shit."

As he reaches into his jeans and pulls out a few dollar bills to give the other men, Natty notices that Jamar's navy polo shirt has a slightly frayed collar and a small red Ralph Lauren horseman emblem on the breast. Like something a successful contractor would wear on the job, since he has drawers full of newer shirts at home.

The Chinese man leaves first, followed out the front door by a messenger in blue Spandex. But the second messenger hesitates, standing in front of Natty and looking him up and down, probably recognizing him as well and wondering what's up.

"Don't go far." Jamar dismisses him with a nod. "We're not done here."

They close the door behind them, enclosing a space full of shattered old surfaces transformed into millions of airborne particles.

"Don't you need a fan?" Natty coughs. "Seems like you shouldn't be breathing this in."

"This a shakedown?" Jamar takes off the mask and do-rag. "I don't think you showed me any ID."

"I'm Nathaniel Dresden, Jamar. I'm sure you remember me."

The eyelid droops just a little more and the mouth becomes a small thoughtful circle, like it belongs to a classical musician about to start playing a long complex piece.

"How did you find me, Natty?"

"Not that hard. You applied for a certificate of occupancy to turn a family house into separate apartments. Doesn't seem like you're hiding at all."

"Nothing to hide." Jamar shrugs. "Got my degree from BMCC and a New York real estate broker's license. Now I own two houses and my own contracting business. How about you?"

He doesn't look much like the way Natty remembered him: a mad and mangy foster kid in a dirty white undershirt and big-man jeans, tall for his age, with an oversized head, crooked teeth, and grabby hands. *Yo, you got so much stuff!* Pulling the GI Joes and toy tanks out from under Natty's bed and leaving them in dismantled pieces on the floor. Precious gifts from Ben, received over the objections of Natty's mother and father. Then there was the Game Boy that went missing right after he arrived. The Sony Walkman that somehow mysteriously turned up under James's pillow a few weeks later, even though he swore he never touched it. The Schwinn bicycle that wound up disappearing when Natty wouldn't let James ride it to the bodega on Seventh Avenue one day. Then the "accidental" bump from the top of the stairs that sent Natty tumbling right before James had to move out.

The man in front of him is maybe just a few shades darker than Natty himself. With his pricey eyewear, close-cropped hair, and tan Red Wing work boots, every inch the New Brooklyn entrepreneur, with nary a suggestion of drug money funding the move into legitimacy.

"I'm doing all right," Natty says. "Got out of the service and picked up my law degree. Staying with my mother awhile. I guess you heard my father was killed."

"Yeah. I know about that."

"Funny." Natty shakes his head. "Most people would say, 'Sorry, man' or 'That sucks.'"

Jamar waves two fingers, his good eye matching the lazy one now. "Where I come from, people got killed all the time and no one said shit."

"But you *knew* my father."

Jamar leans back against an unpainted radiator, as relaxed and leisurely as a man sunbathing at the stern of his yacht while the singer on the boombox keeps pleading "baby, don't hurt me."

"What do you want, Nathaniel?"

The sustained animal-like moan of a saw tearing into a heavier piece of wood upstairs startles Natty. He hadn't realized anyone else was in the house. He puts his hands in his pockets, butt of the gun sticking into the small of his back, as he tries to resettle and remember the sequence of questions he had in mind.

In Army Intel, they taught at least sixteen approaches for interrogations. There was Love of Comrades and Hate of Comrades, which played on feelings of loyalty and betrayal of former fellow combatants. There was Good Cop/Bad Cop, of limited use here since he's alone. And of course, Fear Down, which involved reassuring a prisoner that no harm would befall him if he cooperated, and Fear Up, which did the exact opposite. But he's in no position here to deliver threats of any kind. The table saw, sledgehammers, and the extra men upstairs are all in Jamar's employ. So unless he's ready to shove the gun in Jamar's face, with all the consequences that could follow, he's left with the never-popular Direct Approach, with perhaps a touch of the high-risk We Know All.

"I just wanted to let you know what I've been hearing." Natty arches his shoulders and bends back, casually checking that the gun is still where he can reach it easily. "I've spoken to the police and to the FBI about what happened to my dad."

"Uh-huh."

"I know they've been looking at connections to the cases he's worked on. Some of them going back to when he represented you as a juvenile."

"Okay. But you still haven't said what you want here."

Jamar puts the mask and do-rag on the mantelpiece over the fireplace.

"I just found out that Ben Grimaldi was the prosecutor who cut the deal that sent your subway case to Family Court," Natty says.

"Congratulations." Jamar nods. "You just told me something I already know."

"It got me thinking that you might feel that you owe Ben more than whatever you owed my dad."

"You got a point you're trying to make, Natty? Because we got a big job to finish in this house."

"I've also spoken to Kenny Holloway's family." Natty puts a hand up. "So I know about Kenny and Shakneela Wilkins."

"That's just nothing coming to nothing." Jamar shrugs. "I gave Kenny a job at one of my construction sites and he thanked me by trying to name me in some bullshit drug case. Then he got himself shot. I don't know anything about that. Except what goes around comes around. Sometimes."

"I also know about the witnesses getting killed in three of Ben's other cases," Natty says, as the hammering begins upstairs again. "And you know some of that is going to lead back to you."

Jamar puts the back of his wrist to his mouth, as if he's stifling a yawn. "I'm going to ask you one more time. What are you doing here, Nathaniel? I'm not part of that life anymore."

"I know you were involved in what happened to my father," Natty says. "I just want to know why, after everything we did for you."

Jamar looks down and gives a small laugh, as he wipes his glasses with the hem of his polo shirt. "What mean 'we,' kemosabe? Your father was my lawyer. Once. That's all."

"My family took you in."

"And that's a reason for me to hang four murders around my own neck?"

"One way or the other, someone's going to answer for them."

Jamar turns his head and exhales. Then he reaches down and turns off the boom box.

"Nathaniel, have you ever been to the Schermerhorn Houses?" he says, with a kind of finicky exactitude.

"I've driven by it maybe a million times . . ."

"Right." Jamar hits the radiator pipes with the heel of his palm twice, as if anger is slowly building behind his back. "You went *by it*. But it's where I'm *from*. You understand the difference? My mother and father weren't like your mother and father. My father went to prison because he almost beat my mother to death. The police came and took him away. Then we wound up living in a city shelter because there were six of us kids and no one in the family had a job. It was like we were the ones who got punished."

"All right, but . . ."

"Okay, you got me started, now let me finish." Jamar holds a finger up. "Fourth of July, '95, I was twelve years old and we were living with my cousins at Schermerhorn. Taking turns sleeping in the bathtub. I saw a cop shoot my friend Tracy Rehborn to death because he was carrying a toy gun in the courtyard. The DA made me come to court three times to testify. And then nothing happened to the cop."

"We were talking about my father," Natty interrupts, trying to get back to his plan.

"Right." Jamar takes off his glasses and starts to wipe them on his shirttail. "Who defended me when I pushed Shamduke Marshall onto the subway tracks after that. Because Shamduke said he was going to kill me and no one in the principal's office cared when I asked them to help me. That's when I knew I had to look out for myself. Because there was no system I could depend on. There's no justice. There's just people with common interests. And lawyers who make money. So you want to know why I got no tears for your father? It's because they dried up a long time ago."

"We brought you into our home, Jamar."

"Where you lied and bullied me every day. You remember that? The first night you told me you'd get rid of me like you got rid of all the others they tried to bring in the house. You remember that yellow Sony Walkman you used to have? I saw you put it under my pillow and then call your parents into my room."

"That didn't happen that way," Natty says.

Almost instantly, though, he has a memory of sneaking into his father's study where the cot was set up. The smell of Final Touch fabric softener that his mother used on the guest sheets. The yellowing pillow cases they gave to the temporary kids. All at once, he's doubting the memory he's been holding onto. Instead he's listening for his mother's footsteps and slipping the player under the pillow. There's a sickening thud in the pit of his stomach as the dust in the air begins to settle. He wonders how many other things he's misremembered so he can live with them.

"I used to resent the shit out of you and your family." Jamar finishes wiping his glasses and puts them back on. "You showed me the good life and then took it away. But then I figured you were just doing what you needed to do. And that was that. It all works out."

"My father still saved you, Jamar."

"It was the DA who cut the deal to send my case to Family Court. That's who I owe. And that's who you should be speaking to."

"You're talking about Ben?"

Jamar stares at him expressionlessly as the drill bit bores into a support beam right above them. "I said what I've needed to say. I'm not living in the past. If you got questions, call my lawyer. Who is *not* Benny G., by the way."

"Why? You don't want to mix your business with your legal representation?" Natty lets his hands go loose at his sides, in case he has to grab the gun suddenly. "I know you've been running drugs out of the firm as well."

"Why would you even say that, Natty?" The lid droops lower as the eye behind it studies where Natty's hands are. "You wearing a wire? Or do you have something else on you I need to worry about?"

"Doesn't have to be like that," Natty says. "We could be on the same side for once. I might keep the information about the firm to myself, if I thought you'd help me get payback for my father."

"Hmm, do I believe that?" Jamar drums his fingers idly on the radiator. "You know what, Nathaniel? You should never take anything for granted. That skinny little Chinese brother who passed you on the way out to get my diet orange soda? He's a straight-up Shanghai Gangsta back home. You fuck with him, he'll cut your dick off and feed it to the fish in the Yangtze."

"I'm going to take that as a no, then, on the helping hands issue," Natty says. "I think that's a mistake."

"Always did like your folks." Jamar grabs a tape measure off the windowsill. "They were your good-hearted help-the-less-fortunate types. Who knows where I'd be if I grew up in a house like yours?"

"Maybe you would have ended where I am, and I would've ended where you are."

"You wouldn't have been any damn good either way." Jamar stands up, draws out the tape to measure the window diagonally, then lets it snap back. "Get the fuck out of here now, Natty. I told you who your business is with."

39

At quarter past five, the glass doors of Dresden & Grimaldi open and police officers flood in, Lourdes following Sullivan and a drug-sniffing German shepherd that seems determined to rip its handler's arm from its socket.

"Excuse me." The young Asian receptionist is on her feet, with her headset attached. "What's going on?"

Emergency Service Unit personnel have come up the fire stairs in heavy black uniforms with rifles, Kevlar vests, and riot helmets. Paralegals and messengers are getting pushed up against the cream-colored walls and frisked by precinct detectives. Uniform cops confiscate bikes parked out in the hall. An oak door at the far end of the corridor opens and Ben walks out, pulling up his tie.

"Are you guys shitting me?" He steps to Sullivan, going chest to chest. "You're raiding my office less than twenty-four hours before I'm due in federal court?"

"We have a warrant, counselor." Lourdes holds out the paper, wondering if she's going to need to pry them apart.

Ben snatches it and starts reading. "You're accusing me of promoting drug sales and murder for hire?" He looks up. "Where's your probable cause?"

"The warrant states the facts," Sullivan says, not giving an inch. "Judge McGregor read the affidavits and believes there is sufficient cause to look for further evidence of criminal activity on the premises. My understanding is that the ADAs literally came to his house in the middle of the night, and once he saw the evidence they had, he didn't hesitate to sign off."

Lourdes studies Ben's expression closely as he reads. The muscles in his face start to sag and then compress with anger.

"Let me explain something," Ben says. " 'Fuck 'Em in the Neck' McGregor has been senile since the Reagan administration. He'd sign away his own grandchildren if the DA sent over a blonde with D cups in the middle of the night."

"I'm sure you'll have a chance to make that argument in court," Lourdes says.

"You're doing the feds' dirty work, trying to cripple me when I'm about to take them on?" Ben turns back to Sullivan. "Violating the Fourth Amendment, the Sixth Amendment, and the entire notion of attorney-client privilege in one fell swoop? If that doesn't bear the stench of a vendetta, I don't know what does."

"Our case has nothing to do with your federal matter, Mr. Grimaldi," Lourdes says.

"Really?" Ben half rises on the balls of his feet, as if fury is causing him to levitate. "You know, despite our differences, I never thought I'd see the day when Kevin Sullivan went around carrying the water for the FBI."

"You still haven't seen it," Sullivan says.

"Where's Natty?" Ben calls out to the receptionist, who's tossing her black hair and huffing like some Tribeca nightclub hostess dealing with a rude customer.

Lourdes chances a look at Sullivan: Bad sign that Natty's AWOL right after they talked to him about Jamar. They'd elected to move on the warrants right away, in case he got a wild hair up his ass and tipped Ben off for some reason. But now that Natty's not here, it could look like he knew about the raid ahead of time.

Ben thrusts his jaw out as he goes back to reading.

"This whole case looks like it's based on anonymous affidavits from a couple of guys who work as bike messengers at this office. What'd you do, catch them running red lights and flip them on old warrants?"

Lourdes gives him a buttery smile, instead of duck face. But truthfully, he's close. The messengers were going the wrong way on Nostrand Avenue, where they were each caught with two hundred Oxys, twelve pounds of weed, and ten grams of heroin laced with fentanyl in their backpacks. It took them each less than ten minutes to start talking about getting the drugs from paralegals in the mailroom here.

"If it turns out that some of these individuals have been up to something illegal here, I hardly think you can hold me or the firm personally responsible," Ben says. "David hired most of them, not me. It's not surprising that they'd continue their criminal lifestyle, despite my efforts to provide an honest way to make a living."

Sullivan shrugs. "No good deed goes unpunished."

"Enough." Ben puts his hands up. "Do what you need to do. Nothing you find here will be admissible anyway. Except as the basis of the massive harassment suit I'll file against the police department. When this is all over, I'll have both of your shields." He looks into his office, where the K-9 officer has been pulled in by the German shepherd. "And if that dog pisses on my silk rug, I'll sue for extra damages."

40

The sound of two hundred or so buttocks shifting restlessly in the pews reminds Natty of the passing moments. The clock above the judge's bench says it's half past ten. The Honorable Saundra Gomez, a self-righteous string bean with a page-boy haircut, big earrings, and major political connections, stares at the vacant seat next to Natty at the plaintiff's table, tapping the watch on her wrist menacingly.

There are a couple dozen reporters present, plus various Justice Department functionaries, assistant U.S. attorneys, FBI agents, legal interns, and law school students. Ibrahim Saddik is in the front row with his family, the four of them more devout-looking than he is. His son Hamid has—unhelpfully in Natty's view—chosen to wear his white man-dress and skullcap for the occasion. Ibrahim's wife and two daughters are wearing black headscarves and all-enveloping robes of their own. Natty's mother is beside them, striking a note of understated glamour in a simple black dress and white pearls, with her hair tied back in a bun.

But still no sign of Ben. Natty has been leaving voice messages, emailing, and texting since last night. When Jen from the office called in hysterics about a police raid. Which, unfortunately, took place while Natty was off talking to Jamar Mack. Who may, in turn, have tipped off Ben about his visit. So now Natty worries Ben may have decided to disappear on the eve of the long-awaited summary judgment hearing, to either go into hiding or arrange retaliation.

Judge Gomez signals for him to approach. "Mr. Dresden, what's going on? Your witness is here and the rest of us were ready to begin thirty minutes ago."

"I don't know what to tell you, Your Honor. Mr. Grimaldi should be along shortly."

But what if Ben, deciding the jig is up, has decided to kill himself? Beating Natty to the punch, depriving him of the opportunity for revenge, and leaving him holding the bag for this case.

"I'll tell you: I'm not going to be happy about rescheduling." The judge aims a finger. "I'm only allowing this hearing because there were allegedly things that the government concealed during discovery. But I could reverse that decision."

The courtroom doors burst open and Ben makes his entrance on cue, tucking the purple handkerchief into his breast pocket.

"Forgive me, Your Honor," he says. "I had to deal with an emergency at the office. I promise no further delays."

"Better not be," she warns him and then turns to the main court officer. "Bring in the witness."

As Natty turns back to the plaintiff's table, he sees that Ben has just shaved the stubble from his head. As if he's shorn himself in a ritual to prepare for battle, or the guillotine.

"I'll speak to you, Nathaniel," he mutters under his breath. "After this is done."

Special Agent Paul Kirkpatrick raises his slab-like hand to take the oath. As soon as he sits down in the witness box, he looks diminished and defensive, his seat so low that he's forced to look up like a chastened schoolboy as Ben approaches with a file in hand.

"Good morning, Agent Kirkpatrick." Ben buttons up the front of his pinstripes, his jacket like a Roman senator's toga across his broad chest. "I've been looking forward to this day."

Kirkpatrick tries to match him with a cocky half swivel, but his chair legs give a loud indignant squeak.

George McArdle, the Justice Department lawyer defending the FBI, rises—triathlon-trim and bespectacled in a Paul Stuart suit and tie. His ramrod posture makes Natty think he was probably with the judge advocate general's office in the military.

"Your Honor," he says in a weary singsong. "Is it necessary to indulge *all* of Mr. Grimaldi's theatrics and sarcasm today?"

Ben retracts his chin in exaggerated Italian Uncle Tom humility. "I'm sure I don't need to explain to Mr. McArdle how much latitude I have to question this witness as I see fit."

The judge nods cautiously. "Mr. Grimaldi can ask what he likes, within reason. But let's not play to the crowd too much."

Ben pivots back to the box. "Agent Kirkpatrick, can you tell us what led to agents you supervised arresting my client, Mr. Saddik?"

"We developed information from a confidential source that Mr. Saddik was using his job delivering mail as a cover to transport bomb parts to homegrown terrorists in Brooklyn."

"Can you tell us who that source was?"

Wasting no time going on the attack. His footwork as bold and aggressive in the courtroom as it was in the boxing ring.

The agent rears back a little on the stand. "Of course not."

"Why?" Ben throws his arms open, going from boxer to grand opera tenor belting to the balcony.

"Obviously, our source's life would be in danger if he was exposed." Kirkpatrick answers in a truculent cowboy grumble.

"Convenient, isn't it?"

"This was a valued asset who'd helped us thwart multiple earlier plots." The agent makes a show of puffing his cheeks out. "When he tells us Mr. Saddik is involved in a plan to blow up the Brooklyn, Williamsburg, and George Washington Bridges simultaneously, we take that very seriously."

"You mean you *took* it 'seriously.'" Ben returns to the plaintiff's table and picks up a file that had been lying in front of Natty. "Yes?"

"I think it's clear what I meant." Kirkpatrick frowns.

With his deep voice and piercing blue eyes, he's probably the kind of superior officer who enjoyed seeing subordinates cower and second-guess themselves, Natty thinks.

"Is it?" Ben advances back to the box. "Shouldn't there be a great deal of difference between what you once believed and what you now believe when you've learned pertinent new information?"

"I see what you're trying to get at, Mr. Grimaldi." The agent takes a long sip of water, trying to break Ben's rhythm. "The premise of your lawsuit is that we arrested Mr. Saddik knowing that he was an innocent party." The agent looks past Ben, raising his deep voice and training his eyes on the spectator gallery. "Nothing could be further from the truth."

"Very stirring." Ben moves within a foot and a half of the box, blocking the agent's view of his audience. "But do you understand there's a difference between what you didn't know and what you *should* have known?"

"Yes, I know there's a difference." Kirkpatrick lays a finger across his upper lip. "But I'm not sure what qualifies you or any of your associates to make that judgment after the fact."

Ben puts his hands out as if he's about to lay them on the rail of the box. "Agent Kirkpatrick, isn't it true you questioned my client, Mr. Saddik, for thirteen hours straight without a lawyer present?"

"He never asked for a lawyer." Kirkpatrick stares until Ben steps back.

The doors at the back of the courtroom grunt as Natty turns to see Douglas Bryce and MG Kelly entering.

"He *never* asked for a lawyer?" Ben rolls his neck. "Or was he told he wouldn't need one?"

"I don't recall."

"Why was the decision made not to record that interrogation?"

"I don't recall that either."

"But you *do* recall Mr. Saddik denied having any knowledge of a pending terrorist attack, don't you?"

"Yes."

"Yet shortly after that questioning ended, you were involved in the decision to send Mr. Saddik overseas. Right?" Ben grabs another file from in front of Natty and comes back at the witness. "That's your signature, isn't it?"

Natty feels the twinge in his lower back as he leans forward, trying to see which papers Ben is offering.

"Yes."

"You were aware Mr. Saddik was being taken to a so-called Black Site in Macedonia for interrogation, weren't you?"

"I was."

The twinge moves to his chest: a thrumming of strings, set off by the word "interrogation." Natty finds himself looking at the empty chair beside him.

"And you were familiar with what went on at these Black Sites because you'd been to them yourself?" Ben absently fans himself with the papers.

"Only as an observer." The agent turns in his seat. "Those interrogations were mostly conducted by Macedonian intelligence officers and CIA advisors."

"You knew my client would be treated harshly, though. Right?"

"It's not a weekend at your house in the Hamptons, counselor."

Ben arches his eyebrows for the audience's benefit. "But you knew Mr. Saddik would be deprived of sleep and kept in a tiny cell with lights on twenty-four hours a day?"

"I knew that was possible."

Natty finds himself looking at the empty chair. As if Dad is sitting there, silently wondering if his son did the same things.

"And you knew he'd be denied food and bathroom privileges, didn't you?"

"Yes, but . . ."

Natty expels a breath through his nose, turning away from the chair. Telling himself this isn't the time for flashbacks or imaginary conversations to justify himself to dead people.

"And you knew Mr. Saddik would be beaten on his head, shoulders, and soles of his feet and waterboarded, didn't you?" Ben is saying.

"Yes, I knew it could happen," the agent concedes. "But not by U.S. personnel."

Natty hears himself breathing harder as he forces his eyes down onto the yellow legal pad page, where he should be taking notes for further questions.

"You knew Mr. Saddik could be rear-cuffed and hung from a doorway with his hands behind his back. Didn't you?"

"I didn't know that specifically." Kirkpatrick's eyes crawl sideways.

"But you knew he would be made to feel he was on the brink of death over and over?"

"Absolutely not. The United States government does not believe in torture."

Stop breathing so hard, Natty tells himself. People are starting to stare.

"But you knew basically what would happen to Mr. Saddik, once you turned him over," Ben says. "Didn't you?"

"Only in a broad sense. I was not an active participant."

"But you didn't do anything to stop these methods, did you?"

"No, sir." Kirkpatrick looks toward the flag pole near the bench, as if considering running Ben through with the sharp end.

"You didn't intervene when Mr. Saddik was being deprived of food and sleep, did you?"

"No."

Natty puts his elbows on his knees and puts his head down. Get a grip, Mighty Dread. This case isn't about you.

"You didn't protest when he was being hung by his arms and sustaining injuries that would prevent him from doing his job again?" Ben raises his chin, as if daring Kirkpatrick to take a swing at it.

"I'm not a doctor, Mr. Grimaldi."

"But you didn't have to be a doctor to know what was happening when interrogators threatened to have members of the Saddik family raped or murdered, did you?"

Natty nudges the empty chair away with his elbow. What he did wasn't the same, he'd tell Dad. He never tortured anyone. Personally.

"Objection." George McArdle rises.

"I'll allow it," the judge says.

"I didn't take those threats seriously," Paul Kirkpatrick insists. "No one sensible would."

"Even though you knew they'd waterboarded him nineteen times and had him gasping and begging for his life?" Ben says.

Natty hears a ragged yelp at the end of an exhalation. It's not him. The sound has been coming from outside his head.

He looks over his shoulder just as Ibrahim gets up with a hand clapped over his mouth and tears in his eyes, exiting the courtroom with his family looking after him worriedly.

"The answer is yes." Kirkpatrick tenses his broad forehead. "I did not believe those threats would be acted on. But, Your Honor, can I say something now?"

"Only if it's to elaborate on what's already said." The judge appears to be rocking on the bench, as if atop a runaway stagecoach.

"It's easy for Mr. Grimaldi and his associates to drag this proceeding into open court and posture to try to embarrass our agency. What they don't say is that shortly before Mr. Saddik was brought in, our nation had been attacked. In this city. We had no idea where we were going to be hit next. Some of us were determined to prevent more Americans from being killed. And some weren't."

"Judge, it sounds like Agent Kirkpatrick is considering a run for Congress," Ben says. "Can you ask him not to do it here?"

"Mr. Grimaldi, I've given you a lot of latitude as well." The judge's glasses slide halfway down her nose. "But yes, Agent Kirkpatrick, try to stay on point."

"Yes, Your Honor." Kirkpatrick sits up. "Just let me add that we haven't had an attack of that scale since and the reason is there are men and women who are willing to risk their careers and their lives to protect our country and its principles. Were mistakes made? Perhaps. But they were made in the service of a greater cause. Which is something Mr. Grimaldi and his associates like to ignore."

"Thank you, Agent Kirkpatrick." Ben tilts up his chin, and the back of his head appears to make a muscle. "I'm glad you got all that on the record. Now let me ask you something. Do you see that young man over there?" He is pointing straight at Natty.

"Yes."

"Do you know who he is?"

"I believe his name is Nathaniel Dresden."

The sound of his own name puts Natty into a stress position, his whole body going rigid to withstand the strain.

"Then you know he is the son of my late partner, David Dresden, and a decorated combat veteran himself."

McArdle is on his feet. "Your Honor, what's the relevance?"

"The relevance is Mr. Kirkpatrick just went on record casting himself as the sole defender of our country in this courtroom. So my question is, how can he do that while actively subverting its principles?"

So this is why he's here. This is why Ben has kept him close, instead of keeping him at a distance or having him taken off the count as well. So he can be used as a prop at a crucial moment.

"Gentlemen, we have strayed far off into the wild blue yonder." The judge gavels down. "From now on, all questions and answers will pertain to the facts of the case or they won't be tolerated. Am I clear?"

"Yes, Judge." Ben bows again and presents the crown of his head as it glistens with light sweat.

Natty puts a hand on the armrest of the vacant seat. Knowing the old man might not have been as effective at this crucial moment.

"Agent Kirkpatrick," Ben says. "You mentioned that Mr. Saddik was taken into custody based on information your office received from a so-called confidential informant, whose identity has never been revealed publicly. Correct?"

"Mr. Grimaldi, you should know better than anyone why that's necessary," the agent says.

Conversations in the gallery rise up and die down behind Natty. He turns to see MG whispering to Doug Bryce and wonders who else might have caught the dark reference.

"Be that as it may." Ben shrugs, playing it off. "During Mr. Saddik's two years in captivity at the Black Sites and the Guantanamo Bay prison facility, did there come a time when you and your fellow agents began to question this informant's veracity?"

"I don't recall that, Mr. Grimaldi."

"Really?" Ben breaks into a ringmaster's grin, which he turns to share with the crowd. "You never had any doubts about this allegedly valuable source?"

"I think I explained that this source had helped us prevent a number of other lethal attacks that had been in the planning stages."

"And for his efforts, was this informant being paid or was this a criminal who'd been caught and had agreed to cooperate to get a lighter sentence?"

"Your Honor, we have to object again," McArdle says, pen clenched in fist. "Mr. Grimaldi is purposefully straying into information that's been classified as matters of national security."

"Judge." Ben composes a look of injured innocence. "We've been through this at an earlier hearing, where I argued that this was a smoke screen thrown up by the government to cover up Mr. Kirkpatrick's wrongdoing."

"Factually, I believe it was Mr. Dresden who made that argument," the judge says with a glance over at Natty.

"My point is that the motives and handling of this cooperator go to the heart of our case and prove deliberate intent."

The judge sighs. "Answer the question, please, Agent Kirkpatrick."

"The answer is both," the agent says, with the stare of a long-distance trucker battling white-line fever. "The source was getting paid and working off a charge."

"How much?" Ben asks.

"The amount was, I think, $6,000 a month."

"Some source, eh?" Ben whistles between his front teeth, eliciting a couple of snickers from the reporters in the rear. "Can you tell us, what was the charge this cooperator was working off?"

"Judge?" The agent looks up at the bench plaintively. "If I'm specific, I risk exposing this source's identity."

"Can you confirm it was a federal crime that carries the potential for a long sentence?" The judge takes off her glasses.

"Yes, Your Honor."

"Mr. Kirkpatrick," Ben says. "Did it ever occur to you that this source might on occasion be less than entirely truthful?"

"That's why we verify independently."

"Only sometimes you don't. Correct?"

"Depends," Kirkpatrick says. "If you find a bomb with a ticking clock, you don't always have time to call the manufacturer in Switzerland."

"So you were aware that this source had borrowed a large sum of money from Mr. Saddik and had no way to pay it back?"

"I didn't believe that was relevant," the agent says.

Natty rubs a thumb deep into his beard, as Ben suddenly rounds back to the table and stops in front of him. He stares down for a second. As if somehow this is the moment where they're finally going to confront each other. Instead Ben picks up one of the Freedom of Information Act files Natty leveraged out of MG and heads back toward the witness box.

"You also put false information in this affidavit to keep Mr. Saddik from discovering who was accusing him of supporting terrorism and depriving him of his right to properly defend himself. I believe the term for this kind of investigation is 'parallel structure.' Which is really just lying, isn't it?"

"Wait a second." McArdle gets to his feet. "Mr. Grimaldi can't use this proceeding to make wild unsupported accusations."

"Not unsupported," Ben says, brandishing the file as he approaches the bench. "My office has worked long and hard to prepare for this day, despite all the government obstructions and obfuscations. We now know exactly who this source is. It's an acquaintance of Mr. Saddik's who happens to be a career criminal."

The murmurs have started up again from the back of the courtroom, along with the flapping of notebook pages. At McArdle's table, other assistant U.S. attorneys are scrambling through their papers, caught unprepared.

"Not only are many of the statements attributed to this individual demonstrably false," Ben pours it on, "we can prove that there was an effort by Agent Kirkpatrick to shield him while he continued to commit crimes. They created a fake person on paper to disguise his identity. They have this source eating three meals a day with Mr. Saddik and then following him to every stop on his mail route. Not only should they have known better, they *did* know better. And they obscured these facts for personal advantage."

"Your Honor, that's outrageous." McArdle approaches the bench. "There's not a scintilla to back it up."

"No *scintilla*?" Ben returns to pick up the next stack of Natty's files. "Agent Kirkpatrick, can you tell the court what a 292 form is?"

Kirkpatrick visibly deflates in the witness box. Blood drains from his face and his shoulders collapse. His blue eyes roam to McArdle and then up to the federal seal on the wall, as if searching for some misplaced core principle.

"It's the form agents fill out when they're informing the Bureau about a marriage or a divorce," he says in a barely audible voice.

Ben thrusts the file at him. "Is this also your signature?"

"Yes, sir." The agent glances at the papers, looks away.

"You were in the midst of a divorce and a child custody case when Mr. Saddik was detained in Brooklyn?"

"I was." The agent sinks further in his seat, as if losing body mass by the second.

"Isn't it true that your wife, who is also an agent, put in for a transfer to the Omaha office and you claimed in court papers that you needed her to stay in the New York area to keep working with you because you'd begun this case together?"

"I don't recall that," Kirkpatrick murmurs, his mouth a little to the side of the microphone.

"Could you speak up, Agent Kirkpatrick? And would it help your memory if I showed you an affidavit from your ex-wife in this 292 file?"

"No. I remember now."

"And isn't it a fact that it was in your interest to make this a major case to keep your wife from leaving and taking your child?"

"I didn't just 'make' this case out of thin air." Kirkpatrick crooks his fingers into quote marks. "We had credible information."

"Credible information from a source who you should have known was a liar?" Ben shouts. "Except that you wanted to support him so that you could make a major case and keep your wife from taking your son to another state. Isn't that true?"

"*No.*"

"You deliberately lied and obscured the facts with reckless disregard for Mr. Saddik's well-being . . ."

"I did not."

"You allowed an American citizen to be kidnapped and tortured with malice aforethought."

"That's enough." McArdle rises, as the talk grows loud in the gallery. "Your Honor, can we get a sidebar here?"

"No, let's take a full-stop break. Mr. McArdle and Mr. Grimaldi, in my chambers now." The judge rises, a small woman trying to relocate herself in the voluminous folds of her black robe. "Agent Kirkpatrick, you may step down."

Ben walks back to the plaintiff's table, puffed up and proud, like a rapper dropping the mic. Natty hears press people scribbling notes, their pens like matches on charcoal, while lawyers in the gallery whisper behind their hands. A court officer at the back of the room throws open the main exit doors while McArdle heads toward the judge's chambers.

It's done. The government lawyers will want to settle quickly to avoid further exposure. A number will be named and countered. He watches Ibrahim come back into the courtroom, looking dazed, and wander into the arms of his family. A price tag will be put on his pain and suffering. He'll mumble a few words at a press conference and then stagger away with his wrecked arm, his own PTSD, and his percentage of the award.

Natty pushes the empty chair away. This should have been his father's moment. What he dreamed of all his life: The pure moral victory, untainted and uncompromised by technicalities, niggling doubts, and dog-faced clients who would commit other heinous crimes. The shining instant where the sun broke through the clouds and found a place where he could stand tall and say his work had been worthwhile. It's been stolen by the usurper.

So why does it feel like they're back at the Silver Gloves, at the center of the ring with their arms aloft? How can any part of him feel elated or even accepting of Ben's happy embrace at the table and then standing by as Ben kisses his mother on the cheek?

He looks past them and sees MG shaking her head as she leaves the courtroom. As if somehow she expected better.

41

If it was a party for anyone else except her aunt, Lourdes would be skipping it. For eight hours, she's been dealing with the fallout from the Grimaldi-Dresden case: typing reports on the law office raid, trying to flip more bike messengers into cooperating, and generally avoiding being in the line of fire as bosses shuttle in and out. But it's Soledad's birthday, same day as Georgie's would have been, so at quarter to seven she shows up at a bar called La Isla Bonita—"the beautiful island"—which turns out to be a concrete box under the Brooklyn-Queens Expressway, right across the street from a pet food warehouse and "24 Hr. Video Xcitement."

The place has a yellow canopy with a desert island and shapely palm trees, and "Poker Face" by Lady Gaga is pounding out the open front door.

Soledad is holding court in the front room, a bottle of Pacifico in one hand, the other hand resting on the butt of a skinny, fortyish brunette in a blue blazer and tight jeans. Meanwhile all her aunt's middle-aged poker buddies and fellow union delegates from the department wear Hawaiian leis and softball jerseys that say "Soledad is Fifty and Foxxy!" as they lean back and bellow along with Gaga about bluffing with their muffins.

"Yo, turn that shit down." Soledad waves her arms. "My baby girl is here. Come here, *guapa*."

She grabs her niece and hugs her, her big warm torpedo breasts a comfort even through her boxy Key West shirt.

"*Que gusto!*" She pulls back and holds Lourdes's face in her hands. "You so beautiful, baby. When you gonna learn to put on makeup?"

"Look who's talking?"

"I'm *distinguished*. I don't need to look good."

"Happy birthday, mi tia." Lourdes gives her the hardcover of *Gone Girl* she bought after her visit to Great Meadow. "I didn't know what else to get you."

"Only good habit you got from Papi." Soledad takes Lourdes by the elbow and starts pulling her toward a booth in the back. "Come on, I need to talk to you." Adding to the bartender. "And bring us a margarita for my niece. And don't be stingy with the salt."

"I shouldn't be drinking on a school night." Lourdes slides against the wood-paneled wall.

"Later for that." Soledad puts the book down and burps behind her fist. "You're getting some time freed up."

"Por que?"

"None of those fucking so-called men you work with got the co-jones to tell you, so it's up to your fat old aunt. You're off the Dresden case."

"You want to run that by me again?" Lourdes studies Soledad for signs of a put-on. "What'd I do?"

"Nothing you shouldn't have. Word is, Benny G.'s mailman case is about to get settled, which means the Justice Department will no longer have a conflict about investigating him. There was a meeting with all the chiefs this afternoon, and they even patched in someone from the attorney general's office in Washington."

"And that's it?" Lourdes squawks, turning heads at the nearby tables. "We're just supposed to turn over all our files, all our witnesses?"

"It's way above your pay grade, sweet thing, and mine. If a white man with white hair wants something on this job, he's probably gonna get it. We're just a couple of *hermosas damas* with badges . . ."

"Feels like someone stole my boyfriend from me." Lourdes slumps.

"Darle lo mismo. What are you gonna do?"

Soledad presses the belly button on the hula girl lamp in the middle of the table, turning on the light to study the beer menu and starting her grass skirt and coconut shell–covered breasts to swaying.

"Sullivan is going to go crazy."

"He already did." Soledad shrugs. "Burst into Chief Gunther's meet-

ing and threatened to quit. Big deal. He's got two, three months before
he has to retire anyway."

Lourdes regards the hula girl's gyrations sadly, hearing the faint tinny
strum of ukulele beneath Lady Gaga's robotic beats. It's just about keeping the machine running, she realizes. "You know the feds are just going
to screw it up again." Lourdes shakes her head.

"Not your problem." Soledad sets the list aside. "Their investigation
supersedes ours. All you can do is get out the goddamn way."

"That's not why I got into this, mi tia. It's not just a job to me."

"Then maybe it should be. Otherwise you'll wind up as crazy as Kevin
Sullivan. And from what I've been hearing lately, you don't want that."

Lourdes feels the weight of her aunt's stare on her, as heavy as when
Soledad used her whole body to pin Lourdes to the sofa in the old days,
to keep her from going out on the streets.

"There's been some talk," Soledad lowers her voice, starting to pick
the label off her bottle. "About how tight you two have gotten."

"That's gross. He's twice my age."

"I'm just passing it along . . ."

"Oh my God . . . Bunch of jealous *maricons* talking. I thought I was
working with *men*."

She frowns as the waiter brings her the margarita, appalled as she remembers there was a moment upstate when she actually did think about
sleeping with him. But that was just wondering what it would be like—
not the same as *wanting* to do it. Conjecture and desire. Completely different things.

"Hey, nothing wrong with robbing the cradle once in a while." Soledad
points her bottle at the woman she'd been next to at the bar, slender and
swan-necked in gold earrings. "My lady Ofelia over there is like ten years
younger than me. She's an assistant professor of Afro-Caribbean studies at
City College." She winks and blows a kiss before turning back to Lourdes.
"Before the word came down from on high, I was going to tell you she was
in some kind of snooty Women's Writers Workshop with Alice Ali."

"No shit: Dresden's widow?"

"Yeah, she said Alice was writing a memoir about the men in her life.
Sounded like she had some issues to work out with all of them. Figures,
with who her father was. Mr. Big Revolutionary Social Equality, who was

always banging two or three women on the side. Sound like anyone we know?"

"She was in this workshop before her husband was killed?" Lourdes leans across the table. "She write anything about Dresden?"

"Just that he maybe wasn't who said he was either, and that disappointed her. But that's how it is sometimes with men and women. Right? People think they want one thing, but they don't. That's why I'm more for the females." Soledad smiles at her assistant professor. "Well, *one* reason."

"Would your girlfriend talk to me about Alice?"

Lourdes finds herself looking over at the bar, where Professor Ofelia is looking over her shoulder and giving the place an ample rear view as she doffs her blazer and shakes what she's got.

"Sure, but why bother?" Soledad takes a swig and puts her beer down. "It's not going to be relevant to the investigation and it's not your case anymore anyway. Just let it go. Sorry I mentioned it."

Lourdes stares down at her margarita, studying the salt galaxies around the rim of the glass. Knowing how close she was to putting this all together.

"My advice now?" Soledad says. "Put the ass on your lip."

"Wha?"

"I'm saying, put the ass on your lip and start kissing it. If you want to stay in this job."

"This was a big one for me, Soledad. How am I supposed to save face now?"

"Who said you were losing face? Sullivan?"

"Big case for him too." Lourdes puts the straw between her lips. "He knew the vic. This was gonna be his last stand."

"Don't go down with the wreck, *niña*. If something negative appears about the FBI taking over online or in the newspapers, you better look like you're a million miles away."

"Or else?"

"Listen." Soledad comes forward on her elbows, confiding. "I'm'a tell you something, 'cause I love you. I pulled some strings to get you back to the squad, but that's it. The next time they reassign you, it won't just be a temporary VIPER detail. You'll be out on your ear. I want to see you live

to fight again another day. And you could have a good career in this department."

Lourdes takes another sip off the margarita and puts the glass down, aware of her aunt's off-duty friends at the bar watching them without appearing to look over. Salt and lime juice find a cut in the corner of her mouth where the straw made a tiny incision.

"How can you tell me to forget about it, Soledad?" She tries to lick away the sting. "You were the one who said always go all in."

"It is what it is, baby. More to life than this case. Today would have been your brother's birthday. And I loved that damn kid. We were only a year apart. When he died, the whole family went to pieces. It was a long time until your mother had you, so I wanna see you get to be what you're supposed to be."

Lourdes sucks the salt from her cut and looks over at her aunt's new girlfriend tossing back her drink and joining Soledad's other friends oohing and ahhing sarcastically as Yoenis Cespedes silently wiggles his butt and grabs his crotch on the TV above the bar.

"Funny that you got with a lady who knew Alice." Lourdes looks back at Soledad suspiciously. "You didn't hit on her because you got wind she knew Alice and thought it would help my case. Did you?"

"You do what you gotta do." Her aunt shrugs. "But check out the *culo* on my lady. It's not always just about work."

42

When the steak finally arrives, Natty finds himself seesawing between unappeasable hunger and grinding nausea.

A part of him still cannot believe he is sitting here, with his tie tucked into his shirt, a white napkin on his lap, and his mother at his side, having a civilized victory celebration with the man who almost certainly had his father murdered. Every time he looks at Ben, his eyeballs broil, his stomach talks, and his hand reaches for the serrated knife.

But then the steak arrives on an oval white platter. His mouth, ignoring his brain, begins to water. His belly yawns, demanding to be filled. A thirty-two-ounce porterhouse, a red plastic cow marker declaring it medium-rare, perfectly aged and marbled, charred brown-black on the outside, and cut into two dozen thick purple-pink juicy slabs. The smell alone—a smoky chophouse aroma—could turn Gandhi into a slobbering carnivore. Pick up the T-bone, the odor says. Take it with both hands. Gnaw on it. Forget social niceties. This is what you deserve. These are your rightful spoils. You are the champion, my friend.

"Alice, you're going to have some, aren't you?" Ben, well into his third scotch of the evening, has a dripping piece in tongs over Mom's plate.

"Ben." She gives him a withering look. "Have you *ever* seen me eat steak?"

"Did David ever take you to Peter Luger?"

"No." She folds her arms. "He knew I hadn't touched red meat since I was eighteen."

It's true, Natty thinks. His childhood diet was a mostly ramen regimen with the occasional jerk chicken or tuna niçoise indulgence. Mom, in the old days, would occasionally rail against spending more than $50 at a restaurant, as if enjoying a meal out was a sign of bourgeois corruption and decadence.

"Just try it." Ben leaves the slice on the side of her plate, half hidden by the foliage of creamed spinach. "It'll change your life."

"I've had enough changes." She shakes her head primly.

"Come on, don't be like that," Ben says. "This is a great night. Natty, tell your mother to enjoy herself."

"Let her be."

Natty chews on one side of his mouth, half disgusted with himself for not only savoring the meat, but for being able to swallow any of this.

The three of them are sitting at a corner table near the front window of the Peter Luger Steak House. While the rest of Williamsburg was losing factories, gaining Hasidim, and, more recently, becoming unaffordably hip—the old restaurant just squatted in the shadow of the bridgeworks for a hundred years, implacable and Germanic, with its sawdust floors, plain yellowish walls, oak wainscoting, and beer hall tables, refusing to adjust to any era or take regular credit cards, unshakeable in its confidence that even in the worst of times somehow the winners of the world would find their way to this Brooklyn Valhalla.

So tonight, pumped and jubilant after his post-hearing session with the Justice Department lawyers, Ben declared they would celebrate. He'd loaded Natty and his mother into his Jaguar XE and drove straight from the federal courthouse with the Stones' *Sticky Fingers* blasting along the Kent Avenue route to Broadway, the sun dabbling melted ore on the rippling surface of the East River, pious Satmar Jews with big furry hats and gangster-black overcoats scooting platoons of children out of the way.

Ben pulled up around the Maybachs and Lexuses already double-parked by the entrance, slipped the valet a hundred-dollar bill, and walked in like he was a silent owner. The bar was three deep with graceless barrel-chested men celebrating their unlikely ascendance to the new urban aristocracy with loud voices, expensive jewelry, and much younger girlfriends. Ben ignored them all, stepped in front of a polite Japanese couple who'd probably been waiting hours, and somehow landed a prime table by a first-floor window through some unholy alchemy of bribery, cajoling, and perhaps veiled threat.

"I'm not going to force you, Alice." Ben leaves a second piece of steak on her plate. "But it's there when you want it. And you will want it. Am I right, Natty?"

He winks, as Natty stares back at him, chewing more slowly and deliberately. Trying to ascertain if Ben has any inkling about his visit with Jamar. Or has any notion about what Natty now knows. But Benny G.'s in his glory. Apparently not even worrying about the police raid at his office or the fact that several of the bike messengers are in custody. No, he's just putting the T-bone on his plate, not bothering to ask if anyone else wants it.

Too bad the nine millimeter that Cuddy gave Natty is back at the house, where he left it after his meeting with Jamar. Instead he just pictures himself calmly picking up the steak knife near his right hand and driving it deep into the spot just to the side of Ben's purple pocket-square.

The sinews in his wrist tense, anticipating the amount of force that would be required to pierce the soft tissue and chest cartilage. He imagines pushing the serrated tip into the center of the heart and seeing blood soaking the white shirt Ben is wearing.

But he knows this isn't right.

If he puts the blade in deeply enough, the pump will just stop.

"Whatever she wants." Natty looks down to cut another piece.

How can he keep digesting? It's an unnatural state, to be sitting across from your father's murderer: watching him eat, drink, and laugh as if he has nothing to fear.

"So exactly what happened in chambers?" Mom asks, with the peevish curiosity of a former journalist.

"With the judge and George McArdle?" Ben dabs his grin. "The Justice Department threw in the towel. They'd seen enough. Another minute on the stand and Kirkpatrick would have risked full liability. Any idiot could tell that he propped up the informant and fluffed the case against Ibrahim so he could keep his family together in New York. The Bureau knew they couldn't afford the exposure."

"They offered to settle right away?" She stops picking at her spinach.

"The way George McArdle put it was, 'What will it take to end this?' I gave him a number and he said, 'I'll make some calls.'"

"Are you going to tell us that number willingly or are we going to have to torture you the way they tortured the mailman?" she asks.

"Heh, heh." Ben gives Natty a knowing glance. "I told them any serious discussion would have to start north of twelve million."

"*That much?*" She fumbles with her fork. "Are you insane?"

"Don't ask, don't get." Ben finishes his drink and shakes the ice cubes at a passing waiter. "They know it's a reasonable place to start negotiating. We killed them today. Right, son?"

He slaps Natty on the back. Maybe I should stab him between the vertebrae, Natty thinks. Don't kill him right away. Leave him paralyzed instead. Incapable of breathing without an iron lung.

"Just finishing what Dad started," Natty says. "Wouldn't have had a case without him. Right?"

Ben's hand grows heavy on his back and his eyes become sedentary on Natty's face, searching for clues and flaws. The sounds of clanking silverware and idle conversations around them die away. A passing headlight through the window half bleaches the room. Natty feels the distant vibration and rumble of the subway rattling beneath the table.

"Okay, but more than twelve?" Mom's fingers scroll around the stem of her chardonnay glass. "That's a lot for pain and suffering."

"Only a small portion of that is for Mr. Saddik's pain and suffering." Ben puts his hand over hers. "Ibrahim can no longer work for the post office because of his injuries. But that's worth maybe one and a half, two million—tops. The other ten million is what the government will be willing to pay to avoid a high-profile federal trial in open court. They might win in the long run, but the cost of what they'd have to reveal would be killing to them. Believe me, they're as anxious to put this behind them as we are. Natty, you still with me?"

Natty stares as Ben's lardy white hand curls over his mother's delicate light-copper fingers on the crystal, enjoying more of the spoils. Almost taunting Natty to challenge him on the spot. I took your father's life. I'm taking his money. Why not take what's left?

"The firm keeps a third of the settlement?" she asks. "The full $4 million?"

"Only if we decide to settle cheap." Ben smirks. "I think we can get them up a little more. Let's see who's got the biggest pair at the table."

Mom drains her wine and sets the glass down with a dazed look of someone just off a Ferris wheel as she sways in her seat, lightly touching Natty's wrist to steady herself.

Natty gives her the once-over to make sure she's all right. These last few weeks she's begun to seem like someone else. As if the edges of her personality, which always seemed so crisp and forthright in opposition to Dad's quiet ironies, have begun to dissolve in his absence. Or maybe it's just that he's unused to seeing her beside another man.

Ben starts snapping his fingers like Sinatra and pointing to the empty glasses on the table. "Natty, you need another? Alice?"

Natty lays a hand on his beer stein. "I'm all right."

"You don't look all right." Ben flags down a waiter, with a twenty between his fingers. "*Garçon*, no more empties tonight. Okay? Keep the drinks coming until I say stop. *Capisce?*"

"Yes, sir."

The waiter, Old World and solemn-faced in his white jacket and disciplined hair, ignores the money and hustles away, obviously a veteran witness to public disgraces. The Japanese couple Ben stepped in front of are at the next table, glaring.

"Ben, maybe we want to slow down a bit?" Mom lowers her voice. "You're getting a little loud."

"Bullshit. I waited a long time for a night like this. A man needs to howl at the moon once in a while. Tell her, Natty."

"*Hooah.*" Natty keeps a tight grip on his mug.

"*Ooh-rah.*" Ben reaches across the table and pokes him with two fingers in the chest. "That's the Marine Corps battle cry. What's with this 'hooah' army crap?"

"Nothing wrong with the United States Army."

"Except that it's not the Marines," Ben says. "I'm sorry you washed out before you got in the corps, son . . ."

"I didn't wash out," Natty says evenly. "The army was my choice. I wanted to be in the Rangers before they sent me to Intelligence . . ."

"Yeah, okay." Ben waves him off. "Whatever you say . . ."

He's a little more than drunk, Natty realizes. Something is putting more propulsion in his engines. It could be the testosterone replacement therapy or it could be something the bike messengers have been distributing. Cocaine, steroids, human growth hormone. Or maybe it's just believing that you've somehow managed to vanquish and supplant your rival without consequences.

The waiter brings them a fresh round.

"I want to make a toast." Ben raises his high-ball glass. "Natty, get it up, son." He snorts, amused with himself. "Alice, you too."

He waits until Natty hoists his mug and Mom reluctantly lifts her third chardonnay of the night.

"Here's to winning," Ben says hoarsely.

"Amen." She clinks her glass against his.

"And here's to us being together." He looks at Natty, his eyes getting small and watery. "Like a family . . ."

"Benjamin," Mom says, cautioning.

"I really mean it," he goes on, oblivious to the fact that half the dining room is now staring. "There's nowhere I'd rather be and no one I'd rather be with."

"You are drunk," she says. "And people are looking."

"I'm drunk but you're beautiful." Ben drops his voice into a furry intimate growl, putting his hand over hers again. "The only thing that'll be different in the morning is I'll be sober. Churchill said something like that."

Ben and his mother have always had a kind of boisterous and occasionally volatile back-and-forth, Natty realizes. The daughter of the revolutionary going at it over cocktails with the son of a beat cop, Dad having to make sardonic interjections of "guys, give peace a chance" to keep them from tearing each others' throats out. But they were both always rudely invigorated and borderline giddy after their sparring, as if they were well matched in their disregard for making other people uncomfortable. For a half second, everything seems so warm and natural between them that Natty wonders if he could have gotten it all wrong. Maybe the feds have somehow fooled him into thinking his benefactor is his enemy. Maybe they've phonied up evidence, paid off witnesses to lie, created a false trail for him to follow.

"You're getting sloppy," she warns Ben with minx eyes, pulling out of his grip. "And sentimental."

"Oh, lighten up," Ben grabs her hand and kisses it. "Both of you.

That's the problem with you guys. You don't know how to enjoy your-selves . . ."

"Uh, Ben," Natty leans close, dropping his voice. "You think maybe we should be a little more low-key? The police were at the office less than twenty-four hours ago."

"Forget about that." Ben pretends to swat Natty. "No one else is going to talk."

"How can you be sure?"

"Everybody knows what the average life expectancy of a rat is," Ben says, the hand now coming to rest on Natty's shoulder. "Or should be. In fact, let me propose a different toast."

"Well, all right," says Mom, beginning to draw out her vowels as she gets drunker.

"Here's to getting rid of all the rats." Ben raises his glass and his voice. "Natty, are you with me on this too?"

Natty takes a small sip of his Heineken, just trying to keep the edge off without going too far. There's a light buzz in his blood stream, a slight angle of elevation, so he can look down on himself and see where he might be about to get into trouble. Technically, he's supposed to be in recovery. His sobriety is court-mandated. Just having a beer in front of him publicly is a risk since the last time he got a load on he broke a fireman's jaw.

"You thinking of anyone in particular?" Natty wraps two hands around his mug.

"All of them. Scum of the earth. The worst quality a man can have. Disloyalty."

"Benjamin, where is this going?" Mom sits up, striving to appear sober and imperious.

"Just saying: a rat is always a rat." Ben drains his glass and sets it down with a thump. "I used to tell David: When you find one, call the exter-minator. Or else your house will be ruined."

"Ben, stop." Mom looks like a taxi passenger beginning to suspect she's been kidnapped.

"David used to say I should be more 'compassionate.'" Ben crooks his fingers again. "'You can't blame a man for wanting to get out of trou-ble.' But you know what I'd say?"

"What?" Natty says.

"I'd say, 'You handle your business. I'll handle mine.'" Ben rests a fist beside his glass. "Never apologize, never explain. Because you know what I hate the most? The whole mea culpa Queen for a Day when they list all their crimes to get less time for themselves. When they're really shifting the blame to someone else, instead of paying for what *you* did."

"Ben . . ." Mom tilts her head, giving him a warning glance from the corners of her eyes.

"I'm speaking to *your son*, Alice." Ben pokes Natty in the shoulder. "Trying to teach him something that he should have been taught before. About loyalty. There's nothing worse than a friend who turns on you. Especially someone you tried to help. I've got no use for people like that. Do you understand me, Natty?"

Some of the other diners are starting to point and murmur behind their napkins. A party of young Wall Street bachelors across the room looking up from their ribeyes and filet mignons in concern.

"Ben . . ." Natty slowly lifts his palms. "Did I do something to piss you off?"

"I don't know, Natty." Ben locks eyes with him. "Did you?"

Natty's brain tries to reboot. He's been found out. Ben knows he's been talking to the police and the FBI. He could have tapped the phones or his computer. Or maybe Ben's got a rat of his own, a corrupt cop or a prosecutor telling him who's informing. Or Jamar told Ben about Natty coming to see him. Trying to figure it out is like having three radio stations playing in his head at the same time.

"I have done nothing wrong," Natty says carefully.

"Did you know a rat killed *my* father?" Ben pokes Natty lower on the arm, close to where the bone was bruised.

"What are you talking about?" Natty looks to his mother.

"Well, I don't know about this conversation." Mom busies herself, trying to wipe a lipstick stain from the rim of her wineglass. "I thought we were here celebrating . . ."

Ben ignores her. "My old man tried to help out this kid named Antonio Birdsong. Sixteen years old, shot a numbers runner in the back in Bushwick. He could have done life himself but my father fished him out of the system, went to the DA himself, and got that little bitch a deal to keep his ass out on the street, dealing heroin and banging hookers. Until he gets jammed up again by Brooklyn Narcotics and rolls on my father for allegedly robbing known drug locations with other patrolmen."

"How come I never heard this before?" Natty looks to Mom.

"My father never cried or complained when the Knapp Commission was trying to make him testify against his brother officers." Ben turns his empty glass around and around. "Kept it bottled up every night when he came home and listened to his opera. I still get tears in my eyes, when I hear *The Marriage of Figaro*. Makes me sick what they did to that man. I was coming home late from football practice in high school every night while he was getting eaten up inside because the prosecutors were threatening to put him away for life if he didn't betray his friends."

"Hash browns." The waiter lays down a platter of wrecked potatoes.

"You know, no one ever proved he killed himself on purpose," Ben says. "It could have been an accident. There was no note. And the back-door was open when I found him, so it could have been someone else." He stops turning his glass. "Why are we talking about this anyway?"

"You wanted to talk about rats," Natty says.

"Here's to wiping out all the vermin." Ben raises his glass again. "It's a shame your father didn't live to see this night. But he made his choices and I made mine."

"And what choices were those?"

"Ben, I'm getting tired." Mom finishes her wine. "I'd like to go home. Will you give me a ride or should I call myself a car?"

"David just had a different attitude than I do," Ben says, ignoring her. "He thought people should have a chance to make up for their mistakes. But you and I know better than that. Don't we, Natty?"

"I'm still not sure I follow you." Natty grips the knife again.

"Of course, you follow me." Ben leans close enough for Natty to smell the whiskey rot. "Because you know life is not about second chances. It's about winning *all the time, every time*. It's about destroying your enemies, stepping over their bodies, and taking what you deserve. Which is the respect of lesser men, the company of beautiful women, and the best fucking steak money can buy."

Ben picks up the fork that's been lying on the side of Alice's plate and holds up the piece of steak she's been ignoring.

"This meat is worth about five dollars a bite," Ben says. "And you're not getting out of here until you try it, Alice."

"She doesn't want it," Natty says.

"C'mon, baby." Ben wags the fork in front of her face. "You know you do."

"I said, let her alone." Natty sits up.

"Knock it off, both of you," she says. "You're being idiots."

"Then I'm the idiot who is about to collect $12 million." Ben puts the dripping morsel right under her nose. "So unless one of you has a bigger wallet, I'm the one who's paying for this meal and I want to get my money's worth."

His mother looks down at the meat. And then stares at Ben, who is not just embarrassing her, but daring her son to challenge him. To assert himself and end this public shaming.

"Stop . . ."

The knife is shaking in Natty's hand. A dark-browed manager is heading over from the maître d' station and the Wall Street guys are halfway out of their seats. A couple of bouncer-sized men wearing the plus-size suits of off-duty cops lurch in from the barroom.

His mother grabs the fork from Ben and puts the steak in her mouth, settling the matter decisively. "There," she says. "Everybody happy now?"

His mother, critic of the hegemony, enemy of the patriarchy, swallowing a prime cut. Natty lowers the knife and watches the working of her jaw. She turns and flutters her eyelashes at him. She's made her choice.

"So what do you say, Alice?" Ben looks at Natty over the T-bone he's started to gnaw on, daring him to say something.

"It's all right." She chews. "Just takes some getting used to."

Natty looks down and pushes back from the hash browns, burnt skin and innards mixed up on his plate. The taste of blood on his tongue. The fat of the slaughtered animal congealing on the platter. His mind is made up. He will not wait. He will kill his father's murderer tonight. And then he will never eat meat again.

43

For a few minutes, at least, everything is about perfect. When she showed up, with her aunt's encouragement, at Mitchell Vogliano's apartment in Carroll Gardens, he was glad to see her. He still had warm Chinese takeout on the kitchen counter and the coconut oil in the bathroom that she left last time she was here, three months ago. *Win-win.* After she took her clothes off, he did his job, inscribing the secret language between her legs that sent waves of pleasure through her body, before he let her climb aboard on his pale wiry frame and ride him home. *Win-win-win!* And now she was lying next to him, her head on his chest, watching a *Law & Order: SVU* rerun that had Olivia and Stabler together again, happy and sated at multiple levels. All Mitchell had to do was avoid saying "I love you" this time.

"So . . ." He kisses her on top of the head, during a commercial break. "Does this mean we're back together?"

"Why does it have to mean anything?"

"I'm just, like—"

She raises up on one elbow to give him the yellow-tape look she always gives lovers who talk too much.

"Okay." He sighs. "It is what it is."

"Something wrong with that?"

"No, it's great. It's awesome. I love seeing you . . ." His voice trails off as the commercial starts listing potential side effects for a diet pill that reduces cravings. "I get curious, that's all. How's work?"

"Good."

" 'Good'? That's all I get?"

"Shut up, Mitchell. The show's coming back on."

On the screen, the side effects have ended and a commercial for Six Flags Great Adventure amusement park has come on with the old man in a tuxedo dancing improbably like a teenager.

"I heard they're taking your case away," he says.

She watches kids' faces diving out of frame on a roller coaster.

"You're up, you're down. Just trying to go with it."

"For what it's worth, Lourdes, I'm glad they let you back in the saddle again."

"Speaking of saddles." She reaches under the covers. "Think you got another rodeo in you, cowpoke?"

"Gimme a minute. We're just talking. What else is doing? How's your family?"

"They're, like, whatever." She lies back, hands behind her head, looking at the ceiling. "I saw my father the other day."

"Really? You drove all the way up to see him?"

"We were upstate to see another prisoner, so I was like, why not?"

"And?"

He hovers over her, preventing her from counting the cracks in the paint, the tip of his aquiline Roman nose almost touching the bridge of her broad Hispanic one.

"He says he was framed, like everyone else in the system." She lets her eyes stray past his shoulder. "Tragic victim of circumstance. What are you gonna do? He's my father. He asked me to send him a murder mystery. I'll probably do it. He likes those. You got anything by Lawrence Block?"

"Hey, Lourdes?"

"What?"

He touches her chin tenderly. "I know how hard you work, to get where you are."

"Oh, here we go again . . ."

She starts to roll away and look for her clothes.

"I just want to say, it's okay, if this is all you got for me right now." He holds onto her shoulder to keep her from going. "I just hope someday, maybe, there could be a little more."

She lies down again, wipes the corner of her eye, and wiggles her butt against him.

"I'd like a little more myself," she says.

"I thought you wanted to watch the show."

"What's the matter, you can't multitask?"

"You sweet dirty girl." He laughs, as she reaches back to help strengthen his resolve. "What do you think you're doing?"

"Let's go, Vogliano." She rolls on top of him. "And don't argue. I'm a police officer."

44

The gun is in Natty's waistband as he comes back to the car. The muzzle is pointing down at his crotch and the butt end is jammed against his abdomen, so it stabs into old scar tissue as he climbs in on the passenger side of the Jag.

"Took a while," Ben says. "Everything all right?"

Through the garden-level windows, Natty can see Mom settling in for the night.

"Yeah, she's just tired." He puts Dad's satchel down by his feet. "Or maybe just tired of *us*."

"I hear that." Ben restarts the engine. "What's up with bringing your father's bag?"

"I figure we're going back to the office, might as well have something to carry the papers in. Seems appropriate since it was his case originally. Doesn't it?"

"If you say so."

Ben steers down President Street, throwing occasional glances at Natty and the bag, as if he can hear something ticking inside it.

Natty's suggestion was to drop Mom and her headache off after dinner, then swing by the office and grab the files that would be needed for the morning meeting with the Justice Department officials to discuss the settlement. Which would seem like a flimsy excuse to be heading back to the office after ten p.m.—if there hadn't been a police raid the night before and eight figures at stake.

"Shit." Natty starts patting his pockets as they make the right onto Fourth Avenue.

"What's the matter?"

"Can't find my phone."

"You need it right now?" Ben asks.

"Can you call and see if I dropped it under the seat here?"

"You know, you're not supposed to be drinking in the first place. How many beers did you have?"

"Not that many."

With a grunt of annoyance, Ben pulls up near a deli on the corner of Union Street. Natty looks around, seeing there's too much light to do this now, too many people his age coming out of the bars and clubs nearby. Ben calls up the number on the dashboard Bluetooth system, the wash of passing high beams making it look like the shape of his skull is changing before Natty's eyes.

By Natty's calculations, his phone should now be vibrating at the bottom of his mother's handbag, since he set it to silent and secreted it near the end of dinner. She's probably in the bathroom, brushing her teeth, unaware a cell tower ping is making it appear that her son is in the house with her at this moment.

"Went straight to voicemail." Ben hangs up.

"Fuck." Natty shakes his head, trying to reconfigure his plan on the fly. "I must have left it at the restaurant."

"Okay, so you'll pick it up tomorrow . . ."

"No. That phone's got all my emails and passwords. We have to go back and get it."

"You want us to drive all the way back to Williamsburg *now*?"

"You're the one who keeps saying we can't be too careful. We're already in the car."

"You know how tired I am?"

Ben exhales, the blare of neon and more passing headlights revealing even more bumps and ridges in his phrenology.

"All right, but you owe me big-time." Ben puts the car in drive again.

"You're a saint, Ben."

"Do I detect a note of sarcasm?"

"I'm saying thanks. You need it in skywriting?"

They steer back into traffic, squiggling off Fourth onto Atlantic and then Flatbush, approaching the right onto the expressway, passing the handful of die-hard discount stores, the chilly new apartment towers, and the army recruitment center where Natty walked in feeling like a choirboy visiting his first whorehouse.

"Guess things got a little testy at dinner," Ben says, his hands flexing into fists on the steering wheel. "Didn't they?"

"Not much of a victory celebration." Natty shrugs. "I thought you were maybe a little heavy with Mom."

"I'm still pretty wound up about the police raiding the office. We haven't talked about that, have we?"

"Wasn't much time before the hearing."

"So where were you when it was going on?"

A pothole jars them on the ramp up to the expressway, new modular-built condominiums casting night eyes over the old bumpy road.

"Seeing the therapist again," Natty says, realizing he should have had a better story ready.

"I thought you saw her the day before."

"Then I was getting the files together. You know how I am with time these days."

Traffic slows down, an ocean of red brake lights ahead. Ben is looking at the side of his face, holding the glare a few seconds longer than a driver in a vehicle going thirty miles an hour should.

"You haven't been talking to the police," he says. "Have you?"

"About what?"

A motorcycle shoots past them on the right, the rip of its engine causing Natty to lurch and wrench his neck a little.

"They seem to have all kinds of crazy ideas about what's been going on at the office." Ben is still staring. "They're accusing our messengers of being drug couriers. They have papers claiming that suppliers and distributors are meeting at our office under the cover of attorney-client privilege. Someone on the inside is talking to them."

"What makes you think it's someone on the inside?"

"We found a GPS device that had been placed in one of our messenger's bags. You know anything about that?"

"Why would I?"

"If this was court, I'd say move to strike as non-responsive." Ben tightens his grip on the wheel. "Should we try again?"

"Are you interrogating me, Ben?"

"I don't know. Should I?"

Natty tries to feel around in the dark for the lever to push the seat back, so he has more room to pull the gun out in one smooth motion if he needs to.

"We still having a problem, Ben? I thought we resolved this at dinner."

"I asked you a question and you still haven't answered. I said, have the police spoken to you? And don't say, 'About what?' or pretend to be confused. We're past that point."

A lane up ahead is closed for a work crew steamrolling asphalt on the road, men in goggles and reflectors watching steam rise from the tar like collective rage from underneath.

"Yes, the police have spoken to me," Natty says quietly. "And so has an agent from the FBI."

"Okay, now we're getting somewhere." Ben stares straight ahead, a lit-up map on the dashboard screen showing their progress. "And did Marygrace Kelly put you in touch with this agent?"

"Yes."

Natty adjusts his seat belt, so the butt of the gun isn't pressing so directly into his scar tissue and the "Infidel" tattoo just below his belly. He realizes now that he should have taken more time to get familiar with the Glock 17. It's not like the Berretta Model 9. No hammer on this. Maybe he should have taken it to a range. But then someone would have seen it in his hand. Fog from hot asphalt clouds the windshield as they pass through. Fuck. Now he can't remember if he chambered a round before he got back in the car.

"What have they been telling you?" Ben asks, hands opening and closing on the wheel again.

"They said that allegations had been made about illegal things going on at the firm." Natty pauses, the roof of his mouth dry. "I don't recall them mentioning anything specifically about drug sales."

"Then what did they say was going on?" Ben puts on his directional signal.

"They said witnesses had been killed in a number of cases the firm had been involved in. And they were looking at that. The FBI, not the police."

"And did you believe them?" Ben steers into the passing lane, as they head toward the Classon Avenue exit.

"I didn't know what to believe. They showed me files from several cases."

"And you didn't think to tell me about any of this before the hearing? After all I've done for you and your mother?"

Natty looks out the window again, thinking about how to answer as the highway elevates, rising above the streets that are no longer so familiar to him. Boutique hotels replacing neighborhood bakeries, the skeletons of post-modern apartment houses dwarfing vacant lots, superstore outlets filling out warehouses that used to be open for raves, and billboard canvases for daredevil graffiti ninjas splattering words like "EAT REAL FOOD" and "PIXOTE RAMBO." Everything changed so quickly that you could be out of town for just three months, land at Kennedy Airport, and not be able to find your way around the neighborhood anymore.

"The police and the FBI seem to be running separate investigations into the firm," he says finally, shifting in his seat and angling the barrel closer to his hip than his groin. "I didn't want either one of them to distract from us winning my father's case."

"*Your father's case?*" Ben takes the exit, leaden with contempt. "Did the FBI happen to tell you who first made these allegations about illegality at the firm?"

"They said Dad did." Natty's tongue sticks for a second. "Before he was killed."

"I see."

They swing past the Brooklyn Navy Yard entrance and skim along the waterfront on Kent Avenue, as Natty tries to estimate how far they might be from the surveillance cameras of the nearby film studio facilities. In the distance he can see the smokestacks of non-functioning factories, threatening to call him back to the minarets of Ramadi and Sadr City.

"So the implication is that your father was killed because he made these allegations?"

"Yes."

"And did they suggest someone from the firm was involved in killing him?"

"Yes."

Ben gazes out toward the East River cargo loaders and shipping containers behind chain-linked fence.

"Do you believe it was me, Natty?"

"I don't know."

They've hit a red light, and now they're idling at the edge of a neighborhood. A rare remaining piece of Brooklyn no-man's-land. To the right, there are three-story brick houses with shredded canopies over their terraces and the occasional bearded Hasid hurrying by furtively in a long black coat and a black hat, like an unusually religious hit man on his way to a contract job after dark. On the left sits a concrete divider and a line of parked cars, partly obscuring a large fenced-in area encompassing an auto auction yard, more shipping containers, truck depots, and warehouses probably containing super-secret government operations, where they could be torturing some ISIS wannabe right now: facilities lit up by klieg light towers and presumably overseen by more security cameras.

"This is unbelievable," Ben says. "Did the FBI happen to tell you why your father came forward with these allegations at this particular time?"

The leather seat beneath Ben crackles as the light changes and he shifts his weight to step on the gas again.

"They said he was upset when he learned about witnesses being murdered," Natty says. "But moral considerations aside, I doubt Dad would have been thrilled about a twelve-million-dollar case being derailed by a separate murder investigation."

"Let me fill you in, Natty." Ben turns. "When you called me 'a saint' before, I guess you were being sarcastic. Well, your father wasn't such a goddamn saint either. He talked to the FBI because he was in trouble himself."

"And why is that?" Natty asks, trying to keep his voice level.

"He got in over his head with this mailman case."

"How?"

"The feds caught him on a wiretap, talking to the mailman's son Hamid about smuggling guns to the so-called rebels in Syria. Did you know about that?"

"No." A car with its high beams on comes at them from the other side of the road, temporarily blinding him. "And I'm not sure I believe it."

"Believe it," Ben says. "The kid got radicalized while his father was getting the shit kicked out of him in Macedonia and Gitmo."

More cars pass on the other side, one set of headlights after another, each whiting out whatever he'd been trying to hold in his head a split second before, and pressing like a pair of fingers on his eyeballs.

"You trying to tell me Dad was mixed up in terrorism?"

"I'm saying he got confused about his role as a lawyer and an advocate. You know as well as I do that he always had a little rebel fantasy that he was something more than a mouthpiece for scumbags in criminal court. He crossed the line at some point, and started believing his own myth."

"Then why didn't they arrest both him and Hamid?" Natty rubs his eyes, wondering if this is what a migraine feels like.

"They didn't have quite enough to get the kid, but they got more than enough to nail David and get him disbarred," Ben says. "That's why he went running to his old girlfriend MG at the U.S. attorney's office to make a deal to save his ass. But they were still going to make him give the mailman case to another firm to avoid the conflict."

Each set of headlights feels like a pair of comets going by now, new facts passing through the universe.

"And how do you happen to know all of this?" Natty asks. "Dad wouldn't have told you."

"Trust me. I know."

The light has turned red again. He looks over and sees Ben reach down toward his pant cuff as his foot rests on the brake. Muscles spasm on the left side of Natty's chest, a warning sign he came to recognize in Iraq. It's the same leg where Ben sometimes wears the ankle holster for his father's gun.

"So are you telling me Dad got what was coming?" Natty asks, keeping his voice neutral and his guard up.

"All I'm telling you is David fumbled the ball at the goal line. All I did was pick it up and run it in."

"And made yourself four million in the deal."

Natty's mind is racing, even as the car stays still. Ben couldn't have had the gun in court. If it was at the office, the police would have grabbed it during the raid. Which means it's either at Ben's house or somewhere in this car.

"Did you kill him for the money, Ben?" he asks, heartbeat smacking to the back of his sternum.

"Is that what you think I did?"

Ben's voice is still even, but the car lurches back and forth a few inches in and out of the crosswalk, as if his foot isn't quite steady on the brake.

"Seriously, is that what you think I'm capable of?" Ben asks. "Killing my best friend for money?"

The sights of the Glock are digging into Natty's scar tissue and little hairs on his stomach have gotten caught in the slide. The friction of metal and plastic against skin is rapidly becoming intolerable.

"Then why did you do it?" Natty asks, trying to shift his position again.

The motor purrs as neighborhood wraiths pass through the headlights. A hunched Hispanic hobo wheeling a baby bassinet full of copper pipes by a tall thin Satmar in white silk leggings, a long black coat, and a round fur hat.

"I don't know who to be more disgusted with," Ben says. "You for thinking I could do something like that or me for giving you a break. I've treated you like a son, Natty."

"You told me yourself that you need the money, Ben. You said you're deep in the hole."

"Not that deep." Ben starts to reach toward his ankle again.

"Why don't you keep your hands where I can see them?"

"Why?" Ben slowly straightens up to Marine Corps posture. "What do you think is going to happen now?"

"I don't know, Ben. What would you do if you were me?"

"This is insanity. David was my brother. Don't you know that you guys are like family to me?"

"You just told me that you thought my father was informing on you."

The car is lurching even more, as if the whole frame is vibrating from Ben's barely constrained anger. Natty's gut is refusing to process the steak he tried to swallow earlier. His head is splitting. His heart is almost exploding against the cage of bone trying to hold it in. A family crosses in front of them. A father in a hat and a beard with a wife pushing a stroller, and five small children in tow. The last of them, the straggler, looks through the headlights, somehow finding Natty through the windshield with wide brown eyes. He realizes now that he never quite registered the face of the boy he shot on the stairs.

You don't have to do this, son.

Yes, I do.

"Let me just ask you one other thing," Ben says. "Okay?"

"Okay."

Ben pounds the horn in frustration and the little boy who'd been staring at Natty gets jerked out of the way by his father.

"If I had something to do with killing David, why would I let you get this close to me?"

"Good question."

Natty stares at the red light, knowing it must be about to change. There's no one on the street looking at them. The parked cars along the divide are probably blocking the cameras. In a time and a city where there is always someone watching.

"The answer is"—Ben starts to reach down toward his ankle again— "I wouldn't."

Natty pulls the Glock from his waistband and steadies it with both hands on the grip.

"You don't want to be doing that, Nathaniel." Ben stares down the barrel. "You really don't."

"Go fuck yourself," Natty says.

In the streetlight through the windshield, the look on Ben's face appears closer to sorrow than anger. The first shot enters through his cheek and exits through the closed window behind him, shattering the glass into a spider-web pattern. Its report is as loud as a light bulb popping inside Natty's head. The second shot goes through the right side of Ben's forehead, leaving a spurting gouge. Ben opens his mouth as if to say something and Natty fires a third time, the trigger going back more easily now, and Ben's left eye explodes with a gelatinous pop.

The right eye keeps staring as the rest of the body surrenders. As if the betrayal of his systems is as astonishing as the shots that hit him. Ben slumps, his throat making gagging sounds, blood and aqueous fluid from the eyeball oozing down his cheek. One hand comes off the wheel and flails in empty space before the dashboard, the organism refusing to yield. But then the fingers clench. The arm stiffens, the knee shudders, and a foul odor escapes, mingling with scotch and cologne. His foot slips off the brake and the car starts to roll into the crosswalk, nearly hitting a disheveled woman dashing through the headlights.

Natty yanks the emergency brake and ducks down. Then angles the side mirrors to check for other witnesses on the street and police lights in the distance. Seeing none and hearing nothing, he shoves the gun back into his pants, rolls the passenger-side window up all the way and wipes the shift with the handkerchief that he brought along. Then he hoists his father's leather satchel onto his lap and takes out the black plastic contractor bag, the oversized green knit cap, and the crooked Ray-Bans he hurriedly packed when he went into the house with Mom. He pulls the contractor bag over his head and shoulders, using a box-cutter to make holes for his appendages, dons the knit cap and sunglasses, and looks out the window to make sure the streets are still empty. Then he gets out, leaving the keys in the ignition.

It's only as he crosses the street, staggering and humming atonally like the kind of deranged homeless man that normal citizens try to avert their eyes from, that he realizes he forgot to account for all his brass. The shell casings are still in the car. He turns to go back for them, but then a young couple wings by silently on bicycles, and he realizes he can't risk it. He'll just have to get rid of the gun.

He walks past the Jacob's Ladder Playground and the Roberto Clemente Ballfield, Hispanic kids from the projects hustling by him, flapping their lips without making any words. A seagull wheels noiselessly overhead, heading for the East River. Then he walks by the Hasidic family with the straggling toddlers and the baby in the stroller, crying without sound.

It dawns on him that he hasn't heard anything since he fired the Glock. Except falling snow in his head again.

He's gone deaf, at least temporarily.

A delayed ripple of panic goes through him. There's just a faint, barely discernable ringing.

What if the gunshots were the last sounds he'll hear? Why didn't he make it Bob Marley? Or birds singing? Or wind in the trees? Or the slap of the sea against a ship's bow? Or a woman's happy sigh on a pillow beside him?

He makes a right on Division Avenue and sees the J train rushing over the elevated track, the window lights flickering like a silent movie projector over the deserted streets. No one even glances at him. It's like he's entered into some kind of phantom zone, where nothing is the same as it was. An oddly familiar out-of-body state, close to the way he felt when he walked out of the house in Sadr City. As if he'd been banished from the world of ordinary sensations and comforts. At the time, he thought it might just be a temporary exile. But now, as he ascends the stairs, money in his pocket to buy a ride back to Park Slope, it seems he's become a permanent citizen of a state where no one else can live.

45

As soon as Natty comes padding down the stairs in sweats and a t-shirt, with bedhead hair and a scruffy beard grown out another quarter inch, Lourdes is onto him.

It doesn't matter that her eyelids are still heavy and her tongue is strained from trying to maintain a civil tone with the supervisors who'd tried to stampede her off the crime scene on Kent Avenue in the middle of the night. She knows Nathaniel Dresden had something to do with Ben Grimaldi slumped behind his wheel with brain matter on the shattered car window.

"Natty, they killed Ben," his mother says.

Alice is still sitting on the couch, looking stunned as she drinks her herbal tea and takes in the news from Lourdes and B.B.

"What happened?" Lourdes clocks the way Natty puts his hand on the banister, more resting it than hanging on for support.

No bruising on the knuckles this time. And probably no gunshot residue either. This boy is no fool.

"We're still figuring it out," B.B. says. "It appears he was shot three times at close range while driving along the waterfront near Williamsburg."

"Oh my God . . ." Natty slowly lowers himself into a sitting position on the last stair. "We'd just been celebrating."

Nothing wrong with his response. Exactly as shocked as anyone would be under the circumstances. But he was involved. She's as sure in her belief as the Pentecostal ladies at the iglesias in her neighborhood who writhe on the floor and swear they know Jesus's heart.

"Do you have any leads?" Natty asks.

"We're in the early stages of our investigation," B.B. says. "That's why we're here."

Of course, Lourdes would have preferred to have Sullivan with her, but word is getting around that the FBI is calling dibs on this case, as soon as the terrorism matter is settled. Which means Sullivan is getting thrown under the bus. Lourdes is only being allowed to follow up because she's interviewed these supposedly upstanding citizens before.

"Are there any witnesses?" Natty asks.

"None so far." B.B. palms the little bald spot at the back of his head earnestly, not as suspicious as Lourdes yet. "It's not the kind of neighborhood where people tend to cooperate."

Nothing off the canvas. The Hasids and Puerto Ricans had congregated behind separate sections of yellow tape last night, ghetto people united only in their fishy-eyed distrust of the authorities.

"What about a weapon?" Natty says.

"Not yet." B.B., ever the dog, allows himself to be distracted by Alice, who looks authentically grief-stricken but somehow even more maturely attractive than usual in the morning light. "There were shell casings recovered from under the front seats and no broken glass on the passenger side, which leads us to believe the shooter was inside the car with Mr. Grimaldi."

"So it was somebody he might have known." Natty nods.

What's off is the well of stillness inside him, Lourdes notices. On paper, he's doing and saying all the right things. But being around Sullivan has fine-tuned her dials, to the degree that she can't quite ignore his energy level being a little *less* implosive than usual.

"It would appear that way." She fake-coughs into her fist. "Your mother was just telling us that you'd all been out with Mr. Grimaldi earlier."

"We'd been at Peter Luger's, having dinner," Natty says. "I guess you heard he'd just won that big court settlement."

Mire, he's good, Lourdes thinks. "*He'd* won," not "*We'd* won." Carefully avoiding the suggestion of jealousy or money as a motive. They aren't going to find the murder weapon, she realizes. If he's done the shooting, the gun was probably in the Gowanus now, and there isn't enough money in all the Fortune 500 companies combined to convince a professional diver to plop into that that cesspool to try to find it.

"You know what time you left the restaurant?" she asks.

"Maybe a little before ten?" Natty cocks his head quizzically. "Mom?"

"I can barely think straight." Alice draws her shawl around her shoulders with a little shudder. "Can't you confirm what time we left with the waiters?"

"We can, but where did you go after you left?" B.B. asks.

"Ben dropped us off here," Alice blows on her tea. "Isn't that right, Nathaniel?"

"It'd been a long day," he says. "We were all beat."

Not quite looking at each other, Lourdes notes. Partners out of synch. Or maybe Alice was not in on it at all. How does that figure with what she heard from Soledad's girlfriend about the writing workshop?

"Nathaniel, did you leave the house at any point after that?" Lourdes gives him a softer look. "For any reason?"

"No, I was in for the night." He pulls on his beard absently, pretending to be lost in thought.

"You're sure?" Lourdes thrusts her jaw out.

"Yes, I'm sure." He gives her the vaguely knowing smile of a man who could either fuck you to paradise or push you down a flight of stairs without warning. "I didn't go out again."

"And when was the last time you spoke to Mr. Grimaldi?" Lourdes asks.

"A few minutes after he dropped us off. He called me on my cell to remind me to bring some papers into the office in the a.m."

"Called you here?" She arches her eyebrows.

"If there's any doubt, I'm sure you can check the records."

He reclines a little, opening his knees and propping his elbows on the steps behind him, just a regular guy with nothing to hide.

Screw him, Lourdes thinks. Scruffy as his father but slick as Benny G. Probably thinks he's got us beat because he made sure there weren't any witnesses to the killing and that his cell phone won't put him in the car when Grimaldi was shot.

"Was there any kind of disagreement at dinner?" Lourdes asks.

"Might have gotten a little boisterous at some point." Natty glances at his mother for confirmation. "But like I said, we were mainly just glad to be celebrating."

"If you should be questioning anyone, it should be your friends in the FBI," Alice interrupts. "But I've been saying that all along, and now look: another man done gone."

"Ma'am, there's no cover-up on our side," B.B. says with a kind of uncharacteristic modulation. "No one's happy about this."

"So again: you have nothing." Natty hoists himself into a standing position. "Amazing."

"Natty, you don't mind giving us prints and DNA, do you?" Lourdes says.

A tug at the corner of his mouth. He knows she's using the nickname on purpose. Letting him know that he's not just a bereaved friend deserving formal deference, but a potential skell.

"Why would you need them?" Alice asks.

"Just for elimination purposes." Lourdes shrugs. "Natty, you understand, don't you?"

"Sure." Natty nods, playing it cool and professional despite bed hair. "Whatever you need. Though you already have me in the system from my previous arrest. And you definitely will find my prints and DNA in the car because Ben gave us a ride home earlier."

"We'll also be checking the shell casings found in the car and skin cells under Mr. Grimaldi's fingernails." Lourdes studies his arms for defensive wounds.

The first time she's seen him in short-sleeves, she realizes. She hadn't clocked all the tats before: a dog tag, a rifle, a list of names, and "Everywhere Is War."

"I don't envy you; you've got your work cut out." Natty strokes his furry neck thoughtfully. "A dead defense lawyer who just publicly made a lot of money and a long list of criminals who know him and would gladly take it from him . . ."

"Why don't you let us worry about how we're going to make our case this time?" she says. "I think you've done enough."

He killed Benny G. Not a doubt in her mind, except whether it was for revenge or money. But there's knowing and there's proving, and a Death Valley of sun-bleached bones between them. And right now he's way on the other side of the desert, high up on a plateau, daring her to try to get to him.

"I'm sorry for your loss," Lourdes says. "I know how close Mr. Grimaldi was to both of you."

"Yes," Alice says. "I'm just waiting for it all to sink in. I don't know if it ever really will."

Lourdes watches Natty come over and stand over his mother. As if she's the one in need of comfort. But Alice stays hunched over her teacup, not even looking up to acknowledge him.

46

When Natty comes back to the kitchen after letting the detectives out, his mother is at the stove and his cell phone is sitting on the butcher block breakfast table.

"I thought you might be looking for that," she says without turning around. "I found it at the bottom of my bag."

"Thanks."

He stops in front of the refrigerator, reassessing where he is right now. He's lived in this house maybe eighteen years or so, give or take a few college vacations and summer weeks   probably in and out of this room six or seven times a day, minimum, before he moved away. Which makes it something like a hundred thousand times back and forth over the threshold. But at this moment, it's like he never set foot in this room before.

"I heard it ringing last night, but I didn't pick it up." She cracks an egg against the side of a bowl. "You want pancakes?"

"I wouldn't say no."

"Check the refrigerator. See if we have syrup."

He opens the white door, dutifully confronting the milk and ketchup bottles in the stark arctic shiver. The hum of an unseen motor in the freezer compartment just barely audible to his still impaired eardrums.

"What time did you come in last night?" she says. "I didn't hear you."

"Not too late."

He stands there, still holding the door open, afraid to move. The rattle of the bottles competing with the tinny continuous ringing in his ears.

"The syrup is on the right side, and get me the milk," she says. "Don't just stand there. You're letting all the cold air out."

He grabs the quart of skim milk and the pale beige jug of Vermont Organic from between the Hellman's mayo and the Heinz relish, realizing he'd been staring right at it for at least ten seconds without seeing it. It's not lack of sleep. After he showered last night, making sure to wash his hands and wrists with Ivory soap to get rid of any gunshot residue, he dropped his head on the pillow and slept for eight hours straight, tinnitus be damned. Not a single nightmare or trudge to the bathroom. How many times has that happened since Sadr City?

"Are we going to talk about this?" He realizes he can distinctly hear the drip of the yolk into the bowl, as if part of his normal auditory range has been disproportionately heightened to compensate for the damage done by the gunshots.

"Talk about what?"

The seething of gas jets rises just above the distant ringing and the brittle papery shuffle of the eggshells being set aside.

"You can play dumb with the police, but you cannot—excuse me, you *may* not—play dumb with your mother."

"What is it you want me to say?"

"You and I know that you went back out with Ben after you dropped me at the house."

"Okay. And I came right back."

"Stop. Look at me."

He gently closes the refrigerator door and turns: she still has her back to him, shoulders pinched and blades protruding.

"The police are going to keep looking at you. Any minute the media are going to come calling." Her fingers tremble as they place the broken shells into the plastic compost container. "I need to know if you're going to prison for what you just did."

"I'm not going to prison." He sets the milk and syrup by her elbow.

"How do you know?"

"I haven't done anything wrong."

"Nathaniel . . ."

He can see the tension go up her spine, her vertebrae defined through the thin fabric of her sweater.

"Did anyone see you?"

"I don't know what you're talking about."

She turns down the heat on the stove, leaving the snappish tick of the igniter repeating without the flame.

"I'm not going to make you breakfast if you're going to keep treating me like an idiot. Forget pancakes. I'm just making you scrambled eggs."

"Okay."

She grabs the milk and pinches the top open. "How did you get home after you left Ben?"

"I took the subway."

She pours the milk into the bowl and then closes the top, making sure breakfast, at least, goes the way it's supposed to. "Did anybody see you?"

"I don't think so. And if they did, they wouldn't recognize me."

He'd taken care to throw the Ray-Bans and garbage bag into separate Dumpsters, after he tossed the gun in the Gowanus. Then he made sure the block was empty, before he let himself back into this house, a few minutes before midnight.

"And you called your own phone while you were out to make it look like you were here?" She beats the eggs and milk more vigorously than usual.

"No one's going to know otherwise, unless you tell them."

"*Why?*" She sets aside the fork she was using. "Why did you do this?"

"He killed my father."

She slumps against the stove, bracing herself with her hands on either side. "That's really what you think?"

"I didn't just take the cops' word. I saw what was going on at the office. I read the evidence about witnesses getting killed. And I talked to other people who would know."

No point in getting into the whole Jamar Mack backstory with her. She's carrying enough already.

"Jesus, child. Do you even understand what you did?"

"It's all right, Ma. I've got it all under control."

He picks up the syrup to put it back in the refrigerator, noticing the bottle is sticky from errant rivulets, and the cap is on crooked. A thick brown crust has formed in the treads, keeping it from screwing on correctly.

He stands beside her at the sink and washes the neck gently with warm water.

"I would've talked you out of it," she says, still not looking at him.

"You couldn't have. I know what he did. He practically told me himself right at the end."

"You don't know anything." She turns the burner back on with a jerk of her wrist. "You don't know shit."

"I know he had my father killed because he was afraid of Dad rolling on him. And because he wanted all the money for himself."

"Dumb ass." She takes the syrup back to the refrigerator and slams the door.

"You talking about Ben, Dad, or me?"

"All of you."

She returns to beating the eggs with a vengeance. "Exactly why do you think your father was talking to the feds in the first place?" she asks, the steel-on-porcelain clank of her fork in the bowl almost more than he can stand now.

"Ben claims he got jammed up for some bullshit about smuggling guns to Syrian rebels."

"It's not bullshit," she says.

"How do you know?"

"Because David told me it wasn't."

She throws a pinch of salt into the eggs and then closes her eyes, momentarily exhausted. "A week after the FBI brought him in and played him their tapes. Talking to that mailman's son about running guns for Syrian rebels."

"That part is true?"

She nods, bringing back some of the high-beam headache from last night. Of course, it's true. A side of Natty knew as soon as Ben said it. Dad trying to play the underground hero. The champion of the oppressed. Sticking his neck out for the rebels fighting the oppressive murderous regime.

"David didn't want to tell me," Mom says. "But then he started talking about giving the mailman case away, and I began hounding him to find out why. Eventually he confessed that the FBI caught him talking about doing something he shouldn't have."

"When was this?"

"Just a few months ago. Right after he beat the motion to dismiss and won the right to keep suing the FBI. At first, he tried to tell me it was all a setup. The things he was talking about on that tape weren't even things he was doing anymore. Back in 2011, he'd been trying to help the rebels when they looked like the good guys. Then it turned out some of them were as bad as the regime, cutting heads off and burning people in cages. So a few months ago, your father got upset when he was talking to Hamid and said, 'Are these the same guys we were getting guns for?' Which is how the FBI caught him so long after the fact."

"And you didn't call me?"

"And what were you going to do, Natty? You weren't even talking to us at the time." Her lower lip pushes up, holding back stronger emotions. "I guess you were going through your own stuff, down in Florida."

"Great." He puts his hands behind his head, as if trying to keep the back of his skull from falling off.

"David was looking at ten years minimum in a federal facility. I sat in this kitchen at four in the morning, listening to him agonize about what to do. That's once he finally told me what was going on. And you know what's funny?"

"I'd find it very hard to believe any of this was funny, Ma."

"He kept talking about you. About how all this was going to affect you once it came out."

"*Me?*"

She pours the eggs into the skillet, returning to the routines of daily life even as the foundations of the house seem to be giving way beneath them. "David thought he'd lose whatever respect you had for him."

"That's ridiculous. Of course I respected him."

"Did you?" She stops to study the hardening of the eggs in the pan. "He saw how you were with Ben. Peas in a pod."

"That was before I knew anything."

"Too late to change that now," she says. "When you were little, you always asked him, 'Why weren't you ever in a war, Daddy?' And he never got over that. I think that's at least half the reason he got involved with these so-called freedom fighters. But then he got caught and went running to his little girlfriend at the U.S. attorney's office, to help make a deal."

"Marygrace?"

"That bitch just wanted to get her hooks into him again. She went to her friends at the FBI and got David a deal to cooperate with a separate investigation, in exchange for keeping him out of prison and letting him keep his law license. And all he had to do was surrender the biggest case of his career and turn on his best friend."

He listens to the sizzle in the skillet as the smell of burning butter works its way into him and starts to convert the wave of cramps in his digestive tract into a series of slow painful contractions.

"You're telling me he did it just to save himself?" The taste of metal fills his mouth.

"I'm not saying that was wrong. The feds already suspected Ben was up to something himself. And your father wasn't involved in any of that business. But let's not kid ourselves. He didn't turn informer just because it was the right thing."

Natty hangs to the back of a chair. "And how did Ben find out Dad was going to turn on him?"

"I told him."

"What?"

"I made a mistake." She reaches into the cabinet above the stove and gets out the Motrin. "When your father said he was going to give the mailman case away and wouldn't tell me why at first, I got scared. We were tens of thousands of dollars in debt and about to get thrown out of this house. So I went to Ben and asked him to talk David out of it. Then I guess they had some kind of confrontation and the truth about everything started to come out."

"Did you tell Ben that Dad was going to turn on him?"

"No, of course not." She clenches her jaw. "I said *I made a mistake.* Your father made plenty of his own. Especially not telling me what was going on when we were in trouble. That's why I went running to Ben, and to see if there was any way he could take over the case and get us our fair share of the settlement."

"And instead he decided he'd rather take all the money and get rid of the problem of Dad rolling on him."

"How could I know what he was capable of?" She raises her voice. "He was your father's best friend and I thought I could trust him."

More ice cubes drop in the freezer, the internal mechanisms going about their functions as the water solidifies and the same bonds form just a little farther apart from each other. It makes sense with the timeline Albert described after his stepson was killed. Everything coming to a head at just the wrong time. She pops two pills into her mouth and uses a glass of water on the counter to wash them down.

"Natty, there's something else I need to tell you. It's going to be very hard to hear."

"Harder than what we've talked about already?"

"I think you need to sit down for this part. I'm serious."

He gradually lowers himself into the chair, increasingly aware of the menace of mundane things around him. The grunt of the chair legs, the steam rising from the skillet, the tick of the kitchen clock, the ice maker doing its business. Each sensation triggering another round of peristalsis, squeezing his gut like a toothpaste tube.

"Okay." He leans forward, elbows on his knees. "What is it?"

"Many years ago, not too long after your father and I got married, we started going through a hard time. It was a different era. A lot of people had open marriages and—"

"There was never a time when 'a lot of people' had open marriages," he interrupts, getting more agitated by the second. "That's just some phony excuse people used to have key parties and fool around in the '70s. Can I get some of those Motrin?"

"*Anyway.*" She hands him the bottle. "There was a lot of tension between us. Some of it had to do with whether we were going to have children."

"All right." He shakes a pill into his palm. "Go on."

"We started seeing other people, for a while. David got back together with that MG, who I hated . . ."

He shakes out a second pill. "And?"

"And something happened with Ben and me."

He hesitates and then pours out a third pill. "Do I need to hear this?"

"I think you do."

He puts back his head and tries to open up his throat. Trying to choke down all three pills at once without water.

"Why?" he says, swallowing.

"Why did I do it or why am I telling you?" she says.

"Whatever."

"Because that little Puerto Rican detective was talking about comparing your samples to what they might find in the car," she says. "On the shell casings and under Ben's nails . . ."

He grunts, the pills stuck halfway between his throat and his chest.

"When I was with Ben, it was about the same time that David and I were going through our stuff."

"No way." He hits himself mid-chest with the side of his fist.

"I'm not saying I'm sure. David and I got back together pretty soon after that . . ."

"No fucking way . . ." He hits himself again, trying to clear the obstruction.

"But we never did have another child, though we tried."

The pills start to descend. More chunks fall in the freezer. The beginning of an avalanche. This will bury me, he thinks. I will never get out from under this.

"That makes no sense." He tries to breathe out.

"Politically, there's no way I can justify it." She looks down into the pan. "Ben was everything I hated: macho, domineering, and full of himself. But politics doesn't have that much to do with what men and women really do. Maybe you figured that out by now."

"But he was Dad's best friend."

"What can I tell you? David was a good man but he did me wrong with other women." She is staring up at the hood above the stove, looking through a window of regret. "And baby, you can talk about female empowerment till the cows come home, but deep down just about every woman alive likes a man that's strong."

"All right, *enough*."

He hears the ice maker disgorging another raft of cubes. I will be trapped here forever, he thinks. Locked inside this terrible feeling. For some reason, he pictures one of those ancient hunters still frozen inside a glacier centuries after falling into a crevice.

"I didn't want to tell you any of this, ever," she says. "But better you hear it from me than from somebody else, I guess. Like the police."

"So did Dad . . ." He catches himself. "Did David know?"

Some querulous expression goes from one side of the dividing line on her face to the other. "David talked a good game about wanting a daughter, but I always knew he wanted a son. And I gave him one." She shakes her head. "He was head over heels in love with you from the day you were born. Had a Mets pennant over the crib and a cap on the bedpost before you were even home from the hospital. He acted like a New Man, but he was just another man."

More cubes tumble. What if the hunter suddenly awakened? Would he try to break free? Or would he just give up and try to be at peace with dying inside a glacier?

"But you don't know for sure," he says. "*We* don't know. No one knows whether it's true or not. David could still be my father."

"He could be. But if the police come back at you and say you did it to get at an inheritance, I want you to be prepared."

He feels the numbness from the three Motrin already spreading through him. "I don't know what to do with this," he says.

"The police may not find anything else. And then it'll be up to you to decide if you want to get down to the nitty-gritty."

His whole physical being is potential evidence now. The size of his hands and feet. The circumference of his skull. The width of his neck, the distance between his eyes, the vault of his chest, and the architecture of his muscles. His genetic encoding. It would probably take less than a month to get a sample from Ben's office and compare it to his own profile.

"What if it turns out that I killed my own father?"

"I wouldn't go there, if I don't have to."

"But what if I did?"

He looks longingly at the kitchen counter, remembering the .357 in the frozen pitcher. Then he thinks about the hunter trapped in the ice. What if after all this time, the glacier has become part of him, fused and inseparable? If he struggled to escape, maybe he'd just tear himself in half and bleed to death. Or maybe he'd just shatter into a million pieces and melt away in the sun.

"There's nothing you can do now," she says. "Except drive yourself crazy."

"Mom." He stares at her back until she turns around. "Did Ben know?"

"We never talked about it."

"But he must have wondered—the timing."

"I don't know what he thought." She goes back to pushing the eggs around. "I'm sorry, Natty."

He thinks about the half second before he pulled the trigger in the car. That look that seemed to be more sadness than anger. It could have been just a trick of the light.

"He helped me by giving me a job," Natty says. "Was it because you asked him to?"

"It was your father's case. You were entitled to a share."

"Did you leverage him because he might be my father or because you thought he might have been involved in killing David?"

"You needed to work. That's all."

"Sounds pretty cold."

Her forehead becomes taut and mask-like as she turns the heat off. "Natty, I don't talk about my childhood a lot, but it was hard. When I was eight years old, my father died of a heart attack at a Motel 6 with another woman in his bed. The prince of our movement. He left me and my mother and my three sisters living in Section 8 housing and begging my mother's parents in Connecticut for scraps. My grandfather could barely look at me, and my grandmother used to give us a hundred-dollar bill in an envelope at Christmas to buy groceries for six months. And then she'd pinch my cheek until it turned white and I started to cry. Let me tell you, I learned to hate that little white envelope. So I'm not going back that way. All right? My father preached, 'Might don't make right.' But he was wrong. Because if you've got the might, it doesn't matter if you're right. Now, I loved David right to the bitter end, but the fact is only the strong survive."

"I don't know if I'm as tough as you, Mom."

"Any way you cut it, you're the rightful son and heir."

Even without the flame, the eggs are burning. All at once, he feels sicker than he's ever been in his life. His forehead boiling and oozing filmy sweat with a pungent chemical odor. His gorge rises, bringing lava-like hot vomit to the top of his throat, but his mouth is brick-dry. He staggers over to the refrigerator and pulls it open, confronting the muted roar of the unseen motor. Trying to recall the look on Ben's face more precisely.

Did he know it might be his own son killing him? The thought is as hard to bear as the sight of the empty sneaker on the landing.

"God." He shuts the refrigerator door and opens the freezer, needing more cold. "Why did you even make me?"

"Pull yourself together." She comes up behind him and puts her hands on his shoulders.

The compartment is full of scattered cubes with more space between them than he would have expected. He pictures the iceman broken free from the glacier. Only now he knows it's not a hunter, but Frankenstein's monster who'd been trapped inside, a creature jerry-rigged from disparate parts, who has now escaped. Somewhere he is staggering through the winter-bare landscape, trying to stay ahead of dogs chasing him through the trees.

"Anyone who asks is going to hear you were with me in this house when Ben was getting shot," she says.

"But what if I can't live with this?"

"Listen to me: you are stronger than David and Ben put together." She lets him go with a pat on the shoulder. "Just take care of business, son. And then let's never talk about it again."

47

Soledad is sitting across from the interrogation room at her squad's office, wilting roses and a half dozen gift-wrapped bottles from the party on her desk, as Lourdes arrives with Sullivan and the case files.

"'Bout time." Soledad looks up from trying to pry open a pale blue birthday envelope with her nubby fingernails. "He's been cooling his heels for like a half hour already."

"Good for him." Sullivan takes a stiff-legged stroll over to the observation window. "Someone once said all of men's troubles come from not being able to sit quietly in a room."

"Most women's troubles too." Soledad thumbs her chin pensively. "You must be Sully. You taking good care of my baby?"

"More like she's been taking care of me," Sullivan says.

He hasn't quite acknowledged the fact that Lourdes demanded he be allowed in the room for this one last interview, calling Chief Gunther's office personally after she'd visited the Dresden house this morning and said no way, no how, were they going to clear this without the Apache, the feds be damned. They deserved to be under suspicion themselves, she argued, since Grimaldi was killed right before the final settlement conference.

Give the man respect, she'd said, ignoring Soledad's advice to keep her head down. Knowing there was no way Sullivan could rest easy if he didn't have a chance to settle his accounts. So it galls her just a little that after all that, he's still too embarrassed to look at her. Like she walked in and saw his dumpy, potato-white, old-man ass in the locker room.

"Here, open this for me, *bebita*." Soledad hands Lourdes an envelope. "You got real nails."

Lourdes slides a talon under the flap and pulls out a card with a pink Cadillac on the front and the words *"You don't have to be a mechanic to work on my undercarriage!"*

Sullivan blushes as he looks in the window. "Who is that in the box with our boy?"

"His new attorney is a Joseph Spiro," Soledad shrugs. "No connection to Dresden & Grimaldi far as we know. And no sign of the FBI yet. I told Doug Bryce that if he wants to get in that box, he'll have to try to get through me, and the last man who tried is still looking for his *gondolas*."

"Okay." Sullivan puts a hand to his chest. "I see where Robles gets it."

"Can we go in?" Lourdes ignores the byplay.

"All yours." Soledad waves. "Sullivan, this your last case?"

"Pretty much." He gives her a grave nod.

"Make it count." Soledad goes back to opening her cards. "And make *mi sobrina* look good."

"Aye, aye."

He opens the door, letting Lourdes enter first. A gentleman to the end. Jamar Mack is sitting beside his new lawyer, Spiro, a black man with a Greek name, a bowtie, and dreadlocks spilling over the collar of a neat glen-plaid suit.

"Okay, can we begin now?" Jamar asks in a modulated voice. "Or do we need someone else in the room?"

Not what Lourdes expected. Jamar could have just walked out of a graduate seminar at Yale or a digital advertising pitch in Chelsea. A nice-looking brother in his mid-thirties, with a lazy eye, Cazal horn-rimmed glasses, and a beautiful white cable-knit tennis sweater with Ivy League–style blue-and-maroon trim on the V neck.

"So you know what this is about, right?" Lourdes sits and rests her hand palm-down on the table, next to the ring for the handcuff chain that hasn't been used yet.

"What I *know* is that patrol pulled me over this afternoon for allegedly switching lanes without signaling, and then claimed that they had probable cause to search my Lexus because they supposedly smelled weed,"

Jamar says, with an air of measured impatience as if he was more concerned about the waste of municipal resources than the threat to his freedom. "They could have just given me a summons for the four joints they think they found, but my *surmise* is that this is a pretext. You all wanted to talk about something else. Am I right?"

This time Lourdes doesn't need to look at Sullivan. They knew coming in this dance would have a different tempo. Jamar isn't your typical lowlife. After David Dresden and Benny G. got him sprung early from his juvenile stint, he'd managed to stay mostly under the radar, arrested just three times on nonviolent drug offenses in the twenty-odd years. A post-jail job resume that went from doing Fresh Direct grocery deliveries to getting his degree at BMCC to helping to manage a Fort Greene print shop to dabbling in East New York real estate. Obviously he's acquired a patina of sophistication from dealing with people in the so-called legit world, while at the same time still keeping a hidden hand in the game.

"I took an economics class once that said all human interaction is either about transaction or affection." Jamar adjusts his Cazals. "So what are we doing here?"

"You're aware that Ben Grimaldi was killed last night." Lourdes flips open the file folder.

There's a crime scene photo of Ben slumped behind the Jaguar wheel with his eye blown out and brain matter sprayed against the window behind him.

Jamar gives it a cursory glance. "Why's that my problem?"

"He was the prosecutor who got your felony assault case transferred to Family Court and kept you out of the adult system." Lourdes turns the picture over and displays the printout of the old *Daily News* story about the juvie arrest. "This jog your memory?"

"Ancient history." Jamar splays open his hands, palms smooth and smelling of pricey lotion, Lourdes notices. "Nothing to do with today."

"Except your family had a business in which they used bicycles to transport drugs." Lourdes flips back to the crime scene picture. "Mr. Grimaldi's law office was raided the other day, because he had bike messengers delivering drugs."

"This is reaching." Joseph Spiro shakes his dreadlocks. "You're looking for connections that don't exist."

"They don't?" Lourdes pretends to pout. "That's odd. Because Mr. Grimaldi represented a friend of Jamar's named Shakneela Wilkins. Who is talking to some of our other detectives upstate right now in Clinton."

"Probably about to put his own damn foot in his mouth," Jamar mutters.

"Mr. Wilkins says he has information to share about business that your client was conducting through Mr. Grimaldi's law firm." Lourdes keeps her eyes on the defense lawyer. "He's talking to the detectives about a drug operation that involved bike messengers and contract murders of witnesses to keep them from testifying."

"And how are you all going to tie me to any of that?" Jamar slouches with a hint of bad-boy insolence. "With testimony from Shakneela and his gout? Good luck finding a jury who's going to believe him on his own."

"Which is why we're looking for you to bolster him," Sullivan says, playing the voice of reason. "Your cooperation would be at least as crucial."

"And why would I help you?" Jamar looks around, with a kind of theatrical curiosity, as if he'd accept an answer from anyone.

"For one thing, Benny G. is dead, so you don't have to worry about him retaliating," Lourdes says. "And for another, we just locked up your own son."

Jamar sits up. "When?"

"About an hour ago." Lourdes glances at the window, knowing Soledad is probably watching. "We got warrants based on information we got from Shakneela and some of the bike messengers we arrested the other day. Tell you the truth, we didn't even know you had a kid until Shakneela gave it up. Then we caught your boy with a refrigerator full of handguns he was looking to sell at his mother's apartment. You had him when you were seventeen, and he just turned sixteen? Means your son could be facing twenty-five years. So you were talking about transaction versus affection before? You decide which this is."

"Fuck." Jamar slouches again as his attorney starts to whisper in his ear.

Law enforcement Kabuki. Everyone playing their accustomed roles with slight variations to have the required result that allows the cycle to continue.

"I don't know anything about Benny G. getting killed." Jamar waves off Spiro. "I was at a club in East Flatbush last night. Like five hundred witnesses saw me."

"We know," Sullivan says, his voice dropping into a husky croak. "No one is thinking you're dumb enough to commit murder in front of anyone. Or even to do it yourself."

"Then what do you want from me?" Jamar takes his glasses off.

"The full story of everything else," Lourdes says. "David Dresden, Kenny Holloway, Shawn Davidson, and all the other witnesses who were murdered before they could testify."

"You allocute to everything or else we don't talk to the DA about your cooperation," Sullivan says. "And then the DA can't talk to the judge for you . . ."

"And then we can't do anything for your son," Lourdes says, finally at the point where she can finish his sentences for him.

Jamar hangs his glasses off the V neck of his sweater, Cali cool, and consults behind his hand with his lawyer one more time.

"Okay." He falls back in his seat, winded from taking an instant exhaustive inventory of his options. "Here's the truth. It was all Benny G."

"Convenient." Lourdes rests an elbow on the back of her chair. "Given that he's already dead."

"Do you want the story or not?" Spiro asks. "Because we can peddle this to the feds if you're not interested."

"Go ahead," says Sullivan.

"It's exactly how I was saying." Jamar takes the glasses off his sweater and carefully breathes on each lens. "There's transaction and there's affection. David was a good guy. He helped me with my case and took me in his house for a little. But it was Benny G. who kept me out of the adult system and staked me financially when I was getting in my own business. He could do more for me in the long run. We helped each other over the years. So when he said David had to go, he had to go."

"He contracted you to murder his partner?" Sullivan asks.

"*Please.*" Jamar raises his hands to shoulder level, plainly offended. "Nothing was ever said that directly. All I ever did was introduce people and collect a finder's fee. Ben would give me a burner cell with a number already programmed in and I'd give it to someone I knew who could do what he needed done, whether it was moving drugs or pulling a trigger. And that was the end of it as far as I was concerned."

"Except you got paid as the facilitator," Sullivan notes. "Right?"

"I owned the bike messenger service and the bicycles." Jamar nods. "So I got my rental fees, but it was Ben's business. He introduced sellers and distributors at the law office and took a finder's fee. But he was always running out of money anyway. He liked to live large."

So this *is* it, Lourdes sits back, knowing she should be relieved. The center is holding. They're on their way. They're going to clear David Dresden's murder, plus Shawn Davidson, Kenny Holloway, and—who knows?—maybe three or four others. The fat lady should be singing, and she's pretty much sure without looking up that even Sullivan must be allowing himself a fraction of a smile, knowing he'll be going out on a high note. But there's still the one question.

"Who killed Ben?" she asks.

Joseph Spiro stops patting Jamar on the back encouragingly, and she's aware of Sullivan going into his preternatural stillness mode.

"Wasn't me." Jamar shakes his head slowly. "Like I said, I have an alibi."

She can feel everyone getting irked with her for breaking the flow. It's like she just walked in while they were watching a Cowboys-Giants game and switched the channel to Inspector Morse on *Masterpiece Theatre*.

"Gonna be hard to help your son, if that's all you're offering," she says.

"All right, I'll give you this much." Jamar tilts back in his seat. "Remember I said I lived at David Dresden's house when I was a kid? His son came to see me the other day."

"Natty?" Lourdes pings a look off the side of Sullivan's face.

"Yeah, pain in the ass." Jamar loosens a corner of his mouth and gives his lawyer a cynical half smile. "I thought he was a psycho when I was a kid. And he's still got the cork in tight. He wanted to know what was up with Benny G. and his father."

"And what'd you tell him?" Lourdes asks.

"Same thing I'm telling you." Jamar shrugs. "I'm just the carpenter. But it was Benny G.'s house."

"You told him you thought Benny G. was responsible for his father's murder?" Lourdes moves toward the edge of her chair.

"Not in so many words, but he might have gotten that idea." Jamar glances at his lawyer. "But who knows what anybody's really thinking?"

"Did Natty say anything about what he was going to do to Ben because of this?" she asks.

"No. I said he was psycho, not stupid." Jamar puts his glasses back on. "And it's not like we were ever bosom buddies. But he understood what I was saying. And I wouldn't be surprised if he decided to act on his own."

"And that's all you can give us?" Sullivan asks. "Even if it means helping your kid?"

"Can't swear to something I didn't hear." Jamar sits back. "I done a lot of things, but I'm not gonna sit here and lie. He heard what I said and then went off and did whatever."

Not enough, Lourdes realizes. No way to make a case against Natty, based on what they just heard.

She looks over at Sullivan, to see if he's got any notions about how to squeeze more blood from this particular stone, but Cochise is distracted. She'd been thinking that he hadn't been looking at her because he was embarrassed about needing help from a young woman. But now she realizes that he's begun to pull away from this plane, knowing his work in this job is mostly done.

"If it wasn't Natty, who else would it be?" Lourdes looks back at Jamar.

"Take a number and stand in line." Jamar gives the crime scene photos of Benny G. a diffident headshake. "Lot of people could have done it. My man Ben had a law degree, but he lived like a gangster. All that happened is he got to die like one too."

48

All through the session, Natty focuses on not getting distracted by the cell phone, intrusive thoughts, the flaming helmet, or the fact of Stacy styling way above established norms in a form-fitting navy dress with big eyelashes, black stockings, and two-inch heels.

"Nathaniel, I want to speak to you honestly. Okay?"

"Sure." He eyes the clock above her head. "I thought that's what we've been doing all along."

"That's what we're *supposed* to be doing." She crosses her legs that are more slender and toned than he'd previously noted.

It's been a month and a half since their last appointment. He got permission to leave the city as soon as the fireman case was officially dropped, so he headed down to Florida for a week to try to repair the relationship with Tanya and her daughter. Reaching the point where he could finally make love facing her, before realizing he still couldn't face himself. Then a couple of weeks bumming around the Keys, fishing and drinking without much satisfaction before he took money from the Ibrahim settlement and headed overseas.

At least he had enough sense not to sign up with some private military contractor and go to Iraq, trying to get it right this time. Instead he put in another two weeks trekking in Iceland and then the Alps, trying to find serenity among the peaks and gorges. But all he discovered was it didn't matter if you were on top of the Concordia glaciers or throwing up in a filthy desolate gas station bathroom stall. If your head is in flames, the view doesn't matter that much.

"You're still very well defended," Stacy says.

"Thank you."

"It wasn't a compliment. I feel like I never got past the walls you put up."

"Nothing wrong with walls. They keep the roof up."

"Deflect, deflect, deflect."

"I'm not drinking." He shrugs. "I haven't been rearrested, and I'm back to practicing law. Maybe I've said all that needs to be said."

"I don't believe that." She leans forward, legs crossed and tilted at a 7 angle from her lap. "And I don't think you do either."

"Then maybe I've said all that I *can* say. Ever consider that, Ms. PTSD Expert? You're all into tearing down the walls. But what about the Pottery Barn rule?"

She half closes one of her false eyelashes. "Remind me."

"What Secretary of State Powell said about Iraq before we went in. You break it, you bought it. Do you want to buy *me*, Stacy?"

She sighs and looks back at the clock, struggling, endearingly, to get the eyelash open again. Five minutes left in the session. He's run her down again. Kept her off-balance and lunging at shadows. So she can't steer him anywhere close to the real Mighty Dread.

He used to think he was the Mighty Dread. But now he knows it's what he's always been hiding from. The unnameable. The unease that never went away. The sense he never belonged anywhere, not even in his own family. The inability to get from red to green. And now he's come to the mightiest dread of all, the question behind all other questions: did you do right by your father or kill him? It's there all the time now, a black abyss at his feet, daring him to look down.

"Unfortunately, this is going to be our last session," she says. "I've decided to go into private practice. I love my work here, but it's just too hard with the bureaucracy and the red tape."

"That's too bad."

"Really, Nathaniel?" She redrapes the hem of her dress over her knee. "Do you care?"

"Sure." He looks around, noticing she no longer has the stems in the vase that kept turning, in his mind, into the gun in the pitcher. "I know you meant well. At least you didn't hurt anyone."

"Well, that's something—I guess." She stands and offers her hand. "Good luck. I hope you find a little peace of mind. Eventually."

"Think I'll just try putting one foot in front of the other, and see where that takes me." He pumps her hand and finds himself smelling her perfume for the first time.

He guesses she's gotten herself dressed up for some kind of interview, but up close he realizes she doesn't need it. The press of her palm against his releases an unexpected flood of warmth in his chest. And he never quite registered that she had such a kick-ass body when she was sitting down. Not ostentatiously skinny like a model's, but lush and welcoming. The body of a mature woman. He realizes that he's been hanging back on her the whole time, figuring her interest in him was merely obligatory, but now that the clock is officially stopped he can finally see her in three dimensions.

"By the way, how's your brother?" he asks.

"Which one? I have three."

"The one you said was in the Tenth Mountain Division."

"Oh, he killed himself six months after he came back."

It feels like she just hauled off and slapped him. "Are you fucking with me?"

"Does it sound like I am?"

"How come you never told me?"

He goes slack-jawed and flat-footed. Realizing he'd been so lost in his own miasma that he didn't notice someone in just as much pain right across the room.

"It wouldn't have been appropriate while I was seeing you in the practice. But I'm not seeing you anymore."

"It would've been different if I knew," he says.

She puts her head down for a second, so hair falls in her eyes. "I was the one who found him in my parents' basement. With a note that said he saw things he couldn't handle anymore. Messed me up for a long time too. So I try to help with other people. And as you can tell, it doesn't always work."

He notices he hasn't let go of her hand yet. "I'm sorry."

"I was in therapy myself for a long time." She looks down at the helmet. "Art helped, a little."

"That's you?" Natty says. "How did I not know that either?"

"It takes a long time before you know anything about anybody." She starts to pull her hand back. "Anyway, I guess I'll leave it here."

"Stacy, I think maybe I screwed up with you. I'd like to talk to you again sometime."

She reaches for the macramé pocketbook resting in a corner and extracts a business card for him. "If you want to see me as a private patient, we can work out a scale to cover what your insurance won't."

"Think you'd ever be up for having dinner instead?" he asks.

"Like . . . on *a date*?" Her eyes bulge like he just put his hands around her neck.

"I got money now. I could take you somewhere decent."

"You think that's a good idea? To go out with your counselor?" Her smile goes lopsided, as if she's surprised to find herself even considering it. "Does that sound professional?"

Natty looks down at the skull. "If you made that thing, we've got more in common than I thought."

"So if I'm as screwed up as you, it makes me more attractive?"

"I was gonna say 'hot.' Don't sell yourself short. You have a boyfriend already?"

"No, but you know this is a total recipe for disaster."

"I think we could do drinks sometime without it ending in a 9-1-1 call. What do you say?"

She gives him a long look, the upstate girl at the back-room pool table working the side pockets. "We've both got a lot we need to figure out. But, you know, life is long. You've got my number."

"I'm going to call you."

"Big talk." She sticks her chest out a little and turns sideways, giving him a last chance to admire the view. "Good luck, Nathaniel."

49

Six weeks, two days, Lourdes realizes.

Six weeks and two days of head-banging, tongue-biting, binge-eating frustration as she tried to put this monster down without alienating whatever friends she had left in the department. She'd missed the early summer radio hits, hadn't seen any of the blockbuster movies, failed to attend both her mother's and her sister's birthday celebrations, and blew off two separate fancy dinner reservations made by Mitchell while she was burning through her overtime and driving the entire squad up the wall by being on overdrive 24-7.

If she hadn't managed to clear ninety percent of her cases in the meantime, she'd be counting pencils. But those were mostly diddly-shit street robberies, stolen iPhones, and break-ins where the homeowners spent $3 million on their brownstones and less than $400 on their front door locks. So as far as 1 PP was concerned, she was still rockstar material.

She almost doesn't recognize Natty as he comes out of Surrogate's Court, an old Beaux-Arts building near the Brooklyn Bridge entrance, and dons a pair of shades. He looks thinner and more tan than the last time she saw him, his hair and beard grown out and lightly flecked with threads of silver that catch the midmorning sun as he shakes his female attorney's hand and walks up to Lourdes and Sullivan on the corner, like he was expecting to see them.

"How did it go, counselor?" Lourdes asks. "Get your fair share?"

"Detectives . . ." He looks over the top of his sunglasses. "I thought I saw you in the back of the courtroom. How have you been?"

"Not as good as you're going to be." Lourdes nods. "Congratulations on the settlement."

Natty is wearing a lightweight gabardine suit, with a white pocket square and a paisley tie like the kind David Dresden would have worn. On his wrist, he wears a flashy Omega Seamaster watch with a silver wristband, worth three grand at least. Like something Benny G. would have worn.

"Your end comes to—what?—a million and a half?" Sullivan pushes off the railing and stands to his full height.

"A bit less." Natty adjusts the watchband. "The firm is entitled to a third of the settlement. But Ben had two daughters, and now I'm paying my mother's rent on President Street. So there goes the yacht."

Even Sullivan has to smile. Lourdes notices he's been in a more re-laxed mood all morning, showing up in a white polo shirt and chinos in-stead of his usual black overcoat. He looks more like a father taking his daughter out for a stroll and an ice cream cone than the Grecian Formula Apache out for one last scalp.

"Anyway, what can I do for you?" Natty pulls a cuff over the watch.

"Just following a couple of new leads." Sullivan makes a point of let-ting his eyes linger on Natty's sleeve.

"I thought you already rolled up Jamar's crew for my dad's murder." Natty gives him a bemused half smile.

"We're still working the Benny G. homicide, though," Lourdes breaks in. "We thought you might be able to help us out."

Natty holds his hands out. "What do you got?"

"Nathaniel, did you know a Staff Sergeant James Randolph Cuddy in Iraq?" Sullivan asks.

"Cuddy, Cuddy . . ." Natty takes off his shades and squints upward, as if he'd never noticed the sun before.

"I'll remind you," Sullivan says. "He was in-country same time as you were. Tenth Mountain Division, First BCT."

"A lot of people in First Brigade." Natty shrugs. "Can't say I knew most of them by name."

"Please, Natty." Sullivan puts a hand up. "I did some digging around with my military contacts. Sergeant Cuddy was involved in an incident over there, in which he lost two legs and you gained a commendation. Does that help?"

It's one of those cloudless bright New York mornings where everything seems stark and plain. There's no shadow or shade on the sidewalks. Everybody on the street has a distinct outline against the passing traffic and every office building is a brutalist block against the blue sky.

"Yes, of course, I know Sergeant Cuddy." Natty puts his shoulders back. "But that's your suspect for Ben's homicide? A double-amputee?"

Sullivan gives a weary laugh. "I kind of thought you might say something like that. But no, we're not looking at Sergeant Cuddy for the murder. However he did have a Glock 17 that he reported missing to the police in Gloucester County, New Jersey, shortly before Mr. Grimaldi was murdered."

"Which is of interest because . . . ?" Natty lets the participle dangle.

"Because Sergeant Cuddy had reported other break-ins inside his new home where he lives with his parents." Sullivan thumbs the corner of his mouth, an artist considering his next brushstroke. "You wouldn't think that would happen so much in a rural area, like the one he's in. But there's a lot of crystal meth, heroin, and paranoia these days, so who knows? In any event, there was an earlier incident, last year, where he'd fired that gun at a suspected intruder. The police in the area responded. Which means they had a shell casing from the gun in their system. Which happens to match the shell casings we found in the car where Mr. Grimaldi was murdered."

"I see." Natty takes his time folding up his glasses and tucking them into his breast pocket. "But what does that prove?"

Lourdes notices that his eyes seem to have receded deeper in his head since they started talking.

"We know you went to see Jamar Mack before Benny G. was killed," she says. "And we know what Jamar told you."

"And what's that?" Natty asks.

"Benny G. was behind your father's murder," she says.

"So is your theory that I might have killed him as an act of revenge?" Natty says quickly. "Or to get at his share of the settlement?"

Lourdes shoots a look at Sullivan, not sure if Natty is getting ahead of them to throw them off-balance or to take a first step toward confessing.

"You want to tell us something, now's the time," she says.

"How's the rest of your case?" Natty asks, little white cracks showing in the arches as he pins back his eyebrows.

"We know you were getting busy on your own, talking to the FBI and going to see Kenny Holloway's father," Sullivan says.

"Which doesn't prove anything either," Natty says.

"A jury would understand where you were coming from, son." Sullivan puts a hand on Natty's shoulder. "Especially if money wasn't the main motive. You had him for killing your old man."

Natty nods and puts his head down. This is it, Lourdes thinks. He's going to give it up. Right here, right now. He must have been dying to get this off his chest. Everything seems to go still around them. Traffic heading toward Brooklyn Bridge halts at a red light. Tourists with foam Statue of Liberty crowns and NYPD t-shirts pause to stare. Even the birds in the trees around the courthouse cease their singing.

"No," Natty says.

"No what?" she asks.

"No, you don't have anything beyond a circumstantial case." He shrugs Sullivan's hand off his shoulder.

"These things take time," Sullivan says. "But someone always ends up paying."

"Well, it's not my turn," Natty says. "At least not for this."

"Your turn will come," Sullivan warns him. "We're just giving you a chance to say when."

The warrior chief making his last stand. Didn't want to use up his vacation days to get out early. Didn't want a racket or even an office party with a cake at the homicide task force to celebrate four decades on the job. Busted Beautiful Bobby when he caught B.B. trying to photoshop one of his sketches into an invite on the computer and nearly throttled Andy when he saw designs for a farewell sweatshirt that somehow misspelled his first name. No summing speeches or tributes. Just wanted to work the case up until the end.

"Sorry, guys." Natty puts both hands up. "But I don't think I can help you more than I have. Peace out."

He salutes them and heads off toward the subway, Lourdes noticing for the first time that even though he's grown out his hair so it spills over his collar like David Dresden's, he carries himself more like Ben Grimaldi, as if every step could crack the sidewalk. She turns to Sullivan and finds Cochise going into one of his trances again.

"Think we ever will get him?"

"On you now, Robles." Sullivan shows her his empty hands. "Your time, your town. Just don't leave it worse than you found it."

"That's all you got for me, Papi?"

He takes in the 360. The street goes about its business, oblivious to the change of the guard: lights from red to green, traffic going over the bridge, young thugs turned into old men waiting for buses, pretty girls who'd inspired gang wars become grandmothers carrying the kids' play-clothes in pink Victoria's Secret bags.

"Yeah, chica," he says. "That's all I got."

50

The house is on a tiny street a block and a half off John F. Kennedy Boulevard in Jersey City. An unthreatening two-story with aluminum siding, storm windows, satellite TV dishes on a new roof, and a chain-linked fence around a postage-stamp front lawn. In the kind of neighborhood where working people let their kids ride bikes down the middle of the street after dark, old ladies in black sit on sidewalk lawn chairs, and the men hang out on porches drinking tea and smoking water pipes.

But as soon as Natty hears the boom from a tractor trailer passing over a steel trench plate down the road, he's back to incoming mortars, smoke in the palm trees, and severed limbs in the road. It takes him a few seconds to reestablish situational awareness and get his respiration back under control. Chill. You just passed a Dunkin' Donuts, an Auto Zone, and a Know Thy Neighbor Christian church. Mop your brow, wipe your palms, and stretch your scrotum. It's all good.

He grabs the heavily padded envelope from between the seats and gets out, the mildness of the summer night a contrast to his rising internal thermometer. He crosses the street, squeezes between a couple of SUVs parked by the curb, steps around a Big Wheel tricycle abandoned on the uneven sidewalk with weeds coming up between the cracks, and dutifully trudges up the porch steps. There's a front screen door, a green wooden inner door with a brass knocker behind it, and the sound of a television situation comedy audible on the other side. But his breathing is ragged and his body is coiled, like he's in the stack with the M4 raised to his shoulder again. Instead of pressing the trigger, he presses the little yellow-white button and gets a gentle lullaby of a door chime.

Inside, the studio audience laughs and footsteps bang up a staircase. He looks back at the rented Saab parked curbside, wondering if he should just beat feet, jump behind the wheel, and tear away before the door opens. A window curtain moves—someone checking him out. His heart tightens. His ball bag shrivels up again. Every muscle in his body screams for him to run.

The green door opens and the old man looks through the screen. "Yes, can I help you?" he says with a mild Iraqi accent.

"Um, yeah. I'm Nathaniel Dresden. You're Muhammad Ramzi. Right?"

"Yes, I'm Dr. Ramzi." The old man opens the door. "I've been expecting you."

He seems to have aged at least another decade since Natty saw him a few months ago in the Rite Aid parking lot in his blue pharmacy smock. His face appears to be permanently in shadow, even as he stands directly under a hallway light. His hair and moustache are no longer just heavily salted with white, but pure ivory as if he's been standing statue-still for hours under a winter sky, oblivious to a snowfall as heavy as the one Natty can hear in his own head again.

"Please." The doctor points to a mat just inside the foyer. "May I ask you to take your shoes off?"

The footwear is lined up neatly, just how it was in Sadr City. A pair of homely imitation Oxfords, polished carefully to cover worn spots. Cheap shoes for a proud man, who works behind a counter where no one can see his feet. Next to them are a pair of glittery women's silver lamé household slippers, a touch of Old Country elegance that only other members of the family get to see. Then two pairs of girly Nikes and New Balances, with sassy purple and pink trim and laces. All carefully arranged on a mat with Arabic calligraphy around the borders. Probably not "Enter in Peace and Security" this time.

At the end of the mat, there's a conspicuous empty space as if another pair of shoes should be there.

"If you would," Dr. Ramzi prompts. "My wife just vacuumed in the living room."

"Yes, of course."

Natty slips off the Italian loafers he's started wearing to the office he's rented on Court Street. Six-hundred-dollor Salvatore Ferragamos with gold buckles that he wore for two weeks before he looked down and realized Ben had a pair just like them.

"Please," the doctor says. "Welcome to my home."

The house feels rented, provisional, a shabby structure given more care than it deserves. The floor in the hall has been waxed and buffed, but it's made of splintered planks with heavy lacquer on them. The walls have been freshly painted white and adorned with hanging fabrics and nature prints, which don't entirely hide the cracks or the unevenness of the trim. The living room that the doctor leads him into has been arranged to look as much as possible like the sitting room at the Sadr City house: same warm wine-red and black colors, though the carpet is acrylic, the chairs look like they come from an Ikea, and there's a flat-screen TV showing a *Seinfeld* rerun.

Natty stops in the doorway, watching steam rise from the tea service on a plastic coffee table. The smell of lavender tells him that the lady of the house was in here less than a minute ago.

"My wife will not be joining us," the doctor says. "She says she doesn't understand what you're doing here."

"Right."

"To be honest, I'm not sure I understand either." The doctor comes to the tea table.

"I thought you got my email that I—"

"Yes, yes. You said that you were a member of the United States military who'd been involved in the operation in which my son died and you wished to speak to me about what happened."

Natty walks in cautiously, following the gold links around the border of the Persian carpet, looking down to avoid looking at the pictures on the mantle.

"It took me a while to find you," he says. "And then even longer to come see you."

"But you said you lived in Brooklyn."

"Yes." He thinks of going through the whole business of how he found a new place just around the corner from his mother in Park Slope, but why would this man care?

"That's less than an hour," Dr. Ramzi says. "Even with traffic. Yes?"

"Yes."

Finally Natty finds the nerve to look at the pictures on the mantle. Half are of the little boy. Riding on his father's shoulders in the same front yard where Natty and his fellow soldiers had stood with their rifles, waiting for the door to get blown off its hinges. Astride a donkey at some kind of outdoor Iraqi festival. Posing with a couple of Marines by a fountain, flashing a peace sign, with a Yankee cap askew on his head.

And then there's the trophy. The same one that Natty clocked in Sadr City as an award from the insurgents. He can see now that it's a golden figure on a cracked white pedestal heading a soccer ball. On close inspection, the inscription plate says it's from the MNF—the Multi-National Force—which included Australia, Poland, the United Kingdom, and the United States of America.

"What is this?" Natty points.

"It's a football trophy for my son, Khalil." The doctor bends over the tea set. "It was given to him by members of the coalition when they tried to organize teams. To help win the support of the local population. 'Hearts and minds,' you call it. My son was a goaltender. Seven years old. Never more than four feet tall. Small for his age. And not particularly fast, because his legs were so short. And clumsy, my God. If the soldiers didn't break his trophy, he probably would have done it himself. But he never let the ball in, because he always dove to put his body in front of it. He had no fear, of anything, ever. Not like me."

"I find that hard to believe."

"I'm afraid all the time," the doctor interrupts. "Especially right now. But he was going to be everything I couldn't be. This little boy with the heart of a lion."

"It's a shame it got broken." Natty lowers his eyes again. "We should have offered to fix it, at least."

"Souvenirs aren't children." The doctor slowly stirs the cups. "Do you take sugar in your tea?"

"No, thank you."

"You were the one who did it. Aren't you?"

The words come out casually, with no more emphasis than the questions about the sugar and the drive from Brooklyn.

"I was there," Natty says, belatedly realizing that at some point in the few seconds his heart stopped beating.

"You were 'there'? Or it was you who fired the shots?"

The power of speech takes its time coming back. "It was me."

"And now here you are." The doctor cocks his head to one side. "In my American home."

"Yes."

"Why?"

Why isn't this man shouting? Raining curses and spittle, instead of going through the gestures of civility and hospitality in a way that makes Natty feel the two sides of his rib cage are coming together, squeezing his insides out through the gaps.

"I don't have a big speech," Natty says. "I didn't even think you'd let me through the door. I just have something I wanted to give you."

"What is it?"

The doctor looks down at the package at Natty's side. His fingers nervously squeeze the eight-by-eleven ochre-yellow envelope, popping several bubbles of the wrapping inside.

"Is it a gun?" the doctor asks.

Natty lets his grip slacken. "Why would I bring a gun to your home?"

Dr. Ramzi slowly gazes up at Natty's face again. "To finish what you started before."

Footsteps go across the ceiling, their nervous tread restarting his dormant heart with a sudden painful jolt. "No, this isn't a gun."

"I thought of getting a gun when I knew you were coming." The doctor looks down, pensive and distracted. "My daughter has a friend who is going out with a police officer, who could have easily acquired one. There's a target range not far from here where I could have practiced. I was going to shoot you when you came to the door, and then say I mistook you for an intruder."

"I see."

"Do you think I would have gotten away with it?"

"I don't know."

"It's America. Such things happen. But I am a brown man. So I can't get away with as much as, say, you could."

"Maybe not."

The doctor starts to pour hot water into the teacups. "So what is it that you've brought?" he says.

"I was awarded a large sum of money in a legal proceeding recently." Natty holds the package in front of his chest with both hands like a shield. "So I came to offer you *fasil*."

The doctor straightens up, leaving the cups smoldering. "You've brought me blood money?"

"My understanding is that it's a custom in Iraq," Natty says.

"Then your understanding is flawed," the doctor replies brusquely. "This is a primitive custom of paying when you cause a death in someone's family. As if money makes it all right."

"Sir, I understand that nothing can make up for what you lost. I was just hoping you would accept this as a gesture of condolence and respect for your traditions."

"Our 'traditions'?" The white moustache twitches. "*Sir*, what traditions are you talking about? I studied chemistry and biology in London. I came back to my native country to be a surgeon at Baghdad. I never heard this word *'fasil'* when I was growing up. It only started up again when your country invaded my country and the government fell and these uneducated tribal chieftains took over as justices. It's atavism. I had to stop being a surgeon because every time someone died in my operating room, their sons came to my house in the middle of the night, threatening to kill me unless I paid them reparations. I had applied to come to America before my son was killed even to get away from this stupid savagery. Now I am here, trying to live my life, filling out prescriptions for Viagra and Prozac at the Rite Aid pharmacy, and you come to my home with *money*?"

"I'm just trying to do something right here." The package feels like it's getting heavier in Natty's hands by the minute. "I saw on the Internet your daughter is trying to raise money for a community lab project. Maybe this could help. Ninety-nine hundred, as a first installment, just enough to stay under the IRS radar. I'd be willing to pay for the entirety of her graduate school education."

"My daughter doesn't want your money. Even though she's assimilated, she won't even be in the same room with you." The doctor stares up as another set of footsteps pound across the ceiling. "You know, it would have been better if you did bring a gun to kill me. Because instead I have to stand here and talk to you like a civilized human being. Which is worse than the worst torture you can ever imagine."

"I know."

"How can you possibly know? Did you ever lose a child? Did you ever have someone else come into your home and take away the most important thing in the world?"

"No, but . . ."

"Mr. Dresden, do you know what I hated you for the most?"

"Go ahead." Natty opens his stance, not fighting it.

"I hated you most because I couldn't say anything after you murdered my son. Because I was *scared*. I was scared of what you would do to the rest of my family. And I was scared of what you would do to me. Do you know what it's like to have to live with that?"

"Not exactly, but . . ."

"So let me tell you: It destroys you, every single day. Because you have to live with this. Knowing that you could not protect someone you loved. And the rest of your family knows it as well. And still they have to try to look up to you. Do you even have *any idea* what I'm talking about?"

"My father was murdered," Natty blurts out.

The footsteps have ceased upstairs. He hadn't expected to say anything about what happened, but now the whole house seems to be listening. No doubt the wife is at the top of the stairs right now. Even the timbers in the walls are groaning, as if anticipating weight to be borne.

"It's not the same," the doctor says. "Your father got to have his life. You killed my son. My only son. And for what?"

"I don't have a good answer." Natty hangs his head. "I wish I did. All I can tell you is that my father was a good man, who raised me the right way. I went against him most of my life and now he's dead. I'd like to do at least one thing that he would've wanted. And I think he would've wanted me to do something for your family."

"So did you come to apologize?"

Natty shakes his head. "I was a member of the United States Army. We did the best we could with the information we had, but we were misled. And that caused the tragic situation."

"If you won't apologize, you should go," the doctor says curtly. "I won't accept your money. The longer you stay here, the worse I feel."

The two teacups sit on the table, unoffered. On the flat-screen, a family sits together on a commercial for a beach vacation, staring silently into a sunset as a cruise boat passes on the horizon.

"You know, I have thought of killing myself," Natty mumbles. "Because of what happened."

The doctor puts his hands behind his back, and looks away as if he didn't hear. "I think about my son every day," he says. "I love my wife and my daughter. But I loved my boy as no father ever loved a son. He wanted to be a surgeon, like me. Seven years old. Every night he'd wait by the front door to take my bag when I came home. At night, he'd fall asleep beside me, pretending to read my medical textbooks. You would be so happy if your own father loved you half as much."

"I'm sure you're right."

Another truck outside hits the steel plate over the trench, making street thunder. For some reason, Natty finds himself picturing what might be beneath. A rusted ladder leading way down into darkness. Cracked stone walls. Damaged water mains. Salt-corroded power lines. Frayed wires sending sparks into volatile gas vapors.

"But now I am tired of talking," the doctor sighs.

"Okay."

"You should go back to Brooklyn. It's getting late."

Natty reluctantly gets up and makes his way toward the door.

"You know, I don't think you should kill yourself." The doctor suddenly seizes Natty's arm.

"No?"

"I think you keep your money and live your life." The doctor releases him. "Do your best and maybe eventually you'll find a way to do what I can't do."

"Which is what?"

The doctor holds the screen door open. "Forgive yourself."

Natty steps out over the threshold and stands on the porch, looking for stars behind the clouds. "Yeah, make it sound easy, why don't you?"

"Of course." The doctor closes the screen door between them.

"Sir . . . ?" Natty looks back at him through the hundred thousand little wire boxes.

"What?"

"If I can't apologize officially, can I at least tell you I wish I could go back in time and have everything be different?"

"Yes. This I think I can accept."

The doctor closes the green door solidly. The brass knocker rattles a little. Natty walks down onto the sidewalk, bubble wrap in his package crackling under the pressure of his fingertips. A boy on a bike rides by with his arm extended behind him, miming shots from a pistol. Two smaller boys chase after him, like they're firing assault rifles. A man and a woman are yelling at each other in the house across the street. Black factory clouds crawl over the Jersey night sky. Another truck hits the steel plate over on Kennedy Boulevard, setting off another seismic boom.

Instead of flinching, Natty closes his eyes.

Here, not there.

Now, not then.

Suck it up, drive on.

It's all good.

But everywhere is war.

ACKNOWLEDGMENTS

I would like to give thanks to the following people for generously sharing their time and their insights.

Jeffrey Wells, Jeremy Todd, Jane Hammerslough, Dwayne Allen, Ron Kuby, Elizabeth Keyishian Wilks, Jim Leckinger, Sonja Batten, Alex Horton, David Denby, Captain Jason Savino, Tommy Markardt, Joshua L. Dratel, Jason Hansman, Bill Tonelli, David Kocieniewski, Jason Cohen, Peter Bloom, Lawrence Schoenbach, Rob Mooney (of course!), Stephen Davis, Mac Blauner, Jonathan Hayes, Chris Cecot, Elizabeth Lacks, Gerald Shargel, "Leonidas," Dr. Michael Kramer, Eric D. and Ginger Ray, Joyce Slevin, Robert Epstein, Kate Hoit, and Matt Mabe.

Thanks, as well, to my agent, Richard Pine, for taking me back; my editor, Kelley Ragland, for signing me on and reining me in; and my beautiful and brilliant wife, Peg Tyre, for putting up with me for all these years.

I'd also like to acknowledge my debt to the writers Dexter Filkins, David Finkel, and Matt Gallagher for their groundbreaking work. I want to specifically mention Matt not only for speaking to me, but for bringing the issue mentioned in the prologue to public attention as a member of the military.

And finally, I want to express my appreciation to the men and women I had the privilege of meeting at Walter Reed National Military Medical Center. I'm told that "thanks for your service" can sound impersonal. Perhaps "thank you for your willingness to serve" is better. But words, this time, are not adequate.